THE MISSING EARRING

BY

Mary K. Mamalis

Copyright © 1996 by Mary K. Mamalis

All rights reserved. No part of this book shall be reproduced or transmitted in any form or by any means, electronic, mechanical, magnetic, photographic including photocopying, recording or by any information storage and retrieval system, without prior written permission of the publisher. No patent liability is assumed with respect to the use of the information contained herein. Although every precaution has been taken in the preparation of this book, the publisher and author assume no responsibility for errors or omissions. Neither is any liability assumed for damages resulting from the use of the information contained herein.

This is a work of fiction. Names, characters, places, and incidents either are the product of the author's imagination or are used fictitiously. Any resemblance to actual events or locales or persons, living or dead, is entirely coincidental.

ISBN 1-892896-14-1

Published by:
Buy Books on the web.com
862 West Lancaster Avenue
Bryn Mawr, PA 19010-3222
Info@buybooksontheweb.com
www.buybooksontheweb.com
Toll Free (877) BUYBOOK

Printed in the United States of America

Published August-1998

This effort is dedicated to my wonderful husband, George, of over a half century - particularly for his eternal love as well as his faith in my ability; encouraging me for many years to share my books with others. Thank you, Agapee mou.

To Charlie
A Heck of a dentist!
Lots of luck & hope
You enjoy it.
Kathleen

Chapter 1

Juan, along with many of his friends and relatives, had fought long and hard to rid his beloved homeland of the guerrillas, only to end up in one of their prison camps. He was now determined to make a break and leave the country, figuring he could do more for his people by appealing for assistance from outside sources. His parents had both died after being tortured and starved even though they were old and knew nothing of any value to the guerrillas. Two sisters and his wife (even though she was pregnant) were forced into working for the opposition as housekeepers, and who knows what else. When his pregnant wife, who had always been a fragile woman, died of unexplained circumstances, it made him even bitterer about what was happening in his country. He was even more determined to make good his escape. Two older brothers were doing hard labor someplace in one of the other prison camps. Their wives had left the country with the children when things first started getting serious, and they went to a small town in Panama where one of the girls had relatives. They also felt they could be of more help outside of the country, appealing for assistance in some way to support their cause. So far things didn't seem to be getting much better.

The Nicaraguan economy had started to decline by the beginning of the civil war in 1978-79; the murder of the opposition leader, Chamorro, had caused nationwide uprising with neighbor fighting neighbor in some districts. Roberto left his job to join up with the military in their fight against the guerrillas. The guerrillas proved to be too much for the military and the group of men with whom Roberto was fighting were eventually captured and made prisoners. Juan and two other men had managed to continue working at their respective jobs, trying to live a normal life with their families. However, eventually they too were captured by the opposition, considered political prisoners because they refused to join forces and were thrown into prison, their families (women, old people and children)also being treated as prisoners and forced to work in various areas around the country.

When U.S.-sponsored mediation efforts failed to oust the Somosas, civil war spread, led by the Marxist guerrillas of the Sandanista National Liberation Front (SNLF). The Sandanistas took power in July 1979, and set up a broad-based coalition government. Tensions over Marxist elements on the program soon broke up the coalition.

Opposition by several groups, including the Catholic Church, to the Sandanistas resulted in tightening controls over the opposition. Conflicts with the U.S. also grew as the Sandanistas forged ties with Cuba and others. The U.S. was criticized for aiding the anti-Sandanistas guerrillas (contras) based in neighboring Honduras.

When SNLF leader Daniel Ortega was elected president in 1984, civil conflict got much worse. The U.S. became more open in its support of the contras, while the SNLF increased its restrictions on the opposition and channeled scarce resources to the military, increasing economic hardships, and making things even worse for the people.

In August 1987, Ortega and leaders of four other Central American nations signed a peace pact and by November the SNLF had somewhat eased political restrictions, and even granted amnesty to many prisoners. Early in 1989, Ortega, along with several regional presidents, committed Nicaragua to democratic changes. Eventually the parties agreed to dismantle contra camps in Honduras and to hold elections in Nicaragua in February 1990. On February 25th elections were held and amnesty was granted to both sides for crimes committed during the civil war, the U.S. economic embargo was lifted, and the contras disbanded.

Chapter 2

It was June 1987, more than two years since their imprisonment and the men were getting very anxious to get out. Juan had discussed the possibility of escape from time to time with his cellmates, once he felt sure he could trust them. He knew he wouldn't get far by himself because he didn't know that area of the country very well. In his mind he had a plan he felt would work if he had the right help, and he really felt he had the right men with him in his cell. He called his cell mates together early one morning before they marched off to breakfast and work; and while it was quiet and most of the men still slept, except for an occasional guard passing by the corner of the building where they were located. They kept their voices to a whisper, knowing full well that if some of the other prisoners found out what they had in mind, it was just as bad as if the guards knew about it.

"OK you guys, tomorrow's going to be our final day in this Hell Hole. I've got a foolproof plan if we play our cards right, so - are you with me?" asked Juan of his fellow cellmates. They all indicated they were behind him 100% in an attempt to make an escape. They also had good reason for wanting their freedom, so they were anxious to hear his plan.

The prison was disgustingly filthy and offered no modern facilities - just big old pots, with covers that didn't fit properly, for toilets, that were emptied whenever the guards decided to have it done. Most of the time one of the prisoners had the job of doing it, having all they could do to keep from vomiting. The stench was sickening to say the least. As for showers, they were allowed only one shower a week; the rest of the time they were allowed but five minutes each morning to wash themselves. Four men had to share a cell with straw mattresses on the floor for sleeping. Many of the men had known the good life - holding good positions and having had a college education - before being considered dangerous to the rebels' cause, and they were rounded up like cattle to be imprisoned for indefinite periods of time, so it was even harder on them.

Juan and two of his cellmates were from the same town of Corinto on the Northwest coast, and were considered political prisoners. Juan had worked in a chemical plant as an accountant and Desi and Shorty were working in a stockyard. Roberto, the fourth inmate lived just a few miles from the prison, in Matagalpa, where he worked for a coffee company before joining up with the government's army, but when the guerrillas got a strong-hold he had been captured and thrown into the cell with Juan and his friends. He had no idea where the rest of his platoon had been taken, or if they were even alive.

I think it would be better to wait until the end of next week," Desi suggested. "There was a full moon just last night and we're better off waiting until it won't be so bright at night."

"Yeh, I forgot about that. Good thinking." Juan responded. "OK, the same plan goes as far as getting out of here. As soon as we get to Estell, we'll split up and then meet two weeks later at the little town of Choluteca just north of the border. Everyone knows where it is, don't you?"

They all indicated they knew where it was and then decided they shouldn't discuss the escape too much more between then and Saturday; nor even hang around together very much in the yard for fear someone may suspect what was going on.

Roberto suggested, "We can go over our final plan the night before after lights out if that's agreeable with you guys."

"Saturday should be a perfect time. I heard some of the guards talking the other day," Shorty commented. "They didn't know I could hear them. They were arranging for a birthday party for the 'warden' - guess they're trying to make points with the ugly bastard, because it certainly can't be because he's a nice guy." [that's what they called the man in charge of the prison] "That's Saturday night. They'll probably all be drinking and be drunk as skunks, with only a skeleton crew on that night. They won't even realize we are gone."

Shorty, as one may suspect was certainly anything but short. In fact he was 6' 6" tall, 210 pounds, and strong as a bull. It had taken several of the guerrillas to subdue him when he was arrested and he is lucky they didn't just end up shooting him.

They all agreed that was the best time to make their move and they then changed the subject in case a guard, or one of the other prisoners might hear any of their conversation - even though the guards rarely came through the prison block. When they did it was to take someone to the warden for interrogation. There were always stoolies around ready to give information to guards in return for special favors. The true patriots couldn't understand why those guys were even imprisoned since they literally worked for the guerrillas; then again maybe that's the reason they kept them there - to act as stoolies.

The men had to decide on the area from which they would make their escape. Since their cell faced the river on one side, they all felt they had chosen an ideal time and had the best place from which to make their escape. The prison wall only extended around three sides - their cell facing the fourth side which had no wall - which would make an escape easier. (During the day if anyone made an attempt they were shot on sight by one of the many guards on duty) Parallel to that side was the northwest end of the Rio Tuma, known to have many poisonous snakes and areas of quicksand near the shoreline. If they succeeded in crossing the river they would be faced with dense woods followed by an area of tall Savanna grass before finally exiting out into level farm land.

Fortunately for the group, Roberto was quite familiar with the entire area, having worked in the main warehouse (the building which is now used by the opposition) for several years. He had friends in a little village north of the area and traveled the route frequently. The owner of the coffee company had been shot for not cooperating with the guerrillas and they took over the place, closing the company down entirely to use the buildings as a prison.

The following few days went by very slowly for the men. The weather was hot and the waiting was becoming frustrating, but the four of them went about their normal duties and routines as though nothing were going on.

Friday was spent doing the usual hard labor in the fields, with all four of them gritting their teeth, being on their best behavior and completely cooperative at all times. They wouldn't want to aggravate any of the guards at this time. All they'd need now was for someone to end up in solitary and not be able to make the escape. After their meager supper all the prisoners were returned to their cells. Juan and his friends checked very carefully to make sure no guards were around where they might be overheard. They also spoke in whispers to each other to be sure other prisoner wouldn't hear them and spoil the plans, possibly getting them into trouble at the same time.

Another thing in their favor was that they had a corner cell which made them even more optimistic that they could get away with their escape. God help them if it weren't successful.

The prison building was an old brick one - all on one floor. It had been used as a warehouse annex and supply building until it was taken over by the opposition to use as their prison, and it was divided up into small cells. The security wasn't the best but with so many guards on duty all the time, they didn't concern themselves with a possible break and, in fact, had never had one.

Over a period of time the men had managed to gather various objects like a fork and knife from the mess hall, plus several rocks with very sharp edges. Someone would bring a different one in each day until they felt they had enough to start their eventual escape. Luckily for them the fact that the building was brick offered them a better chance of escape by digging out the mortar between a block of bricks as a means of escape. They were very cautious even though they felt everything was still in their favor.

Loosening up a portion of brick large enough to squeeze through was very slow and tedious, and required doing it when outside noises were loud enough to cover the noise of their scratching, but little by little they succeeded. The closer the time came for their escape the more they realized that Saturday night (the night of the party for the warden) was the ideal time for their escape and made them all the more confident they would succeed. All but a small amount of mortar had been removed; a little at a time and was put in their pockets and disposed of while at work. One of the straw mattresses blocked the area where they had been removing mortar so it wouldn't be noticed. Besides, the building, being so old, had signs of crumbling mortar in many areas on the outside walls.

Chapter 3

It was 10 PM on a warm Saturday night, the lights in the prison cell blocks had just been turned off and Juan and his friends could hear loud music and talking and laughing coming from the building the guerrillas referred to as the community center. The commanding officer and the guards used it for their mess hall as well as a recreation hall. One end had been partitioned off and made into a couple of offices where they would interrogate prisoners from time to time - trying to convince them they should join forces. A radio for contacting other prisons was in one of them, to be used mostly by other guerrillas to call on them for help in the event of a skirmish they couldn't handle. The kitchen was also located in this building. They had already gathered for their night of drinking and carrying on, leaving just a skeleton crew to watch the prisoners.

"Shows how stupid those guys are," Juan commented. "They're more concerned with having a good time than guarding the place properly. Their stupidity is our good fortune I'd say. We sure are lucky Shorty overheard those guys discussing the party.

"Yeah," Desi agreed. "I've been checking those guys and a guard comes by every 45 minutes. Guess he stops for a drink before continuing his rounds, and he is due in a couple of minutes. I'd suggest we go about five minutes after he goes by, though I doubt if they will miss us before morning. And, unless I miss my guess, they'll be drinking so much they just might oversleep tomorrow, and by that time we'll be long gone."

The men quietly gathered their meager belongings and a few minutes after the guard passed, they pulled away the corner mattress gently and quietly removed the loosened block of bricks, and one by one they slipped through the hole and into the dark of night. The last man through pulled the mattress as close to the wall as possible and then carefully replaced the block so it wouldn't be noticed on future rounds by the guard.

They then headed for the river, crouching down as they ran across the prison yard. Once into the water they crouched low and followed Roberto as he slowly lead the way across the river and into the dense wooded area, carefully following each other, Indian style, in the pitch dark. As they emerged from the woods they came into some tall Savanna grass, known to harbor several species of snakes (many of which were poisonous). Roberto knew exactly where to go, even in the darkness and within four hours they had made their way to level farmland where there was just a few low bushy areas for protection. By this time the men were very tired.

"We made it," Juan said with a sigh. "Now where do we go from here?"

"We'll stay together until we reach Estell," Roberto announced. "At that point we'll separate and head north to the border, which is not very far. We'll find something to eat in town. I know where there is a little cabaret just at the edge of town. Well, actually it's a dive, but it's open all night. Just keep low as we go through the brush just in case someone spots us and asks questions."

Before he could say anymore, Desi asked, "How do we know the guerrillas haven't taken that over? If anyone suspects we're escaped prisoners, we've had it. These prison clothes don't help any either."

"Don't worry," Roberto told him. "A friend of mine agreed to patronize those bastards and got on their good side just so they would have a place to blow off steam. At the same time he would have a place to protect anyone in case they decided to attempt to leave the country rather than being imprisoned - like us. He has a few rooms on the second floor of the place that he rents out. Believe me, he can be trusted and will have food for us."

"What's the name of the place?" Juan asked.

"He calls it the Jealous Jaguar," he answered. "It's a real dive, with girls available all hours - day and night - who will give a guy anything he wants for a price. That's why the guerrillas allow it to stay open; so they can come in any time and force one of the local girls to fuck him or suck him - whichever he feels like at the time. Even though they are local girls, they have been told in no uncertain terms that if they or any member of their family want to live to see another day they will keep those bastards happy and, in return, the village will be relatively safe. Some girls actually don't seem to mind it and call it doing their bit for their country! I'd sure as Hell hate to think of my wife or daughters or sisters having to entertain those crumbs. But I'm afraid that because of the situation, many young girls are unwillingly lead into a life of prostitution these days."

"Yeah, that would sure be quite a sacrifice for a decent young woman," Shorty said. "You're right though. That sounds like a real classy dump." Then, changing the subject he added, "but are you sure there will be some good food? I'm starved after that prison garbage they called food, not to mention from the long walk."

"Believe it or not the food isn't bad; at least it used to be pretty good. I understand the guerrillas make it possible for the owner to get good food. After all, they eat there too," Roberto answered. "But don't worry Shorty, I'm sure there'll be plenty for you!" and they all laughed.

It was very late at night when the weary travelers finally reached the Jealous Jaguar and decided to fake being drunk, staggering into the dimly lit place just in case there were rebel soldiers there - even though it did seem rather quiet around the area. Roberto had his fellow 'drunks' follow him and before they reached the bar his friend recognized Roberto in spite of all the weight he had lost in prison.

"Well you old son of a bitch," he called out. "Imagine seeing you here at this hour. What can I do for you and your friends? I assume they are your friends. Maybe the place will liven up now. It's been dead all night."

As the men approached him in the dim light he recognized the uniforms they were wearing and said, "Holy shit. Well I'll be damned. Now I understand why you're out so late. Don't tell me you guys actually managed to pull off an escape from those good for nothing bastards." "Yeah, they're my friends and yeah, you guessed it. We managed to get out and we wanna make sure we don't go back. Are any of the local scum around?" Roberto asked. "We're famished - haven't had a decent meal since before we were arrested, and we need a place to rest a while; that is, if you can safely accommodate us."

With a nod of his head, acknowledging the introduction, Chico replied, "No problem my friends. Those jackasses have all gone south of here. There was an uprising north of Chinandega, about 40 miles south of the prison you just came from; they needed extra help so everyone was pulled from this area for a while. In fact, some of the guards from where you were probably had to go there too. Actually I was thinking of closing in a while because it's been so quiet. The girls all went home after the guerrillas left.

"Sit down, all of you, and I'll fix you some food. How the Hell did you guys get out? I thought they were more careful than to allow four guy to break out all at once. They've had a reputation as an escape-proof prison you know."

"Well, we just ruined their reputation," Roberto told him. "They must really be pissed off. Those idiot guards were so engrossed in celebrating the warden's birthday, probably trying to make points with him, they forgot what their duties were. Now that you mention the uprising, they'll get no help from that place we just left. In fact, they'll probably be in big trouble for not having their radio on so as to know they were needed. The noise of the music and their carrying on would have drowned out the radio anyway. Pity those poor inmates tomorrow, because the guerrillas really get mean if things don't go right. I'll bet this is the last party they'll ever have. Hope they all get shot for not being on guard. Anyway, we made our break and are heading for friendlier territory, like over the border until things quiet down. Figured we could raise some money for arms to send back here. Do you wanna go with us?"

"No, I'm afraid I can't." he answered as he placed the food and drinks on the big wooden table. "Right now I'm better off right where I am, running this joint. It's available for those bastards when they want to relax and my family is free to come and go. I'd rather have a better class of people as customers but for now this is the way it has to be."

The four men ate ravenously, like they hadn't eaten in weeks. Roberto was right - the food was very good. While they ate and told of their escape, Chico sat down with them listening intently; amazed at how they got away with it and that no one had seen them between the prison and his place.

"You guys couldn't have picked a better time to get out," he said. "I doubt if there's a guerrilla between here and the border because of this latest skirmish. Our countrymen are becoming better organized and are gathering in larger numbers to fight these bastards instead of just small groups. They have been getting some arms from over the border from sympathizers up north. I'd be with them myself if it weren't for this damn game leg that slows me down so much."

Then a puzzled Desi asked, "If I'm not being too inquisitive, what happened to your leg? Would an operation help make it normal again?" "I'm afraid not." he answered. "At least not in this country. I was cutting some trees down and when we were sawing the logs, one of them rolled off the platform we had them on and crushed my leg; broke it in several places. I've got metal pins holding it together in several places. By the end of a long day, it hurts like Hell.

"After you fellows eat, you can get a little sleep." he told them. "Then, at dawn a guy near here - someone you can trust - will be taking a load of hay up north, just a mile from the border. I'm sure he won't object to you guys hitching a ride. That should help you some, and a damn sight better than walking all that way."

"Hey, that's great." Roberto said. "Instead of splitting up here we'll wait until we get closer to the border. We figured we'd be better off if we didn't travel together, in case some of the opposition sympathizers are around. Ya know what I mean? Listen friend, I think I can speak for my buddies here when I say we'll always be grateful to you. I really owe you, and I'll get in touch with you as soon as I get settled again. Trust me my friend."

"What are friends for if they can't help each other during rough times?" Chico answered. He then showed them to a large room with several cots where they were to bunk down. "Not much but they are clean and fairly comfortable. I'll call you later. By the way, I have a little money I can spare for each of you. And I'll give you a change of clothes and fix some food for you to take along. Who knows when you'll find a place to eat. Believe I have some clothes that careless travelers have left behind. There's sure to be something that will fit you guys - even Shorty. You sure as Hell can't travel in those rags. I'll burn them."

At 6:30 A.M. they were awakened and, by the time they shaved, showered and dressed; and had some coffee and sweet rolls, the hay wagon had arrived and they climbed onto the old stake-bodied truck where they stayed until they reached their destination, about two hours later. In less than an hour after getting off the hay wagon they were over the border and in Choluteca, Honduras, where they said their good-byes and, as previously planned, went their separate ways - promising to keep in touch with one another by running an ad in the personal column of several different newspapers, figuring each would definitely see at least one of them.

Chapter 4

Juan decided to stay in Honduras for a while where he worked wherever he could find employment; at the same time trying to contact family or old friends he had back in Nicaragua. After an unsuccessful attempt at locating anyone, he decided that as soon as he could save enough money he would make his way to the United States in hopes of starting a new life for himself and continuing in his effort to locate any of his family who may still be alive. Eventually he would head for the Northeast part of the country where he felt he could get a better job and where the weather wasn't so hot. For a while though he would find work in the southern part of the country, like Texas or New Mexico, working until he could put aside some money to send back home.

He was fortunate enough to locate his second cousin, Renaldo, hoping he had some news from home. However, he didn't know much more of what was happening back home than Juan did. They promised to keep in touch though and Juan also asked Renaldo to notify him if he ever noticed anything in the personal ads of the newspapers addressed to him, explaining what he and his friends had agreed to. Juan told Renaldo he'd get in touch with him as soon as he was settled, so he asked Renaldo to give him his address and phone number so he would be able to contact him, if not by phone then by mail.

For over a year Juan worked hard, saving every penny he could and taking courses in English at night at the local schools where he was living in Amarillo, Texas. He learned fast and he soon incorporated some computer courses into his curriculum, figuring it would result in better jobs. Even though he was an experienced accountant, he felt he needed to be computer knowledgeable as well.

Several months after he finished his basic computer course, he had saved enough money to fly to Portland, Maine where he bought an old used car and drove to a town a short distance from the coast of Maine - Lakeridge - located in the southeast area of the lakes region near Sebago Lake, where he was fortunate in securing employment in a small but growing company called, Total Graphics, Inc. It was an equal opportunity company and was willing to pay the tuition of any employees who were eager to further their education. This way Juan was able to work days and continue his schooling nights at company expense, completing the computer courses that would help in his work in the accounting department. For the first six months he did nothing but work, go to school nights and study. He figured the time for socializing could come later.

Chapter 5

Eighteen Months Later

Things had been going very well for Juan at Total Graphics. He was a good worker, a fast and willing learner, but was not a good mixer and didn't associate with most of the other employees, to the point where he was considered very anti-social and most of the people didn't like him - just tolerated him. His main concern was making money in order to send as much as possible back to his brother and his family, whom he had finally located through his cousin. He said he wasn't trying to win any popularity contests and as long as his boss was happy with his work that was all that counted. Even though the fighting had pretty much ended back home, the economy was still not good and people were left very poor, so Juan's concern was to assist them in any way he could. Juan did have some female friends (not everyone would have classified them as ladies when they saw him with any of them). It had taken him quite awhile before he started dating without feeling guilty, because he and his wife had been very close. Then he told himself she would have wanted him to go on with his life, that he was too young to just sit around and spend the rest of his life alone. Unfortunately, he didn't frequent the better parts of town so the women he dated weren't the best - many of them being prostitutes. His only steady, as such, was a young girl he called Bunny. He was much older than Bunny but they enjoyed each other's company and she enjoyed listening to good music, as did he, so they made it a point to go to Boston occasionally to a concert. However, he also spent much of his time in noisy, smoky dives with the other kind of women.

One evening, just as he arrived home to his small apartment, the telephone was ringing. When he answered it, it was his old friends Desi and Shorty who had been told by his cousin where they could find him. They decided to look him up so they could have a reunion of sorts and exchange news as to what they had been doing since coming to the States and what news they had from their respective homes. They had been living in Texas and decided it would be cooler in Maine than it was there during the summer and they drove up in Shorty's pickup truck. They were staying at Chaplin's Cabins on Route 302 in Naples. Juan told them he knew where it was and that he would be there as soon as he could get there.

Juan got into his old beat up Ford Taurus and headed for the motel which was about a 20-minute drive from where he lived. Traffic was light so he made the trip in plenty of time. His friends were standing out in the motel parking lot waiting for him.

"You guys are a sight for sore eyes," he shouted as he got out of his car and headed to where they were standing. "What a great surprise." he added as he met them. "Sometimes it gets awfully lonely not having anyone from home to talk to. This is a nice place and I have a good job, but there's nothing like home. I'll admit one thing, you sure picked a good time to come up here. Late spring and early summer is a beautiful time. Actually the fall is the most colorful and attracts loads of tourists but by then it is also starting to get a little cool."

When they met, they greeted each other with a big hug and handshake, Shorty towering over both of them and looking as though he could squeeze them to death. He had gained some weight since they last saw each other and must have been 280 pounds on his tall frame; an unusual size for a person from Nicaragua. He had told them he inherited his size from his mother's side. His mother was not from Nicaragua, but was Polish and Shorty never did find out how she and his father ever got together.

"Damn, it's been too long," Juan said. "Let's go someplace where we can get a beer or a glass of wine, and maybe something to eat. Are you hungry? I don't have to ask Shorty, because you guys don't look as though you've missed any meals lately.

"I have a few groceries at my apartment but if we were to get the least bit noisy, I'd hear about it," Juan told them. "Maybe we should just go to a bar I know where we don't have to worry about raising our voices. I'll pay. Besides, I not only don't like to cook, I'm a lousy one and I eat out most of the time, except maybe for breakfast."

"OK," they both agreed. "That sounds good. We'll take your car, if you don't mind, and then you can just drop us off back here."

Everyone thought that was a good idea and then proceeded to get into Juan's car. The bar where they were going was just a short distance from the motel. It wasn't a fancy place, but it was cleaner than most and it also offered short order meals as well. When they entered they asked for seats where it would be private so they could talk over old times. The owner led them to a booth towards the back of the place.

"So, how have you guys been? What are you doing and do you have steady jobs?" Juan asked them excitedly. "There are so many questions I have to ask. But then you guys probably feel the same."

"Well, we are thinking about going back to Nicaragua. The fighting has stopped and the elections are over, and I understand people on both sides have been forgiven their crimes, as they refer to them. There is still much poverty and unemployment, but things are improving." Desi told him. "Right now we are working in Texas on a cattle ranch. It's not a very good job; hard work and doesn't pay very much but it is a job and keeps a roof over our heads. Right now is a quiet season so they let us take some time off."

"I thought I'd be returning home by now but my job here is a good one and I like the climate - pretty cold in the winter but otherwise it's great," Juan said. "I hope that next year I will have saved enough to take a vacation and go back home and try and locate more of the family. My cousin Renaldo, who lives in Austin, Texas, keeps me up-to-date on things back home, which he claims haven't really changed much. Someone told him they knew at least one of my brothers was still alive, but I already know that. In fact, he is taking care of my daughter. When the economic conditions improve and it looks as though there is a future for me, job-wise, I'll probably leave my job here and go back home. So far it is just a possibility. I too miss my old home and family, but I was lucky enough to locate my older brother, and I may try to talk him into moving up here with his family and bring my daughter with him, if I change my mind about going home permanently."

"So, have you seen any mutual friends along the way?"

"As a matter of fact," Shorty said, "we saw Roberto once but he was planning to go to Arizona to live. He finally met the girl of his dreams, after all these years, and wants to get married and settle down - said he's had enough moving around. I figured him for a confirmed bachelor, but you never know about people."

"Yeh, we asked him about his friend who helped us get out of the country - what was his name? Chico?" Desi said. "The poor guy was sent to prison about a year after we left. Seems they found out he had been helping people escape from the country. They took over the cabaret and arrested him - took his home and forced his family to work for them. The poor guy really suffered at their hands. They didn't make it very easy for him and, having that bum leg made it even harder on him. It was less than a year after he was arrested when the war was over, thank goodness. The government pardoned him for his so-called crimes and gave him back his home and cabaret. They were able to locate the rest of his family, who had gone through an awful lot, but at least they are all together again. We started a fund to help pay the expenses for him to come to the U.S. and have his leg fixed up.

Roberto said there was a doctor at the New England Medical Center in Boston who was willing to repair his leg, but Chico didn't have enough money to make the trip. So, I figured it's the least we could do for what he did for us. I've managed to save a little and have collected a few hundred from other people who knew him. What do you think of the idea?"

"Hey, that's a great idea." Juan agreed. "He was a heck of a nice guy and we all owe him a lot. Before you guys leave I'll give you some money. I've managed to save quite a bit since working here. You can also give me his address and when I go home again I'll look him up. By that time he should have had his operation."

The three men had several drinks and had a fairly good meal, considering it was just a bar, before leaving several hours later. Juan left them off at their motel, apologizing for not having room for them in his little apartment which was really just one big room with a small kitchenette and bath. They said it was OK and they understood. Juan offered to show them around that weekend, if they were planning on staying that long. "We are pretty busy at work right now, or I'd take a day or two off and we could do some real good sightseeing." he told them. "But, we'll have evenings and this weekend. I'll take you guys to some good restaurants where they have fantastic fish. You haven't eaten fish until you have it here in Maine. Betcha neither of you ever had lobster! Well, you're going to have some before you leave and you may just want to stay just to have good shellfish meals. We'll plan on driving up the coastline where you'll see real beauty - nothing like you've ever seen before. I must admit it is really different as well as beautiful around here. The lakes area here is nice, but personally I prefer the coastline."

"Sure, we'll be around for a few days and speaking for myself," Shorty said, "I'd love to try some lobster. I can't recall eatin' much food that I didn't like. How about you Desi, are we staying for awhile to see the sights and eat?"

Desi agreed that it was a good idea. He was anxious to see this part of the United States too before he returned to Central America.

That weekend the three men toured around the East Coast of Maine, seeing the sights and eating at many of the nicer places. One day he drove them to Kennebunkport and told them that President Bush had a home there, and he drove as close as they could get to the property. They were impressed. He found a nice restaurant facing the ocean where they enjoyed a delicious lobster and steamer dinner. Shorty had developed a taste for raw oysters as well as boiled lobster - and ate lots of both. Each time Juan insisted on paying the bill and always with big bills from a roll of money he had in his pocket. The other two would look at each other in wonderment at times, but never questioned Juan as to why he carried so much money around.

When it was finally time for his two friends to leave Maine and return home, Juan kept his promise regarding a donation for Chico's operation and gave Desi a check for $5000 for the fund. "Here, guys, this should help some in getting his leg fixed up." Juan told them. "Tell him I wish him luck and my prayers are with him. Let me know how things turn out."

"We sure will," Shorty told him. "Boy, you sure must be doing OK to afford a donation like that. We were thinking if we got a few hundred we'd do well. Thanks again."

"I don't make it a habit of spending money foolishly and I got lucky recently. Besides, I can't think of a better cause on which to spend it," he told the men. "Just don't forget me and keep me informed of things. If you ever get up this way again, be sure and look me up, and I'll take you guys up to Acadia National Park where the beauty will knock your socks off! We should plan to get together more often. So long good friends. We went through an awful lot together and I'll never forget either of you."

The three of them then gave each other big hugs and a sturdy handshake and Desi and Shorty departed in their old Chevy pickup, promising they would be back the first chance they had.

Chapter 6

Total Graphics, Inc. (T.G.I.) was a relatively small firm which, for the past 12 years had specialized in computer software packages. Prior to that it had been just a family project started 40 years ago as a printing company, selling a limited amount of office supplies on the side. In a few short years business had increased to the point where they employed 27 people. As automation and computers became the big thing and the company started to lose business, the founder realized it was time to modernize and become more diversified. At that point his employees were compelled to become computer knowledgeable or find another job. After replacing his old printing presses with computers and related equipment and, gradually educating his employees to the modern way, almost immediately his business boomed. Additional space was soon required as the company expanded to a total work force of 89 people, and they leased office space in a large office building near the downtown area.

Benjamin Wilson, President and founder of Total Graphics, Inc. is still in charge of operations at the company, working every day, even though he is in his mid sixties His wife, Marge, has occasionally assisted with the books, especially during income tax time - just to stay abreast of what is going on is the way she puts it, even though she isn't really needed. She had worked for the company in the early days.

The Wilsons' only daughter, Angie, is married to Alex Christou, the Vice-President and Chief of the Accounting Department. They have three children. Their son, Steve, went to work for his father after completing college 15 years ago. Steve, being the oldest of the three children, could some day take over as president and inherit part of the business when his parents passed on. He is extremely intelligent and outstanding in his job. However, he was spoiled and in recent years turned out to be an arrogant, conceited man with an outrageous temper, and lacking responsibility. To make matters worse about two years ago he started drinking heavily, though he managed to always be sober on the job, and he is suspected of using drugs. He has never taken after either of his parents, his sister or his younger brother. Ben tries to keep him in tow as far as the company is concerned - told him in no uncertain terms that he would pull his load with the company, and be civil to the employees, or out the door he will go and would be disinherited in favor of his sister and younger brother.

For that reason, and that reason only, Steve complies with his father's orders while in the office, but away from the company he is often referred to as that rich, pompous ass who must have been given to the Wilsons by mistake. How could a couple as nice as they end up with such an impossible son?"

Many people wondered why Steve's wife had stayed with him so long unless it was the money, although she was always such a quiet, gentle woman and an excellent mother to their three children. No one was surprised when she finally took all the abuse and cheating she could stand and filed for a divorce, as well as requesting a restraining order forbidding Steve from seeing her or the children without other members of the family being in attendance. Until a thorough investigation into her allegations of wife beating and child abuse is completed and the divorce is granted, he is not to be seen anywhere near their home. He took a small apartment near the edge of town, near bars and night clubs.

His parents see their grandchildren regularly and enjoy visiting them and their mother, as well as having them as guests in their home. The children like that arrangement because they get to use the big swimming pool their grandparents have. Ben and Marge feel sorry for the grief their daughter-in-law has gone through because of Steve. Everyone still has hopes he will change.

The Wilsons' youngest son, Michael, lives in California where he has an excellent position with a large hotel in the Bay area. He never showed any interest in his dad's business, went to college (maintaining a 3.95 average) where he earned a Masters in Business Management at Northeastern University. Since he also enjoyed cooking and bartending - having done some during the summer while going to college - he decided to combine both with hotel and restaurant management, enrolling at Johnson & Wales in Rhode Island, where he also excelled. He is an extremely likable, handsome young man with a dynamic personality. His father always said he was such a charmer he could sell someone the Empire State Building and the buyer would think he had cheated Michael!! Ben was always sorry Michael didn't care for the family business because with his charm and charisma, he could have done wonders for TGI. However, he was proud of his young son for his accomplishments at such a young age. He wished Steve had been as caring and ambitious as Michael.

T.G.I. had become a very lucrative business in spite of a nationwide slumping economy (recession as the so-called experts were calling it), mostly due to the tremendous influx of foreign imports. Mr. Wilson preferred to keep it on a small business level after having seen many computer oriented companies over-extend themselves and grow too big, too fast, only to fall in debt over loss of business - some having gone bankrupt and losing their company entirely. Partly due to Mr. Wilson's honesty and integrity, T.G.I. managed to win contracts (some for the Government) over other small businesses in the east and, for that reason, employees' jobs were considered relatively secure which wasn't the case in much of New England at this time.

Chapter 7

On the occasion of the fortieth anniversary of the company the owners decided to show just how grateful they were for their success by celebrating. Ben and Marge had a dinner party at their home for their closest friends and business associates, which was comprised of many well-known business men in town, in addition to a few local politicians. The Wilson's home was a large, stately, colonial-style house situated on an enormous, immaculately landscaped 4 acre lot in the suburbs, overlooking Sebago Lake; ideal for entertaining large groups. There was a large patio and lawn in the back, where in warm weather most of their entertaining took place. A similar celebration with dinner and dancing was to take place at a nearby hotel for the entire company at a later date.

The night of the party their home had been beautifully decorated with fresh flowers placed in prominent places throughout the house. Marge looked exquisite in a silk, lavender colored cocktail length dress with the proper matching jewelry. She had traveled to New York recently to find just the right dress. She couldn't have chosen a nicer color to go with her soft, grey hair and fair complexion. She took one last walk-through of her home to make sure everything looked just right to her. She always worried that things wouldn't go the way she wanted them to, even though she had a reputation around the area for being the perfect hostess.

Extra help had been hired for the evening, to serve drinks, hors'deuvres and to prepare the buffet style dinner which she felt would be more appropriate than a sit-down meal. Fifty-eight guests gradually arrived, with only a few late arrivals.

One of the late couples was Ben's daughter and her husband, which was most unusual for them. Still later Steve arrived with a slim, young girl in a tight, low-cut, red mini dress; long red and gold dangling earrings, and very heavy makeup; hanging tightly to Steve's arm as though she were afraid he'd try to escape her clutches! His parents were very embarrassed that he would be seen with such a person (much less bring her into their home), even though he was separated. People who knew the family well weren't too surprised, knowing Steve's reputation. His choice in the women he dated left much to be desired and this one did not fit into a group such as there was at the Wilson's that night. Many of the guests felt that for this occasion he should have had his wife with him even though they were estranged.

The girl was exactly the opposite of his wife, Laura, who was always very gracious and smartly dressed. Marge and Ben had warned him earlier that he had better watch himself and be on his best behavior that night, also letting him know how they felt about his choice of date for the evening - meaning for one thing to go easy on the drinking. They wanted no trouble from him to spoil the evening.

The party went off very well with everyone appearing to be having a good time. A group of city officials approached Ben about the possibility of his getting involved in local politics. He tried to convince them he was no politician and was too old to think about getting involved even if he were so inclined. They didn't agree with him and assured him there was a place for a man of his caliber and experience in business. The fact that he was also very well liked and respected in the area would be to his advantage.

"Thanks for your vote of confidence," Ben told them. "But I really don't think I would care to get involved in politics. I'm happy where I am. However, I will sleep on it and let you know what I come up with.

"Right now the business is my main concern and whatever I do I must give it my undivided attention. I don't believe in trying to split my time between two important things." Ben explained. "It has to be either my business or politics - not both."

"Well now," Clyde Foghorn, the mayor said. "I'll accept that. We certainly hope you come to the realization that it would be a good idea and that you'd be very successful in whatever office you would choose to run."

"Even yours?" Ben kidded.

Mayor Foghorn didn't take this remark as being a bit funny, but the rest of the men laughed, and that was the end of any conversation encouraging Ben to enter politics.

Except for Steve drinking too much and making a fool of himself near the end of the evening (which didn't surprise many of the local people), everyone enjoyed themselves and, as they were leaving, each guest thanked Marge and Ben for a lovely evening.

After the last guest left Ben put his arm around Marge and said, "As usual my darling, you were a perfect hostess and the party was outstanding. I don't know how you do it, but you sure are well organized. That woman, Pearle Mesta, sure didn't have anything over you, and you're much prettier. I love you my dear and, in case I haven't told you lately, you're a very beautiful woman and I'm very proud of you." And he gave her a tender kiss on the cheek.

"Well thank you sweetheart for those very nice compliments," she answered, smiling into his eyes. "I consider myself lucky to have someone who loves me so much. I'm just happy things went so well. We always have a good staff to help set things up and clean up afterwards. I'll have to admit though, I am tired. Shall we go to bed dear? I'll tell the help to make sure they lock up before they leave."

Chapter 8

Four Months Later

A staff meeting was called in the conference room at TGI; mandatory for all section managers. Even though the company had always been quite stable, Mr. Wilson - being a natural worrier - was concerned with things going well, in particular the financial department. Therefore, he held frequent staff meetings.

As soon as everyone had arrived and were seated around the large conference table he asked each manager to give a report on the work being done in their department. Included, he had asked for efficiency reports on how employees in a particular area were performing. The shipping room, the software designers, the records department, and the general offices all gave a highly satisfactory report on their respective personnel. The trainees were all very conscientious and cooperative they said.

Ben then asked Alex, Vice President and General Manager of the Accounting Department to give a report.

"Alex, I happened to glance through some of the books the other day and they didn't seem to make sense to me." Ben told him. "So I thought I had better let you explain things to me. Perhaps I didn't have everything on hand and, of course, I am not as much of an expert at books as you and your people are. That's why I hired you - for your expertise in accounting. Don't know what the company would do without you. So, if you will give your report, to set my mind at ease, that things are fine, financially, with the company, you will make me very happy."

"Don't give it a thought," Alex said. "It's like you said, not all the books are in the same place because right now we are starting our own audit. I'm sure if we were to go over them all together, you'd find everything in perfect order. I have the best bookkeeping staff in the state and trust them implicitly. We do have our regular meetings too, to discuss any problems there may be on anyone's mind. I did worry for awhile about Mr. Marcos, the fellow from Nicaragua, that we hired about a year and a half ago, but he has shaped up to be a very good accountant. He went to school nights and finished getting his degree; said he had started college before the war in his country. He's not the friendliest of people but as far as his work is concerned, I don't think I have to worry about him. In other words we seem to be in good shape."

"I'll take your word for it Alex," Ben told him. "If you should have any problems with any of your people at all, don't hesitate to bring it to my attention and we'll work it out." Then turning to his son, Steve, he asked, "And how is Rose doing with her training? I realize she is older than many of our personnel, but she has always been a hard worker and I hope that it isn't too difficult, at her age, to learn computer programs."

"Oh, she is doing fine." Steve answered his dad. "What she doesn't pick up on right away, the others help her with. Martha has helped her a great deal.

"She is a smart woman and is eager to learn. Too bad everyone isn't as conscientious and dedicated as she is. Of course, she can be a little outspoken at times, though nothing like her friend Martha, but that certainly doesn't have any effect on her job."

"Well," Ben said, "I guess it is safe to say the company is in A-One condition and I have the best staff around to make certain it remains that way." Then, turning to Alex, he said, "I do want to get together with you one of these days and go over the books - no hurry though. Sometime when we both have plenty of free time. We wouldn't want the auditors to come in and find a few pennies missing. By the way, how is Harry doing? He impresses me as a pretty smart, young man, someone who is very dedicated and should go far as an accountant."

"Sure Dad, any time." Alex assured him. "Right now we are pretty busy but in a couple of weeks or so, whenever you say. As for Harry, we couldn't have anyone more dependable and the younger, less experienced people really look up to him. Don't know what I'd do without him. By the way, just so you know how valuable I think he is, I recently made him my assistant. I wouldn't be surprised if he had an announcement to make one of these days. Don't know if you've noticed that very attractive girl he's been seeing for a while; well, it looks pretty serious."

"That's good. I'm always happy to see people get ahead," Ben commented. "As for his girl, I'd say he's the right age to settle down. I wish him luck.

"Thank you everyone. We can all get back to work now. I appreciate everyone's loyalty and putting up with these frequent meetings."

Chapter 9

"Peter, we need to talk," Stephanie said to her husband, sounding very serious. "Come sit by me on the couch, please."

"OK Steph, what's with the oh so serious sound to your voice?" Peter asked. "You sound as though you have a big problem," and he gave her a light kiss on the cheek, which was more than she had been used to the past few months.

"Don't try and humor me at a time like this," she told him. "I need to know why we argue so much lately. I'm worried about us. I love you very much and lately there are times when I feel you don't even know I'm around. If I've done something to cause this please let me know. Or if I'm not pleasing you in some way tell me what I can do to make things better."

"Nothing is wrong," He told her. "You're imagining things. What's the matter, are you going through your change early? I understand that makes women act rather strange. Everything is fine with me. Nothing is wrong. Is that clear?"

"You know there is," she told him. "We never go any place together; you are always off on these trips. You used to always make time for us no matter what stresses there were at work. Another thing, when I went to the bank to make the mortgage payment, I was told there was insufficient funds. How can that possibly be. I'm always very careful about the money I spend. Between our combined salaries we should never have to worry about insufficient funds. Have you been entertaining some of your buddies where you work? if so, you really must be a big spender."

"I told you everything is OK," he insisted. "I've just been too tired to dress up and go out after all that traveling. You can't possibly know how much it takes from a person to be constantly traveling around whether it be flying or driving. As for the money I'll have to go down and give that bank a piece of my mind. There's no reason why we shouldn't have plenty to make monthly payments, unless you've been buying some more of those expensive outfits you think you have to have to keep up with your job. You act as though you are the president of the company instead of just a secretary."

"Don't start in on my company again," she told him. "As secretary to the president, sure I have to look my best. But I haven't bought a thing for over six months. You are pretty good at spending money too when you go on your trips - probably trying to impress everyone about what a big shot you are. If it isn't that then you'd better set them straight at the bank because I have utility bills to pay this coming week, and I don't want any checks bouncing. I never thought we would have to discuss money problems."

"You have an overactive imagination lately, Stephanie, and I can change that with one good punch." He yelled at her. "If it isn't me who is not paying enough attention to you, it's something else to complain about. This time you decided you'd blame me because you couldn't pay the bills. I don't want to hear anymore about it. I'm going out to get some fresh air before I lose my temper. Maybe when I get back, if I decide to come back tonight, you'll be in a better mood." and he grabbed his jacket and went out the door, slamming it behind him.

Chapter 10

Early one morning, about a month later, Ben stopped by Stephanie's desk to ask her to make a call for him. He found her in tears.

"What in the world is the matter, dear?" he asked of his favorite secretary. "Is there anything I can do for you? Do you care to talk about it?" "I'm sorry, I should have better control of myself than to break down here in the office," she sobbed. "But I just couldn't help it. I'll be OK in a minute."

"Maybe you'd feel better if you talked about it," he told her. "I have strong shoulders and a good ear for listening, if it will help."

"It's my husband," she answered. "All of a sudden he is a changed man, after all these years. No matter what I say or do, nothing pleases him and he's always yelling at me. It doesn't do any good to try and reason with him and when I ask him what the problem is he tells me nothing or, 'you should know'. I think I still love him, but he just isn't the loving, considerate man he used to be. This morning he was really in a strange mood and refused to talk to me at all. When I tried to get him to answer me he hit me and told me to 'butt out'. I have no idea what time he gets in at night, or if he comes home at all because he sleeps downstairs so much. He can be so sweet when he wants to be but those times are getting further and further apart."

"Would it do any good if I or someone else spoke to him?" Ben asked. "I'd be happy to do anything I could, you know that."

"Thanks, but I don't think so. Peter would just get even madder and tell me I had no right involving anyone else in our life. I'll just have to try and catch him in a good mood and then ask if we can talk seriously to each other, and see if he will tell me what is wrong. I did that a few weeks ago but we didn't resolve anything. Right now I am so upset. Thank you for talking to me and letting me pour my troubles off on to you. You are a very kind man. Mrs. Wilson is certainly fortunate to have a husband like you.

"I'm OK now. What was it you came out to ask me to do Mr. Wilson?"

"I'd like you to call Rose and see if it would be convenient for her to come to my office about 9 o'clock this morning." he said.

"Should I tell her why you want to see her?"

"No, that won't be necessary. She already knows."

Stephanie was rather puzzled that he didn't tell her why he wanted to see Rose. She couldn't imagine why her boss would need to discuss anything with Rose. Perhaps if she hadn't been so upset when he came to her desk he may have told her. However, she called and gave Rose the message and, later when Stephanie told the other girls that Mr. Wilson wanted a private appointment with Rose, as in so many office places, there were all kinds of speculation. Why would he possibly have anything so secret to discuss with Rose, the girls wondered. Could she be getting a promotion and, if so, to what? Or maybe he was not satisfied with her work and she was getting a reprimand, though most of them couldn't believe it would be that. When she finally came out of Mr. Wilson's office she said nothing to Stephanie and just headed back to her own office.

Later, during their morning break, several of the girls gathered in the employee lounge and Martha asked Stephanie if she had found out what the secret meeting was all about. Martha was nice but she thought she should make everything her business - didn't want anything going on that she didn't know about.

"What's wrong Martha?" Stephanie asked rather impatiently, realizing right away she never should have said anything to any of them, especially Martha. "Do you think Mr. Wilson wants to have an affair with Rose? Actually, he didn't confide in me and I didn't ask any questions. Figured if he wanted me to know he would have told me."

"How can you not be curious?" Martha asked. "Don't tell me you wouldn't like to know what it's all about just as much as I do. What could Rose have or know about that your boss would possible be interested in?"

"I don't know, and I don't really care. Besides I'm pretty busy right now, so I have to eat and run. Why don't you ask her when you see her? I'll talk to you later. And don't worry, if I hear anything earth-shattering or at all exciting, I'll be sure and let you know."

"Boy, she sure isn't in a very good mood this morning." Martha said. "Wonder what her problem is. It can't be that time of the month; that was last week. That's a little unusual for her to be in such a mood."

"So why don't you go to her office and ask her, if you're so curious?" Valerie asked. "Are you afraid she might tell you to get lost?" and she walked back towards her office before waiting for an answer.

"Gosh, but there sure are a bunch of grumpy people around here today," Martha thought to herself. "I should have had my coffee break at my desk. I just might decide to ask Rose."

Chapter 11

About two weeks later

Saturday evening, everyone associated with T.G.I., in addition to a few business associates, arrived at the ballroom of the local hotel to celebrate a delayed 40th anniversary celebration of the company. Because it was a very busy time on the actual anniversary date, the party had been postponed until work slowed down, everyone would be back from vacation, and things were back to normal.

Their spouse or a date accompanied most people. Mr. Wilson wanted to show his appreciation for their loyalty and hard work and had spared no expense to make this a gala occasion for the employees. He figured without them the company wouldn't possibly be the success it was. There was a cocktail hour followed by a full course filet mignon dinner, a few special awards, followed by dancing until late. Everyone had been invited and most of them showed up.

Ben and Marge, Alex and Angie, and Steve and his date were at the head table. (Steve had a different girl this time who wasn't quite as bad as the other one) Ben's parents, who were both 92 years young, and still very spry, had been flown in from Florida on the company jet for the occasion and they too were at the head table.

Their youngest son, Michael, also surprised his parents by flying home from San Francisco for the occasion, which pleased his mother and dad very much. He was accompanied by a beautiful, dark-haired young lady named Jennifer, whom he announced was his fiancée - an unexpected surprise for the family since they didn't realize Michael had been going steady, so the evening turned out to be a double celebration for them. Stephanie and her husband, who seldom went to any company get-togethers because he supposedly was rather shy and felt out of place, (at least that was what Stephanie always said) were there for a rare evening out. He was strictly a home body she had indicated at one time - actually she was trying to cover up for his usual bad mood towards her. However, this evening he certainly didn't appear very shy. In fact, after dinner, Stephanie found herself alone several times while Peter mingled with the single girls. She was visibly aggravated at times, but told anyone who mentioned that he seemed to be enjoying the girls, that she figured it was good he was coming out of his shell and getting to know people from the company about whom she talked so much.

Peter was a senior draftsman and trouble-shooter with an architectural and construction firm out of Portland, and was required to make many business trips to wherever the company may be involved with a building being constructed at the time. He was really a highly qualified employee and his services were very much in demand. For that reason, allegedly, he preferred staying home when he wasn't called upon to work overtime (or at least that was what he claimed). The rest of the time his excuse was that he was just too tired and preferred to stay home and relax. In recent years, however, his attitude at home with Stephanie was definitely bitter.

"You're awfully quiet tonight, Steph," Rose commented. "Aren't you feeling well? Your husband seems to be having a good time though. Can I get you anything?"

"No thank you," she replied. "I'm OK. But I wouldn't be surprised if my 'bashful' husband has had too many drinks and is making a fool of himself, acting as though he's in his second childhood. I've never seen him drink so much. In fact, I've never seen him have more than a glass of wine."

Interrupting the other two girls, Martha said, "I don't believe what I'm seeing - Juan with a girl who doesn't look like a well-used pickup. I hate to say this but most of his dates usually look like hookers. I apologize; this is too fancy a place for talk like that," and she laughed, thinking she was quite funny.

"Never mind, I'm even more surprised that he is here at all. I wonder why?" Dennis questioned, suspiciously.

"Why shouldn't he be here too?" Janet, his date, asked Dennis. "He does work for the company and has as much right to be here as you or I - perhaps even more so since I'm just your girl friend."

"Hey honey, you're not JUST a girl friend," he told her. "You're my very special one and only beautiful lady; and don't you forget it."

"Here he comes. I'll tell you about him later, Janet." Martha said as she turned her attention to Juan and his date.

"Well good evening Juan," Martha remarked with a very friendly tone to her voice. "We're surprised you could make it but glad you did. Who's this lovely young creature you have with you? How do you rate someone like her?"

"Hi everyone," Juan said, adding rather sarcastically, "Its nice to know you're all so happy to see me. This beautiful young lady just happens to be my niece who is visiting the states for a few days before going back to school in Honduras. Isn't she pretty?" and he proceeded to introduce her to the people at their table. "I didn't think I should bring one of my regular girls to such a fancy affair - you all know what I mean. I have been taught how to conduct myself properly, when necessary, even though you people may not believe it. Try not to let the shock be too much for you. Now, if you will excuse us I would like to introduce Monica to the boss." and he took his niece by the arm and left the little circle of fellow employees to gossip about him.

"It has been a pleasure meeting all of you," Monica told them in broken English as Juan was about to lead her away. "Don't mind my uncle. His bark is worse than his bite, as you say here in America. He is really a very nice person and he paid for my trip to the United States. He is very generous. I'll see you later."

There was utter silence at the table, as the two of them left. They couldn't believe what they had just heard since no one had ever wanted to see a good side to Juan. Were they being unfair to him because he wasn't friendly? After all he had gone through before coming to the U.S., he had reason not to trust some people.

"Why are these people bad-mouthing that fellow Juan?" Stephanie's husband, Peter, asked Valerie, who just happened to be sitting nearby. "I don't see how anyone could be so bad and still be retained with a company."

"Actually he minds his own business most of the time," she said. "But, he's kind of a loner, really isn't very sociable and is very opinionated, so many people don't like him. I've never really had any quarrel with him," and she proceeded to tell Peter a little of Juan's background.

"Maybe the guy has reason to act the way he does under those circumstances," he answered her, and walked over to the table where Stephanie and he were assigned.

Juan and Monica had been placed at the same table as Rose and her date, Edward; Paul, from the mailroom and his girl friend,

Sandra; Mitch, a programmer, and his wife Penny; and Roberta, an analyst and her husband, David. Everyone was very cordial to Juan for a change and they found he could be quite pleasant and well mannered - or was it Monica's presence that prompted his gentlemanly manner? They also found him to be very knowledgeable about many subjects. The meal was delicious, the conversation interesting and everyone had a good time.

After dinner Juan made it a point that everyone eventually met Monica, and the most critical of the group appeared very surprised that Juan could have such a lovely, well-bred niece - so friendly and out-going. Most of the men had hoped to dance with her, but Juan didn't give anyone much of a chance. He and Monica danced several numbers together when Mr. Wilson cut in and asked her to dance with him, and he proceeded to steal her away from her uncle. Juan certainly wasn't about to tell the company president he couldn't dance with her.

He had told some people they had another engagement and would have to leave early. Then, before anyone else had a chance to ask Monica to dance they left, Juan having told others that he had to get his niece back early. He couldn't seem to keep his stories consistent.

"Well, I'll be darned," Carlos said. "He's the last person I expected to see here tonight. I wonder why he decided to join the party - never has before - probably wanted to show off that gorgeous niece of his. He made sure the people at the head table met her, and he acted like a perfect gentleman. I didn't realize he could be such a good conversationalist, and be so proficient about so many subjects. I sure can't figure this one out."

"Who exactly is he?" asked Rita, Carlos' recent bride. "If he works for the company too then why is it such a surprise that he came?"

Carlos proceeded to explain to Rita about Juan, at least what they knew about him, and how impossible he could be some of the time in and out of the office - when he wasn't taking time off. It seems his attendance record wasn't very good.

"However," he related, "we heard from a good source that he was a prisoner of the guerrillas in his country for over two years. When he escaped he came here and settled, hoping that he could eventually save enough money to pay someone to locate some of his family, if they hadn't all been killed as a result of being taken prisoner. I suppose we shouldn't be too hard on him after what he has gone through, but he could make an effort to be more civil. He is well educated so he shouldn't be so hostile. After all he is in friendly territory now."

"Not meaning to change the subject," Valerie said, "but I wonder where Debbie is tonight. I thought she had planned on coming. In fact, she told me she was looking forward to the big bash, as she referred to it."

"I think she told me she had some finals coming up and needed more study time." Dennis told her. "She really is intent on getting good grades. I'm sure it must be rough working days and having to study and go to school nights. She evidently doesn't have much social life these days, but I shouldn't think this one night out would have hurt her grades. She is just as serious and conscientious at work as she seems to be about school. She sure is an ambitious girl and should go far with her career."

"I'll have to let her know what a good time she missed and that it would have done her good to get out and relax for a change," Martha commented. "She is such a lovely, likable girl and very smart; but she should get out and enjoy life more while she is still young."

"Well, listen to our philosopher," Carlos said. "I didn't think you could be so serious and concerned over another employee."

"Hey, there's a lot about me you don't know, and never will," Martha kidded.

"Wow," Carlos explained. "Listen to our Martha everyone. She's trying to make us think she is a mystery woman."

"She has a point, you know," Valerie commented. "Too many girls take life too seriously when they are young and the next thing you know youth has passed them by and they're no longer kids and never got to enjoy the things kids usually do - know what I mean? Believe me I know what I am talking about."

"Gosh Valerie, I never realized how serious you could be." Jerry remarked. "If I'm not being too inquisitive, are you speaking from experience?"

"Yes, as a matter of fact I am," she told him. "With me it wasn't a matter of choice. My parents just believed in study, study, study for me. There was never time for play while I was getting my education. Since they never had a chance to go to college, I was to fulfill their dream. While other girls were dating and having fun I went to college, then home to study and then help around the house after I finished studying. That in itself wasn't so bad; but then why am I telling you all this. I've no right to bore other people with my life story."

"An attractive girl like you should have had lots of dates." Carlos told her, after over-hearing the conversation. "I'm very sorry to interfere with your conversation, but I'll bet you could have broken many hearts. You're a beautiful young lady."

"Well thank you Carlos," she said. "That's very sweet of you, but I doubt if there are any broken hearts on any paths behind me."

"I agree 100% with you Carlos," Jerry said, and then turning to Valerie he said, "See, I'm not the only one who thinks you're very attractive. I've noticed you many times around the building, and hoped I'd get a chance to meet you. By the way, do you have a ride home tonight? I know you didn't come with anyone because I've been watching you. It would be my pleasure to drive you home, that is, if you don't mind."

"As a matter-of-fact, I had figured on taking a cab," she told him. "That's the way I got here. But, thank you very much, I'd really appreciate a ride home."

Chapter 12

It was a very quiet ride home for Stephanie and Peter. Both of them wore statue-like faces, neither speaking to the other. The evening hadn't been what Stephanie had hoped for and she was almost glad he had suggested leaving early. The rest of the people at the table were aware all wasn't rosy and right between them, but didn't say anything. Long before they actually left, he was very friendly to everyone else at the table, as was Stephanie, but neither addressed any comments to each other until he told her they should go because he had some work to catch up on.

Finally, as they were nearing the street where they lived she asked him, "What work do you have to catch up on a Saturday night? Since when is there such pressure in your job that you have to work after hours? I simply don't understand your attitude lately. We used to have fun together and could always talk things over if anything were wrong. You ignored me the entire evening."

"First of all, what the Hell do you know about construction? Why do you always have to think something is wrong? There is nothing wrong. You're always blaming me for being so quiet and anti-social at the office parties. Tonight I thought I was very charming and now you claim something's wrong. My God, Steph, make up your mind how you want me to act. And don't bring on the tears like you always do when you're not happy with what I say."

He turned the corner almost hitting another car due to his anger and careless driving. Then he made a screeching turn into the driveway where he came to a sudden stop. He got out of the car, slammed the door and rushed up to the front door, not even bothering to open the car door for his wife, like he usually did. She got out of the car and followed him into the house.

After they were inside he told her he had to go back to the office and finish a drawing that they needed early Monday morning. He would have finished it tonight if she hadn't insisted on dragging him off to the party.

"You seemed to be having a good time," she told him. Then she asked very sweetly, "Do you have any idea what time you might be home? if you do, I'll wait up for you and we'll have a drink, like the old days, and we can talk for awhile and unwind before going up to bed; maybe even sleep late tomorrow if you want, since it is Sunday. How would you like that?" she suggested, hoping to get him to calm down and pay some attention to her.

"Never mind staying up. You need your sleep the way you've been lately. Besides, I have no idea how long it's going to take me. After your attitude tonight I'll probably have difficulty concentrating on what I'm doing anyway," and he picked up his jacket ready to leave.

"Well, I certainly hope you're not blaming me for that too," Stephanie called to him from the kitchen. "Frankly I'm beginning to wonder about you with all these late nights and frequent trips. That, in addition to my being ignored when you are in town makes me wonder what's happening to us. You wouldn't have a girl waiting in the wings, would you?"

"Oh for crying out loud. Stop talking like a crazy woman," and he threw an ashtray at her, narrowly missing her. "And don't bother staying up tonight hoping to see me. I may decide not to come home." Before Stephanie could comment any more, he left slamming the door behind him.

Chapter 13

In the meantime, the ride home for another couple, much later, was equally as quiet for a while. Neither Valerie nor Jerry could figure out how to start a conversation.

Finally, Valerie decided to break the ice by being the first one to speak and said to Jerry, "I like your van. You have very nice interior colors. How come you chose such a big vehicle? Do you have a family - or maybe it isn't any of my business?"

"Thank you, I like it too." he answered. "Actually I have had it for three years. My wife wanted one to have for when we went on trips. We used to travel quite a bit - short trips of a week or less. It is very comfortable and we didn't have to worry about how much luggage or other stuff we took with us - much better than flying where you're rather restricted as to what you can take.

"Oh," she explained, "I didn't realize you were married. I have never seen you with anyone at office parties, so I assumed you were single."

"You don't know?" he asked. "My wife passed away a little more than two years ago. It's still not easy talking about it, but she was killed in an automobile accident. She and her girl friend were on their way home from a baby shower one of the girls had, and a drunk driver ran them off the road. They were both killed. The girl she was with had a Jeep. The top was down, since it was a warm night, and they were thrown from it landing on a pile of rocks."

"That's terrible. I'm so sorry." she apologized. "I shouldn't have asked."

"That's OK, Val." he said. "It was such a tragic loss of life - never should have happened. The guy had a long record of driving drunk and he only got 5 years in prison. Hardly seems fair to me. But that's the criminal system these days.

"But, what about you?" he asked. "If I'm not being too nosy - and tell me if I am. I've heard that you were divorced. If you weren't allowed to date, how did you ever manage to get married?"

"No, I don't mind telling you, and after all my questions about your wife, how could I object to your questions?" she said.

Then continuing, she told him, "Unfortunately, I had to marry a guy my parents arranged for me. Bet you never thought that arranged marriages still existed, especially in this day and age. Well, I've got news for you. I stuck it out for almost two years and then we both finally realized it had been a big mistake from the start and that we could never love each other, so we got up the nerve to tell our parents how we felt and we got a divorce.

"We were friends, and still are. It's just that we didn't love each other and were smart enough to know it. He has since married a very attractive girl and they have a little boy and are very happy.

"Our parents were pretty angry at first. Luckily there were no children to complicate things. In fact, except for the honeymoon, when we really tried to act like husband and wife, we never even had sex. We couldn't see making love when we didn't love each other. Don't get me wrong, I'd love to have children, but I'm just glad I didn't have any by him."

"Do you have your own place now?" he asked. "Or are you still living with your parents?"

"No way would I have gone back home. They lived in Pennsylvania, a little farm town near Altoona, which is where I grew up. That's why I originally moved to Maine; so I wouldn't be too close to them. They were pretty upset about the divorce; much more so than we were, that's for sure. I told them I was a big girl and intended to live my own life. If I make mistakes I will have no one to blame but myself. They finally realized too that the marriage had been a mistake. Thank God we were back on friendly terms before they died - killed in a plane crash in Europe, on their way home from what was their second honeymoon.

"So lately I read a lot, I have my bowling team, and I treat myself to an occasional trip into Boston to a concert. This past 4th of July I was at the Esplanade for the annual concert at the Hatch Shell. That was quite an experience. I rarely ever date because I haven't found anyone who seems to have the same interests as I. Most guys these days think they have to sleep with a girl on the first date, especially if they find out she's been married.

"I have a small condo at the Sebago Estates. It's very nice; has a swimming pool, tennis courts, and access to sail boats at the lake. It's really very nice and the grounds are always kept in perfect shape. The people are nice and there's never been any noisy, inconsiderate neighbors. I really like it. But listen to me rambling on about myself. I'm not usually this talkative."

"You sound like a very private person; enjoying quiet times and good music? And don't worry about talking too much because you haven't."

"I guess you are right; I really hate loud, boisterous people, as well as this loud music people go for today. They seem so crude, as though they were doing it just to attract attention - or maybe to annoy other people." she said. "I guess maybe I'm just a dull person. It's probably because of the way I grew up."

About that time Jerry had arrived at the gateway to the condo property and she directed him to the street where she lived. He pulled up to the spot that was reserved for a car for her apartment, 323B. He got out and then went around the van to help her out.

"Thank you. Not every man will do that these days. Either that or the girl doesn't care." she said as he assisted her. "Personally, I think it is a very nice gesture. It shows that the age of chivalry is not gone."

"Thank you very much. By the way, where is your car parked?" he asked her. "I only see one space designated for your apartment."

"I don't own a car." she told him. "That is another thing for which I can thank my parents. They didn't think it was necessary, and when I was married my husband drove me wherever I needed to go, or I would take a bus. Since then I just haven't taken the time to take lessons. Besides, right now I can't really afford a car; at least not the kind I would want."

"When you get around to learn, I'd be happy to be your instructor," he told her.

They walked up the few steps to the patio that led into her apartment where they stopped. She got her keys out of her purse and started inserting them into the lock.

"Let me unlock that for you," he said. After unlocking the door, he told her how much he enjoyed their ride home and asked her, "Would you like to go to dinner with me some night? I really enjoyed your company and would like to get to know you better."

"Yes, I think I would like that," she told him. "It will be sort of like my first date. In fact, it will be a first for me. Doesn't that sound crazy, at my age? Well, see you at the plant Monday. Thanks again for the ride Jerry."

As he went down the steps to his van, he felt better than he had in a long time about the possibility of dating again. Valerie was such a nice girl, he thought he could really get to like her a lot. He had to admit she sounded a little pessimistic about life but he felt he could change that if given a chance. All she needed was for someone to show they cared for her. He had noticed her for some time when he saw her in the corridors but never had the nerve to find an excuse to talk to her. Besides, since he never saw her being friendly with any of the single men, he assumed she was married. This evening gave him the opportunity he was looking for. Until this moment he had never given a thought that he could possibly get serious with another woman, always trying to compare them with his late wife, which really wasn't fair. However, he wasn't intending to rush into anything. After all, how could he be sure Valerie liked him enough to go steady?

Jerry was not the only one with thoughts of dating again. Valerie was contemplating on how wonderful it would be to go out with somebody she had chosen - a chance to actually date Jerry and maybe get serious. She wondered if it really was happening and could it possibly develop into something permanent. She didn't want to try and rush him, but he was a very nice man and very much a gentleman. True he was a few years older than she, but not so much that she shouldn't date him. She had heard girls discussing dates and how some men would want to come in on the first night and make love. Or, in some cases, the girl would take the initiative and invite the guy to spend the night. That idea didn't sit well with her at all and she wasn't about to sleep with Jerry. She felt sure she had made a good choice for herself - but how could she be sure the feeling was mutual?

She threw herself on the chaise lounge and just lay there daydreaming of her ride home, and the possibility of becoming serious with Jerry when her telephone rang. She couldn't imagine who would be calling at this hour and at first wasn't even going to answer in case it was a crank call.

"Hello," she said, rather timidly.

"Hello yourself. Is this the lovely Valerie Ansara?" the voice on the other end said. "If not, you will do because your voice is as nice as hers."

"Jerry, did anyone ever tell you you're crazy?" she answered, laughing. "What in the world are you calling for at this hour? I almost didn't answer. You just left my place. Either you drove home awfully fast, or you live close by."

"I'll answer the first question first," he said. "No, I'm not crazy, but if you would allow me to see you often enough I think I could be - about you. The answer to the second question is that you didn't say how soon we would be able to get together for dinner. How about tomorrow night? As to your last remark, I did not speed and I live less than five miles from you. So how about tomorrow night and then I won't bother you anymore tonight.

"Oh heck, I'd love to go to dinner with you, but tomorrow night is my girls' bowling night and I can't miss it because we are in first place. I can't let them down. Maybe the next night as long as you promise not to take me to McDonald's. I hope you feel I'm worth some place better." she kidded.

"Surely you jest," he answered. "I wouldn't dream of taking a lovely lady to a place like that. I'm really disappointed that bowling has priority over me. Maybe we can get together at the company cafeteria at lunch and determine an agreeable date for us to get together and where we may want to go. Right now though, we'd better get to bed. I'll probably cry myself to sleep because I was turned down in favor of a bowling ball," he told her. "Sweet dreams anyway

Chapter 14

Rose and her younger sister, Olga, had decided to share the expenses of the big house in which Rose and her late husband had lived. She had so many happy memories and memorabilia that she just didn't want to give up any of it, which would have happened had she moved to a smaller place. She convinced Olga that it would be to their benefit for Olga to give up her apartment, since her divorce, and come and live with her.

Olga had a successful catering business, which she started several years ago with a young man to whom she had just married. He soon lost interest in the business and in her, and left for the West Coast six years ago, leaving Olga to manage the business alone or sell it. She chose to keep it operating and was determined to make it a success without him.

The business eventually became so lucrative that it required hiring several people full-time and others who were on call in the event of an extra large function. Things worked out very well. She leased the first floor of a small building where she could install a good-sized kitchen in which most of her preparations were performed. The business also required at least one large truck outfitted to carry food to its destination without spilling any, in addition to some smaller trucks for other uses.

"Olga," Rose told her one day, "why don't you use the kitchen at the house for smaller jobs and save having to go back and forth each day? It's such a beautiful, big kitchen with all the modern conveniences you need, it's a shame it doesn't get more use. I really don't mind. You know how much cooking I do. I hate it as much as you like it."

"You don't really mind, Sis?" Olga asked. "Gosh, that would be wonderful. I always wished some of my work could be done at home but never had enough room in which to do it. You do have a fantastic kitchen that is just longing to be used more. I'll tell some of my associates that we will be doing that. We'll keep it clean, you can be sure of that. My assistants do a great job of cleaning up after a job."

"Hey, that's OK, Sis. I'm sure not worried about it not being clean. I know how neat you have always been," Rose said. "I guess you could say there's a little bit of selfishness involved where I'm concerned, because I will have someone to keep me company in the house, since it does get very lonesome in this big old house - and you know I don't want to give it up. At the same time I'll have some decent meals for a change. You know what a lousy cook I've always been. Henry did most of the cooking when he was alive - said he'd rather do it than eat what I cooked. Isn't that awful? It's a good thing someone in the family took after our mother in the kitchen."

"It would be a pleasure to prepare anything you want." Olga told her. "I love to cook and the fact that you are willing to let me live here, much cheaper than I did at my apartment, and to allow me the use of this fantastic kitchen, it's the least I could do. By the way, who cooked when Billy was alive?"

Billy was Rose and Henry's little boy, their only child. Unfortunately, he died a tragic death when they were visiting friends, for a cookout. They had a swimming pool and somehow he and some other children got into the fenced in pool area and Billy fell in. Before anyone could get to him he had drowned. He was only 4 years old. It took many years before Rose could talk about it without breaking into tears.

"Henry did it then too and Billy thought it was funny that his daddy cooked the dinners instead of mommy," she told her sister.

"What are you planning for Mr. Wilson's big shindig?" Rose asked. "You know, the girls at the plant are going crazy trying to figure out why he and I have been having meetings behind closed doors. Even Stephanie doesn't know. The one who is suffering the most though is Martha. I've told you about her haven't I - the inquisitive one? I think she is developing ulcers trying to figure out what is happening."

"Thanks so much for mentioning me and my service to him. It will really be a feather in my cap and probably result in even more work, if this party is a big success."

"Don't worry little sister. It will be a fantastic success, and I don't know why I hadn't thought about having you arrange his parties before. His wife could have used you when she had the anniversary party at the house a few months ago. There were all kinds of big shots there from the area business world as well as some politicians," Rose told her. "You would have doubled your employees after that. Sorry I goofed up."

"Don't be silly. I've had plenty of jobs lately. As for Mr. Wilson's upcoming party, plans aren't 100% complete yet. You can be sure it is going to be a biggy though," Olga assured her. "As a matter-of-fact, this will probably be my biggest effort to date so I want to make sure it is super nice. He told me money was no object and that's what I like to hear from a client. He wants a buffet and I agreed with him that in view of the number of people expected, that would be the best arrangement. I guess he will have the usual stuff you find on a buffet, plus more."

"Don't tell me he hasn't talked about the possibilities of lobster as well?" Rose asked her sister. "That would really be something. What about the decorations, or a theme? Does he want that sort of thing?"

"Gosh, you talk about Martha being curious." Olga laughed. "I'm just kidding. Yes, we have discussed the possibility if a theme of sorts and also asked me what colors we should use in decorating the place and tables. And, yes, he does plan to have lobster. I told him it would be difficult to calculate how many because people either like it a lot or they won't eat it at all. He said to allow one two pounder for each adult; then what one did not eat, the people who did like it would take care of most of the rest. I told him I thought two pounders were quite big along with all the other food; that perhaps we could just have the tails available to eat with the cocktail fork and use the rest of the meat to make lobster salad. That way it would give a little variation. he thought that would be a good idea."

"My gosh, are you going to have enough room in your place to prepare all this stuff. I know you have a pretty good sized kitchen there, but this is going to mean an awful lot of food." Rose remarked. "Perhaps you could plan on preparing certain portions here and the rest at your place. You're going to have to get an awful big truck to pack all the stuff to the building too. May I ask you how you will keep the hot dishes hot?"

I wish you hadn't asked that one." she answered. "As soon as we have decided exactly what the menu will be comprised of then I'll know what problems, if any, we may have as far as hot dishes are concerned. I'm sure there are plenty of outlets in the atrium, but I'll no doubt be using chaffers in which to keep hot dishes warm. He probably won't want very many hot dishes.

"Your suggestion to have some of the dishes made here at the house is a good one. Maybe I'll have my people prepare the desserts here."

"Now, what about decorations?" Rose asked. "Mr. Wilson didn't talk too much about that to me. He will probably discuss it with you when you see him. By the way, when are you having your meeting with him? Do you want him to come here to the house, or would you rather see him in his office?"

"I'm not sure," she replied. "I do have to go over there anyway to check out the atrium before I can come up with any ideas for decorating. That would be interesting for me to come over there. I don't think I have ever met anyone from the company, so they will have something else to talk about. And, since we don't look alike and our last names are different, they probably won't even associate us with each other. This could be more fun than I had expected. Do you suppose you could set up an appointment with Mr. Wilson. After all, we have never met. He just hired me because you convinced him how good my service is."

"Yeah, Sis, I like that idea. I'll ask him to have Stephanie set up an appointment for you to see him, and not tell her who you are." Rose suggested. "I'd sure love to see Stephanie's reaction to that - having Mr. Wilson tell her to make an appointment with still another woman and not tell her what it relates to. But most of all I'm anxious to see Martha trying to figure this one out. This will really be mind-boggling for her. I've never mentioned to any of the girls that you live with me or what you do for a living. Somehow the subject has never come up and I never volunteer information in front of Martha or I'll get the third degree."

"But don't they know my first name? Certainly you have mentioned me to them in conversation at some time."

"Oh sure," Rose said. "When I speak of you I mention my little sister and when they asked your name, as you know they have, I refer to you as Cooky, my pet name for you. I told them you got it a long time ago, since you were so cute when you were little, and somehow the name stuck. Fortunately, I've been lucky that Martha hasn't given me the third degree about you; like what do you do, are you married, why not? - plus at least a dozen more questions."

"Boy, she really must be quite a character. In that case I'll continue to be Cooky and we'll keep them guessing as to why Mr.

Wilson has another secret woman, this one named Mrs. McKenzie."

"Well, I'll start the action tomorrow and call Stephanie and tell her I have to speak with Mr. Wilson on the phone and then tell him our plan. He will take the ball from there because he gets quite a kick out of the fact the girls are all suspecting him of some sort of clandestine affair," she told her sister. "I hope Stephanie is in a better mood than she has been the past few days. She used to be so happy and carefree and all of a sudden she looks sad; as though she were going to break out in tears. She didn't seem herself at the anniversary party either. I hope everything is OK on the home front. I'd find it hard to believe anything is wrong with her marriage. But then her husband has had to do a lot of traveling lately, so she's probably just unhappy about that. I'm not going to let myself be another Martha by asking a lot of questions that are really none of my business.

Chapter 15

"Hurry up woman," Dennis called out. "We're going to be late for the concert. You know what a crowd there always is at that place. I'm not really that crazy about this group tonight, but I promised you we'd go wherever you wanted for your birthday."

"Yes honey, and I appreciate the sacrifice you are making for me," Janet kiddingly responded. "Don't forget, I've gone places that didn't exactly thrill me either; like when we went to the Whitney Houston concert. You know what I think of her. That's what I like about our relationship; it's a matter of give and take and we always try to make the other one happy."

"You are worth pampering and I can't think of anyone else I'd rather have," he told her. "You always do the same for me."

"Janet, how long do you think we should allow to drive to Boston at this time of day? I had hoped to stop someplace for dinner, but I'm not so sure there's going to be time. We may have to just grab a burger someplace along the way and then tomorrow night I'll make up for it by taking you someplace special. How does that sound?"

"That's fine with me," she responded. "By the way, not meaning to change the subject, but is Jeff and his girl - what's her name? - going with us? They had mentioned the possibility last time we saw them.

"No, they had an argument a few days ago and still aren't talking to each other," Dennis replied. "They are both so darn stubborn that neither one wants to apologize. I'm sure they'll get over it eventually. That would be nice if we could have made it a foursome for the evening. Actually, we never know what kind of a mood they are going to be in. I never saw two people who supposedly love each other so much but who argue all the time. What's it going to be like when and if they ever get married."

"Yes, I know what you mean. By the way honey," she asked. "What's happening at the company where you work these days? Is that Latin guy getting along any better with people? I can't understand how anyone who has apparently gone through so much can be so antagonistic towards people who aren't of the same race as he. Is he anti-black towards all of us or just you?

With so many different nationalities at the company, I just wondered if he dislikes all ethnic groups because if that's the case, who does he think he is, anyway."

"I don't know. He just hates the world, I think. It seems at times he is taking it out on everyone because of what happened to his own country. I don't know, but frankly I'm not so sure I even care. I tried to be nice to him when he first started working there, but he wanted nothing to do with me; told me he didn't associate with "niggers" so that ended that. If he feels that way about people who aren't of his own race, then you know what he can do?"

During the drive south they made better time than they had hoped, traffic being much lighter than usual, so they stopped at Warren's in Kittery, near the New Hampshire border and had a fried clam dinner. As usual they weren't disappointed in their meal there. They then got back on Rte 95 and headed for Boston and the Gardens, where the concert was being held.

"Have you thought about a good date for our wedding?" Dennis asked Janet. "You know we have to allow enough time to make up a guest list, hire a hall, arrange for the minister, and all that stuff that brides are responsible for. Is next spring too soon to figure on? I don't know about you, honey, but this living together would be much nicer if we were married; especially if we're ever going to have a family. The more I think about it the more I feel we should have married right from the start. Maybe we should just elope and save all that money for a big, long honeymoon. What do you say?"

"Gosh, I have been waiting for you to say something about setting a date," she told him. "I didn't realize you were ready to go for it. Are you really serious about the idea of an elopement? I never really thought about that - always figured on having a big, splashy wedding, but let me think it over. I may just like that idea. The sooner we can become Mr. and Mrs. the better I'll like it. Don't know about you but I'm anxious for a real house and kids running around. I agree with you, this living together is not so hot. We have to be so careful that I don't get pregnant, and I don't want to conceive a child if I'm not married. Was there a particular reason why you suggested we elope? This weekend will give us plenty of time to think about it and decide whether it is to be a quickie or a big, expensive wedding. Whatever you want to do is fine with me sweetheart."

Before Dennis had a chance to answer, she told him, "If we were to plan for a big wedding, you know the bride's parents usually foot the bill and neither of ours can afford to pay for anything but a very small affair, which would mean not being able to invite everyone we would want to."

"If it's the bride's responsibility, then you do what you want and I'll be with you 100% of the way. I suppose if you should decide on a regular wedding we could help pay some of the expenses. But we should give it a little more thought before making a final decision. A lot of people will be disappointed."

"No, I want to give the elopement idea more thought," she answered. "We could always do that and then maybe one of our friends or family would throw a reception for us after we have announced that we're married. And, if they choose not to, that's OK too."

"That sounds fine to me, honey. Like I told you, whatever will make you happy."

Almost half an hour passed with no one saying a word; each of them concentrating on wedding plans. All of a sudden Janet squealed, "We'll do it. By gosh, I've decided. This bride-to-be wants to elope. To heck with the big wedding. We'll do that on our 25th anniversary. What do you say to that, sweetheart?"

"Well, first of all, don't scare me to death with your squealing," he told her. "I say that's a fantastic idea. So when did you plan on consummating this union?"

"This weekend, silly. We'll find some place where we don't have to wait three days or whatever it is, and we'll return to work as Mr. and Mrs. What do you think of that idea? It would certainly shake up a few people, both at your office and at the hospital," she said. "OK, it's all settled. I'm so excited, I'll only be thinking about that during the entire concert."

"I've got a brilliant idea," Dennis suddenly said, after almost ten minutes had passed. "Since you don't care for this group anyway, let's forget about the concert and find a place where we can get married. There must be some state that doesn't require a three-day wait."

"The only one I know of off hand is Maryland," he told her. "As far as I know none of the New England states allow quickie weddings. Shall we go down there? We can always pick up some extra toilet articles and some other clothes to take us through a couple extra days. Better decide soon, we're close to where we turn off for downtown Boston."

"Let's do it. We'll surprise the bunch at work, not to mention our families. It is OK if you take a couple of days off isn't it honey?" Janet asked him. "I know there will be no problem at the hospital where I work. I'll just call one of the girls I know who would like to get in some extra time and have her arrange it."

"Sure. So, when we find a hotel we'll check in and then I'll call a friend of mine and have him notify my supervisor that I needed an extra day and I'll be back to work by Wednesday. OK?"

"Then we'll have to look for a mall so we can get some clothes appropriate for the wedding. After all, since we didn't plan on any of this when we left home, all we have are our casual clothes, which won't do for a wedding. Oh honey, I'm so excited just thinking about it. Imagine, within a couple of days I'll be Mrs. Dennis Colby. Gosh that sounds good."

"Well, thank you my dear; it does have a nice ring. No pun intended, but speaking of rings we'll have to find a jewelry store too. so we can buy wedding rings. Most malls have at least two or three. We can buy new clothes at the mall too. How far do you think we should plan on driving tonight?"

"How about the outskirts of New York City?" she suggested. "We should be able to find hotels or a motel where we can spend the night. Then we'll start out early the next day and drive to Annapolis. It is a nice town, and we should be able to find a nice place for our wedding night."

"That sounds good to me," he told her. "In fact, that's a great idea."

They carried out their plans and by late Monday afternoon they were married in a little chapel they found in the outskirts of Annapolis. They then checked into a small but nice little hotel as Mr. and Mrs. Dennis Colby. The hotel, small as it was, did have a lovely, little bridal suite. Janet was ecstatic over being able to sign her new name.

When they reached the door to the room, Dennis unlocked the door then swept her off her feet and said, "Welcome to the bridal suite, Mrs. Colby." and he carried her over the threshold, gently putting her down, at which time he gave her a big hug and a kiss and told her how beautiful she was and how much he loved her.

"Well thank you my handsome husband." she answered. "I love you very much too. Now what's on our schedule?"

"You really have no idea? I can't believe that. Actually, the bridal suite includes a champagne dinner in our suite," he told her. "Just as soon as we are settled and ready to eat we can call downstairs and they will prepare our meal. I guess we picked a pretty nice place. We'll have to remember it for when we celebrate our anniversaries.

"In the meantime, I'm not quite ready for champagne or food. I just want to know how it feels to make love with my wife, and hope you are thinking along the same line."

"I sure am," she said, as she was about to undress. "I was hoping we could make love before dinner."

They slowly undressed each other and, after admiring each other's naked body, they embraced tightly, then laid down on the bed to make love for the first time as husband and wife. A short while later, after showering and getting dressed in something more comfortable than their wedding clothes, Dennis called the front desk to let them know they were ready for dinner.

"To a long life and many happy years together, my darling." Dennis toasted, as they were about to eat the delicious gourmet meal the hotel prepared.

"And may we have a house full of kids." she added. "I love you very much Mr. Colby. This is much nicer than attending a noisy old concert."

"Hey! Hey! I'll drink to that. It's also much more fun, darling."

Chapter 16

Wednesday morning when Dennis returned to work, he asked to see Steve, his supervisor, for approval of two weeks leave.

"What's the occasion, at this particular time, to want some leave?" Steve asked. "Are you and Janet going to sneak off someplace and get married? You've been looking rather love sick lately, if you want my opinion."

"As long as you mentioned it, I may as well let you know, we are married." Dennis confessed. "We eloped while we were away for the weekend. I highly recommend marriage for everyone. I realize we have been living together for the past few months, but had we known married life was going to be so wonderful we would have done it long ago instead of just living together. We need the two weeks to go on a honeymoon. Haven't decided yet whether it will be Hawaii or a Caribbean Cruise. They both sound rather romantic to us. All that really matters is that we are together. "By gosh but it's nice to hear that two people feel like you do." Steve commented. "I'll have to tell my dad about this and see what we can come up with for you two - a party of some kind to get you started off right. He and his wife are such romantics he'll definitely want to do something for you two. Of course you may have the leave. How much time did you say you need? You kids have my blessings for a wonderful time and a long life together. Hell, just because my marriage hasn't been what I had hoped for doesn't mean I don't approve of it for others."

"We haven't made reservations for any place yet. We wanted to make sure we had the leave approved. I'm sure Janet won't have any problem getting some so, hopefully, we can get out of here the end of the week. Thanks ever so much, sir." Dennis said, and he left the office with a smile on his face.

As he was walking back towards his own office, he met Harry and Mitch coming in his direction.

"Hi Dennis, you sure look like one happy guy this morning," Harry commented. "What did you do, win the lottery? I can't think of anything else that could put such a happy face on a man."

"Heck no, man - much better than that. Janet and I just got married over the weekend and I have to be the happiest guy around. You're engaged aren't you? Then why not go all the way; you'll never regret it. I wouldn't want it any other way now."

"Well, I'll be damned." Mitch interrupted before Harry could say anything. "When did you say you took the plunge? Are you sure you know what you've gotten yourself into? Well, good luck pal."

"Don't knock it if you haven't tried it." Dennis responded. "I just talked to the boss and he's given me an OK on a two weeks leave so Janet and I can go on a honeymoon. We are both so happy we can't understand why all married couples don't feel the same way we do. See you guys later. Right now I have to go call my bride so we can decide just where we're going."

"How about that Mitch?" Harry said, after Dennis went his way. "I just knew something had happened. It's not normal for a guy to look the way he has all morning; like a darn Cheshire cat just waiting for someone to ask him what the reason was for his look. He did say they had eloped this past weekend didn't he? I thought they were going to a concert when all the time they had other plans."

"Who did what over the weekend?" Juan asked as he approached Mitch and Harry. "Don't mean to appear nosy, but I couldn't help but hear you."

"Old Dennis and Janet got hitched over the weekend." Mitch told him. "Must have been a spur of the moment thing because they didn't say anything last week about marriage plans. I sure wish them good luck."

"Big deal. Is that all?" Juan responded in his usual sarcastic manner. "I thought something important happened. Don't we have enough niggers running around these days. I suppose they'll produce another dozen or so kids to infest the country with."

Before Mitch could respond to Juan, Harry interrupted, asking him what he had against the Black people. "They're no different from any other race, under the skin - some good and some bad. Jerry happens to be one of the good ones. He's smart, ambitious, and a darn pleasant guy to be around. So what's your beef, Juan? How'd you like it if people ran your people down like that? He has never done anything to hurt you."

"You people just don't understand what I've been through do you? Have him for a friend if you want. It's no skin off my nose, but don't expect me to feel the same way as you," and he turned and walked off in the opposite direction.

"Boy, what a terrible attitude that guy has." Mitch commented. "One of these days he'll get in trouble; he'll make one of his not-so-smart remarks to the wrong person and they'll knock him on his butt, if not worse. I think sometimes he even hates himself."

"Hey, let's forget about that Latin jerk and go tell Martha the good news about Dennis and Janet. You can be sure if we tell her the news will be all over the building within five minutes."

"Great idea Harry," and they both headed off in the direction of Martha's office.

Chapter 17

It was early Thursday morning when Olga placed a phone call to Ben's office. Stephanie answered the phone with a cheery "Good morning, T.G.I., may I help you?" Olga asked Stephanie to please put her through right away, that it was a very important personal matter.

"Mrs. McKenzie is on the line sir," Stephanie announced to Ben. "She just said it was an important personal call."

"Yes, thank you, Stephanie." he said. "Hold any other calls I get, or have them call back. Thank you."

He wasn't on the phone very long when he called Stephanie on the intercom and told her to make sure any appointments he may have between nine and eleven the next morning are canceled, and to reschedule them. Instead, please write in Mrs. McKenzie's name for those two hours.

Olga and Mr. Wilson chatted for just a short while. Meanwhile Stephanie called some of the girls and told them what was up. None of them had ever heard of a Mrs. McKenzie and all wondered what in the world was going on with Mr. Wilson.

"The pay off," Stephanie said with disgust, "was that this time this woman asked for him by his first name. No one ever does that. She's going to be here tomorrow morning."

"I'll bet he is planning something that involves his wife," Valerie told them. "He seems like the type that would do nice things for the woman he loves. I suppose you have more sinister thoughts on your mind though, don't you Martha?"

"Well, I don't know. Until this came up I was sure he and Rose were up to something," Martha commented. "But now I'm not sure what to think. He has suddenly become a rather mysterious person lately. What did this McKenzie woman sound like, Steph. Was she old or young? Did she have a sexy voice?"

"Oh come on now, Martha," she answered. "Let's not get ridiculous. I told you she would be here to see him tomorrow morning. I, personally, find it hard to believe that Mr. Wilson would ever have an affair. He's too much in love with his wife. There has to be a perfectly legitimate reason behind all this. But in the past he has always let me know what's going on. That's the only reason why I'm so curious."

"Yeah, Martha," Kim said, "If you want to know so badly, have Stephanie give you an appointment with Mr. Wilson so you can go in and question him about what he's been doing with those women! Or you can wait until she arrives and ask her."

Hearing Kim speak up like that really surprised everyone. She seldom voiced an opinion and only spoke when spoken to. They were all rather taken back; especially Martha who, for once in her life, had no comeback.

Finally Valerie came out with, "Three cheers for our little one. You're OK Kim. You should speak up more often."

"I never know what to say, so I just keep quiet and listen," she admitted. "Besides, I don't know all you guys very well yet."

"Well now, you should join us more often when we have our chats, and get to know us. You'll never learn any younger." Valerie told her. "We get kind of silly at times but we all work for the same cause - the good of T.G.I. - and we'd love to have you as one of our gang. How about it girls? Do you all agree?" When they all nodded their head in agreement, she looked at Kim and said, "See, what did I tell you?"

"What about it Kim, aren't you just a little bit curious too?" Martha asked. Then, addressing all of them she added, "You guys can make fun of me if you want, but I sure wish I knew what is going on. I can hardly wait to see her."

"Actually, Martha," Kim said, "I'd rather talk about our newlyweds. Isn't it romantic what Dennis and Janet did last weekend; running off and getting married without telling anyone?"

"I'm sorry Kim, but that will have to wait for another time. I'm sure we are all happy for them. As for what Mr. Wilson is up to, time will tell." Stephanie said. "In the meantime we'd all better get back to work or we won't have a job." And she left them, rushing off down the hall to her own office.

"Gosh, wouldn't you think she'd be thrilled to death for them?" Martha grumbled as they left the area for their own offices. "I've never seen Stephanie acting so strange before. She must have gotten up on the wrong side of the bed."

"No," Valerie told them. "It's not just the past few days. She has appeared very unhappy and melancholy for quite a while, and one day I could swear I saw a bruise on her face. However, I figured it was her new hairdo that was sort of casting a shadow on her face. Now, the more I think about it the more I think I was right about the bruise. Do you suppose her husband could be abusing her and she doesn't want anyone to know?"

"I don't know," Martha said. "He doesn't really seem like the type. In fact, he has always appeared rather shy and quiet whenever I've seen them together. But then I guess you can't always tell about people. He could be one thing in public and altogether different at home. One of these days I'm going to be so curious that I'll go up and ask her. I'll say, 'friend to friend, what's happening between you and Peter'?"

"She may just tell you to mind your own business, you know." Kim told her.

"Then, as far as I'm concerned, that's the same as a confession that there is something wrong." Then Martha reminded them they'd better get back to work.

Chapter 18

The following morning when it was time for the morning break, several of the ladies gathered in the coffee room in hopes Stephanie would be there to let them know the outcome of the visit to Mr. Wilson by their mystery woman. Stephanie hadn't shown up yet and the rest of them were going crazy with curiosity. Martha hadn't arrived yet either.

Just as they were considering leaving, Martha walked in with Stephanie not far behind. "Girls, you'll never believe what Mrs. McKenzie looks like. She is a very attractive, dark-haired lady of maybe about fortyish. She's tall and very smartly dressed. They didn't stay in his office very long when they left and went out to the atrium. I didn't dare try to find an excuse to go out there. Steph, did you find out anymore than what I just told the girls?"

"No, I'm afraid I'm just as much in the dark as you. I had to stay at my desk for a while, until I could find someone to cover for me. That's why I'm so late for my break. I'll say one thing, Mrs. McKenzie is sure a very pleasant person. She speaks like one with a very proper upbringing - good schools and all that; and you should see her clothes. They sure don't look as though she has to worry about sales, or buying off the rack. Believe me, I know good clothes when I see them. If it means anything, they did talk about when the best time would be, but they never really spoke up enough for me to hear anything worthwhile. The door leading into Mr. Wilson's office wasn't closed tight, but I didn't dare leave it open a little or he would have seen it and asked me to close it. Sorry girls, but that is the latest report, such as it is, on Mrs. M."

"Well Martha, do you care to speculate on what Steph just said?" Valerie asked. "You always have a good imagination and can come up with something from just a little information. You've been rather quiet all of a sudden."

Everyone laughed at Valerie's remark, but admitted they had the same thought about Martha's ability to come up with a reasonable explanation of things.

"Have you noticed something strange girls?" Martha finally asked. "Who is missing from our little morning break group, and she has been missing on more than one occasion in the past? In fact, she was with Mr. Wilson a couple of times?"

"You must mean Rose," Cindy, one of the secretaries, said. "I thought about that, but she was meeting with him some of those times. But she's not with him now. I'm wondering why she didn't join us today. Could she be mad at one of us for some reason? Maybe she's involved in this mystery."

"I don't know what to think." Stephanie told them. "She hasn't shown any interest in the fact that Mrs. McKenzie has been contacting Mr. Wilson. Do you think she and Mrs. McKenzie might be friends, or something?"

"I doubt it very much," Martha commented. "They are just so different from one another. From what Stephanie tells us about this gal's personality and all, she isn't the type Rose would have for a friend. Besides, there has to be several years difference in their ages. No, I can't believe there can be any connection. Mrs. McKenzie is too high-class; probably comes from a wealthy family and went to the best of schools. Guess we didn't learn much today about what's going on. I have to get back to work; see you all later."

"Wait just a minute girls," Kim called out. "I have an idea. Why doesn't one of you ask Rose if she has seen Mrs. McKenzie and what she thinks of her, and then see what her reaction is? I think Martha is the best one to do that."

"Thanks, Kim. Thanks a lot. If you are that curious why don't you do it. In fact, Rose may be more apt to tell you than me. Besides, I don't have time right now." and she left.

Chapter 19

A Night in Early October

"Hey man, I know what you've been up to and it's going to get you in big trouble some day," Roger said to Juan. "Don't tell me you don't know what I'm talking about either because I know just enough to start an investigation."

Roger had been waiting outside the bar so he could follow Juan when he took his girl home. He was anxious to talk to him and figured this was the best opportunity he would have. What he wanted to talk about couldn't be discussed at work. Someone might overhear them.

"You're crazy," Juan responded with fire in his eyes. "I don't have any idea what the Hell you're talking about. And even if I were doing something wrong it wouldn't be any of your damn business, so get lost."

As he raised his arm, indicating he was going to strike Roger, Roger was ready for him and landed the first punch. It wasn't a hard one but enough to startle Juan.

"Don't you try anything with me, you lying bastard. I've been watching you for some time, and I know you're being paid off regularly, which can mean one of two things. Either you've been extremely lucky at the track, you're selling drugs, or you're involved in blackmail. I haven't found out which one it is yet, or why, but the why doesn't really matter. And don't you raise your fist at me again or I'll really knock you on your ass. I didn't spend all those years, as a kid on the streets without learning how to defend myself," Roger responded angrily.

"You don't know anything and if you did you couldn't prove it," Juan replied. "What gives you the right to accuse me of anything? I thought we were friends but I guess you're no different from anyone else around here. But if it's a fight you want, I know a little about self-defense myself - didn't last all those years in prison without learning something. The next time you take a poke at me, I'll make damn good and sure it is your last one."

Juan started to walk away but Roger wanted to settle things right then and there, so he grabbed Juan from behind and spun him around. "Don't walk away from me," he demanded. "Maybe we can work a deal and whoever is paying you can shell out a little of his wealth my way too. I could use a few extra bucks. I know you're doing it - just haven't figured out who's paying you, but I will get to the bottom of it and when I do I'd better be part of the action or I'll tell the police what I know."

"Threats like that aren't good for your health, man," Juan warned him. "But just to prove I'm a good-hearted guy, and because we have always been friends, I'll consider your offer. Maybe we can work together."

"Hey, thanks man. I couldn't ask for more." Roger said. "Let me buy you a drink, just to show there's no hard feelings. - sort of celebrate our partnership. There's a little bar a couple of blocks down the street that's open practically all night - Moody Street I think it is. Should still be open and at this hour it will be quiet so we can talk."

The two men walked down the dark, dimly lit street. The noise of their heels, in the otherwise quiet of the night, echoed against the cobblestone street as though they were in a canyon, causing the dark street to have an eerie atmosphere. It wasn't one of the better sections of town, with mostly small, independent neighborhood markets that closed early for fear of being held up; their doors and windows all protected with heavy bars in an attempt to save them against burglars breaking in. In addition, small, cheap Neon signs pointed out bars that were still open. The men stopped at the second bar they came to, with a flashing red and blue Neon sign reading, 'Jakes Bar. Open All Night'. As they entered the place, only a half dozen or so people were sitting at the bar watching late night TV and sipping their beers. Juan and Roger sat in a booth nearby, ordered a beer and proceeded to discuss their possible merger in crime.

"What makes you so sure I'm being paid off as you call it?" Juan asked. "That is, assuming I really am, and mind you I'm not saying it's true."

"I've seen envelopes being passed to you from time to time, not always in the same place or on the same day of the week." Roger answered. "I could search you right now and find a big wad of money - right? But I don't want just a sample of your action by robbing you when I can get more. So, what's your take each week?"

"OK, you win," Juan admitted. "I won't tell you who is paying me, but I get five grand a month. I can spare you one grand now and, considering I'm the one really taking all the risk I think I'm being very generous. A lot if it goes back home to my friends to help them rebuild the country after what those bastards caused. They made a real mess of my country and left everyone in poverty."

"Sorry friend," Roger replied. "I can understand your problem but I have some of my own. Inflation, you know - it has done a job on my wallet. You'll have to ask for a raise to six grand. Tell them prices have gone up and then give me two grand, which I think is more reasonable.

"Hey man, I was lucky to get him to agree on this much. Don't push it or he might decide to cut me off and take his chances, even though it will mean trouble for him too," Juan told him.

"Well now, that will depend on what your supplier does for a living and who he works for. I doubt if he would take a chance on being caught himself - for whatever reason - just to turn you in for a mere $5000 a month. He would probably be in a lot more trouble than you would." Roger answered. "And now I can assume your supplier is a man. I wasn't real sure until now. Anyway, it's worth trying for a raise. When do you see him again?"

"I don't deal directly with him anymore." Juan told him. "He sends the money - only cash - with a messenger to deliver it. Somehow he always manages to find me. If you've really been tailing me you'd already know. It's always a different place and not always by the same delivery boy. But I'll be getting another payment the end of next week because he was short this week."

"I knew most of that. I just needed you to confirm it. That's good; gives you time to contact him. I assume you do know how to contact him, don't you? - and let him know you need a raise. In the meantime I'll settle for the grand you gave me."

"OK. I'd give you more but the rest of what I have was promised to my family back home. I never spend much on myself," Juan told him. "Hey friend, that's a real sad story but then it's also a personal problem. Frankly, I don't give a shit about your family. To me, I'm Number 1, and I'm the only one who counts. Sorry if that sounds selfish but I've always had to scrimp and scrape to make ends meet. It would be kinda nice to have some of the pleasures of life. You must know what I mean."

"Let's get out of here," Juan suggested, ignoring Roger's last comments. "I don't like this dump and I'm not too thrilled with some of the conversation from someone who is supposed to be a friend and partner. Besides, I have to get up early for work. Can't afford to be late."

Roger paid the bill and said goodnight to the bartender, ignoring the men at the bar and the one who had crowded ahead of him to pay his tab first. The two men then proceeded to walk back up the street to where they had left the car neither man having much to say to the other. It was now raining hard, the streets like small streams with water rippling off towards the nearest manhole and gutters. It suddenly seemed even darker and more desolate.

Chapter 20

Meanwhile, back at the Christou's house the same evening.

"Alex, I need to talk with you." Angie told her husband. "That is, if you plan to be home this evening so we can have some time together for a change. The kids are all asleep now. I gave them supper early so the two of us could be together."

"So what's so important we should have privacy to talk?" he asked. "I had hoped to go back to the office for awhile, but I guess I could let it go for tonight. What did you have in mind?"

"Actually, I thought maybe the two of us could eat out. It's been ages since we had dinner out together. How about it Alex? Mrs. Fairburn, next door, will be happy to sit for the kids, if we decide to go. We haven't been out to the club in a long time. Do you mind going there? The service and food are both good and we will be home early."

"I guess we could go out there." he told her. "But it's not the best place to talk if you're looking for privacy, and you sound as though that is what you want. We'd better leave as soon as possible if we're going to get home early. I have to make a phone call first. One of the guys and I were going to work tonight on the accounts. It's always easier to work at night when there are no interruptions."

"OK dear," Angie responded. "After you make your call, I'll call Mrs. Fairburn and get my coat and we can leave in about two minutes."

They left the house for the country club about 8 o'clock. Very little was said between home and the club. Even while they were eating there was nothing but small talk - the kids and what was going on at work. Alex didn't ask her what she wanted to talk about, even though he could tell by her conversation with him that something was on her mind. He realized that but didn't want to ask her because he was afraid she just might know what was happening where he was concerned. They did have a nice meal and were back home before ten thirty PM.

When they returned home, paid Mrs. Fairburn, and were alone, Angie asked Alex to have a cup of coffee with her in the kitchen. He thought she was acting very mysterious, but joined her in the kitchen.

"Alex, are you having an affair with someone?" she asked with no warning. "You're not always at the office when you say you are, you haven't been doing much traveling lately, so what else are you doing? And you've been spending money like it was going out of style. I've looked at the latest bank statements and feel I should know why there are so many withdrawals of large amounts, and for what?"

"Are you crazy? What makes you think I could possibly have an affair?" he responded. "I have a wonderful family and love my kids, and here you are suspecting things like that. I should be asking you what's wrong with you. You've been acting rather peculiar lately yourself, and are usually ready for an argument. As for the money," he added, "I shouldn't have to answer to you what I do with the money."

"Just a darn minute, Alexander Christou," she shouted. (When she was particularly upset with him she called him by his full name) "I certainly have every right to know when large sums of money are withdrawn at a time, and often. We have always been honest with each other, including as far as our financial affairs are concerned. Why not now, all of a sudden? Besides, if nothing is wrong you shouldn't be so touchy about it."

"OK honey, calm down and don't get all upset." he told her in a very sweet, calm voice. "I guess I should have told you; I know you used to be a bookkeeper with your dad's company. I should have realized I couldn't keep anything from you. I'm afraid I made some bad investments by buying in on some bad stock, but I was hoping I could make up for it by buying some different ones. I didn't want to worry you. It will all be taken care of soon. Let's go to bed and forget all this nonsense. The only important thing is that I love you and the kids."

She accepted his explanation as to what had happened with the money but asked him why he would want to invest so much money nowadays without consulting someone who was an authority in the stock market. He told her someone had given him a tip and he thought at the time the man was knowledgeable where the stock market was concerned. The man was supposed to be proficient where the market was concerned.

The subject was closed for the time being when he got up, walked over to her and gave her a big hug and kiss; the kind she hadn't been getting from him for a long time. She wondered why he couldn't be like this all the time, still she wondered if he was really being sincere. Why hadn't he asked her dad or one of his brokers, she wondered. But she didn't want to ask any more questions at that time. he was being real sweet to her and she wanted it to stay that way.

"Well now," she said, sweetly, "This is more like the Alex I once knew. You don't know how much better you have made me feel. Let's not keep things from each other any more. I would have understood if you had just told me from the start what the problem was. Let me get these dishes rinsed and in the dishwasher and I'll be right with you."

A few minutes later they went arm in arm upstairs to their bedroom, like old times. Alex became very passionate and romantic with her after getting into bed. She actually allowed herself to believe their problems were in the past and that she could believe what he had told her.

"Oh Alex, my darling, I'm so sorry I mistrusted you. I love you so much I guess I just couldn't stand it if anything or anyone ever came between us. Can you forgive me?"

Chapter 21

Back on Moody Street, as Juan and Roger hurried down the wet pavement, a dark figure jumped out of the alleyway where vandals had broken the street light. It was pitch black, windy, the rain was coming down in sheets, and before either man had a chance to get a good look at the form, he had knocked Roger to the ground. Juan struggled with the form, but to no avail. The figure was too overpowering and had given him a blow to the side of the head, knocking him out. The figure searched the pockets of both men, taking all the cash they had.

An hour later, Roger awoke, shook his head and gradually things started to clear up and he remembered where he was. It had stopped raining but he was soaked to the skin and had a terrible headache. He looked around to see if Juan was OK but, to his surprise, he was alone on the wet cobblestones and Juan was no place to be seen.

"Well I'll be damned." he sputtered as he searched through his pockets. "That no good SOB knocked me out and took his fuckin' money back. He'll be sorry. No one makes a Goddamn fool of me and gets away with it."

As soon as his head had cleared sufficiently and things were no longer fuzzy, he walked in the direction of where he had left his car - wondering if Juan had taken that too. A few minutes later he saw it parked where they had left it. Actually, he wondered how come Juan hadn't taken it too, and how did he leave? He certainly didn't walk all the way home from here. He drove home slowly, trying to figure out his next move and how he was going to get back at that no-good Juan.

Roger got very little sleep. It was almost 4 AM before he arrived back at his apartment. Immediately he got on the phone and called Juan. An answering machine came on, which didn't surprise him too much, so he left a message. "You son of a bitch, you're gonna be sorry you stole my money and left me out there on that crummy street in the rain. I should have known I couldn't trust you, but I'll get you yet." He had assumed Juan was responsible for what happened to him - especially his aching head caused by the blow on the back of his head.

After showering he put an ice pack on his head for a while before getting some sleep. Although he hadn't intended to sleep very long he didn't awaken until ten AM. He wouldn't have gone to the plant at all that day but he liked Don and was anxious to be present for his retirement party; so he shaved and dressed and left for work - still raging inside over what had happened. He figured he'd see Juan there too, if he had the guts to face him after the events during the night.

When he reported to the shipping room for work the first person to see him, a janitor, who's name he didn't even know, asked him, "Hey pal, what happened to you? You look as though you had a rough night. Are you sure you should be here this morning?"

"Thanks, I needed a compliment like that." Roger replied. "You don't know the half of it. I'm lucky to be here at all the way I figure. Just don't drop anything heavier than a feather or my head will blow up. But, where is everyone? They haven't started the party already have they?"

"That bad huh? No, the party doesn't get underway until near noon. I guess a lot of them are helping out in any way they can and the others are just goofing off until it's time for things to start."

"Have you seen Juan Marcos yet? We were together for awhile during the night and then someone knocked me on the head and I passed out. I don't know if Juan did it or if he got it too, but when I finally woke up he wasn't any place to be seen."

"As far as I know he hasn't shown up yet." the janitor replied. "That's strange though, because lately he's been here every day right on time; sometime before I get here. As for you, you'd better get a cup of strong, black coffee, something to make you look more like you're still one of the living."

"Yeah, I guess I'd better. Well, thanks for listening to me. I'd better make an appearance so someone knows I'm here. See you later. If that Latin so-called friend of mine shows up, tell him I'm looking for him."

Chapter 22

The foliage was beginning to peak in that area and somehow Mother Nature must have worked overtime because the colors were utterly resplendent this year. Only in New England do the colors come out so brilliantly and varied, and attract so many tourists throughout the Northeast. After the heavy rain during the night, the sun arose brilliantly, drying out the foliage as well as the streets.

Several months had passed since the big anniversary party. This time the atrium of the Kessler Building had been decorated for a farewell party that afternoon for the Chief of the mail room. This area was used by all of the companies who occupied the building as it was so big and ideal for decorating for big affairs.

Don, the honored guest, had been with the company 38 years and had seen many changes through those years, as the company grew and modernized, always keeping up with the times. But now he decided it was time to retire and take life easy in a warmer climate.

Mr. Wilson made sure everyone had done their part in making it a party to remember. The company was noted for giving fantastic going-away parties. Little did anyone know just how much this one would be remembered. Just about everyone had indicated they would be there. Even Juan, who had become a little more amiable the past few weeks, had planned to be there early to help out in any way he could.

Ben had decided to keep Juan on with the company in view of a few things about which his niece had enlightened him at the last party. In addition, Ben had had a talk with Juan a few days later in his office. He decided what Juan needed was more understanding in view of the tragedies in his life. He was a good worker, after all; it's just that he wasn't socially inclined.

As the hour approached for the party to begin for Don, everyone started to assemble in the atrium. Gifts were stacked neatly near the head table where they would be presented at the appropriate time. A dais had been assembled with chairs for Mr. Wilson, the honored guest and his wife and several other special people. Following the presentations there would be a buffet style meal with plenty of time for eating and drinking and socializing for as long as anyone cared to stay.

One of the first people to arrive was Martha, the Senior Data Base Maintainer. She has been with the company for many years, and is extremely competent in her line of work. However, she is also very inquisitive and outspoken and doesn't hesitate giving her opinion about anything, or telling people what she thinks of them, if she doesn't agree with their philosophy. In spite of that she gets along with most of the employees, except for Juan, and they are thorns in each other's side. She has refused to believe he could ever change from the anti-social, loner type he was at first; nor did she ever show any sympathy for what he had gone through before coming to the states.

Harry, who followed her in, had a totally different attitude. He is easy going and shows compassion for people in uncontrolled, bad situations, but, at the same time, he never allowed people to walk all over him. He is an assistant accountant, in his mid thirties (and still single), and has been with the company for almost nine years. He doesn't consider Juan a best friend by any means but he has always been friendly, as a co-worker. He has been sympathetic towards him over the loss of most of his family.

"What's going on here? You guys look like a bunch of sad sacks." Carlos commented. "This is supposed to be a party, not a wake. It should be a great get-together even though we hate to lose a terrific guy like Don. He's going to be hard to replace."

"Yeah, it's sure to be a super party - especially since we haven't seen anything of that jerk, Juan." Martha commented with her usual sarcasm for him. "Too bad he isn't the one leaving, but then I sure as heck wouldn't be here if it was for him. He could spoil the best of affairs."

"Knock it off Martha." Carlos told her. "Enough is enough. We all know you don't like him. But the guy's gone through Hell. Maybe if one of us had been in his place we wouldn't be very friendly either. He's still bearing the scars of his homeland and probably still doesn't completely trust people. Besides, he's been pretty sociable since Mr. Wilson had that last talk with him. So just drop it and try to be civilized. After all, this affair is to honor Don, not to bad mouth Juan. Come to think about it I haven't seen him all day."

About that time Stephanie came by and interrupted, before Martha had a chance to make any more nasty remarks. She commented about how nice the place looked, not realizing the tension caused by the conversation taking place between Martha and Carlos.

Stephanie is the executive secretary for Ben and Steve. She is very fair with everyone with whom she deals, gets along with most people, and is very well liked. Stephanie is a very attractive woman with some formal education, extremely good manners and personality, and impeccable taste in clothes, as well as her hair and makeup. Ben couldn't have chosen a better person for the job. She came to work for Ben almost 12 years ago and he tells everyone he'd be lost without her.

Stephanie was not overly fond of Juan, more because she had never been able to understand his attitude with many of the other employees, and showed little respect for anyone regardless of age; though she had to admit he was always nice and polite to her, and his general attitude had changed a little recently.

"Didn't they do a terrific job? This place never looked so good. Whoever was responsible sure did a fantastic job." Stephanie commented. "I'm glad Don finally decided to call it quits and take it easy; though the mail room will never be the same. I for one am really going to miss him. But I'm happy for him and hope I can do the same thing in a few years."

"I couldn't agree with you more about Don," Martha said. "Not like some other guy I know."

About that time Valerie and Jerry walked in hand-in-hand. Seeing them, Martha forgot about Juan and remarked. "Hey folks, look who's here. If you guys have missed these two love birds the past few weeks then you are all blind."

"Yes, folks, isn't it nice to see two such happy people," Stephanie said. "When did you two discover each other? You do make a terrific looking couple. Is this serious or is this wishful thinking on my part?"

"Steph, you are starting to get Martha's habits of giving people the third degree." Jerry remarked with a big grin on his face. "We aren't talking just now, right Val? Besides, you can't consider us the happiest, necessarily. Have you ever seen two more love sick people as the newlyweds, Dennis and Janet? By the way, I wondered if he was going to be able to break away from her long enough to be at the party today. However, I saw him earlier on the phone; no doubt talking with her. It's a wonder they manage to separate long enough to go to work."

Everyone laughed, but before anyone could come up with a clever answer, they noticed that Ben had arrived and was trying to get everyone's attention to quiet down and listen to what he had to say.

"May I please have everyone's attention?" he called out.

Someone had forgotten to arrange for a microphone so he had to raise his normally soft-spoken voice. "Since someone in this organization goofed and failed to supply me with a mike, I promise no long-winded comments. So, let's get this party under way." he said in a voice that was very loud for him. Everyone cheered and whistled and he wasn't sure if it was due to his promise there'd be no long speeches or because he was anxious to get the party under way.

"First, I have an announcement that doesn't pertain to this afternoon's event. In case word hasn't reached everyone, although I imagine it has by now, Dennis and his lovely lady, Janet are now Mr. and Mrs., but that will be an event for us to cover in the near future, since they just returned from their honeymoon.

"Now for the big event of the day; not that we want to see Don leave because I'm sure everyone shares my sentiment that we are really going to miss him." Again everyone applauded and cheered, agreeing with Mr. Wilson.

After several more minutes of praising him, Ben proceeded to call on different people who planned to roast or toast him and present him with a gift. When they were finished, Ben called Don and his wife, Madeline, up front. He presented Don with a U.S. flag neatly folded in a triangular-shaped shadow box - a flag that had been flown over the U.S. Capitol. He then gave him a plaque with the usual engraved message on it. And, finally, for his 38 years of dedicated work, he was presented the traditional gold pocket watch engraved with dates of his employment and thank you from the company for a job well done. He then addressed his comments to Madeline.

"For you dear Matty, we thank you for your many years of patience and understanding on those numerous occasions when we had to keep Don here to work late hours - and we weren't playing poker or entertaining pretty girls. (He jokingly remarked). We also thank you for your own dedication, volunteering when we needed extra help on community projects in which the company always seemed to get involved. For all this, and for just being a heck of a nice gal, we want to present you with a small token of our esteem."

He then presented her with a Sterling Silver Revere bowl, appropriately engraved with words of appreciation from the company, as well as giving her a dozen long-stemmed red roses.

"Oh," he apologetically commented. "I almost forgot. There is one more thing. Just to get the both of you in a relaxing mood for your retirement years, we want you to take two weeks and relax in Hawaii. I just happen to have two airline tickets with your names on them. Since I didn't know which islands you may prefer, here is a check which should cover your hotels and anything else you may want to do while over there. Have a good time kids. By the way everyone, Don is the first retiree from our company. We have had a few people leave to go on to other careers but he is the first to be able to take advantage of our retirement plan."

After the final applause and cheering, both the honored guests made short thank you speeches, with more than a few tears shed by many people. Ben then, in his usual cheerful, soft-spoken voice issued an ultimatum - that it was high time to eat, drink, and be merry; and no one need go back to work that day; that is, unless they wanted to, and he gave a little snicker. First though he wanted everyone to know who had done such a magnificent job in preparing the food, as well as the beautiful decorations and table setting.

"Don't think I'm not aware of the gossip going around about Rose and me and, more recently another young lady. Martha, you can relax now," he added, knowing full well she was the one having started the rumors. "I will put your mind at ease regarding the many meetings we've had together. Ladies and gentlemen I want you to meet Olga, Rose's kid sister, who so skillfully and beautifully arranged all this for the affair.

"By the way, if any of you ever need to have a party catered, this is the young lady you should call. Folks meet Olga McKenzie, owner and manager of Unlimited Caterers. Just another little piece of information, I couldn't believe that my treasured secretary was just as curious and suspicious acting about what was going on as some of the other ladies." Then, jokingly, he said, "Stephanie, I think Martha is getting to be a bad influence on you."

There was a big cheer and a standing ovation for Olga. And both Stephanie and Martha blushed over his remarks about them.

"May I say something?" Olga asked Ben. He gave her a nod and she continued. "You folks will never know how much fun the three of us had keeping some of you people in suspense. This type of thing is not really what I do best - keeping secrets, that is - but my sister, Rose, decided we should be very mysterious about the project and it appears we were quite successful. Of course the fact she has always just referred to me as her kid sister, Cooky, helped a lot. I hope you are all pleased with the results. Thank you."

"Now that the big mystery has been solved, let's get on with the party," Ben told the crowd. Then getting in another dig at Martha, he added, "However, frankly Martha, it is kind of a compliment to think someone might suggest that anyone could possibly be interested in me other than my beautiful wife. I'll be sure and tell her about it."

Everyone cheered and applauded once more for the caterers and then proceeded to the long tables to enjoy the fabulous display of culinary art as well as a large selection of drinks, both soft drinks and liquor. Someone remarked it was a shame to disturb anything because it all looked so picture perfect. Many people did manage to get pictures, in addition to video taping the decorated atrium and the tables before they were disturbed. They also made sure they recorded the gift giving procedures and speeches.

It wasn't very long after all the people had served themselves, found seats and started to eat when a piercing scream was heard from outside and in ran Donna, the receptionist from the main lobby of the building.

Donna is what the average man would consider quite a dish - the kind he'd never kick out of bed! She has long, blonde hair, brown eyes and olive complexion. She is tall and slender, very pretty and knows it, curves in just the right places, and almost always wears mini-skirts to show off her long, shapely legs. Her personality, along with her appearance makes her just the right person to be a receptionist in a large industrial building such as this. It wasn't very often that a man didn't find an excuse to stop and chat with her, before taking care of any business he may have in the building. Donna seldom showed any sign of emotion, was always very much in control, but this time she bordered on hysteria.

As soon as Ben could calm her down to the point where he could have a fairly rational conversation with her, he found out that she had gone to the parking garage to get something from her car and found Juan lying on his side, his eyes wide open, as though he had been surprised by someone. She was sure, considering his appearance that he must be dead but she didn't want to touch him, and she started to cry.

"Calm down Donna. Did you call the police?" Ben calmly asked.

"No sir, I was too frightened at what I saw and I came running right here because you were the closest people around." she answered, still trembling and sobbing. "I'm sorry if I spoiled your party."

"Steve, call the police and tell them to get right over here. And Rose, get Donna a drink please, and see if you can calm her down some. In the meantime I think everyone should remain here and not go into the garage. Let the police handle it when they arrive. In fact, as difficult as it may be, I suggest we try and continue with the party for now." he told everyone.

Naturally, from this point on the topic of conversation was the probable death of Juan. In spite of the fact he was far from the most popular person in the company, no one honestly wanted to see him dead. Going on the assumption he had been murdered, the conversation went accordingly; each one trying to speculate how he got there and who did it.

"I shouldn't be saying this even about him, since I have been so happily married recently, but I can't help it. He was a jerk," Dennis said. "Someone did us a big favor, although I must admit he was very sociable and well-mannered at the anniversary party - probably trying to impress his pretty little niece though. Maybe now the office will run more smoothly. Who needs characters like that around? All he was good for was running around with trashy females. Too bad he couldn't have found someone more like his niece. Now she was a real classy gal. However, today is for Don, so let's not forget that and try and have some fun."

Dennis is head of security for the company, generally gets along with everyone and is a cooperative, hard-working employee. He did have a definite dislike for Juan and the feeling was mutual, mostly because Juan hated Blacks, and he tried to walk all over Dennis because he was Black. Dennis, at the same time, felt Juan was only good for complaining about everyone, except for those whores he always managed to pick up, and he bragged about that.

Dennis was in his late 30's, had a liberal arts degree from some New England college, in addition to a few credits in law enforcement. He had worked hard to get out of the environment in which he had lived as a child and make something of himself. He had finally been bitten by the love bug recently and eloped, even though he once claimed he would never get married.

"Be careful how you talk," Rose told him. "The wrong ears could pick it up and you'll end up as a suspect. Oh, I realize you wouldn't do such a thing, I'm sure, but someone else may not believe that."

Rose, a middle-aged lady is an analyst trainee. She had never worked with computers before coming to T.G.I., though she was bright and learned very quickly. Only recently she had decided to return to the job market, since she was getting bored at home alone. She had tried working with her sister in her catering business but didn't like that kind of work - said she wanted something she felt would be more challenging and rewarding. She had been a widow for three years (her husband's death had been a very tragic and sudden one and she still found it difficult to talk about it), and she decided it was time to get out among people, so she went to school to learn about computers. Besides, financially, she needed the extra income. She couldn't understand dissension in a work area and thought everyone should at least try to get along with each other. She had her own opinion of Juan, which wasn't a very high one, but she didn't care to express it at a time like this.

Martha, after hearing the conversation of some of the others commented, "Why should we worry. We've been in here since before ten this morning, and most of us have been available to help set up for the party, so we didn't have time to even think about Juan, much less murder him. But, if I knew who did it I would congratulate them for getting rid of him - NO, I don't really mean that; because I'll have to admit I did feel kind of sorry for him. He has been through an awful lot in his lifetime what with prison and losing his parents and his wife while they were still so young. It's just that he has always been so unbearable around here."

"Hey, listen everyone. Martha almost admitted Juan had some good points." Carlos commented sarcastically. "Maybe there's hope for her yet. But how can they suspect one of us anyway? He could have had lots of other people who didn't like him. It could even have been one of his so-called girl friends. He was always cheating. He bragged to me a lot about all the different women he slept with and how crazy they were about him. It's hard to believe he was ever married. I wonder what his wife was like."

Carlos was originally from Central America - Honduras - and still had a trace of an accent. He is also a data processor and the newest member of the company. He is a very pleasant, likable man in his early 30's. The young girls in the company think he is cute and handsome and felt terrible when they learned he was already married. Although Carlos hadn't had a chance to know Juan very well, based on what he had seen and what everyone had been saying about him, not to mention the bragging he did, Carlos didn't attempt to socialize with him. Besides, he felt they had nothing in common since they apparently had an entirely different set of values where life was concerned. Carlos was not totally aware of Juan's complete background or he may not have been so harsh on him - both having come from Central America.

Martha couldn't resist making more nasty remarks about him and said, "He seemed to think he was God's gift to women - some crummy gift! It makes me want to throw up just thinking about ever having sex with him. He was disgusting. What kind of women did he have? Probably real dogs. But he did get a lot of calls from women during the day at work. There's one in particular who called all the time. She even came by the office one day to meet him - she wasn't quite as bad as some."

Before she had a chance to make any more derogatory remarks she was interrupted by Rose who told her, "Knock it off. The poor guy is dead now." She then noticed the main door opening. "Oh, Oh, here are the cops. You know what they're here for."

Chapter 23

"I am Officer Lanza," exploded a loud voice from a tall, burly police lieutenant, as he entered the atrium, nearly scaring some people out of their wits. "I hate to disrupt your good time. However, we seem to have a murder on our hands which we feel is the number one priority at this time. So, I don't want any of you to leave until we've had a chance to ask some questions to try to get to the bottom of this. As you all must be aware by now, Juan Marcos, one of your fellow workers, was found in the garage of this building, presumably murdered.

"Since most of you worked with him and he was found in the garage, I must consider the possibility one of you did it. Mr. Christou tells me he wasn't very popular here, so I will expect everyone to make themselves available for questioning. In other words, don't anyone plan on leaving town. Do I make myself clear?"

As he glanced around the room to see if he could get a response from someone, he noticed Stephanie leaning against a supporting column. He was temporarily speechless and, as he couldn't help but stare at her, he thought to himself, "At last I've found the girl of my dreams, but how do I get to meet her?"

After regaining his composure and returning to reality, he told everyone, "First of all, assuming you are all innocent - and that remains to be proven - do any of you know of anyone who hated the victim enough to want him dead?"

Since no one spoke up immediately he continued, "Until the coroner can establish the time and cause of death, we won't take any official statements from anyone as to their whereabouts. But you'd all better try and remember where you were during the past twenty-four hours. By the way, when was he last seen alive? Did he report for work today? Was he here yesterday? Your timekeeper should know when he was here last if no one else did. Who is your timekeeper?"

All his questions were fired on the group so fast no one had a chance to interrupt and answer any even if they wanted.

Finally a soft, meek little voice from the area of the punch table said, "Sir, I am the timekeeper."

It was Kim, the little Oriental girl from the Accounting Department who offered the information. "He left yesterday about 3 PM - said he had a bad headache and was going to see his doctor. He gets migraines; or he did. He didn't come in this morning but some girl called early this morning and reported him sick," she told the officer.

"Do you happen to know his doctor's name, or the name of the girl who called?" asked Officer Lanza.

"I'm sorry sir, I don't know the name of his doctor but the girl he goes with most is Bunny. Since I don't know the sound of her voice, I can't be sure that's who it was that called, and I don't know Bunny's last name. That's all I can tell you sir."

"Does anyone else have anything to say at this time that might be of some help?" the officer asked, as he glanced around the room to see if anyone looked as though they may have some information.

"I saw him last night with a girl at the Mad Dog Club down on Corsica Road." Carlos volunteered. "It's not the best of places - like a place to take someone only if you don't want to be seen. Know what I mean? I sure wouldn't dream of ever taking any girl of mine there."

"You mean a real dive?"

"You got it, officer. It sure is a dive - dark and smoke-filled - but it has a great dance combo and the sushi is fantastic, if you like sushi, and I do." Carlos responded.

"Did they see you?" the officer asked.

"I don't think so; they were too wrapped up in each other, literally. They were really making out - as the kids say - back in a corner booth. Doubt if they were aware of anyone else in the place. The lights weren't very bright, but it was definitely Juan and Bunny." he assured Lt. Lanza.

"Do you recall what time that was?" he was asked.

"Well, I left there right around 11:30, and they were still very much wrapped up in each other." Anticipating the officer's next question, Carlos proceeded to tell him, "I know what time it was because the late sports news had just ended. I had waited for the results of the football games and as soon as I finished my drink I left." Again he answered what he thought would be an inevitable question. "I was completely sober because I can't and don't drink hard liquor. I just had a club soda."

"How do you know the girl's name was Bunny? Did he introduce you to her?" asked Lt. Lanza, as he glanced in Stephanie's direction. She was walking towards the dessert table at the time.

"I told you I didn't talk to them and they didn't see me. I had met her out in front of the building one day last week when Juan and I happened to be leaving at the same time. She was waiting for him and he introduced us." he answered. "You know officer, I just had a thought. How do we know that someone from his home country didn't find out where he was and killed him for some reason unknown to us. That's something to think about."

"I guess you could be right," the officer said. "First though I have to eliminate the possibility of someone here doing it. Besides, why would they want to dump his body here in the building where he worked? No, I really think it was someone in town, if not right from the company. However, I'll keep an open mind about that possibility," he assured them.

"We're definitely going to question all of you more but for now I won't detain any of you any longer. Just don't forget what I told you all - be prepared for questioning as soon as our investigation is more complete and we establish the time of death." he reminded everyone. "Now, go on with your party and enjoy yourselves.

As he started to leave the area, he made it a point to walk in the direction of the dessert table. Winking at Stephanie, as he passed by, he said, "Don't eat too much of that stuff pretty lady."

The police officer, having departed, the party continued with everyone wondering who the killer was and if he or she was among them.

"That's sure a heck of a way for Don to have to remember his last day here," Rose commented. "I feel sorry for poor Mr. Wilson too. He's too nice a man to have to get the publicity that will no doubt come out of this. He wanted so much for this party to be a big success and then something like this had to happen."

"Hey, it's not his fault one of his employees was murdered. I don't think Juan wanted to die. Mr. Wilson will make out OK." Dennis assured her. "The old-timers are a lot tougher than most of us. I'm sure the company has gone through many rough times in the forty years they have been around and I'm sure they will come out of this incident just as well."

From this point on, the conversation between different people was much more quiet and the party finally broke up earlier than expected since the atmosphere was no longer as cheerful as it started out. In spite of how many people felt about Juan, none of them ever thought anything like this would happen and they certainly didn't want him killed; not to mention the bad publicity the company could get as a result of the murder.

Chapter 24

The Following Evening

That evening after dinner, Ben and Marge were discussing the events of the previous day, wondering who could have murdered poor Juan.

"Do you really think it could have been someone from the plant?" asked Marge, his wife of 38 years. "I just can't imagine who would be capable of such a thing, and for what reason? All our people seem to be so nice and friendly. To think that poor man went through so much before escaping from that awful prison, only to be killed in what he thought was a safe and friendly country."

Marge was a very likable, middle-aged woman in her early 60's, who started with the company as a file clerk before transferring to what was the bookkeeping section, and later married her boss. She is a petite lady, a perfect hostess at the many parties they have and is always extremely well-groomed, wearing the latest in fashions for women of her age. Her small stature and chic hair style gives her a much younger appearance. She was in charge of the bookkeeping office in the earlier years but rarely goes to the office anymore - not that she is no longer interested in the affairs of the company. Quite the contrary; she keeps up-to-date on everything going on there, even though she doesn't know much about computers. She turned the reigns over to Mr. Christou shortly after he was hired. Everyone likes her pleasant disposition and caring manner, and the fact that she and Ben always appear to be such a loving couple. "They act as though they are still newlyweds," is the usual comment.

"I have no idea who could have done it or why, dear, but we still don't know any of the facts surrounding his death. The possibility Carlos brought up is certainly something worth looking into and I guess the authorities will be investigating that avenue as well. The police so far haven't given us any information to speak of, but perhaps further investigation and the coroner's report will produce some leads. Something should break soon; it was yesterday morning that it happened," her husband told her. "After all, we don't even know how long he was dead before they found him. It's strange that he wasn't found before, with so many people going back and forth to the garage. It's also possible he wasn't even killed there but was just placed there to make it look like someone here did it. At any rate, I sure hope they solve it in a hurry. This kind of publicity can't help us or the community in general. All this speculation that is taking place here is not good. It made the headlines not only in the Portland papers but in the Boston papers as well."

"Well, I'll be glad when this investigation is over and things calm down. At this point it seems our employees are all suspicious of one another and chances are good that none of them had any part in it. It just doesn't make sense," Marge sighed.

"Now don't you worry my dear. Things will be OK. Let's change the conversation and talk about something more pleasant, like the plans we have to take the grandchildren to Disney World during their school vacation."

"Ben, there's someone at the front door." Marge remarked. "Who could possibly be calling at this time of night; it's almost 10:30? Would you mind answering it, dear?"

Ben went to the front hall, looking out the side window before opening the door, just to make sure it wasn't some stranger. "It's Harry. Put some coffee on, dear. I'm sure he'd like a nice, hot cup on a cool, rainy night like this." he called to her.

Upon opening the door he saw not only Harry but his girl friend, Linda, and asked, "Harry, what in the world are you two doing out on a miserable night like this? Come on in." The weather had taken a drastic turn-around and what started as just a light rain earlier in the evening had turned out to be a heavy rain with bone-chilling wind - hardly the kind of weather to go out in unless it was really necessary, and it was doing a job on the foliage which wouldn't last long at this rate.

"I'm sorry to bother you and Marge at home," he apologized, "but I felt it was something that couldn't wait. At least I think it's important. Oh, by the way Mr. Wilson, this is my fiancée, Linda. Linda, this is my boss, Ben Wilson. I believe you met at the 40th anniversary party."

"It's a pleasure," Ben told her. "Nice to see you again. Come into the living room where it is warm and comfortable. We have a fire in the fireplace tonight to take the chill off the room." He proceeded to lead them into the large, comfortably furnished room. The huge fieldstone fireplace lent a warm, cozy glow to the room. As they entered, Ben's wife got up to greet their guests. "Dear, it is Harry and his fiancée, Linda. You remember her from the anniversary party, don't you?" he politely remarked. Then he told the couple to make themselves at home.

"Yes, I certainly do remember them. How nice to see you both again. Let me take your coats and hang them up," she said. "May I get you something warm to drink? Seems like a good night for a cup of hot coffee - or hot chocolate if you prefer. I'm just getting ready to make some for us. I'm afraid we aren't much for liquor."

Then she asked, "By the way, have you two set the day yet? I assume since Ben called her your fiancée, Harry, that you are engaged. You had better plan on having us on your wedding guest list or we'll be very unhappy, won't we Ben?"

"Well, actually we aren't officially engaged - not yet." Harry responded. "But you know you two will be high on our list of guests when we do get married. Right honey?"

"Of course they will, when we decide on a date." Linda agreed. "Do you know something I don't, Harry?" Then before he could answer, she said. "We did get quite a chill. It is a horrible night. I'm afraid it is doing a terrible job on the foliage as many leaves have been blown off the trees and, as you know, they can be treacherous to drive on; almost as bad as ice if you have to stop fast." Then, turning to Marge she said, "May I help you in the kitchen so the men can be alone to discuss whatever they need to talk about?

"Yes dear, that's a good idea," Marge said. "Come with me, Linda."

When the two ladies left the room the men chose the comfortable easy chairs near the fireplace to discuss the reason for Harry's late night visit.

"OK Harry, you must have something very important that it couldn't wait until morning," Ben remarked. "You're definitely not here on a social call. I knew that as soon as you walked in. You aren't in any trouble are you?"

"Heavens no," Harry answered with a chuckle in his voice. "I'm not even married yet and Linda already keeps me in line. But I love it." Then with a very serious tone to his voice, he remarked, "There is something I found out this evening, which I think you should know about. It could be just another rumor but I still want to tell you first, before word spreads around fast and someone starts their own investigation. I surely hope that's all it amounts to - a rumor - but either way I think you should know what's going through the grapevine."

He then proceeded to let Ben know what it was that he had heard - from an allegedly reliable source, he told him. Ben promised he would look into it first thing in the morning but hoped it turned out to be just malicious gossip and not fact. He did appreciate Harry coming to talk to him about it and asked him not to say anything to anyone else.

They then joined the ladies in the kitchen where they had coffee and cake and chatted for a little while. By that time Harry and Linda commented that it was getting late so they had better leave.

Chapter 25

Harry and Linda didn't want to stay very long because they lived across town from the Wilson's and it was a long drive back to the apartment they shared. Besides, it was getting quite late and they both had jobs to go to the next morning. Like so many young couples of the day they lived together even though they were contemplating marriage eventually.

The ride home was a quiet one, Linda not knowing if she should bring up the subject of Juan, so she kept quiet. She figured if Harry wanted her to know the details of what he and Ben discussed he would have told her. She also wasn't sure just how much Harry had told Ben.

It was a tense ride late at night, through the pouring rain, the wet leaves, and the strong wind. The windshield wipers on his Mercury Cougar were going as fast as they could - luckily there was very little traffic at that late hour.

As they entered the apartment, in order to break the somber atmosphere of the tense ride home, Linda said, "OK lover boy, time for bed - last one in the shower is a rotten egg," and she ran for the bathroom, kicking off her shoes and starting to disrobe along the way. Harry got the hint and was close behind her.

After a warm shower together, taking turns washing each other's bodies, they dried each other, got into their king-size waterbed and snuggled together, their warm bodies in a tight embrace.

"Honey," (figuring she could mention it now) she said softly, "I worry a little about having told Ben what you did. Do you want to give me the details?"

"Not now, but don't worry," he replied. "Ben will get an investigator on it and find out soon enough. There's no reason for you to worry your pretty head about it, at least until it is checked out. Besides, that's Ben's problem. We have problems of our own."

"Really?" she replied in a very concerned voice. He sounded very serious to her.

"Yes, woman, our problem is how soon are we going to make love?"

"Oh, you're impossible and I love you," she whispered in his ear, and they embraced each other tightly, just enjoying their closeness. Then, after showering each other with tender kisses, they assumed the proper position and consummated their love act.

Before finally going to sleep Linda whispered, "Harry, my darling. I never thought I could be so happy."

"Me too, sweetheart. Good night and sweet dreams precious."

The following morning Harry was very quiet while they showered and dressed. Then during breakfast he asked Linda how much she loved him.

"Do you mean to sit there and ask a ridiculous question like that after last night?" she asked him, looking him straight in the eye.

"Well, you could be just another over-sexed broad. But as long as you were serious and you do love me, you won't object if I give you this," and he took a beautiful 3-karat diamond ring out of a box and slipped it on her finger. "Now, sweetheart, how soon do you want to marry me?"

"My God, I thought you would never ask I began to think I would have to do the asking. But this ring, Harry? It must have cost a fortune." she told him. "Can we really afford it?"

"Well, can I assume that means yes?" he asked. "And never mind can WE afford it. That's my problem. The money is from my bank account. It won't be ours until after the wedding."

"Of course I'll marry you silly. The sooner the better, but I do think we should wait until this murder at your company is resolved. However, there's nothing preventing us from setting a date," she responded.

"Yes, I agree with you darling, and I can hardly wait for that day." he answered. "But now I must finish breakfast and get to work before I'm fired - and we can't afford that with a wedding coming up; and hopefully, a little bundle of joy soon after that."

"I've gotta get ready for work too," she replied, ignoring the last remark. "See you tonight sweetheart. What do you want me to fix for supper?"

"Hey kid," he answered. "We have some celebrating to do - no supper at home tonight. I'll think about it and call you later. But plan to wear something special. We're really going to celebrate. Nothing but the best. And we'll talk about a good date for the wedding at that time. Talk to you later honey. Have a good morning."

Right after lunch that day Linda received a phone call from Harry telling her to ask for the rest of the day off, then go home and pack her toothbrush and fanciest dress - something sexy - because they were taking the weekend off to celebrate their engagement and discuss wedding plans.

"We are leaving no later than 4 PM. Didn't I tell you our celebration called for the best? Well, I decided the only place to celebrate our engagement is to have dinner at the Ritz Carlton in Boston, and spend the weekend there." He then let her know he was able to get reservations and they would just relax, do whatever they felt like at the moment, sleep late and come home Monday or maybe even Tuesday.

"My, aren't we the demanding one now that we're getting married," she kidded. "And the Ritz no less. Wow, I'm really impressed. I'm not sure I'll know how to act in a fancy place like that."

"Hey honey, you're every bit as classy as any woman who ever stayed there. But listen, lady," he said, "if you don't want to go with me, just say so and I'll find another dame who will be happy to spend two or three nights with me."

"Like heck you will! I'll be ready before two o'clock."

They were on the road a little after 3 PM, much earlier than Harry had expected.

"Any regrets my lovely lady?" he asked her. "I should have insisted on being engaged long before this and I hope you don't want a long engagement because I don't think I could stand it. Dennis was telling me there is nothing like being married. He claims it is altogether different than just living together and he wishes now that they had married right from the start. I know my parents thought it was terrible when I told them about us. I know when I was younger I promised myself I would only have sex with one girl, and that would be my wife. Maybe we shouldn't have weakened last month."

"Well, I'm afraid my folks were absolutely dumfounded too to think their little girl would do such a thing. And, you know, maybe they were right. Fortunately we both know we were virgins when we met and never had sex with anyone else, but that's not the case with most other couples. Makes you wonder how many mates some people may have tried out so to speak.

Anyway, that is all going to be in the past. If it's agreeable with you, sweetheart, I think Christmas would be a beautiful time to get married. How do you feel about that honey?"

"I think that's great," he responded, giving her a tender kiss on the lips. "We'll have time over the weekend to discuss the details. I can hardly wait to call you my wife, in addition to being my best girl. I love you so much that it's going to seem like an eternity before our wedding day finally comes."

Chapter 26

A couple of days later a memo was circulated to all employees to meet in the main auditorium at 10 AM sharp. It didn't indicate why, but it was mandatory for the entire crew to be there, and Mr. Wilson signed it.

Most people were reasonably sure it had something to do with Juan's murder because it had been very quiet around the building since the day of the party. If anyone were going to be suspected it probably would be Carlos since he was the last one from the company, as far as anyone knew, to see him alive. By a quarter of ten many of the employees had already started filing into the auditorium, anxious to know if their guess was right, and what the police had found out, if anything.

"Anyone wanna make a bet as to who killed Juan?" Dennis asked - a remark made more to break the silence. "We should start a pool - winner take all."

No one seemed to appreciate his humor and ignored his remark as they went into the auditorium.

As soon as everyone was seated, Ben walked to the front and approached the mike. (Nothing had been discussed regarding Harry's visit to Ben and, with Harry and Linda having been out of town since the following day, Harry thought this meeting may be relative to that.)

"Ladies and gentlemen," Ben said, with a very stern, business-like sound to his voice, "I'm sure most of you realize the purpose of this meeting. At this time I want you to meet Lt. Lanza once more. He will give you instructions as to what will be done here today.

"Thank you Mr. Wilson for allowing this interrogation to take place here. I won't be doing much of it myself. Instead, I have assigned Det. Sgt. Greg Petrakos and his partner, Detective John Stilkowski, to this case. I expect all of you to cooperate with them so the guilty person can be brought to justice and you folks can get back to your respective jobs. So, if you know anything at all, no matter how insignificant it may seem to you, please tell them. Thank you." And he left the podium, walking back towards the exit. Luck was with him he thought when he noticed

Stephanie near the exit door. He smiled and told her to have a good day, wondering when he was going to have an opportunity to meet her so he could ask her for a date.

The two officers walked up to the podium, Sgt. Petrakos being the first to speak. "We can now tell you that Juan Marcos was definitely murdered by a person or persons unknown at this time. The murder was also not committed in the parking garage. The body was brought to the garage from another area and we are working on where the killing actually took place.

"It will be necessary for us to question all of you about your whereabouts prior to the time he was found. We believe we have a couple of fair leads but until we question all of you we'll try not to draw any definite conclusions. I have a crack detective assisting me with this case and he will be questioning some of you. We decided to do the questioning here instead of at the police department, which should make it easier for you folks. We will use those two small rooms next to the auditorium, if that's OK with Mr. Wilson. And, Mr. Wilson, I will depend on you to make sure everyone who was at the party will be around for questioning."

"Sure," he said. "No problem at all. And I will make sure everyone is available. The rooms will be free for as long as you need them."

The officers had questioned less than half the people the first day and indicated they would have to return the following day. Most of them were eliminated at once, for one reason or another, and were no longer considered possible suspects. However, those who worked closest to Juan would be questioned at greater length, since it was determined many of them didn't like him and the police were anxious to know just how deep their dislike was.

Mr. Wilson was not considered a suspect but was asked to stand by in case the officers had additional questions of him about any of his employees. That is, did they have a criminal record or any minor infractions of the law at all, or problems getting along with other people.

He assured them that, to his knowledge, all his people were law-abiding citizens with nothing more than a possible parking violation. As for rapport with each other, everyone seemed to get along OK in the office. Some wouldn't have associated with others outside the office, but at work things were fine; except for

Juan, because they felt he was so anti-social they wanted nothing to do with him, unless it was business.

When Det. Stilkowski questioned Debra about her whereabouts the evening before the body was found, she told him she would rather not tell. He convinced her she could be the main suspect if she didn't cooperate and answer his questions. There was no reason for her to get special attention so, "answer all my questions," he told her.

"Well, don't tell anyone but I was with a gentleman friend of mine at the West Shore Motel," she confessed. "We were there all night. The night clerk will vouch for us. In fact, my friend dropped me off at work the next morning. Besides, I could never kill anyone, no matter how angry I might get."

"What is your friend's name, so we can verify it?" asked the detective. "We'll try not to involve him, if it is at all possible, but I must have it."

"Do I really have to?" she asked. "He's a married man and he could get into a lot of trouble if the wrong people found out he was having an affair - know what I mean? But he's going to divorce his wife soon and then marry me. He promised me and I know he will keep his promise."

"They all say that, miss, just to get in bed with a dame. But you'd better let me know. We'll find out one way or another and then he and you could get in even more trouble if we have to find out our way. Ya know what I mean?"

"OK," she said very reluctantly, and Debra whispered a name in his ear. "Now you can understand why I don't want anyone else to know"

His eyes opened wide with astonishment. "Wow, no wonder you wanna keep it quiet." He was definitely surprised at the name she revealed. He assured her he would not mention the name to anyone unless he absolutely had to, but it could possibly come out anyway, eventually.

Sgt. Petrakos had the dubious task of questioning Carlos, whose story he wasn't at all satisfied with from the start, because he never indicated where he had gone when he finally left the club.

"OK Carlos, let's have your story one more time and this time I want to know exactly where you went and what you did when you left that dive."

After repeating his story one more time, he added, "Then I went right home. I had to be up early for work the next day so I didn't want to stay out too late. Besides, I've never been one for real late hours."

"Do you mean to tell me you weren't the least bit curious about Juan and the dame with him? - like where he picked her up - when they left - where she lived? - that sort of stuff. I find that difficult to swallow," he said. "Did you meet anyone on the way home who will corroborate your story?" he continued, as though Carlos were his favorite suspect.

"Hey, listen man." Carlos answered, obviously very agitated. "I had no quarrel with Juan, even though we weren't social friends by any means, but we weren't enemies either. I couldn't have cared less who he chose to run around with. That was none of my business. If he chose to hang out with those sluts, so be it. I just happened to see them there in the same club I just happened to go to. Besides, I told Officer Lanza the other day that I had seen her outside the building after work a couple of times, obviously waiting for him. Why don't you find her and question her? She was with him the last time I saw him."

"OK, don't get smart," Sgt. Petrakos warned him. "I strongly suggest you think hard about who may have seen you after leaving the club. That's all for now."

"Well, actually sergeant, the next person I saw was my wife," he admitted. "I know because I went right home. She was just saying good-bye to two of her girl friends."

"Not that it's any of my business, but do you two always do your own things? If I were married I'd expect my wife and myself to do things together," Petrakos told him.

"No," he answered. "She has several girl friends who get together the same night every week, so I go to the club and watch sports on TV until I think they've all gone home. We've only been married about 6 months and I see no reason for her to give up her friends. She doesn't object to my night out."

In view of the line of questioning, those who had been interrogated had come to the conclusion that Juan had been killed very late at night, making it all the more difficult to prove where they were. After all, who can prove they were home in bed?

"Well, OK, that's all I need from you today." the Sergeant told them. "But all of you make yourselves available in case I have more questions, which I no doubt will. Have a good afternoon.

Chapter 27

"It looks like someone beat us to the punch." Sgt. Petrakos remarked to Tony Osborne, as they entered the door. Tony was a young police officer assigned to assist him in searching Juan's apartment for any possible clues. "They sure turned the place upside down. I was afraid something like this might happen before we got to it. I just hope we are able to find something in this mess that hasn't been too badly disturbed."

"We'd better call the guys in right away to dust for prints, before we move or touch anything." Petrakos said. "I don't want to disturb anything anymore than it already is until they finish."

Two men from the fingerprint department came in with their equipment and started their job of dusting for prints. They commented on the big mess in such a small apartment and asked why anyone would need to leave the place in such shambles.

"How does it look guys?" Petrakos asked. "Are there any worthwhile prints?"

"Yeah, boss, there sure are more than one person's prints. One should be the victims, and we'll soon know who the others are." Gus replied. "They left some beauties on the door knob and some more over here on the bureau. They certainly weren't professionals or they would have been more careful; probably would have worn gloves. We'd better get these right down to Headquarters and start tracking them down. We'll probably have to send them to Washington for identification, and hope these prints are on file. Then you shouldn't have any problem solving your case. Someone sure didn't think ahead about the possibility of being caught. See ya later Sarge. Have a good day." He then gathered up his equipment and left the other two to finish their job.

"Where do we start first?" Tony asked, staring at the small apartment in disbelief. Whoever did this sure made a terrible mess - it would seem they were in a big hurry to find whatever they were looking for and get the Hell out before someone walked in on them - or maybe someone did interrupt them and they had to make a quick get-a-way."

"Let's look through the bureau drawers, and we probably should check through the sofa bed too." Petrakos suggested. "He supposedly had a lot of money; whether it was cash or deposited in a bank account is something we will have to determine. You might check that desk in the corner. He must have had a bank book of some kind - right?"

"Hey Sarge, here's a little book; looks like an appointment book with a section for telephone numbers. Maybe we'll find something in here that'll give us a clue - like who he'd been seeing or scheduled to see. There seems to be some names with numbers and here's a couple of pages with just telephone numbers, without names next to them. Maybe the number for that girl, Bunny, is here so we can call and see what she knows."

"OK Tony, hang on to that. Now I wonder where he kept any jewelry he had. Since he was known to wear an earring, I doubt if he could buy just one, so there has to be a mate. The place is such a mess; the intruder could have taken it plus other jewelry and we'd never know if he even had any." Greg commented. "Did you happen to find a box of any kind that could be used for small jewelry?"

"No, but I just found something just as good if not better." Tony replied. He pointed out a long envelope taped to the bottom of a drawer he had just pulled out of the bureau - one of the few things that wasn't already on the floor. "Don't touch it. Just give me a plastic bag and I'll pull it off with this file and let it drop in the bag. My guess would be there's money in it. They really were in a hurry to have missed this - unless someone had interrupted them. But then, amateurs probably wouldn't think of looking there."

In a small drawer of the desk, under some neatly stacked handkerchiefs, they found a small box. Upon examining it carefully they opened it to find a goldtone chain with a cross on it, a pinky ring and several pair of earrings, all of which appeared to be cheap costume jewelry, except for one pair of expensive Sapphire earrings. These the officers dropped in the bag of things to take back to Headquarters for further examination. Whether the burglar had missed the drawer or had seen the jewelry and recognized it as inexpensive stuff and just left it, they couldn't imagine. On the other hand, why would they have left that drawer neat and intact, then leave the others in such a mess; especially since the missing diamond earring should have been there too. Hopefully there would be fingerprints on the box other than the victims.

"Eureka!" Sgt. Petrakos called out. "I do believe I've found something very important. Going over to where Tony was in the kitchenette, he showed him a bank book from one of the local banks. "This was in the drawer next to the dish towels. What a strange place to keep a bank book, but it looks very promising. Look at all these deposits and withdrawals he made just in the past year or so. Very little of either up until then. Doesn't that make you wonder how, all of a sudden, he could make deposits of that size on his salary? They range from two to four thousand dollars each month. And here's one that's for sixty-five hundred."

"Yeah, I doubt if Total Graphics paid him that kind of money," Tony responded. "And certainly no part time job would pay anything like that. Even if he were a betting man, he wouldn't have exact amounts to deposit each month."

"My guess would be blackmail," Petrakos answered. "But, who could he have been blackmailing and why? He must have found out something that could be dangerous if he exposed a certain person. All this stuff we have to take back to headquarters should certainly tell us something. Do we assume the person he was blackmailing was also the killer; if not who killed him and why? He must have had something they wanted and since it wasn't on his person they trashed his apartment. Boy, there are so many possibilities.

"Well, let's put some of this furniture back where it was. It's a shame that this place is such a mess. I think the victim must have been a very neat person because everything is a wreck, except for the kitchen, and that is immaculate. I'm sure the rest of the apartment was just as neat. Wait just a minute; here are some bills up on this little shelf. I think we should check the phone bills and see who he'd been calling lately - good idea?"

Tony agreed it was a good idea and promptly included the bills in with the things to take to headquarters. "I think it would also be a good idea to check his answering machine, while we're at it. There are a couple of messages on it." The first message was, 'Hey man, the well has run dry. You're on your own from now on. The boss said to go to Hell and tell the police if you want. You'll just get yourself in trouble too. Blackmail is a crime you know. I'll call you again later.' ` The second one was the message Roger had left when he returned home following his attack the night of the murder. They decided to take the answering machine with them too and see if there was any way they could identify the first voice.

After loading up all the bags of possible evidence they had accumulated, they left, locking the door behind them and fastening up the usual yellow police line ribbons alerting people to keep out.

As they were starting down the walk they encountered Desi and Shorty coming their direction. "Hey officers, what's up?" Desi asked. "Something happen to Juan Marcos? Is he in some kind of trouble?"

"What do you fellows know about Mr. Marcos?" Sgt. Petrakos asked. "He was murdered a few nights ago. Do you know anything about it?"

"Oh my God," Shorty exclaimed. "We are friends of his from back in Nicaragua - just arrived last night and decided we'd surprise him - give him news from home and talk over old times. We also had a mutual friend who just had a serious operation in a Boston hospital and we wanted to let him know he's now OK.

"So why did some bastard want to murder our good friend. He never hurt anyone. He was probably the most generous and caring person we know." Desi added.

"Well, I'm sorry you guys had to make this long trip." Sgt. Petrakos told them. "We were just here checking out his apartment to see if we could come up with any clues as to why someone would want to kill him. From what you tell me, I guess you couldn't be much help. You could notify someone in his family, if you know where they are. They may want to come up here and claim his belongings."

"Yeh, OK. We don't know where members of his family are in Nicaragua, but we know of a cousin of his in Texas, and we'll notify him. Thanks sergeant," Desi said as they turned and left, both wondering how and why this could have happened.

On their way back to the precinct, the officers stopped at a small diner for lunch, since it was past their normal lunch time. It also gave them an opportunity to discuss the case, at which time they both agreed it was becoming more and more complicated.

Chapter 28

"Everyone sit down and make yourselves comfortable." Ben ordered in a stern voice he hadn't used in many years with his children. "I hope my source of information is proven wrong but there is reason to believe someone in this family is involved in the murder of Juan - either by their own hand or by hiring someone else to do it. If this is so then what the Hell has happened to this family since we've become successful. When we were struggling to get ahead everyone was thoughtful, considerate and honest with each other. Has the money gone to your heads? Have you lost your sense of value as to what you are expecting out of life, and how to treat your fellow man; not to mention your family?"

Ben was furious but before anyone could respond and say anything in their defense he continued, "Now I'm holding my own interrogation and I don't want any arguments or complaints. Like it or not, even though you are all adults, I'm still the head of this company as well as the family, and don't intend to have its good reputation shot to Hell because some selfish SOB can't be honest with his family or anyone else. When did selfishness enter this family? He then turned to Marge and apologized, saying, "Excuse my language, darling."

Continuing, he said, "Now, since no one seems to want to volunteer anything I'm going to address you one at a time and hope to get to the bottom of this." It wasn't at all like Ben to show such anger - and he rarely raised his voice or swore, so the shock of his manner of speaking left everyone wide-eyed and speechless.

"By the way, Angie, where is Alex? Whether you realize it or not, he is part of the family if only by marriage."

"He had to go someplace, Dad," she told him. "He said he would be home before the meeting ended. I told him it was very important."

"I expected him to be here from the start, not when he chose to arrive. However, we will start without him. Now, I don't want any interruptions - absolutely none - when I'm questioning anyone. OK Steve," Ben said, "What have you got to say for yourself? You are sober at the moment, aren't you? You've caused me and your mother more headaches the past couple of years than even the worse parent could possibly deserve. So for once in your life answer my questions truthfully. You know I will do everything I can to provide the best lawyers to defend the guilty one, if any of you are, in fact, involved in this mess or know anything about it."

"Hey dad," Steve responded, as he stood up. "Why the Hell is it always me you point your finger at first? You think your precious son-in-law and my sister are so perfect they could walk on water. Well, damn it, I've got news for you...."

"QUIET!" demanded his dad. "I will not have this kind of carrying on in my home or that kind of language in front of your mother. I told you I was doing the questioning. Now sit down and be quiet until you're spoken to.

"Steve, why are you always on the defensive as though you have something to hide, like a guilty person?" his dad asked him. "Just relax and give me straight answers, with no comments or accusing remarks about anyone else and we'll all get along fine.

"First, exactly where were you the night of the murder? If you were with one of your girl friends tell me so. I don't care which one it was, but I want an honest answer and if you left her presence for even five minutes I want to know. Do I make myself clear?"

"OK Dad," he answered. "I was with a girl friend, but she wasn't a local girl. She was someone I met on one of the business trips who just happened to be in town. She is a very nice young lady; even you would agree to that. I don't care to get her involved. But we were together all night. She doesn't even know Juan so there is no reason to implicate her. Now, that is the truth. You'd have been proud of me because I was completely sober that night too. I wanted to make a good impression on her. By the way, in case you're interested, we did not sleep together - had separate rooms. We just talked business. Do you believe me, because that is my alibi? She will back me up as will the manager at the Sebago Lake Lodge where we stayed. This is basically what I will tell the police when they get around to questioning me."

"You sound very sincere, son." his dad remarked. "I think I can believe you this time. Why can't you always be this calm and cooperative instead of being on the defensive and going into a rage whenever we say something you don't like. I will ask one more thing of you however; if you hear anything that sounds like it could be fact, or if you think of something you may have forgotten, please let me know. I just want to get things back to normal in this company. Is that asking too much?"

"No dad, it isn't and I promise to let you know if I find out anything." Steve answered in a tone quite unlike the way he had been of late.

"Now, Angie, where is that husband of yours?" Ben asked rather impatiently. "Much as I hate to say this, I have some important questions to ask of him but I don't want to say anything until he gets here. In the meantime, has he said anything to you about the case, or anything in particular going on in his office?"

"No dad." she replied. "In fact we haven't discussed much of anything lately. He seems to be so busy all the time, and has been away quite a bit so we haven't had much chance to discuss the case or anything else. I think I see his car coming in the driveway now." From where she was sitting she had a view of the front yard.

"Well, I was hoping you might know something," Ben responded. "But obviously you don't so I'll question Alex as soon as he gets inside. Do you want to open the door for him? I'm sure he doesn't have a key."

"OK dad." and she went to the door. "Well, Alex, it's about time you got here. Don't you think you could have arranged your schedule so you'd be at Dad's meeting on time? You know he wouldn't have asked us to be here if it weren't important."

"I'm here aren't I?" he responded with a snide sound to his voice. "Why do I always have to bow when your dad speaks? I have important things of my own to take care of too."

"I heard that Alex, and I don't like it." Ben told him. "You are not only an employee of the company but you are a member of the family, like it or not. Therefore matters pertaining to either should have first priority. Now, if you aren't too busy, please sit down and answer a few questions for me. What has happened to you lately? You're never around when I want you.

"I know you couldn't have been the murderer because you were in Ohio on business at that time. However, I have some very disturbing questions on a different matter to ask you. I have been hearing some ugly rumors lately, and I'm trying to get them cleared up by questioning members of the family."

"I'm sorry, but I didn't mean to sound like I did but Angie has been too darned touchy lately. Seems we very seldom can talk like we used to so I just stay away from the house." He was making it sound like she was the bad guy. "So what is it you want to know? I really don't know much about the murder if that's what you're insinuating."

"Well, that's not exactly what the grapevine says," his father-in-law said. "We...."

"Now just a damn minute. I don't know who is spreading rumors about me, or why, but you know I have been loyal to the company since day one....."

"Don't interrupt me, Alex." Ben shouted. "Just let me finish and then you may say whatever you want in your defense. But I'm going to let this family know what I have been told about this situation, which involves you a great deal - not so much about the murder but something far more serious where the family is concerned. Then you may tell your side of the story. At the moment I have an open mind and it is up to you to make sure I keep it that way. Now, sit still and listen."

Continuing, Ben slowly turned to his daughter and said, "Angie, I hate to have to tell you the rumors going around, but I have it on good authority that Alex has been running around with another woman; who or how many I'm not sure of at the moment....."

"Well, Well, so Mr. Perfection isn't so perfect after all," Steve said with a sneer. "guess I'm not the only one who....."

"No, not you Alex. Tell me it isn't so," Angie interrupted, and she sounded as though she were going to cry. "Please tell me they are all wrong."

"Oh stop it Angie." Alex answered. "Are you so naive that you didn't suspect something was wrong? What have you given me recently to make me want to stay home? You've been the most boring wife a man could ever have lately and always complaining. You used to be warm and exciting. Now you're like an ice box - no warmth or romance left in you.

"The rest of you may as well know. I don't know how you found out, but sure I've been seeing another woman. I'm simply not the type who can go home to a cold potato. I need some love and attention." he told the rest of them. "I'm sorry I let you down as a family, but I need to know someone cares about me and, if getting it from another woman is what I have to do, then so be it. It's that simple."

Just as Steve was about to say something else, his dad interrupted. "You be quiet Steve, and let me ask the questions.

"I can't believe what I am hearing, Alex," Ben said in amazement. "If you felt your marriage was so bad why didn't you discuss it with Angie, or us. Heck, if necessary you should have gone to a marriage counselor, or the priest, anything but running around with other women. You're right, I am extremely disappointed with you. I thought I knew you better than this.

"So this is why Angie has been so moody and depressed lately. What are we going to do about the situation? First of all, do you still love her? And, if you do, how can you possibly expect to make up for what you have just done, not only to Angie but to your children when they learn what you are doing?"

"Of course I still love her. I just did it to see if I could shake her up and get her to change and be more loving again." he claimed. "Actually, I thought there for a while she was back to her old self but it didn't last long and she's even more distant than before. I've always felt I was very fortunate to be a member of this family and wouldn't want to intentionally do anything to spoil it. But it looks like I may have gone too far."

"I can't believe what I'm hearing. Only a short while ago we went out, had a very pleasant evening together; at least I thought we did. Then we came home, talked for a while and made love before settling down for the night - the first time in a long time. Do you mean to tell me that I was just another lover for you for that night? That's why you told me at first you had to work late. You made that phone call to tell your little whore you wouldn't be able to see her that night. You lousy creep; you were probably thinking of her all the time you were making love to me. You're a damn fool if you think I'd take you back after you've been fucking around with God only knows who." she screamed, shaking her fist at him. "What the Hell do you think I am? You weren't thinking about me or the kids - just your own stupid self. What a damn stupid excuse to use to change me; change me from what to what, pray tell?"

"Angie, that's enough. Stop it this minute." her dad ordered. "That language does not become you and I will not have that kind of talk in front of your mother. I realize you're upset but you don't need to use that kind of language."

"I'm sorry mom, but I'm just so sick and disgusted with him. I simply can't believe this is happening to me," and she started to cry.

"Now dear, don't cry." her mother said, trying to comfort her. "We'll work something out. You two have been together too long and seen so many good years. And we must consider the children. There certainly must be some way of patching things up."

"Really mom," she cried. "How can I ever want to sleep with him, much less make love to him again after what he has done. I saved myself for him before we were married and I have never even looked at another man. How could he ruin our lives like this? He can't think very much of me or the kids."

"So Alex," Ben asked. "What do you plan to do now? At this point, anyway, I don't intend to dismiss you from the company - you are too valuable to me as an employee and I feel what has happened between you and Angie has nothing to do with your work. However, this is certainly an insult and an embarrassment to us. I always gave you credit for being smarter than this. Naturally, it will depend on Angie as to what arrangements will be made for you and her. I'll give Steve credit for one thing - he never pretended to be something he wasn't. When he started cheating and walked out on Laura, the entire family knew right away. He didn't try to hide it. I'm just at a loss to know how to handle this."

"You can't possibly understand how I feel, Ben." he pleaded. "You and Marge have such a perfect marriage; always out to please each other; and once I felt that was the kind of relationship Angie and I had. I'm the kind of man who needs a lot of love and, until recently I had that love. Then all of a sudden it was gone, but Angie didn't want to talk about her problem; instead she just complained about everything. I'm surprised she allowed me to make love to her the last time we did. I know that's probably a rotten excuse. Maybe you should talk to her too, if you can get her to calm down enough to speak rationally. If it's any consolation to her though, I never had intercourse with the girl I was going with - and it has been just one. It was always just oral sex."

Angie let out a scream. "Oral sex, intercourse; I don't give a shit which it was. What's the difference? You cheated on me and broke my heart and now you try and make it just a simple 'oral sex'. Big deal! Are you bragging about it or are you just plain crazy?"

"Angie, is it possible for you to calm down and answer some questions without getting too emotional?" her dad asked. "I know this hurts and you are very angry, but I'd like to know your side of the problem, and let's face it, it is a problem."

"I'll try dad, but I don't know what to say. This is such a personal matter and downright embarrassing; but maybe it would help to talk about it.

"When I had that miscarriage early last year, it left me very depressed at times and I had to force myself into allowing Alex to even touch me much less make love to me. I made all kinds of excuses, but didn't want to say anything about how I really felt. I really don't know why I had that feeling, but I felt like something within me had died, when I wasn't able to come home from the hospital with a baby. Can you possibly understand that? The feeling didn't change, I got more depressed, and he didn't seem very sympathetic, so I guess, in a way, I was blaming him for what had happened. "

"Alex claims he asked you on several occasions what the problem was." her dad said. "Is this correct? Did he question you?"

"Yes, I guess he did, now that I think of it," she admitted. "And I told him nothing was wrong - nothing."

"Not that I'm trying to condone what he has done," her father said, "but do you think it was fair to him not to have explained the situation? It could have avoided all that has taken place lately. Try looking at it from a man's point of view. How would you have liked it if the situation were reversed and he had something bothering him but refused to share it with you? You often wonder why your mother and I have had such a long, happy marriage. Well, it's because we talk to each other and share each other's problems; always trying to do things to make the other one happy. You two obviously do not follow our policy and look where it has gotten you?"

"As usual, you are probably right, dad," she admitted. "But he has done a terrible thing and I don't know whether I should try to forgive him or not. How can I be assured he won't do the same thing again, and could I ever really forget and forgive? I don't feel, at least at this moment, that I ever could."

"Maybe you both need some time apart. If you both feel your marriage is worth saving, perhaps it's worth discussing with your priest. Angie, how do you feel about that?"

"I'm willing if Alex is, but for now I just want to be by myself for a while," she said. "Right now I have to find an excuse for the kids as to why he won't be coming home tonight. I don't want him in the house until I've had a chance to think about what you have said."

"OK Alex, how about you?" Ben asked. "Is this marriage salvageable? Do you want to give it another try now that you know Angie's problem? Another thing, I personally would like to know who the other woman was. I don't think Angie should know though. It could only make it worse for her."

"Had I known a long time ago what was on her mind and why she was acting the way she was," he confessed, "I wouldn't have dreamed of looking for another woman. I would have insisted on some therapy, or maybe even told you and Marge what was happening. Angie, why didn't you tell me? Oh, I know it doesn't make it right, but I longed so much for some affection. I would like very much to give it another try.

"As for the other woman, Ben, let's go in the other room and I will tell you her name so no one else will hear." After the door was closed, he told Ben who the girl was.

"You're old enough to be her father," Ben exclaimed. "What the heck prompted you to go after someone that young? You know I will have to let her go don't you? I do not want her working with this company under these circumstances. It's a shame because she is a good employee. But I blame her as much as you. She knew who you were and that you were married and still she was willing to go after you."

"I don't know." he said. "She is young and exciting and used to flirt with me whenever she saw me. She made a big fuss over me and was very warm and romantic - that was what I was looking for and that was what she was willing to give me. I'm sorry I caused her to lose her job. I guess I really fouled up good. Maybe I can help find her another job."

"That's not a good idea." Ben told him. "I will do it, and at the same time, I'll write a letter of recommendation for another position, and find some excuse as to why we let her go. She has some pressing expenses and can't afford to be without a job. I probably shouldn't bother with her because she is just as much at fault as you, but I just don't want her to ruin her life at such a young age. Don't expect me to help you out of anymore embarrassing situations though. Now let's go back to the others and discuss how we are going to resolve your's and Angie's problem."

Chapter 29

The following day the questioning continued with Sgt. Stilkowski calling on Martha first, followed by Rose and Kim.

Martha, who lives in a fashionable apartment complex some distance from the company, overlooking Long Lake, was asked where she was that night. She assured Sgt. Stilkowski that she had been home all evening watching her favorite television shows. During the 11 o'clock news she had fallen asleep with the TV on. Eventually one of her neighbors banged on her door, awakening her, and telling her to 'turn off that damn TV'. When asked what time that was, she said it must have been about 1 AM, and she was sure her neighbors would back her up because they're always complaining she plays her TV too loud and have threatened to call the police. She added that after taking her medication - which she should have had much earlier - with a glass of warm milk, she took a shower and went right to bed.

The sergeant felt there would be no problem checking out her story and no longer included her on his suspect list. However, he warned her he hoped he would never get a call about her TV being on too loud, and for her to be more considerate of her neighbors and keep the sound down. She wouldn't like it if the situation were reversed, or if they had a party until late at night and kept her awake.

Martha promised she would keep the volume down. Then she offered one other thing that Det Stilkowski might find of consequence to the case. She indicated that Juan had been flashing wads of big bills around the past few weeks. He never indicated where the money came from and she didn't know whether or not he was a betting man, but it did offer an interesting angle to the case and she suggested it might be relevant and worth looking into. Another thing she asked the detective was whether or not they had searched Juan's apartment to see if they could find any clues that might help solve the case.

He answered very abruptly, saying, "Listen lady, do you think we are stupid? Of course we checked the place and dusted for prints. We're not exactly amateurs at this business, you know. We're just waiting for the results. Does that satisfy your curiosity? Don't try to do my job for me."

During the lunch break there was much speculation among different employees as to what actually happened and exactly what the police did know about the murder.

"Well, I think someone found out about all the cash he was carrying around," Martha said, "and they killed him for the money."

"That doesn't make any sense." Dennis responded. "If someone robbed him, then where did they kill him and why did they dump his body in the parking garage after all of us had started working? Another thing, how could they possibly have known where he worked anyway, unless it was someone who knew him very well? No, I don't go for the robbery angle. It must have been for other reasons as well."

"I'm afraid the police will find out that it really was someone from the company although I can't imagine who it would have been, or what the motive could have been." Rose commented. "It has to be something far more important - like maybe drugs?"

"No, he wasn't a very sociable person but he sure wasn't stupid and was definitely not the type to get involved in drugs." Carlos said. "Besides, he was too busy entertaining all those tramps he slept with. He wouldn't have time to deal with drugs. But seriously, guys, I could never be convinced that with his family roots and upbringing he had before all the trouble in his country, drugs was a definite no, no for him. He was too busy saving money to send back to Nicaragua."

"Then maybe he was dealing in drugs and sold them in order to get money to send home. Or do you suppose he could be the type of person to blackmail someone?" Martha said, suspiciously. "All that money might indicate either possibility. But then who could he have been blackmailing if that were the case? There are so many possibilities, you know."

"Martha, you have a really wild imagination and a suspicious mind. Maybe he was the head of a whore house - what do they call them - a pimp or a john? I don't know; whatever it is. That would pay very well too, from what I've heard," Rose kidded. "I think you read too many murder mysteries."

All of a sudden meek, little Kim spoke up. "I was scared I was going to get arrested just for being with the company. That officer sure was gruff. Heck, I very seldom even spoke to Juan so what possible motive could I have to want him dead?"

"Hey, Kim, we were all given a real third degree and then some." Rose told her. "Don't think you were singled out for the rough questioning. I think he just likes to pick on defenseless women."

"Well," Martha commented. "I was kind of hoping that cute Sgt. Petrakos would question me. Instead that other guy really gave me more than the third degree - practically threatened to arrest me if I didn't keep the volume on my TV down at night. I was stupid enough to tell him I had gone to sleep with it on too loud and the neighbors complained. Of course that was my alibi, so this time I was glad I did have it on loud. But still, if the cute one had interrogated me, I wouldn't have minded so much."

"Well, Well," Rose kidded. "So Martha has a crush on a cop. What next?", and they all laughed as they went their separate ways back to work.

Chapter 30

Everyone had returned from lunch when Sgt. Petrakos requested to see Dennis. He too offered testimony that backed up what Martha had said, the officer later learned after comparing notes. He mentioned the money, which he always had - much more than what he made. Dennis said he thought he was just trying to impress people, but figured he hit it lucky at the track until he asked Juan one day if that was where he had been. If so Dennis would sure like to know his system for picking winners.

"So, was he lucky at the track or did he get it from some other source?" the officer questioned.

"'Hell No' he told me," Dennis said. "He said he got it easier than that - in fact he would be getting more that night. His job paid pennies compared to what he had going for him then." He was almost sorry he had said anything about his conversation with Juan because it just led to more interrogation.

"And just where were you that night?" Sgt. Petrakos demanded.

"I went to the health club to work out, like I do every other night. A guy's gotta keep in shape these days you know; hafta look good for the little lady." he said. "I was home by ten-thirty. I just got married recently and I didn't want my bride to sit at home alone for too long. She didn't mind my going because she had some things to catch up on anyway. We had a diet soda while we watched the late news and then we went to bed?"

"You seem to know so much about Juan and all his money, I think you know where he hung out and you went down to the bar where he was and when you saw his car you waited until he left. Then you tailed him and, after he took the girl home you slugged him, took his money and killed him. Now why don't you admit it so we can wrap this thing up!" he charged.

"That's a lot of bull shit and you know it! You've got a wild imagination," Dennis yelled. "I didn't kill him. Why would I want to ruin my life and my marriage over scum like him, just for a few bucks? Do you think because I'm black I have to be guilty? Well, you're dead wrong. Find yourself another patsy. If I did it, how did I get the body into the garage the next morning. Did you ever think of that? I was there early helping the others get ready for the party. Since no one saw Marcos lying there as they were coming to work, someone obviously had to have put him there after the rest of us arrived. Use your brain Sergeant."

"Well, actually we haven't figured that one out yet. Perhaps you have an accomplice." the officer answered, obviously trying very hard to make Dennis the guilty party. "In the meantime I'm going to keep close watch on you. After Det Stilkowski and I discuss our findings, I think he will agree you're our man." he said.

"You're 100% wrong because I'm not your man - MAN! If you check you'll find I've never been in trouble and don't ever expect to, so bug off." Dennis was furious that they were pointing an accusing finger at him.

After they had been questioned, Rose and Valerie were discussing the tough interrogation they had gone through.

"Boy, that detective is a rough one." Rose said. "I got the feeling if I didn't give him the answers he wanted he would start beating me with a rubber hose. Couldn't that be considered harassment, the way he talked to us?"

"I don't know." Valerie answered. "But they sure aren't very nice. I realize they have a job to do, but do they have to be so nasty and assume we are all guilty? I always thought people were innocent until proven guilty, so why is it so hard to be civil? I think if I were ever stopped for speeding he would cuff me and place me under arrest." she added with a smile. "What about you Steph? Was Sgt. Petrakos just as tough on you?"

"No, he wasn't bad at all. In fact, he didn't ask me much and when he finished he said he was sure I had nothing to do with it." she told them. "He wasn't like that officer who came here the first day; the lieutenant I mean. He's the one who made me nervous. He kept staring in my direction, no matter where I was standing and, as he was leaving I'd swear he came by the dessert table on purpose. In fact he gave me a big smile and winked, and then told me not to eat too much of it. Actually, it's too bad I'm married. I would have appreciated attention like that more if I were single, because he is rather good looking."

"I didn't realize that. But then again he might have been just as gruff if he were doing the questioning. By the way, do you think they will be questioning the big bosses?" Rose asked, ignoring Stephanie's last remark.

"Why not. They should be considered just as capable of murder as any of the rest of us," Stephanie replied. "I've worked with most of them for a long time and can't imagine any of them doing something like that, but people are not always what they seem to be in different situations. Who knows what they are capable of doing. A good example is Mr. Wilson's son, Steve. He is a heck of a nice guy on the job, but a total jerk where his family is concerned and, I understand, didn't have any trouble abusing his wife and kids at times. That's why she is divorcing him, you know. He is a heavy drinker outside business hours and gets mean when he is drunk. I've heard he takes drugs at times too."

Chapter 31

Word got around fast the next day when Sgt. Petrakos was seen entering the building. Before he reached Mr. Wilson's office, Stephanie had already been notified of his pending arrival.

As soon as the sergeant arrived, Stephanie called Ben on the intercom to tell him he had company and then she told the sergeant to go right in. She wondered why the sergeant had returned so soon. He supposedly had finished questioning everyone the day before.

"Mr. Wilson, sir, I hate to bother you again," Petrakos apologized. "Where is the young lady who discovered the victim? I haven't seen her around here. She may have something else she could tell us. We sure didn't get much out of her the day she found the body."

"Actually, she doesn't work for us. She's hired through the company that owns the building, but I can arrange for you to see her," he replied, and he called Stephanie and asked her to see if Donna was at her desk and to tell her he wanted to talk to her.

"Hi Donna." Stephanie said, when Donna finally answered her phone. "That nice Sergeant Petrakos is back again. He wants to ask you a few more questions. Guess he figured you were too upset the other day when he was questioning you. Do you mind coming into Mr. Wilson's office for the questioning?"

"Gosh, no." she answered. "By the way, sorry I took so long to answer but I was away from my desk, you know. No problem at all. Just let me find someone to sit at my desk for a little while and I'll be right there. Can't imagine what else he could want but, what the heck, I don't mind.

"I understand you wish to ask me some questions officer." Donna said in a low, sultry voice - as though she were trying to imitate Lauren Bacall - and she proceeded to slink into the office as though she were auditioning as a model - nothing like the hysterical girl of a few days ago.

"Yes miss," he answered. "Please be seated. I need to know exactly what you saw out in the garage, and what time it was when you discovered the body - anything at all that you can tell me that might be of some significance in this investigation."

"Well now, let me see," she drawled with a slow, deliberate tone to her voice. Then, crossing her legs, her tight skirt more than half way up her thigh, she continued. "I went out right about eleven because I had left my sweater in my car and it was a little drafty at my desk with the doors being opened so much, you know. A girl can't be too careful about catching a chill you know."

"Never mind the sweater for now," he responded, thinking if she's so worried about catching a chill why doesn't she start with some skirts that don't show almost everything she has. "What about the body?"

"Oh yes, the body. That poor Mr. Marcos. Well, when I walked around my car to the side where my sweater was - I just happened to be parked right there, you know - and lo and behold, there was that poor man, just laying there all crumpled up and those big brown eyes a starin' at me. I shiver every time I think of it. It near scared me half to death," she drawled. "His jacket was all dirty and his shoes were all dirty with sand, and leaves were stuck to them. I thought that rather strange because he was always very neat, you know. Don't know where he could have been. There's no sand between here and the lake. He was a mess and it was plain to see he had to be dead, you know.

"I saw that man practically every morning as he came to work and this was the first time I ever saw him without that gold wrist watch he always wore. It was really beautiful you know. He told me one day it was a gift and I believed him. It had to have cost a lot of money. Believe me, I know jewelry. My daddy is in the business, you know. And that's all I can tell you, sir." she added, sounding a bit out of breath.

"You did very well miss," the officer remarked in a very soft voice. "Thank you very much for your cooperation. By the way, where were you the night he was killed? We never have had a statement as to your whereabouts."

"Well now, let me think." she said. "I do believe I had a date that night. Yes, as a matter of fact I did. We went out for dinner and dancing and then just drove around a while before my friend took me home. If I remember right, I was home before 12:30. I invited him in for a nightcap but he told me he'd better get home or he wouldn't be able to get up for work the next day, you know? Then I told him he was welcome to spend the night if he'd like because I have plenty of room. He kinda liked that idea but said he would have to go back home and get some toilet articles and some fresh clothes for work the next day."

"What time did he return to your place?" Petrakos asked.

"Well now, if I'm not mistaken it was around two-thirty AM, give or take a few minutes." she told him. "I had made some coffee and put together some little sandwiches; a little snack for us for when he returned, you know. I thought that would be a nice gesture, don't you? So, I wasn't paying too much attention to the time. I think it was about three-thirty before we went to bed. And that's about all I can tell you."

"OK miss, I guess that will do it for now. If I need to ask any more questions I'll know where to find you. If you should think of something else that would be helpful to the case, don't hesitate to give me a call."

Since the door had somehow been left ajar, some of the girls had stopped by Stephanie's desk to listen to what Donna had to say. As soon as the interview was over they scurried away, only to meet again later at a coffee break to talk about it.

"Well, la-de-da - Miss Glamourpuss sure impressed the sergeant. Boy, he never spoke to us like that." commented Valerie. "With some of you he roared. I guess it depends on what your legs look like and how much you are willing to display. And I noticed he didn't ask her who she was with. She really had him hypnotized, and I thought he was so nice."

"No, from us all he wanted was the facts, just the facts, and no more!" Rose responded, trying to sound like Sgt. Friday on that old TV series Dragnet. "She could have told him the story of her life and he wouldn't have interrupted. He would have just stood there gawking at her legs. But then we didn't talk to him that way either, you know?"

"Yes, she drove me crazy with her, 'you know'," Stephanie remarked. "But I guess you guys didn't notice the earrings she was wearing. They were identical to the ones Juan used to wear. I think it is stupid for men to wear earrings and that is why I had noticed them on him. They were beautiful diamond studs; must have cost him a few paychecks. I think I should ask one of the officers if there were earrings on the body when it was found. If not, Martha, you will have something else to add to your book of mysteries. What do you guys think? Another thing - she said she always noticed the watch but what about the earrings he also wore each day. She didn't mention them."

"Hey Steph, I must be a good influence on you." Martha chuckled. "I remember those earrings too now that you mention it. In fact, I kidded him about them one day and he just frowned and didn't say anything. They could definitely be important to the case. Someone should compliment Donna on her earrings and see if we get a reaction. Another thing, if she thinks she is so much of a jewelry authority, why didn't she comment on his earrings at the same time she mentioned the watch. I think she knows more than she is telling."

"No, I don't think that's a good idea." Stephanie remarked. "I think we should find out first if Juan had his earring on when they first found the body. If not, then I agree with you; maybe our sexy receptionist isn't as innocent as she seems to be."

They all agreed she had a point and that the detective should be told about the earring and have him check on it. Besides, who would want to steal just one earring?

Chapter 32

"Now, Mr. Wilson, I'm afraid we must question Mr. Christou and your son," Sgt. Petrakos said. "I'm sure everything is fine, but we do have to find out where they were and what they might know that would help us."

"I understand officer." Mr. Wilson replied. "I will notify them. You do have your job to do." Then turning on the intercom he said, "Stephanie, please tell my son that Sgt. Petrakos wants to ask him a few questions. Have him come to my office. Then he told the officer he was welcome to use his office because he was getting ready to leave for his summer house on Long Lake for a few days. He was beginning to feel the stress of the past few weeks and Marge felt he should relax for a few days and he couldn't do it at home.

A few minutes later Stephanie announced that Steve was in the outer office. Mr. Wilson said a fast hello and goodbye to his son and left him with Sgt. Petrakos.

"What can I do for you?" Steve asked, very impatiently. "I'm pretty busy so I hope this won't take too long."

"It all depends on you, sir. We'll make it as short as possible, but I do need to get the answers to a few questions about the night of the murder; like, where were you between 11 P.M. and 3 A.M.?" Petrakos asked him, thinking how very much different he was from his father - like they were made from different molds.

"I was with a friend all night." he responded. "My friend will back me up, if necessary."

"And just who is this friend? Does she have a name? I assume it is a lady friend since you don't look the type to spend a night with a man." the officer answered.

"You sound damn sure in assuming that my friend is a girl. I didn't have to tell you who I was with. I could have just told you I worked late. Besides her name isn't important to you or the case." he replied in his usual sarcastic manner.

"Hey mister, don't be flip with me. If everyone else can cooperate with this investigation, so can you, unless you have a special reason why you don't want to talk. You don't have to be such a smart ass just because you're the boss' son. It doesn't cut it one bit with me." he snapped. "Now, where does this girl live? We may want to question her too. I want proof of your whereabouts - something other than just your say so. Now, would you like to cooperate for a change or shall we go down to the station for this questioning?"

Steve suddenly calmed down and told Sgt. Petrakos, "We weren't at her place; she doesn't live in town. We were at the Sebago Lake Lodge - checked in about 9 PM and didn't leave until 5 AM, so I could go back to my apartment and change before going to work. I have a place of my own since my wife and I separated. The girl's name is Gloria Watson and she is staying at the Lodge until she decides whether or not she wants to live in this area. She's originally from Ohio where I met her one time when I was on a business trip. She doesn't know anyone in town but me. By the way, I already told all this to my dad when he questioned me."

"Now that didn't hurt a bit, did it?" Sgt. Petrakos remarked. "What do you know about the victim? I understand he wasn't very popular."

"Hell, I only know him from work and that was enough. We didn't exactly travel in the same circle - he just wasn't in my league. The only time I ever saw him outside the office was when my dad had the company party. I doubt if many people here liked the guy, but I sure don't know why anyone would kill him. Sorry I can't give you anything that would help in this case but I just don't know anything. I apologize for the way I acted at first. This hasn't been one of my better weeks." he added.

"Thank you for your help, Mr. Wilson. We'll keep you posted but, unless I feel I have reason to do so, I probably won't need to talk to you again."

Sgt. Petrakos was actually disappointed he didn't get any more information from Steve because he couldn't stand his superior attitude and would have loved to see him involved. He had heard of his reputation as a womanizer, and already knew why his wife was divorcing him.

He then asked Stephanie if it might be possible to talk with Mr. Christou at this time so he could finish questioning everyone, in order to start putting the pieces together in hopes of finding out who the murderer was. What his/her motive was and where it was actually committed.

Stephanie called Mr. Christou's office and asked that he report to Mr. Wilson's office for interrogation by the police. "Mr. Christou will be down as soon as he finishes a phone call. In the meantime, why don't you have a seat. Would you care for a cup of coffee? We make pretty good coffee here." She smiled, adding, "I sure wouldn't want your job officer. By the way, how is Lt. Lanza, the officer who was here the first time. He has a very nice smile."

"I'll tell him you asked about him. And, yes, I believe some coffee would be fine." he told her. As he took a sip he remarked, "This is very good - much better than we ever have at the precinct. That's more like mud, depending on who makes it."

Before he could say much more, Alex appeared and said, "I understand you have some questions to ask me. I really don't know what I could possibly contribute to your investigation because I was out of town the day of the murder, but I'm willing to answer your questions. Let's use Mr. Wilson's office where it's a little more private." Then turning to Stephanie he said, "Stephanie, if anyone is looking for me, you know where I am, but it has to be something important for you to interrupt us."

"Yes sir. I understand what to do."

After the two men were seated, Sgt. Petrakos said, "I'll start by asking you the same question I have asked everyone else. Sorry to take you away from your busy schedule, but it shouldn't take very long and Mr. Wilson made it quite clear that everyone should be expected to be questioned; at least those who may have had any dealings with Mr. Marcos. We are anxious to get this case solved."

"I understand," Alex said. "Like I told you, I don't know of what help I can be, but what would you like to know?"

"What can you tell me about the deceased? How well did you know him? He did work in your department, didn't he? Can you think of any reason why someone would want him dead?" Sgt. Petrakos questioned.

"Well, I really didn't know much more than anyone else I guess," he commented. "He was from Nicaragua where he had been a prisoner during their uprisings in the late 70's and 80's. He escaped and eventually made his way to the States and later to New England where we hired him. Yes, he did work in my department. He was a quiet fellow, did his job, but didn't socialize much with anyone else, except maybe for Mr. Philips in the mail room. As for anyone wanting to have him dead....."

"Sorry to interrupt at this time, Sergeant," Stephanie said as she opened the door, "but Mr. Christou has an emergency call from his department. They need him downstairs right away. Do you mind completing your interrogation at a later time?"

"No, that's OK. I don't think we have very much more to discuss at this time. I'll make another appointment to see Mr. Christou if necessary."

"Is Mr. Ben Wilson around, miss?" Petrakos asked Stephanie, having forgotten what Ben had told him earlier about his plans to be away for a few days. "There is someone else I would like to talk to. I think I missed him during the questioning the other day. Do you know Roger Philips?" he asked her.

"Sure. He works in the shipping department. By the way, Mr. Wilson left for a few days R & R, but I'll call Roger to come down here so you can talk to him." She then made a phone call asking Mr. Philips to report to Mr. Wilson's office on a police matter.

"I'll be right back," Petrakos told Stephanie. While I'm waiting for Philips I'm going out for a smoke. I'm trying to quit but some days are very trying and I have to have one. I'll be back in a few minutes. By the way miss, I'll tell Lt. Lanza you were asking about him."

"No, I'd rather you didn't. He might think I'm flirting with him. I was just curious as to why he is always staring at me when he comes to the office. Good luck with your attempt to stop smoking. I'm sure you will feel better if you do. By the way, call me Stephanie; not miss."

Chapter 33

As Sgt. Petrakos was walking down the corridor toward the elevator, he met Martha along the way.

"Good afternoon officer." she said with a smile on her face. "How are things going with the case?"

"Pretty good ma'am," he told her. "Why? Do you have a special interest in this case?"

"In a way, sir," she told him. "Some of us girls were noticing the earrings that Donna - she's the receptionist with the legs - was wearing when you had her here for questioning. They were identical to ones Mr. Marcos used to wear. Well, actually, he only wore one, but I'll bet it was part of a pair. After all, you can't go to a jewelry store and ask to buy just one. Do you think it should be pursued further? It's not too likely they would both be wearing identical jewelry. At least that's how I feel. And, if they are real good ones it's quite possible he had them engraved someplace with an identifying mark in case they were lost or stolen. I know I have a few pieces of good stuff that my late husband had ID'd for that reason."

"You seem to know quite a bit about things like this." he commented. "I don't suppose you are an amateur sleuth of sorts?" he laughingly said.

"Are you making fun of me Sgt. Petrakos?" she asked in a sort of flirting manner. "I do read a lot of mystery stories. But this murder sort of strikes close to home, where it involves one of our employees. You know, Sergeant, as long as we all had to be given the third degree - and that is what it seemed like when that partner of yours got through with us - I was wishing you had questioned me instead. You seem to be much nicer." she commented, acting as though she were 20 again.

"Why, do you think you know something else that could be important?" he asked her. "I'm willing to listen. Perhaps we can get together later over a cup of coffee and talk about it. Right now I have to get back to the front office and talk to someone up there. They probably wonder what happened to me. Is that OK with you? By the way, what is your name?"

"That would be fine with me," she told him. "There's a little coffee shop across the street. I should be through work by the time you finish your questioning, so I'll meet you there a little after four. By the way, my name is Martha." She walked back to her office very pleased with herself, feeling if she played her cards right he might even ask her for a date.

"How come you have a cat that killed the canary look on your face?" one of the girls asked as she came into the office. "Just what are you up to anyway? Did you manage to pry some juicy information out of someone?"

"Don't be silly. It was nothing like that. This is a very personal thing and you will just have to keep wondering what it is. Goodbye dear." and she went to her desk and pretended to be very busy before anyone else bothered her.

Chapter 34

Valerie met Jerry at the door. He was a half hour early and she was still in a robe with her hair wrapped in a towel. She had just come from the shower.

"Oh my gosh," she exclaimed. "I didn't expect to see you this soon. I just got out of the shower and am certainly in no condition to greet a guest. Sit down and make yourself comfortable while I go in the bedroom and get dressed."

"OK Val," he answered. "Do you need any help? Just kidding but maybe the day will come when you'll change your mind. I'll sit here and read the paper."

"Have you decided where we are going tonight?" she called out from the bedroom. "I want to know whether to dress fancy or casual. Just want you to know what a terrific time I had the other night. The music was fantastic and the food really delicious. But, I think we should maybe go casual tonight and maybe spend a little less. I'm not crazy about modern music but if you dance, let's go to a nightclub just for the heck of it. We can grab a fast snack someplace on the way and come back here for a late supper. I know just what we can have."

"My! My! aren't we wound up tonight." he said. "I don't think I've ever heard you say so much at one time. I like it. It means you are finally getting comfortable with me. As for your suggestion for tonight; sure, I don't mind going to a place like that once in a great while, but I sure can't stand that stuff as a steady diet. Most of all, I like the idea of returning here for a late supper.

"OK. Here I am." she said, as she walked out of the bedroom modeling a red mini-skirt and a pink jersey top. Her hair was neatly arranged in a French braid with a big red bow in the back. She looked more like a teenager. "How do you like it? Are you impressed? Do I look good enough for you to take out and show off?"

"WOW! What a dish," he remarked, staring at her legs. "I didn't realize you were so well built. At work you dress so conservatively. You're awesome, as the kids say. You have sure changed since we started seeing each other - and for the better. You're not as shy; not that that isn't a good thing but I just can't explain how I feel about you the more I see you. I think I'm falling in love with you and that's not bad either." And he gave her a big hug and kiss.

"Gosh, had I known this outfit would get this kind of reception, I'd have worn it sooner." she said. "I've had it for some time but was reluctant to wear it until I felt I knew you better. I was afraid you might tell me to grow up and put some decent clothes on. I know it's a little kooky, but I'm glad you like it."

We're going to have to stop by my place so I can find something that will go with your outfit better than what I have on now." he told her. "Are you ready to go?"

They arrived at his apartment about fifteen minutes later. He had a typical bachelor pad; a huge living room with mostly leather furniture, a little alcove where he had his computer set up, a small but adequate kitchen and a huge bedroom with a king-size water bed, and a large bathroom with a Jacuzzi. Off the living room were sliding glass doors leading out to a patio. It was nice but strictly furnished for a man.

"I like it." Valerie said. "But it sure needs a woman's touch. Oops, sorry. I didn't mean that. After all it is yours. You didn't tell me my place needed a man's touch. But you really do have a very nice place. How long have you been living here?"

"About a year." he told her. "I'm glad you like it. It's comfortable and meets my needs very well. If you'll excuse me I'll go change and then we can be on our way."

As Valerie wandered around the big room she saw some pictures on the baby grand piano. One was obviously his dead wife and the others probably his parents. Another one had what she assumed to be either a brother or a sister, their spouse and three children.

"Hey Jerry, if I'm not being too inquisitive, who are the nice looking people in the pictures?" she called out to him. "I like seeing family pictures around a house. It makes it seem more like a home."

About that time Jerry was on his way out of the bedroom dressed in jeans and a T-shirt with musical notes splashed around on it.

"These are my parents, my big sister and her family, and the other one is my wife taken about six months before the accident. She was a pretty lady, wasn't she?"

"Yes, she sure was a beautiful girl. You must have loved her very much and found her death to be devastating."

"Yes, we did have a wonderful relationship," he told her as he made his way over to the piano where she was.

"Gollee!" she drawled, as she turned around and saw him coming towards her. "That outfit sure shows off your muscles. Where do you work out to have such a build as that. I don't think I have to worry about not feeling protected with you for an escort. I really like what I see."

"Thank you, fair lady." he said as he made a sweeping bow. "Actually, I can attribute my muscles to my Marine Corps training. I served about six years in the Corps right after high school, not knowing just what I really wanted to do yet. It was good training for me in more than one way."

Never having been in a local night club before, they chose one in the outskirts of town, managed to find a parking place and went inside. A small combo was playing some popular soft rock - something they could dance to and still be near each other.

"I have to go to the powder room to check my makeup," Valerie said. "I'll only be a few minutes."

"OK Val," he said. "I'll just sit at the bar until you come out and then we'll get a table and have a drink before we start dancing, if that's OK with you."

"Sure thing." she said as she left the bar area and headed for the rest rooms.

"Hi there friend." said a voice coming from the stool next to Jerry. "You have quite a physique,"

"Yeah, thanks," Jerry answered. "I attribute that to my Marine Corps training and clean living."

"Do you come here often? Don't think I've seen you before because I'd remember a nice looking guy like you with those beautiful, big muscles." the guy said. "By the way, my name is Lloyd. Can I buy you a drink? Then we can take it and sit over at my table and talk in private. Who knows where it might lead us."

About that time Jerry had realized what was happening. The guy was gay and was looking for someone to pick up; and it sure as heck wasn't going to be him.

"Listen, Lloyd. It's not OK. You've got the wrong guy. In the first place I'm not your friend. In the second place, shove off and find someone else, or I'll make you wish you had."

"Oh come now. Don't play hard to get." Lloyd told him. "I know one of my kind who really wants to be picked up but who likes to play hard......"

POW!! Before he could finish the sentence, Jerry landed a right jab to the man's jaw and sent him flying. "That's my answer about wanting to be picked up," he yelled at him. "I'm no damn fag, so get lost."

About that time, Valerie had come out of the rest room to see the guy still sprawled on the floor on his back.

"What happened Jerry? Did you do that? Let's get out of here. Some darn Lesbian tried to pick me up in the rest room. I thought I was going to have to punch her in the nose to get my point across."

"That's funny," Jerry said and started laughing. "We must really be beautiful people to get propositioned by the likes of them. I think I put my point across to that one on the floor. Of all the clubs we picked for a night out - this is a gay bar. Let's get out."

They had a big laugh over their experience with the gays, and went to a place in the next block where the atmosphere was entirely different. They had a drink, danced a few numbers to some soft rock and then left. Jerry commented that Valerie was a very good dancer for someone who had led a sheltered life. She told him that, as a child, she had several years of dancing lessons - ballet and modern jazz - so this kind of stuff just came natural.

It was 11 o'clock when they returned to her place, still reminiscing and laughing about their visit to the gay bar.

"So, what's for supper, woman? I'm famished."

"Do you like spaghetti? I hope so because I make fantastic meat sauce and while the spaghetti is cooking I'll throw a salad together. How does that sound? Besides, it's the fastest way to a good dinner. I may even have a bottle of wine around here to go with it. How about garlic bread? If.you like that I can make some of that too."

"Fantastic. That sounds good but don't make too much work for yourself." he told her. "Is there anything I can do to help?"

"No, just stay nearby and keep me company. After that big encounter you had with your friend at the bar, you must be exhausted." she said, kiddingly.

"Valerie, honey, I wish you would get serious just for once, so I can tell you how much you've come to mean to me these past few weeks. Every time I want to talk seriously, you change the subject. Put that stupid spaghetti box down and come over here." As she neared him he threw his arms around her giving her a big hug and an extremely passionate kiss. "Does that tell you something about how I feel for you?"

"It sure does and I have to admit I feel the same for you but have been afraid to admit it." she told him. "I have wanted someone for such a long time that I could really and truly love, but right now I feel as though if I pinched myself I'd wake up to the same old dull situation. I do care very much for you Jerry. Now, let me finish dinner and we'll talk about it later."

"Sounds good to me honey."

In a little while dinner was on the table. After a few bites, Jerry said, "Hmmmm, this is delicious. I didn't realize I had found such a wonderful cook, and one so beautiful. How lucky can a guy get?"

As soon as they finished supper and Valerie placed the dishes in the dishwasher, they sat next to each other on the couch, each one waiting for the other to speak. They then chatted about unimportant things at work, about the newlyweds, and both agreed that Stephanie had changed the past few weeks.

Finally she said, "Jerry, it's terribly late. Would you like to stay here for the night? I have tomorrow off and you could take a day off too, couldn't you? That way you wouldn't have to be driving home so late and we could plan on doing something together tomorrow. I have plenty of room here."

"Well, I don't really live very far away, as you know. However that would be a nice idea; but wouldn't people talk?

"Who cares about what other people say? I have a nice guest room that you are more than welcome to use. It doesn't have a waterbed, like you have, but it is quite comfortable."

"OK, that's a good idea, but it would be far less work for you if we just forgot about the guest room and shared one room," he suggested. "I'm not rushing things am I? I don't mean to be but I just want to be near you as much as possible."

"Well, I don't know whether or not we should do that. I've never even considered sleeping with someone I wasn't married to. But it does sound very exciting and risqué." she admitted. "OK. What the heck. It's time I got a little daring. My life has been dull long enough. You talked me into it. If people are going to talk we may as well give them something worthwhile to talk about."

"That's my girl." he told her. "You won't be sorry. I can promise that."

When they first got into bed they were both very quiet and for a while kept their distance from one another, neither saying a word - like two little kids doing something wrong. Finally, Jerry asked her, "Do you mind if I cuddle up close to you for a goodnight kiss?" And before she had a chance to respond he had turned over and moved very close to her, kissing her neck and resting one of his hands on her breasts, caressing them gently. She started breathing heavily and it was obvious she suspected what was about to happen, but she offered no resistance. It wasn't long before they had completed a very romantic love scene, expressing how satisfied they were with each other.

"I didn't think it was possible to love someone so much," she told him. "You have made me very happy. Would you believe this is the first time I have made love to a man since my first unfortunate marriage? What a difference when it is with someone you really love."

After showering together and drying each other they went back to bed and enjoyed a very restful night's sleep

The following morning Jerry awoke first and, resting on his elbow, stared at the lovely lady asleep next to him. After gazing at her shapely body, he leaned over and gently kissed her lips. As she slowly opened her eyes, he said, "Good morning sleepy head. Are you going to sleep all day? It is almost 10 o'clock. Did anyone ever tell you you're beautiful first thing in the morning? If they didn't then they must be blind."

"Good morning to you too, Jerry. First of all I don't make it a habit of allowing anyone to make love to me, morning or night. And, I didn't plan on sleeping this long, but I haven't had such a relaxing night's sleep in ages. You sure are good for me. I don't suppose you can spare a hug and a kiss before we get up." Then, realizing she had nothing on, she asked where her nightie was. "This is the first time I have ever slept in the nude."

"It was in the way last night when we were about to make love. You do remember doing it don't you?" he asked, with a sheepish grin on his face.

"Boy, do I ever. I'll never forget. Making love with someone you really love can be so beautiful. As for the nightgown, you just taught me how wonderful it is without one; especially when you are snuggled up close to the one you love.

Before anything more could take place, Valerie slid out of bed saying, "If we are going to go any place today, we'd better get dressed and have some breakfast. Staying here could lead to almost anything."

As she started for the bathroom he gave a loud wolf whistle and he followed her to the shower.

Chapter 35

"Hey Rog, you're wanted in the front office." one of the men in the mailroom called to Roger. "What did you do now."

"Didn't you know, Phil. He's just been made Vice President, and we'll all be working for him." kidded another one of the men, and they all let out a big laugh.

"Don't be a wise guy," Roger responded. "How the Hell am I supposed to know what they want. I've been minding my own business, so I don't know why they want me up there. The cops never got around to questioning me yet, since I was on vacation, so maybe that's all it is. I'm not worried about that. See you guys later."

When he arrived in Stephanie's office a little later, he asked her what was up. He said he couldn't imagine why he would be told to report there.

"Sgt. Petrakos realized you hadn't been questioned when he was here the other day, so he'd like to talk to you about Juan." she told him. "He's in Mr. Wilson's office. I'll let him know you're here and then you can go right in."

"Come right in Roger - that is your name isn't it? - and have a seat." Sgt. Petrakos told him. "I need to ask you a few questions concerning Mr. Marcos. I understand you were a friend of his."

"Yes sir, we did go places together occasionally, but I wouldn't consider us buddy, buddy." he told the officer.

"I heard that you and Marcos were at a bar having drinks together the night he was killed. Is this true? Tell me what the two of you did and what time you last saw him?"

"Well sir, I just happened to be on my way home around midnight when I saw him coming from his girl's home." he related. "I caught up with him and offered to go have a drink with him at the bar a few blocks from there. He mentioned that it was late, but he guessed one wouldn't hurt, so that's what we did. I'm not sure what time it was when we left; some time after 1 A.M."

"Where did you go from there? Think carefully, because so far it would appear you are the last person to have seen him alive. Exactly what happened after you and Marcos left the bar?"

"That's about all, sir," he stuttered. "I went back to where my car was and I guess he went to where his was. We went in different directions. That's it."

"Would you like to go over your story once more fella?" Petrakos asked, impatiently. "I think you left a considerable amount out. I may as well tell you we have a witness who saw you in the bar. Now tell me exactly what you two were doing there. Didn't he give you something?"

"Yes sir," Roger answered rather nervously. "I may as well tell you everything from the start. You obviously know part of it anyway and it won't take long for you guys to figure out the rest."

"I think that would be a very smart move," Petrakos agreed. "Let's start with just before you got to the bar."

"OK." he said. "I had seen Juan with a lot of money recently and was curious to know just how he got it. If he was playing the horses or gambling someplace, I wanted to know his system for winning. Actually, I doubted if it was anything like that because on different occasions I had seen a guy slip him a thick envelope, and he was always flashing big bills around. I guess you could say I was sort of blackmailing him because I told him what I knew and if he didn't share it with me I'd report him and have him questioned about the money.

"At first he denied my allegations." he continued. "Then he admitted he was blackmailing someone but he wouldn't tell me who or why. He finally did admit he was getting $5000 a month so I told him I wanted a grand for myself or I'd report him. At first he didn't want to share that much with me but said he would sleep on it. In the meantime he gave me a grand in good faith and the next day he would let me know how much more I would get, if any. I settled for that at the time."

"Did he ever even hint who was giving him the money? What about the guy who delivered it to him?" the officer asked.

"He told me a different guy delivered the pay-off each time and it was never the same day of the week or at the same time of day. They would get in touch with him and he would go after it. That's what he told me." Roger related.

"Did you ever see any of the delivery guys well enough to be able to identify them?"

"Not really. They always seemed to do it in dimly lit places and at night. One was very tall though, I remember and still another one was short and very heavy. They all wore heavy coats and a hat, no matter what the weather was."

"OK, after you left the bar, where did the two of you really go?"

"Well, it was raining hard that night and my car was parked about three blocks away. Actually, from where I had met him, we took my car to within three blocks of the bar, and walked the rest of the way." he told the officer. "We couldn't have been more than a block from the bar, on our way back to the car, when we went by an alley. The light was very dim because the street light was broken. I caught a faint glimpse of a dark figure coming out of the alley and I don't remember anything more until I awoke almost an hour later. I had a big lump on the back of my head. I checked my pockets and all my money was gone, including what Juan had given me. The first thing I thought about was that he had done it to me and taken his money back. I was absolutely furious to think that he would do such a thing over $1000 bucks, and I was cursing him all the way home.

"When I got home I called him. There was no answer but the answering machine cut in and I told him what I thought of him and that I'd get even with him when I saw him again. But, I never saw him again because he was later reported dead. This is the honest truth Sgt. Petrakos, If you were to check his answering machine you'd probably find the message still on it. I showered, and put an ice pack on my head because it was really hurting. Then I went to bed, intending to get up early enough to see if I could help out at the party the next day, but I didn't wake up until 10 A.M. When I reported in at work, I met one of the janitors and he told me how awful I looked - wanted to know what had happened to me, but I didn't tell him. This is all I have to tell and it's the truth."

"That's quite a story. Of course you know I will have to check out certain parts of it." Petrakos told him. "Are you sure he didn't tell you anything else; not even a hint as to who he was blackmailing. I need to know everything or I may have to hold you on suspicion or as an accessory. Do you understand? Oh, by the way, how come you didn't find him when you came to work, if his body had been placed there sometime during the morning?"

"Of course, what I told you is the truth. I did not kill him, nor did I have any reason to want him dead. I didn't park in the garage that morning. I figured there probably wasn't enough room anyway, that late in the morning and I found a space across the street that had just opened and didn't have a meter. I really lucked out that morning, in that respect."

"That was not the answer to my question. I'll repeat it. Did he tell you anything else at all; like who he was blackmailing?"

"OK officer. He finally did admit to me that he was blackmailing Mr. Christou because he had seen him running around with another woman - someone from the company, in fact. If word got around about it there would be big trouble for Mr. Christou and the girl. They were seeing each other in secret, but he happened to see them several times; one time when they were just leaving a motel, and once was at a park where they were sitting on a bench under a tree, really hugging and kissing." He indicated that Juan said they weren't being very discreet for people who were trying not to be seen.

"He deserved to be blackmailed for doing a dirty thing like that." Roger said. "Mr. Wilson trusted him so much and Mr. Christou's wife is a real nice lady and doesn't deserve a guy like him. Actually, if someone was going to be murdered he should have been the one. To make matters worse, the girl is probably young enough to be his daughter."

"It's not for you to appoint yourself judge." the officer told him. "I agree that was a terrible thing to do, but you could be in trouble yourself. Just stay around town and make sure you're available for further questioning. By the way, I meant to ask you, did Juan have his earring on when you saw him last? The girls claim he was never without it, but when we found his body there was no earring."

"Yeah, I used to kid him about that earring. He told me once they were a gift from his late wife and he treasured them like a girl might her engagement ring. He was wearing it when I saw him last. Someone must have taken it, but I don't know who would want just one earring, unless it was another man." he told the officer. "Girls don't normally wear just one."

"That's all the questions for now, but stay around town in case we want to talk to you again." Petrakos told him.

Chapter 36

Lt. Lanza had just completed a staff meeting with his men and given them their assignments for the day.

"Greg." he called to Sgt. Petrakos. "Do you mind staying for a few minutes? I'd like to talk with you about the Marcos murder."

"Sure, Chuck. I'll be glad to. Guess you know we went to Marcos's apartment, dusted for prints and picked up quite a bit of stuff that could help us in the case - some bills, his checkbook, answering machine. We also found a little box of jewelry which included a pair of Sapphire earrings that appear to be the real thing. I thought we could check for an I.D. on them too and see if they match up with the I.D. on the other ones."

"Sounds good to me, Greg. I heard someone say it's possible he was blackmailing someone. Is that what you have determined too, and who is he? I haven't had a chance to go over all the reports you guys have made based on the interrogations. Not meaning to change the subject but did you happen to see that pretty secretary in Mr. Wilson's office? I'd give anything to meet her and be able to ask her for a date. She sure is one pretty lady."

"About your question as to a possible blackmailer. That fellow, Roger, told us Marcos was blackmailing Mr. Christou. We'll be checking on that possibility. As to Mr. Wilson's secretary, strange you should say that, Chuck. By the way her name is Stephanie. She was asking me about you and told me she thought you had a very nice smile. For a married gal, I can't understand her interest in you. However, I just happened to overhear some of those girls talking and someone said, and I quote, 'things are not very happy in her house'. I got the impression her husband is not a very nice guy. Maybe there's hope for you if you're really interested."

"Oh, I'm definitely interested. Wouldn't you know; after all these years I find the girl I want and she turns out to be married. You say her name is Stephanie? A very pretty name."

"But about the murder. What do you think about the people at T.G.I.? Any good suspects in your opinion? This sure is puzzling. I just don't understand why the killer went to all the trouble of disposing the body in that garage."

"Well Chuck, it seems to me if anyone in the company did it, they certainly wouldn't be dumb enough to move the body there. Someone is trying hard to throw suspicion on an employee of the company. So we have a murder case as well as someone being blackmailed. I wonder if the two are tied together. I doubt if Christou killed Marcos but he could have had someone else do it.

"Right now I have to get over there and talk to someone else. Then one of the girls thinks she may have a clue to this. She works there, is a nice gal., and it won't hurt to talk to her. She loves murder mysteries and I think she makes a hobby of trying to solve murders. Like I said, she is a heck of a nice gal and I'll be meeting her after work for coffee at a little coffee shop near the company building. Good luck with your attempt to date the secretary. See you later."

"Yeah Greg, I'll probably need it. Maybe someone should have murdered her husband too. Then I would have been able to step right in. Just kidding pal. We don't need any more murders to try and solve. On the other hand, if her husband has been mistreating her, something should be done."

"I didn't mean to be listening in Lt. Lanza, but I heard you mention someone was beating his wife," Sgt. Nelson mentioned as he came in the room. "We were just sent out on a call for the 2nd or 3rd time where the neighbors were complaining of fighting in this house over on Waverly Street."

"You don't happen to remember the name, do you?" Greg asked.

"Yeah, it was a Greek sounding name - started with a K, but I'm not sure what it was. I can find out for you if you're really interested."

"I'm interested, Nelson. Please check into it and get back to me. Right now I have to get to work. I'll see you later, Chuck."

Chapter 37

Martha entered the coffee shop and asked for the booth at the far end so she and Sgt. Petrakos would have privacy for what they would be discussing. And, with any luck, if he wasn't already married, she might be able to end up with a date with him,

About five minutes later he walked in, saw where she was sitting and went down and took the seat across from her.

"Have you ordered yet?" he asked her, as he took a cigarette from his pocket. "I took a little more time than I had expected since we had a staff meeting. Sorry Martha."

"That's OK, I only got here a couple of minutes ago," she told him, as she added, "I hope you don't plan to light that in here, near me."

"In fact, the waitress hasn't even been here to take my order. I'm glad you joined me. I was afraid you might think I was a nut, or something, and not show up. Like maybe you had to get right home for some reason. By the way, what is your first name? I don't want to keep calling you Sergeant, or Sarge."

"My name is Gregory, but call me Greg. All my friends do." Then he said, "Why would I not show up when I said I would. If you're hinting that I might be married, relax." At the same time he replaced the cigarette in the package, telling her she wasn't the first one that day to tell him not to smoke.

"I'm single. Had a very foolish marriage when I was nineteen, got out of it fast and have been too involved in my work to bother since. And now you know all about me. What about you, other than the fact you like murder mysteries but you don't like smokers."

"I get the feeling you're making fun of me. But I'm used to that. The girls are always kidding me about trying to solve crimes, in addition to telling me I'm too nosy at times. It's really just that I'm naturally inquisitive and anxious to know the why and wherefore of everything - know what I mean? Other than that there's not much to tell about me. I've been a widow for ten years, like reading - especially mysteries, don't date very often, and I work for T.G.I."

The waitress finally came to their booth and they each ordered coffee and a sandwich. As soon as she left they continued their conversation.

"What I really wanted to see you about Greg," she said, "was to tell you my feeling about certain aspects of the case. I was serious about my suspicions about Donna. She mentioned seeing the gold watch but didn't say anything about the earring when she discovered his body. Now, I can't ever remember seeing Juan without that earring. I'd be willing to wager he used to wear it to bed. I'll bet if you were to question her more - like where did she get them - she'd give you a phony story. I think they should be checked for any identifying marks, like maybe his initials or birth date. It's possible, you know, to engrave something on earrings, as small as they are. It would be very small but with a magnifying glass it could be seen. She never wore expensive earrings like that before, just cheap costume stuff to work. My father was never in the jewelry business like hers but I also know good jewelry. Another thing, I don't remember you ever asking her who her date was that night."

"My gosh, Martha. Don't tell me you girls were listening. That wasn't very nice, but you really are observant and have a worthwhile point. I'll remember to check on that, and, since you are so interested, we will be questioning her again. There has been some other evidence which has surfaced, but I can't discuss it with you."

"Another thing, if it isn't classified stuff." she asked. "Did you happen to find any other good jewelry in Juan's apartment? If you did, there probably will be identifying marks on those too. Then you can be pretty sure she was lying. One other thing, unless the killer pawned that watch, I'll bet when we find our suspect, he will be wearing it because it really was a nice one."

"As a matter of fact we have thought about that." he told her. "It's just one other thing that has us baffled about this case."

"Now, Martha, don't you think we have talked enough about the case for today? I really didn't think we would spend the entire afternoon talking only about that. What are you doing for dinner tonight?" he asked

"I don't have any particular plans. I usually just go home and have a light supper and then read or watch TV. Why, do you have something in mind," she asked, as if he would be asking for any other reason.

"Yes, as a matter of fact I did have something in mind. Do you like Greek food?"

"Love it, if it is good, homemade Greek food." she told him. "I've had some that has been awful. I take it you know where we can get some?"

"Well," he replied. "I believe I make the most delicious Souvlaki and spinach pie, as you non-Greeks refer to Spanakopita, that you can find. And I just happen to have some Baklava left over that I made a few days ago. That is one thing that improves after a few days. Can I interest you in a Greek dinner at my house? If so, I'll pick you up around seven-thirty."

"Wow! A man who not only is handsome but can also cook. How lucky can a girl be? That really sounds terrific and very yummy. I'll be ready and waiting. Your menu sounds fantastic and I can hardly wait to get there, providing you don't smoke. By the way, is there anything I can bring to add to the meal?"

"OK, it's a date, and just bring your appetite. I have everything we need. By the way, I've been trying to quit so I promise not to smoke." Then he told her, "Right now I have to report back to the precinct, so I'll see you at seven-thirty." He paid the check and then, before Martha left he asked her, "by the way, what is Stephanie's last name? I never noticed it before."

"It is Kaknas. Why? Is there some special reason you want to know?"

"Yes. Lt. Lanza and I were discussing battered women and one of the sergeants, who overheard us talking, said he had gone on a call the night before, for the second time recently, over on Waverly Street. Seems a couple with a Greek name....."

"That's Stephanie's address," Martha interrupted. "Don't tell me that rat of a husband is really beating up on her. I have suspected something like that for quite a while but never asked her about it. Figured if she wanted anyone to know she would confide in one of us. Thanks for the information. I'll see you later."

Chapter 38

Martha was ready and anxiously waiting when Greg rang her doorbell at exactly twenty-five past seven.

"Hi Greg," she said cheerfully. "I told you I'd be ready when you got here. I'm looking forward to the Greek dinner - don't recall ever having had any homemade Greek dishes; only those made in restaurants."

"OK then, ma'am, your chariot awaits you." and they went down the walk and he assisted her into his Grand Am convertible. I'm sorry I have to pick you up in uniform, but we had a special briefing and I didn't have time to change."

"You don't have to apologize for your uniform," she told him, adding, "Why could I not imagine you driving anything else but a convertible after being in a police cruiser all day? It just seems the right kind of car for a macho man like yourself, and I don't mind riding with you in uniform. Of course, one of my neighbors might think I'm being arrested," she laughed. "Oh, is that what you refer to me as? I often wondered just what a Macho man was, but I didn't think I fell in that category."

"So, what's on the menu for tonight?" she asked. "I can hardly wait. I'll probably eat more than I should, which I always do when the food is good - and I have a feeling this is not going to be any exception."

When they arrived at Greg's house he let her out of the car first and then drove into the garage. They entered by way of the kitchen door, which she thought was rather unique, telling him it was the first time a date had taken her in the back door instead of the front.

"I believe in being different. Never let it be said Greg Petrakos was a traditionalist." he told her. "Now, you may either sit out here and watch me or go into the living room and find something to do alone. Personally, I like the homey feeling of the kitchen and when we were growing up we spent more time in the kitchen than we ever did in the living room - sort of like the modern day family room, if you will."

"Well, the kitchen it is then," she said. "I just didn't want to get in your way since I don't know if there will be anything I can help you with. If so, just say the word. I'm a pretty good cook, but only for plain stuff."

"Before I start dinner, let me get out of this uniform and change into something more comfortable." and he went to the bedroom, returning in a few minutes with sweat pants and a snug fitting T-shirt with a picture of the Parthenon on the front. He put a cigarette to his lips but when he saw the 'you'd better not' look on her face, he took it out and threw it in the wastebasket.

"Now I can go to work. How about a glass of wine while I make dinner? I have some wine I think you will like, if you like red wine. It is called Mavrodaphne. I also have some Oozo, if you want something that will really make your toes curl! Have you ever tasted it?"

"No, but I've heard a lot about it and I'm not so sure I want to try it. Maybe later I'll get brave enough to try it. Right now I'll settle for the red wine. Thank you," she said, as he gave her the glass. "Mmmm, very good," she told him as she took a sip. "I like it."

They continued chatting, mostly about Greek food and tradition - never about the case - until Greg had the food on the table.

"My gosh, how many other people are coming for dinner?" she asked. "You have enough food for an army!"

"Whoa there lady. Bite your tongue! We do not speak of the Army in this house; only the Marines. Actually, it's just for you and me, baby." he kidded. "The Greeks know how to eat, fight and make love. And when they do any of these they put their hearts into it and do it better than anyone else.

"Now that I have taught you about my people, let's eat. And be sure and tell me whether or not you like the food. I'm sure you will, and if you don't then you just don't know good food." And he leaned over and gave her a kiss on the forehead.

"What a guy. You really surprised me. Underneath that tough guy facade is a little pussycat - a soft loving person.

"But at the same time, there's nothing bashful about you." she told him. "Has anyone ever told you there could be a little conceit in your family, namely you? But that's OK, as long as the conceit turns out to be the truth. Anyway, as someone used to say, the proof is in the pudding; so let's eat."

"Don't spread it around, if you think I'm a pussycat. It will ruin my image at the station." he told her. "Now, pass your plate and I'll give you a meal fit for the Gods."

After having a traditional Greek salad, he served her some baked lamb, roast potatoes and Greek-style vegetables. At first she didn't say a word, just ate as though someone might take it away from her. "Ummm, this is scrumptious. I haven't had anything so delicious in ages. Why hasn't some girl grabbed you - good looking, an absolutely fantastic cook, and good protection? What more could she hope for? I hope you don't think I'm crazy."

"Hey, I like to see people enjoying a meal, especially if I am the cook. I take it from that response you do like it. Be honest now; if there's something you don't care for, say so. Oh, I almost forgot to put the olives and Feta cheese on the table. And I'll get the spinach pie for you too," and he went to the refrigerator and returned with them. "Try these, if you still have room. These are Calamata olives and I prepare them myself. The ones in the market are generally terribly salty. Olives are supposed to make one passionate, you know, so take several. The cheese is called Feta and is made from goat's milk. Try it."

She took a couple of olives, ignoring his remark about them - and then some Feta cheese, and then a piece of spinach pie, tasting each of them. "Oh, this must be Heaven," she said. "I never had anything so good on earth. I swear I'm going to be 200 pounds by the time I get out of here. How do your people stay in shape when they eat so much yummy food?"

"They burn all the calories by making lots of love. Why do you think they have a siesta, like many other countries, after lunch? You don't really think they spend all that time sleeping do you?" and he laughed.

"Now you're teasing me again." she told him.

"Well, I never believed it possible to make anyone so happy with food." he commented. "When we're through, you have a choice of Baklava, rice pudding or some Diples. Don't think you have ever heard of Diples, but they are light and crispy and sweet, as are most Greek desserts. Would you like some now or perhaps you'd like to wait until later and we'll have dessert with coffee. I frankly don't see how you could possibly have room for anything else at the moment."

"That's an excellent idea. Let's go into the living room for awhile and chat and then try the dessert later. While you're getting that ready, I'll make the coffee. I can do that pretty good."

They sat in the living room telling each other a little about their respective jobs. Greg talked about Greece; that his mother was from Thessaly and his dad from Kalamata, he told her about his trip over there when he was a teenager and how he always wanted to go back just to visit and see more of the country because it was so beautiful.

"You can't imagine what a beautiful place most of it is. Of course, you have to get out into the smaller towns and villages where the real people live to appreciate it. And you should visit the Acropolis and the Parthenon in Athens - absolutely breathtaking. I often wondered if the Greek people really appreciate all the beautiful historic places they have, like a little further north of Athens, up around Delphi. I've had to take trips over there on business; like when an American gets in trouble and they need someone to bring him back here. I've had to make several trips because I speak fluent Greek. I'm not sure how I first got roped into these trips, but I never get a chance to enjoy the country. It's all business.

"I'm sorry Martha. I didn't mean to take over the whole conversation. I'm not giving you much chance to talk, but if you ever have the opportunity, you must visit Greece."

"Gosh, if it's even half as nice as you say, it must be awesome. I haven't really done any traveling to speak of. Not that I wouldn't like to but my salary doesn't give me an opportunity to spend money on travel. Besides, I don't think it would be much fun going alone, and I don't think I'd care for these tour trips.

"Since you speak fluent Greek, maybe sometime you could teach me a little."

"I could do that, but I have to warn you it isn't an easy language to learn. We'll get together some evening and just concentrate on learning some Greek words - simple ones to start, like: How are you, Good morning, Good night, I love you. And I'll think of a few more before you come over next time."

"That sounds good. But I think it's about time for dessert and coffee and then I'll let you take me home. I promised a dear friend of my mom's that I'd go over to her house and help her clean up her yard in the morning, and she likes to get out early.

She can't afford to hire someone and I enjoy working outside. You should meet her sometime. She has a little house a couple of miles from me. She's almost 85, but very spry. I have trouble keeping up with her at times."

"You are full of surprises, Martha." he pointed out. "I doubt if many people appreciate how caring and thoughtful you are. I think that's nice."

"Thanks, but let's get to the kitchen and tackle that dessert. I'm anxious to see what that's like."

She enjoyed the pastry just as much as everything else and wondered how the Diples were made. "They are so fragile. I can't understand how you can handle them without breaking them while you're making them."

"I'll show you sometime. It is a little tricky and you have to work fast, but once you get the hang of it, it's a piece of cake."

"I hate to eat and run Greg, but I do have to get up early. I'll probably dream about the wonderful meal I had tonight."

"Heck," he said, as he snapped his fingers. "I was hoping you'd be dreaming about me; instead you expect to dream about food. Well, you can't win them all. Maybe next time."

All the way home she talked about the dinner and how anxious she was to learn to make some Greek dishes and how to speak some Greek.

"Good night Martha." he said. "I really enjoyed the evening. We'll have to do it more often." and he gave her a kiss on the cheek just before he unlocked her door to let her in.

"Me too, Greg," she told him, and she blew him a kiss as she was about to close her door.

Chapter 39

It was Saturday morning when Steve insisted on visiting his children even though there was a restraining order against him because of the alleged child abuse filed by his wife in her divorce proceedings. He wasn't to be deprived of an opportunity to be with them by the judge or anyone else as far as he was concerned. A few drinks to start off the morning put him in an extremely foul mood.

It was a foggy, damp morning when he roared up to a screeching stop with his bright red, late model Corvette. The car barely missed the well-trimmed shrubs bordering the walk and driveway up to the front entrance of his wife's house. Slamming the door, he rushed up the stairs and pounded viciously on the front door.

He no longer could use his key because his wife had the locks changed in an effort to protect herself and the children for when he had been drinking or taking drugs - in moments like this when he blamed her for all his short-comings.

"Open the Goddamn door, before I knock it down." he screamed in rage. "I wanna see my kids and you'd sure as Hell better not try to stop me. Do ya hear me?" and he continued to pound.

With the safety chain still on, Laura called to him to lower his voice and to leave or she would call the police.

"You crazy fool. You're waking the whole neighborhood. Can't you lay off the booze, or whatever it is this time, long enough to pay a civilized visit to the kids?" she told him. "Besides, it's only 7 o'clock in the morning. Come back later. I'm not waking them up at this hour."

"Don't give me that shit." he yelled. "They're my kids too and I have rights and I want to see them now. Don't tell me what to do. Now, open the damn door."

Temporarily ignoring his pounding and screaming, Laura quickly picked up the phone in the front hall and called Ben.

"Dad," she cried. "Steve is pounding and screaming at the door, insisting on coming in to see the children. He's either been drinking or is on drugs, but he certainly isn't in any condition to see them. Besides they are sleeping - or they were before he got here. Please do something for me. I'm afraid of him. If he doesn't stop the neighbors are going to call the police again."

"Calm down dear." he told her. "I'll call the police and then come right over to your house myself. Try to quiet him by telling him he will have to calm down or you won't let him in because, in his present state, he will frighten the children. Stall him as long as possible until we arrive."

She said she would try, and hung up and went back to the door trying to think of some way to reason with Steve. Luckily Ben didn't live very far from her and, being early Saturday, traffic should be very light.

"Where the Hell did you go? Did you tell the kids to get up and get down here so their dad could see them?" he asked with a slurred speech. "I'll give them just five minutes; then I'll break the damn door down and, if necessary, get em out of their damn beds myself. Why aren't they up anyway - everyone should be up by now."

"Steve, don't be ridiculous." Laura told him. "It's only a little after seven and it's Saturday. There is no reason for them to be up so early. They are up early school days so they deserve one morning to sleep. Besides, aren't you out rather early, even for you, or maybe you never went to bed at all last night. You look as though you could use a cup of black coffee and a shower. If I were sure you'd behave I'd let you in and give you some coffee while we're waiting for the children to dress and come downstairs.

She was trying to calm him down and, at the same time stall for time so Ben and the police could get there before Steve got even more violent. In his present condition though, she didn't believe he could pound his way out of a paper bag.

"If you're trying to patronize me," he said, having some trouble getting the word 'patronize' out of his mouth, forget it. The longer you wait to get this damn door unlocked the sorrier you're gonna be. I'm sick and tired of not being able to see my kids when I want; it just isn't fair. I really miss them you know."

All of a sudden he started getting very melancholy and broke into tears. Laura was quite sure from his actions he was probably on drugs instead of being drunk. In any event she wasn't about to let him in the house in case his mood changed and he went back into a rage. She had no intention of taking a chance on his beating up on her or the children. About that time she noticed Ben's Town Car coming down the street with a cruiser following close behind.

"Steve, please don't cry. We'll work something out." she assured him in a very soft voice, so she wouldn't get him raging again. "The kids are almost dressed and will be down in a couple of minutes. I don't want them to see you crying. Just take it easy and when they get here I promise I will let you see them, and we'll have some breakfast together. You'll feel better after having something to eat."

Hearing car motors Steve looked around to see his dad's car coming to a stop in front of the house, followed closely by the police. Getting out of their cars they immediately rushed up the walk to the house. Just as suddenly as he had become melancholy, he reverted back to a raging bull.

"You fuckin' whore; you were just being nice until the old man and the cops got here. You'll be sorry." he threatened. "You have protection now, but I'll get you yet. They won't always be around. You're turning my own kids against me."

Laura didn't say anything more because by that time Ben and the police had come up the steps onto the porch and the police were ready to restrain him.

"We heard those threats Steve," his dad said, "and it's not very smart. When you sober up or get off the drugs - whichever you're on right now - you may visit your children, but not in the condition you're in now. So calm down and don't act like a maniac and make it any worse than it already it."

"Do you want me to arrest him sir?" the officer in charge asked. "He has actually threatened the lady with her life."

Before Ben could answer, Steve cried out, "Lady? What lady? I don't see no lady around here. All I see is a damn liar and traitor. She wants my kids to hate me and won't let me in my own home. Whatta you think of someone who'd do that, officer?"

"You are fully aware of the conditions of your visitation rights, and this is not your house - not anymore." his father reminded him. Then turning to answer the officer he said, "No, I don't think it will be necessary; at least not at this time. I'll take him over to my house and my wife and I will dry him out or whatever it takes to get him to look presentable and to sound a little more rational. Then maybe we can talk some sense into him."

"I'm sorry sir," the officer said. "But since I was sent out in a situation such as this, I have to search your son for anything that may be incriminating - a weapon of some kind, or even drugs - because he did threaten his wife."

"I understand," Mr. Wilson replied.

The officer made Steve spread his legs while he searched him. There was no gun but in one of his pockets he found a small plastic envelope. He sniffed the contents and said, "OK, I'll have to arrest you for possession of cocaine. I'm sorry Mr. Wilson, but I have no choice in a matter of drugs but to arrest him. I really hate to do it because of you, but maybe a night or two behind bars will give him some time to think about his actions. We will also have to impound his car until he can see a judge, and the judge makes a decision about him. You may follow me to the station if you want, but personally I don't think you'd be doing him any favors by bailing him out."

As he and the other officer dragged a raging, cursing Steve back to the cruiser, he read him his rights.

"I'll be back to see you later Laura," Ben told her. "Don't worry, I'll see what I can do for him even though he brought the whole thing on himself and doesn't really deserve my help. I feel there must have been something I didn't do as a father to cause this."

"Thanks dad. Thank you very much. In spite of all that's happened between Steve and me I don't want anything bad to happen to him. He was once a real nice guy. And please don't blame yourself for what is happening now. You did all any father could possibly do. Unfortunately, Steve is his own worst enemy."

Steve was forced to spend the weekend in jail. Ben didn't visit him, nor did Marge or Laura. Ben felt it best to leave him alone and let him have time to think about his actions.

Early Monday morning, still with wrinkled clothes and unshaven, Steve was called into court. His dad did ask one favor of the judge (whom he had known for quite some time), though he normally didn't do such things; and that was that his case be heard first. Ben had called one of the company lawyers, filled him in on what had happened and asked him to be present at the hearing.

Steve could consider himself lucky that morning. After hearing the case, the judge let him off with a year's probation plus the promise he would have himself admitted to a drug and alcohol rehab center. If he came out of it clean and stayed drug and alcohol free for one year, he would wipe his record clean. But, if he ever saw him back in his court again, even though he was Ben

Wilson's son, he would go to jail for the maximum time. Steve promised him he would never see him there again and, that he had learned his lesson the hard way, unfortunately. He offered no argument when he was taken to the rehab center, realizing what a mess he had made of his life.

Chapter 40

Monday morning

Jerry called Valerie to see if she would like to attend a concert that night.

"I'm sorry honey, but you know this is my bowling night." she told him. "We are in the finals and I can't possibly let the team down at this point."

"Can't you get a substitute for tonight, honey? I really would like to take you out tonight. I haven't seen you for several days since I had to go on emergency leave. Are you sure you won't reconsider?"

"I'm sorry, but I happen to have the highest average on the team and they really depend on me when the playoffs come along." she told him. "We have an excellent chance of coming in first the way things have been going. You must understand, don't you? I know what we can do. Why don't you come over to the bowling alley and watch us. As soon as we finish we can go someplace for a while. If it means victory for us we won't be having our annual banquet for another couple of weeks anyway, so we can leave as soon as the bowling is over. How does that sound to you?"

"Well, I guess that's better than nothing." he said, sounding rather disappointed. "I had hoped my first night back we could be together. I missed you something awful."

"Oh sweetheart, I'm sorry," she apologized. "I missed you too but I do feel I must not let my team down. We have worked hard all year to get to this point. We'll make up for it. I love you Jerry. You can either pick me up at home at 7:30, or meet me at the bowling alley around 8 o'clock."

"I'll meet you at the alley," he told her. "If I come to your apartment I'm liable to be so happy at seeing my gorgeous, sexy girl that I'd rape you and your team would never win. I love you too." Then he hung up.

Everyone was on time to start the playoffs. Since they were the team to beat, Valerie's team actually wouldn't start for about an hour and a half later but they all had to be there from the start, so she and Jerry sat and watched. She introduced him to all her friends, but was very intent on cheering on the different teams. It was team "D" that they were most concerned with. If someone else beat them, then Valerie's teammates were fairly confident they could beat any of the remaining teams.

It was finally time for the Bears (her team) to play the Ravens for the trophy and the championship for that year. She was a little nervous, as they had never come that far before. Having Jerry there also made her even more nervous and she almost wished she hadn't suggested that he come by. She made up her mind she would treat these three games like any other ones and just do her best. (The two top teams had to play three games, and the team with the highest total pinfall would be the winner).

"Yeah Val, let's do it." the girls all yelled, as she got up in the fifth frame. "Let's do a high five," meaning they wanted her to get her fifth strike in a row. "You can do it." And she did. In fact, she rolled a 219 her first game and, along with what the rest of her team rolled, they had won the first one by 34 pins. The other team took the second game by just two pins, so they still had a fairly good lead, but one bad break on their part could change that in a hurry.

Just before they started the third string, Jerry came up to Valerie, gave her a big kiss and said, "Go to it Tiger. Knock 'em dead. I know you can do it. Love you."

She was so surprised because, up until then, she had the impression he was angry with her for not going out with him right from the start. Instead, he had been yelling and cheering her team on too and then when he came up to her and wished her luck it gave her an altogether different feeling - like it put more life in her.

"Thanks honey." And she walked up to the alley and picked up her ball. She glanced back at him and then rolled the first ball - right down the middle and into the pocket for a strike. This happened seven more times. Then in the eighth frame, she left the 10 pin (everyone moaned), but picked it up with the next ball for a spare. She finished the rest of the game with all strikes, giving her a total score of 279, the highest she ever had; and, along with the scores of the other girls, they won that game with a big 68 points over the other team.

Everyone yelled and screamed and clamored around Valerie, hugging her and congratulating her on the high score she got.

"Boy, you were really hot tonight. Your boy friend should be here much more often." one of the girls told her. Valerie was then presented a special trophy for the most valuable player, not only of the tournament but for the entire season. She also received a cash award of $500 for the highest average of the season.

While all this was going on Jerry went to a telephone and made a call.

"Thanks everyone, for the award but you all helped me. I couldn't have done it alone. We all had a great season," she told them. "I hate to leave you so early but my boy friend just returned from a trip and we'd kinda like some time together. You do understand don't you? I'll see you guys at the banquet.

"OK honey, let's get out of here." she told Jerry. "Aren't you proud of me? I know bowling doesn't exactly excite you but I love it and we have a lot of fun each week. Besides, it also keeps me in shape."

"I don't find anything wrong with your shape kid." he answered. "Maybe if I knew how to play the game it would be OK, but I never really had that much interest in learning it. Guess I may have to if you're so crazy about it. I'll have to admit I did enjoy myself tonight, cheering you girls on. But right now I have more important plans for us."

As they left the bowling alley Valerie couldn't imagine what he meant by his last remark. She was so happy about her victory and the check that she couldn't imagine what he could come up with that would make her any more excited. But she was very happy that he was finally home.

"So what's up, Jerry? How are things at home? I really missed you while you were gone. Guess you could say I've become quite attached to you and hate it when we can't see each other every day, if only for a little while."

"Well, if it weren't so late, I'd suggest we go home and get dressed up and go out someplace special, but since it is so late, we'll have to go over to my apartment. I have something for you that I brought back with me. It is special just for you. And don't start asking what it is because I'm not even telling you if you're warm. I just want to get you alone with me. I missed you so very much it hurt. I do love you, you know."

"I love you too. But, you know what; maybe you should take me right home tonight and we'll get dolled up and go someplace special tomorrow night when we will have the whole evening to ourselves." she suggested.

"No way, my love." he told her. "End of subject."

She said no more and soon they arrived at his apartment. He parked the car, helped her out and up the stairs into his apartment. He hadn't said anything else to her for the past few minutes.

"Sit down and make yourself comfortable," he told her. "I'll be right with you," He went towards the kitchen where she could hear him doing something but she didn't know what. She thought she smelled food but couldn't understand how he could have cooked anything so fast. What could he be up to.

He finally returned, gave her a kiss and took her by the hand. Together they went to the kitchen where he had the kitchen table set up with a linen tablecloth, candles lit, fine china and silverware and a delicious gourmet dinner all set up, with all her favorite dishes.

"It's beautiful, darling. But what - how? - who did it?" she stumbled over her words, absolutely dumfounded at what she saw. "What is this for, honey?"

"It's for you silly. I had to let you know how much I missed you. This is why I tried to talk you out of bowling. But I'm glad now I didn't. This is much more cozy than a crowded restaurant, even if it is in the kitchen. I know the chef at that big restaurant on the lake and told him what I wanted. I had intended to take you there tonight but I called from the bowling alley and told him our plans had to be altered, and he took care of the rest - timed it just right. I'm glad you like it. Now let's eat while everything is warm."

Before they started he poured some champagne and they drank a toast to their love and to better days. He then told her to take the cover off the soup plate that was at her place. As she raised it up she let out a scream.

"Oh my God." she gasped. "What in the world is this? It is the most gorgeous thing I have ever seen. It has to be at least 4 karats," she said as she looked at a huge diamond with small emeralds surrounding it.

"It's yours if you will marry me," he told her. "I don't believe in long engagements, so you'd better think fast." he kidded her. "It sounds as though you like it so I hope you like it enough to keep it."

"Oh, I love it, really love it, but I might get mugged if I wear it outside." she kidded. "It is absolutely gorgeous and of course I want it. And yes, you know I will marry you. Oh, thank you so much. But how did you know Emeralds were my birthstone?"

"I have my ways, my darling." Then he said, "Just a minute," as he got up and came to her side of the table. "I want to put it on your finger." As he did, he said, "You have just made me the happiest man in the world by accepting this. Thank you for loving me so much, my darling. Now let's eat."

She told him she was so happy she didn't think she could eat, but he told her she'd better after all he went through to get it delivered at just the right time. They both enjoyed the delicious meal that had been so expertly prepared, chatting about the events of the past few days. He let her know that the crisis had passed for his dad and that he would be released from the hospital in a few more days. He was going to have to retire but otherwise could lead a fairly normal life.

"Did you tell them about us? I'm very anxious to meet them, and hope they will like me."

"Sure I told them all about you and showed them your picture. They are sure you will make a terrific daughter-in-law. Of course, the next subject was how many children are you planning? I told them we hadn't discussed that but I felt sure you would want a family. I wasn't wrong was I? Oh yes, another thing my mom made me promise - that we wouldn't live together until we were married. I assured them there were no plans to do so and that we both have our own place."

"I'm so glad they were pleased about me. Come to think of it, you certainly were sure I was going to say yes when you asked me to marry you, weren't you?" she remarked. "Well, you should have been. As for us having a family, I certainly hope we are successful in that respect. If necessary, I'd give up my job to take care of any children we have, if we couldn't find a competent sitter to come to the house. As for our living together, you know I don't go for that. If you recall, I was very hesitant about your staying over that night. But it is too late now to do anything about that. Anyway, I'm not sorry that we ended up having intercourse that night. It just made me realize how much I really loved you.

"I think I'm going to like your parents. In fact, I think I will write them a little note and also send your dad a nice get-well card. Do you think that will be OK?"

"They would be very pleased. Dad is extremely sentimental so if you send him a card you can be sure he will cherish it."

She then changed the subject and told him about how Martha had discovered Sgt. Petrakos, and he was surprised about that. She then brought him up-to-date about the murder and how she and some of the other girls wondered if Stephanie's husband might be involved because the police had gone to their house. They decided it probably had no connection as they could have gone there on another matter.

As soon as they both cleared the table they went to the living room. Jerry told her the restaurant would send someone over the next morning to clean everything up and take the dishes back to the restaurant.

"What time is it Jerry? I should be getting on home. This has been a very exciting evening and I really do need to get some sleep, if I'm not too keyed up and tense to relax and go to sleep," she said, admiring her ring once more.

"Would you believe it is almost 2:30 AM. You're not going home tonight, as late as it is. You can stay right here. I promise I will not bother you tonight. In fact, just so I won't weaken, I'll sleep on the couch and you may have the bed. How's that for being strong and very much a gentleman? I'm afraid though that we are cheating each other tonight."

"Holy smokes! I never realized it was so late. No wonder I'm so tired. Between the bowling and all the other excitement of the evening; especially your proposal and the beautiful ring, the time just slipped away. OK, I'll stay here but only on the provisions you promised," and she proceeded to go to the bedroom to get undressed.

After getting undressed, she stood at the bedroom door clothed only in a short, sheer nightie which she had left there the other time she stayed overnight, and said, "Wait a minute. What do you mean, cheating each other. Explain yourself darling."

"Well, I think a proposal of marriage and receiving a beautiful engagement ring should be reason for a special celebration by the two lovers involved; like expressing their love for each other by more than just a goodnight kiss. Besides, how can you stand there in that sexy thing you call a nightie and expect me not to get excited?"

"I don't know," she said coyly, her curvaceous figure showing through her nightie and her voice sounding as though she didn't know what he was talking about. "Do you have any particular idea in mind?"

"I suggest this is an occasion to practice some of the things we will be doing when we are married. At this point he removed all his clothes, displaying his well-built muscles and manly physique.

"Well," she said reluctantly, "I had hoped to get right to bed, but you have me so excited now, realizing you are ready to make love, I won't be able to sleep until we do. Besides, I've never made love on a waterbed." And she removed her nightie, tossing it on a nearby chair, displaying a sexy, curvaceous body, which he interpreted to mean that she was ready for anything he wanted to do.

It didn't take long before their sighs and heavy breathing indicated a most successful and romantic interlude had just culminated.

"Good night my darling, they told each other," and after relaxing in each other's arms for a short while they fell into a deep sleep.

Chapter 41

"Is Sgt. Petrakos there?" a voice asked. "I have some information I think might be very important in that murder case he's working on."

"I'm sorry but he isn't here right now." said the desk sergeant. "If you will give me your name and number, I'll have him get right back to you as soon as he arrives."

"Well, OK. My name is Stewart Woodley and I work the bar late at night at Jake's Bar on the east side of town." he told the officer. "My number is 555-4231. After 9 P.M. I'm at the bar and that number is 555-8796. Be sure he gets the message. I'm sure the information I have will be very helpful."

"Sure thing." the sergeant answered. "I'll make sure he gets it right away."

About a half-hour later Mr. Woodley received a phone call from Sgt. Petrakos.

"Mr. Woodley, this is Sgt. Petrakos. I understand you have some information that could be important to the Marcos murder. Do you want to tell me about it? Or better still let's meet someplace and discuss it."

"Yes sir, I do. First of all, please call me Stu. Everyone does and I'm more comfortable on a first name basis, if you don't mind. Where can we meet to discuss what I have for you? I'd rather not do it over the phone, if it's OK with you."

"No, I don't mind." the officer told him. "In fact, it's a good idea not to talk on the phone. I'll meet you wherever you suggest. I'm free for a while this evening, so whatever is convenient for you, as long as it's private and no one can over-hear us."

"It's a pleasant evening." Stu told him. "Let's meet down by the lake. There's a little picnic area two blocks north of the amusement park, near the jogging trail. It should be quiet down there. We'll meet at 8 o'clock. Since we've never met, I'll be wearing my Tazmanian Devil sweatshirt my kids gave me. I'm medium height, red hair and weigh more than I should. OK?"

"That sounds good." Petrakos told him. "I guess I'll recognize you by that description. As for me, I'm over six feet tall - 6 ft 3 inches to be exact. I have dark brown hair, cut short of course - regulations require it. Since I'm off duty this evening, I won't be in uniform. I'll probably be wearing sweats too - one with a bulldog on it - the Marine Corps mascot - but I will have an ID badge with me. See you at eight."

At precisely 8 o'clock Sgt. Petrakos arrived at the designated area. Stu was sitting at the first table, obviously out of breath, and was easy to recognize, even in the semi-darkness.

"You must be Stu," Petrakos said. "How many other red-headed, grown men would be sitting alone after dark at a picnic table, wearing a Taz shirt? Hi, I'm Sgt. Petrakos and you sound like you're all out of breath.

"I brought some pizza and a couple of sodas to have while we chat. Hope you don't mind that I didn't bring beer but I don't drink when I'm on business. By the way, here's my badge," and Greg took it from his pocket to show Stu. "You may call me by my first name too, which is Greg."

"I thought I would run for a while. I do as often as I can. Nice to meet you Greg, but you didn't really have to bring anything to eat. As you can see I don't need it," and Stu laughed. "Let's get right to business, if you don't mind, because I have to be at work by ten."

"OK, Stu, what do you have for me? It's really very nice of you to volunteer information, and don't think the police department doesn't appreciate it."

"Well, you must realize bartenders see and hear all kinds of stuff; especially when they work in the kind of joint I do." he told Greg. "The night Marcos was allegedly murdered, a couple of guys came in and asked for a booth as private as possible, which doesn't mean much in that joint. A few minutes after they got there, it was obvious they were in a heated argument. Then they quieted down and the one guy (the victim) took a thick, brown envelope from his jacket and took a wad of bills from it. He handed some of them to the other guy. In the meantime one of my customers at the bar struck up a conversation with one of the other guys at the bar. I couldn't help hearing what he was saying."

"Yes, go on. What did he have to say?" Sgt. Petrakos asked.

"He told the other guy he recognized both of them because they worked where his wife worked. He said that the one with all the money was not very popular and many people wished he'd go back to where he came from. Then, as soon as the two men in the booth asked for their check, this guy who was doing most of the talking at the bar, all of a sudden paid his check and left the bar in a big hurry. Strangest thing I ever saw. Now, I could be imagining this, but the guy who left first seemed mighty suspicious to me. I had this gut feeling he was up to no good when he hurried out before the other two; like maybe he was hoping to cash in on some of their money. If I give you a description of the guy, it shouldn't be too difficult to find out which female employee's husband was out drinking late that night. What do you think?"

"I'd say you have a good point, Stu. Why don't you stop by the station tomorrow sometime and we'll do a composite of the man." Greg told him. "It is definitely worth checking out and I'll let you know what I come up with. If you think of anything more that might be worthwhile, let me know." and he handed him one of his cards and a $50 bill. "Thanks a lot for your cooperation. I'd give you more for what you told me but I can't afford any more and the department doesn't usually pay for information, unfortunately. Now you had better get to work if you don't want to get fired."

"I don't want any money." he said as he gave Greg back the $50. "I feel it is my duty as a citizen to help when I can. I just hope I was of some help. Don't worry about my being fired. Who else would be willing to work those hours in that section of town? I'll be at the station probably sometime late in the morning. Goodnight Greg. Nice to meet you. Good luck on the case."

Chapter 42

"Hi Val, have you seen Martha this morning?" Rose asked as they were on their way to the cafeteria. "She looks as though she hasn't been getting much sleep lately - sort of walking around in a daze. I think she's been keeping late hours but I wonder why. Do you think maybe she's watching too many late, late Perry Mason reruns?"

"You mean you don't know? Our miss has-to-know-it-all has been dating who else but that handsome cop, Sgt. Petrakos."

"No, you've got to be kidding. Our Martha dating a cop? Does she think she can help him solve his cases, or maybe she just wants him to help her solve her mystery stories. I can't imagine her dating anyone, much less a cop. No wonder she hasn't been around much asking us all kinds of questions. Don't get me wrong, not that she isn't attractive enough, but she just has never dated much. By the way, have you shown her that big chunk of ice you're wearing? That should make her sit up and take note."

"I know she has always seemed like kind of a home-body but perhaps the right guy just hadn't come along yet. She's been widowed for over ten years. Look at me, speaking of my life. I never thought I'd ever find the man just meant for me, after that terrible marriage my parents got me into. But, no, I haven't had a chance to talk to her about this." she said as she held out her left hand, displaying the ring.

"Hush, here she comes." Rose whispered as Martha approached them.

"Hi girls." she said with a happy sound to her voice. "How goes it? It's a beautiful day isn't it? Anything new on the murder case?"

"We're on our way to lunch. Would you like to join us? We'd be...." Valerie started to ask Martha, but was interrupted by Rose.

"Whoa, kiddo. Shouldn't we be asking you that?" Rose commented, at the same time apologizing to Valerie. "How are you making out with Sgt. Petrakos these days? You didn't think we knew about it, I'll bet. But we have our spies too. I'll say one thing, whatever you two are doing it has sure put a happy look on your face lately. How long has this romance been going on and is it serious?"

"Rose, you are sounding like Martha when she questions someone," Valerie kidded. "No offense Martha."

"Heck no, we are just two almost middle-aged adults who enjoy each other's company. Why does everyone think that just because a lady is dating a man they have to be lovers, sleeping together, and not just good friends. You two are really something. He asked me out soon after he started working on the case, if you must know. and we have become very good friends."

"Well, what does he have that's so appealing? I must admit he is kind of good looking. But what do you two have in common, if I'm not being too presumptuous?" asked Valerie.

"Val, you should realize, they both are interested in solving crimes. You should know that by now."

"OK you guys. That's enough. Greg hasn't always been a police officer. He has traveled a lot before he joined the force. He spent some time in the Marine Corps too. He has had a very interesting life and is fun to be with. He's also a fantastic cook, especially of Greek food, and I love good Greek food. I think you guys resent the fact I'm dating and am happy. Before I just stayed home and spent my spare time watching TV and reading books. There are other things in life, and fortunately I have found one of them - having a very nice male friend. Now, does that satisfy your curiosity?"

About that time Valerie extended her left hand to ask for the salt when Martha spotted her ring.

"Holy Cow! What bank did you rob to get that gorgeous ring? They don't put prizes like that in Cracker Jack boxes! Don't tell me you and Jerry are officially engaged. I'll be darned. Why were you keeping it a secret? Here you're both teasing the Hell out of me when all the time we should have been talking about you. Congratulations. You got yourself a very nice young man." Martha told her. "I'm really happy for you both."

"Well, thank you. I think so too. He is such a sweet guy, and very romantic." and she promptly went about telling the girls about how he gave it to her. "By the way Martha, I'm sorry we teased you so much about the sergeant. I'm glad you are looking so happy these days. Boy, this company all of a sudden has all kinds of romance going on - Dennis and Janet running off and eloping, my getting engaged, and now you have found someone you enjoy being with - maybe even Mr. Right. I think it's great."

"That's OK. I've done my share of teasing over the years. Hey, I've got to get back to my office. I was late this morning and have a lot of work to finish today. But first, have I got some startling news for you guys. I know now why Stephanie has been so unhappy looking at times. Greg and I just found out her husband has been beating up on her. One of the other sergeants was telling him yesterday how he and another officer had been called to their house at least twice because of complaints by the neighbors. Isn't that awful? Someone should beat him up."

"Well I'll be darned," Valerie said. " I just knew things weren't like they should be. She is too nice a person to have a rat like that."

"I've got to get going. We'll talk about it later," Martha told them, and she left.

"Well, what do you think Rose? Don't you feel it could be just a little bit more than friendship between Martha and Sgt. Petrakos? I hope she realized we didn't mean anything about what we said to her. She admitted she has done her share of kidding and for someone who has been out of circulation, as far as men are concerned, I guess I can understand her feelings. I wonder if Stephanie has heard the latest about Martha and her 'friend'. Maybe we should tell her."

"I don't know. Stephanie isn't exactly herself lately. After what Martha just told us I guess she has reason to look downcast. She sure tries to put on a good front. I'm not about to ask about her problems. A bad marriage is not something you question anyone about. One day I could have sworn her right eye was swollen, but I didn't say anything."

"Yes, I noticed that too but since no one else said anything I thought maybe it was just my imagination." Valerie said. "I heard someone say they saw the police over by her house one day. I guess Martha knew what she was talking about. Of course, if the sergeant told her that then it has to be true.. I'm sure glad Jerry and I have a good relationship. Our only problem is when do we think is a good time for a wedding." Then she asked if Rose was having anything more to eat.

"No, I've had plenty. Besides, I have to get back to my office. See you later. By the way, has Stephanie seen your ring?"

"No, but by now she has probably heard about it. I wasn't sure if she would care about something like this the way her life has been lately. I feel terrible for her because she is such a nice girl."

Chapter 43

The phone rang at Ben Wilson's house. It was seven AM and Ben and Marge were just getting ready to sit down to breakfast. Unlike many families these days, Marge always insisted they have breakfast together before leaving the house each morning.

"I'll get it Marge." Ben said, as he picked up the portable phone next to the refrigerator. "Hello, this is the Wilson residence."

"Good morning, sir. This is Lt. Lanza. I hate to bother you at home so early, but I wanted you to know that we think we know who the murderer is. Would it be too much of an imposition for me to drop by and talk to you about it?"

"Well, you caught us just getting ready for breakfast, but you're welcome to join us if you're coming right over and we can discuss it after breakfast with a second cup of coffee."

"As a matter of fact, I haven't had a chance to eat yet, so you can count on me. It will take just a few minutes to get there from where I am, and thanks a lot."

During breakfast the conversation was merely chit, chat about the previous days' events, the problems with young people today, crime in small towns as well as in the big city, and uncertainties in the far East. Somehow Lt. Lanza managed to bring up Stephanie's name, telling Ben and Marge what a pretty girl she was. They didn't say anything but glanced at each other with a quizzical look. When they finished eating Lt. Lanza remarked what a delicious breakfast it was and how much he appreciated it.

After breakfast, Marge made another pot of coffee and brought it to Ben's study where the two men were sitting. "Thought you'd like this in here where you can talk in private." she told them, and she closed the door as she was leaving.

"Your wife is a terrific hostess, Mr. Wilson. Not every wife has good looks, a gracious manner and is a good cook. You are indeed lucky."

"Well thank you Lieutenant. I feel I hit the jackpot when it came to a wife. They just don't make them any better. If all

marriages were like ours, the divorce lawyers would be out of business. But I'm sure we didn't
meet to discuss my marriage. What's on your mind so early in the morning?"

"Like I told you on the phone, I think we may have our killer. Thanks to some terrific detective work and a little help from a concerned citizen, we're reasonably sure we know who it is; it's just a matter of proving it.

"I'm afraid, in a sort of a way, it involves your secretary. Her name is Stephanie, isn't it? - Stephanie Kaknas?"

"Why yes, she is a top notch Executive Secretary in my office. I wouldn't know what to do without her. But she certainly isn't the killer. It would be ludicrous to even imagine her killing someone."

"I didn't mean to say she was. I'm sure a nice lady like she is wouldn't do such a thing." Lanza said. "But I have a description of a man who could very well pass for her husband. When Sgt. Petrakos described him to me, we went to the plant and asked a couple of people to identify the composite we had and they said it resembled Mr. Kaknas. I would like to talk to both of them and see what I come up with. But I'll want to talk to them separately.

"Just how much do you know about Stephanie and her husband? Do they have a happy marriage, and what kind of a job does her husband have? I'd like to know his story about where he was that night."

"I really don't know her husband very well." Ben admitted. "I believe he works for a construction company someplace out of town. He hasn't come to many of the family get-togethers the company has had. He seemed personable enough when I met him. However, I must admit, I don't think things are going too well lately."

"Why do you ask about her marriage?"

"Because, yesterday Sgt. Petrakos found out one of his friends had been called to her house more than once lately because of complaints of them fighting. Do you know anything about it?"

"One day I found her crying at her desk. When I questioned her she just said she wished she had the kind of marriage Mrs. Wilson and I have. Then, one day I could have sworn she had a bruise on her face, and lately she definitely has not been her usual cheerful self and at times seems to be off in another world. I don't like to pry too much into my employees' private lives, but she was willing to admit her marriage was not what it used to be. However, she still keeps a picture on her desk taken on a vacation a couple of years ago."

"Well, I'm intending to check into that but right now it looks as though we may have to bring him in on suspicion. Too many things are not right....."

The study door opened and Marge told Lt. Lanza he had an important phone call.

"Thank you," he said as he picked up the phone in the study. "Hello, Lanza here. Hi Greg, what's up? What? You're kidding. You don't say. Well, I'll be darned; that is interesting. Stay where you are and I'll meet you in twenty minutes to look over what you have and then we'll do what we have to do. Thanks for calling."

"Well, it looks like we have our man, sir." he said to Ben. "I must rush off to meet with Sgt. Petrakos. Some very important developments have come up. As soon as I have the details, I'll notify you. Thanks again for breakfast. Say good-bye to Mrs. Wilson for me."

Ben wondered why he didn't take the time to tell him at least a little of what they had discovered, but when he told Marge what had happened, she said they should just be patient and wait until later.

Chapter 44

Shortly before lunch, Lt. Lanza called Ben at his office to see if it would be possible to meet with him again.

"Of course. Come on right over. I'm not very busy right now. What's up?" he asked.

"I'll tell you all the details when I see you. In the meantime, did your secretary report for work this morning?"

"As a matter of fact she didn't." Ben told him. "She called in sick. What's this all about anyway?"

"I'll let you know when I get there, Mr. Wilson."

Ben was really puzzled about what Lt. Lanza had said and the way his voice sounded. He couldn't imagine that Stephanie might be involved in any way with Juan's death. He was definitely quite concerned with regard to the conversation, and anxiously awaited the officer's arrival.

As soon as Lt. Lanza arrived, the secretary notified Ben and he was told to go right into Mr. Wilson's office. Mr. Wilson stood up as soon as the officer entered and asked what was going on.

"I'd like you to come with me to the Kaknas home, Mr. Wilson, if you don't mind," he told him. "I have a warrant for the arrest of Mr. Kaknas on suspicion of murder, and I thought maybe you'd like to be there for moral support for your secretary. I'm sure it's going to come as quite a shock to her and she will need a friend." (He thought to himself, 'how I wish I could be that friend')

"Of course lieutenant. Let's get going.

"Lisa, if anyone is looking for me, I had to leave on an urgent matter and will probably be gone most of the day. Have a good day. If a real emergency comes up I may be reached on Lt. Lanza's car phone. I don't think I had any appointments for this afternoon, but if I do, reschedule them, please."

On the way over Ben asked Lt. Lanza if he could tell him anything more about why they suspected Mr. Kaknas. Lt. Lanza told him he'd rather not discuss it at the moment but that he'd find out when they got there. He did say there had been a call during the morning from a neighbor complaining of what seemed to be fighting <u>again</u>, next door at the Kaknas house. So they would be checking into this in addition to picking him up on suspicion.

"You know sir," Lt. Lanza remarked. "It's too bad your secretary is married. I'd love to have a lady like her in my life. If what you said about her is true, plus the phone call we just had, how could any man abuse someone like that?"

"She is a lovely girl. I know I'd be lost without her as my secretary. I can't understand why she ever married that man either. From the little I've seen, they don't seem to have anything in common. I guess they were happy when she first married him, and they say love is blind, but he just doesn't seem to be the right type for her."

Lt. Lanza pulled up to Stephanie's house about 20 minutes later. Sgt. Petrakos and his partner were parked across the street, ready to join Lt. Lanza when he got the signal. Ben and Lt. Lanza went up the walk and rang the doorbell. It wasn't until the third ring that Stephanie answered the door, dressed in a bathrobe and slippers, her hair askew, instead of in it's usual neat coiffure, and looking as though she had been crying.

"Mr. Wilson, Lt. Lanza, what are you doing here? What's the problem?" she asked, with her head down and her hair covering one side of her face. "Forgive me for looking like this but I had a rough night and really don't feel well at all. You really didn't have to come all the way over here Mr. Wilson."

"Is your husband here?" Ben asked. "Lt. Lanza would like to ask him some questions."

"Why yes, he is upstairs taking a shower." she told them. "But why would the police want to talk to Peter? Is he in trouble? He was here with me all night. What do you think he has done?"

"You'll find out soon enough, unfortunately. Right now please just tell him someone wants to see him. Don't tell him it is the police or he might just try and get away." Lt. Lanza told her. "If he does that, it is just going to be that much harder on him."

Acting very confused over the visit she said, "Sure," and when she turned around to leave, they both realized she had a bad bruise on her forehead, which her hair had been covering, in addition to a cut lip.

"Wait a minute Stephanie," Lt. Lanza said, "What happened to your head? Don't tell me you ran into the proverbial door; and how did you get the cut on your lip? From reports I've been hearing about your husband, I won't buy that story. We had another call from the neighbors. Has he been abusing you again? He could be in even worse trouble if that's the case. Right now I'm here on another matter."

"I don't care to talk about it. I'll tell him someone wants to see him," and she left the room and started up the stairs. "I won't guarantee he'll be willing to come down right away. He's been acting rather strangely lately."

Ben and Lt. Lanza heard a loud commotion and a voice shouting, "What the Hell do you want now? Didn't I tell you I didn't want to see your miserable face around me today?" Stephanie obviously told him he had company because he then yelled, "Well, I got the message bitch, so get out of my sight so I can finish dressing. I'll be downstairs in a minute. Tell him to keep his pants on."

She came down and gave Ben and the officer the message, which she realized they already knew. She acted very nervous and didn't seem to know whether she should stay or find another room in which to go. Ben couldn't believe it was really his secretary who always looked like such a fashion plate and who was always so much in charge on the job. He felt very badly for her but wasn't sure what he should or could say.

"Do you want me to stay here or is your business personal? Why don't I put on a pot of coffee and we can all have some." she told them, trying to put on an act as though nothing were wrong.

"Never mind Stephanie." Mr. Wilson told her. "This is strictly police business and you probably should be here. Is this the reason you have been so unhappy at work? Your husband has been abusing you lately, hasn't he? You know you can confide in me and Mrs. Wilson. You've been like a daughter to us over the years and we don't like to see you unhappy." he said, speaking very softly.

It was the wrong thing for him to say at that time because she burst into tears, and didn't know where to go so they wouldn't see her crying.

About the same time her husband came down the stairs, looking like a tiger ready to strike. "What the Hell is she crying about now. Women; all they are is trouble. Ya wanna see me officer? What's the problem? She didn't call you claiming I was beatin' her up did she? She's so darn clumsy these days; always running into things, then she blames me. I think she's going crazy or....."

"Enough, Kaknas." Officer Lanza interrupted. "It wouldn't take much to get me to beat the Hell out of you for abusing this lovely lady. As a matter of fact the neighbors have called saying there had been yelling and fighting in the house this morning and it hasn't been the first time. From the looks of her I'd say it was true. But that's not why we are here." At that point he whispered to Ben to signal Sgt. Petrakos to come on in. "We're here on an entirely different matter. Where were you the night of October 2nd?"

"Hell, how am I supposed to remember that long ago. I can't even remember what I eat for breakfast," he sarcastically remarked.

"I don't need any smart remarks from you. This is serious business. You'd better start remembering, or perhaps we can shake up your memory. I suggest you were at Jake's Bar on Moody Street on the East Side sometime after midnight. Does that ring a bell?"

"Yeah, I could have been there. So if I was, is that a crime, having a drink with a friend? What else was supposed to happen that night?"

"It's not a crime to have a drink at any time but it certainly is a crime when you follow someone else out of the bar and murder him. We're placing you under arrest for the murder of Juan Marcos. Sgt. Petrakos, cuff him and read him his rights. Take him to your car and we'll be with you shortly," Lt. Lanza instructed Petrakos.

However, it wasn't that simple. Just as the Sgt. started to put the handcuffs on him, Peter unexpectantly swung at him, landing a punch to the jaw. At that point Lt. Lanza drew his revolver and told him to stop or he'd shoot. That ended the struggle and Sgt. Petrakos cuffed him. While Lt. Lanza kept the revolver pointed at him, Sgt. Petrakos went out to his car and called in for backup, telling them to send two of their biggest and strongest men because Kaknas was a fighter, and was giving them a hard time. Peter was a big man and very strong so they preferred not to take any chances.

There was a chair in the front hall. Lt. Lanza told him to sit there and not try anything foolish because from all that had happened there that morning, it wouldn't take very much for him to accidentally shoot him. Peter all of a sudden didn't have much to say. That didn't last long however, when he saw Stephanie standing near the living room door.

"So what the Hell are you looking at? After all the things I've given you through the years. Now you are letting them do this to me. Did you report me? You know Goddam well I'm with you every night - tell them that's the way it is or you'll be sorry. You know they don't have nothin' on me. Why the Hell would I kill any damn Hispanic I didn't even know? Well, say something. Don't just stand there looking like the dumb broad you are. I give up." Then looking at Lt. Lanza he said, "Hey cop, do you want a fuckin' dame? She's no damn good, so you can have her. Maybe you can make her happy." and he started laughing.

"Peter, how can you talk to me like that. You're embarrassing the officer. You know I've always loved you and even now if I could do anything for you I would. If you know something tell them. Do you want me to call a lawyer for you?" she asked.

"Why the Hell would I want a lawyer. They don't have a damn thing on me. Besides, I don't need your help. I don't ever want to look at your ugly face again. Do you hear me. GET THE HELL OUT OF MY SIGHT!!" he screamed at her. "And if you know what's good for you, you won't be in this house when I get back."

About that time Sgt. Petrakos and the other officers arrived and took a fighting, raging, swearing Peter out and put him in the cruiser. One officer mentioned to the other, "You know Bill, this is the 4th time I've come to this address in the past few weeks. It's about time they arrested him."

"I'm sorry you had to see all this Mr. Wilson." Stephanie sobbed, and she apologized to Lt. Lanza for what Peter said about giving her to the lieutenant. Then she said, "I never would have realized he was implicated in Juan's murder. Just how serious is it Lt. Lanza? Do you really think you have a case? I can't believe this is happening to us. How can a once sweet, gentle man turn so angry and mean?"

"Tell me dear," Mr. Wilson, asked in his usual gentle voice. "He has been abusing you, hasn't he? You didn't get those bruises from a fall. I thought you were smarter than that - to let a man treat you like that. He's certainly not much of a man to beat up on a defenseless woman. Well, Mrs. Wilson and I will help you in any way we can dear."

"Yes sir, he has been beating me up off and on for some time. Only lately it has gotten worse and he told me if I reported it to anyone he'd make me wish I hadn't. Every time a neighbor reported fighting over here, he would hit me that much more, blaming me for the police coming here. I tried to cover the marks with makeup or a different hairdo so no one would notice it." she confessed. "I just can't figure out when things started to go bad. Thank you Mr. Wilson for all your kindness. This is very embarrassing having you see me like this. I'll put some ice on my forehead and take a sedative and go to bed. I'll be at work tomorrow morning. We'll work something out. Lt. Lanza, let me know what happens with Peter, even though I don't know why I should care. In fact, after everything that has happened, by morning I may even have changed my mind and won't care what happens to him."

"I understand. We'll leave you now as long as you're sure you'll be OK. Would you rather stay someplace else the rest of the day, or call someone to stay with you? You're safe until, or if, he gets out of jail. But with the murder charge against him, more than likely he won't be out on bail. If you need anything, here is my card and you may call me any time. I really do care, you know." and he smiled and winked at her, like he had many times before.

"No thank you. I'll stay here. With him out of the house I'll be fine. Thank you for your concern - both of you. Let me show you to the door." She then told them both to have a good day and she closed the door and locked it.

After Mr. Wilson and the lieutenant left she went upstairs feeling safer than she had for a long time and, looking at the card Lt. Lanza had given her, thinking seriously about what the lieutenant had said to her, 'Call me any time'. "I just may find an excuse to do so," she told herself.

Chapter 45

Harry called Mr. Wilson and, very excitedly said. "I really need to talk to you about the discrepancies we just found in our accounts. Mr. Christou refused to listen to me before he left, when I tried to tell him about it. I'm really quite concerned and you are the only one I can talk to. I'm sure there is a considerable amount of money missing. I just can't get the books to balance. I'm sure there's nothing wrong with the computers."

"Don't come to my office Harry. I'll be right down to yours since the books are all there. There must be a simple explanation."

Ben arrived in the Accounting Department a few minutes later and asked to see where the problem was. Harry had always been such a conscientious employee he would worry if he thought a penny were missing.

"Upon cursory examination it would seem that the profit ratio is off each month for the past several months. The ratio of assets versus liabilities has taken a drastic drop." Harry told Ben. "Based on this and other signs several of the other fellows and I estimate that approximately 200 thousand dollars is missing.

"That's an awful lot of money in such a short time." Ben replied. "Get on the phone and arrange for the auditors to come here as soon as they can make it. If Mr. Christou isn't interested in this discrepancy, I certainly am. What trip is he on now?"

"He's in Nebraska, but said you had approved it - should be back in two or three days. I hate to say this sir, because it will sound like I'm being critical, but he seems to be taking a lot of trips lately. Are they all really necessary? And he's been acting rather strangely, as though something is weighing heavily on him - that is eating at him. Might I suggest you question him when he returns; or am I out of line?"

"No you are not, especially since you're concerned with the company. Believe me, I will talk to him. He has been having some marital problems lately, but I thought those had more or less been resolved. As soon as he returns I will definitely question him. In the meantime, just as soon as you reach the auditors, make sure I am notified as to how soon they can get here. They won't necessarily be able to make it today."

About two hours later Stephanie received a call from Harry for Ben, that the auditors had arrived and were waiting for Mr. Wilson before starting.

"Already? Fantastic!" he remarked. "That's wonderful. Tell them I'll be right down there. I'm surprised they were able to see us so soon," and he told Stephanie where he would be if anyone needed him.

"Good afternoon sir, I'm Ben Wilson," he said, extending his hand. "I'm glad you were able to accommodate us so soon."

"My name is McIverson. You're lucky we just happen to have some time this month. Now, do we have all the books ready? It helps you know." he told Ben in a very gruff, stern, no-nonsense voice, as though he were in a hurry to get the audit over. "Do you have any idea how much we may be looking for?"

"Possibly two hundred thousand, maybe less." Harry told him. "These are the complete set of books and you're welcome to use this and the adjoining office, if you need them."

"Mr. Taylor will be available to answer any questions you may have." Ben told him. "You will find him very knowledgeable and cooperative. Call me if you need me."

As soon as Ben left, Mr. McIverson (a portly, middle-aged man with thinning red hair and a short cropped beard) grumbled, "Well, young man, you can expect us to be around for the better part of four days if we're lucky, so don't plan on taking any vacation time during this period. We'll have your books up-to-date as soon as we can."

For the next four days the auditors were busy with the books, seldom saying very much to each other - a grunt or a groan and sometimes just an uh-huh or hmmm. Occasionally Harry would call Ben about the progress or Ben himself would make his way to the Accounting Department to check on what was going on.

Everything had been very tense during that time with the rumor-mill working overtime as to the presence of the auditors at this particular time.

Finally, on the afternoon of the fourth day, Mr. McIverson asked Harry, "Are you the head of this department young man?"

Harry hated being referred to as 'young man' instead of by his name, but he answered, "No sir, I'm not. I'm the Deputy Chief. Mr. Christou is Chief of Accounting."

"Then why hasn't he been here," he demanded abruptly. "I don't like dealing with underlings. Where is he?"

Furious at being considered an 'underling' (sounded like something from a sci-fi movie he thought!), Harry told him, "He's on a business trip out west and should be back tomorrow night. If you wish I will call Mr. Wilson to talk with you. He is the president."

"Yes, yes, get him down here so I can give him my report and get out of here."

"What a grouch!" Harry thought, as he dialed Stephanie's number to relay the message that Mr. McIverson wanted Mr. Wilson downstairs as soon as possible.

As soon as Ben arrived he was told the bad news - the company was short by one hundred and ninety-five thousand dollars. "I'd say you have an embezzler in your company Mr. Wilson, and the sooner you get to the bottom of this the better. Do you have any idea who might be behind it? What about this Mr. Christou who is out of town? Usually ends up being someone high up when something like this happens. Can you trust him? I'd advise you to get him back here right away and question him. That's a Hell of a lot of money, if you'll excuse my language, in anyone's books."

"I don't want to accuse anyone falsely." Ben told him. "Even though he is a long-time employee, I intend to have him on the next flight home if at all possible. And you can be sure there will be plenty of questions to ask. Thank you so much for your quick response. I appreciate it."

"Yeah, Yeah. That's my job. That's what you pay me for." Mr. McIverson grunted as he and his men gathered up their attaché cases and went out the door.

"Boy, what a cheerful fellow. I think his face would crack if he were to smile. He couldn't possibly be married." Harry commented.

Ben, smiling, said he had to agree he wasn't a very friendly fellow; at the same time reminding Harry of their latest problem.

Chapter 46

"Have you gone to see Peter since his arrest?" Ben asked Stephanie. (Even though the auditors were at the company Mr. Wilson still found time for his secretary's problems.) "He may have calmed down enough now to want to see you."

"No, I haven't. You don't know him very well Mr. Wilson. If he wanted to see me he knows where I am and he would have called me. I did call Sgt. Petrakos and he said the bail had been set for a half million dollars. The judge here is a tough one and he feels that if they let Peter go he will either skip town or come after me; either way he will be a fugitive from justice. He's not only concerned about the murder charge, but also the fact he has threatened me. There is no way he can afford that kind of money and I'm not about to pay for a lawyer for him. I have decided to be smart for once in my life,. and the only lawyer I intend to hire is a divorce lawyer so I can be rid of Peter forever. Don't tell anyone but I called Lt. Lanza and asked if he knew a good divorce lawyer. Oh, by the way, Sgt. Petrakos also told me they took a considerable amount of money from Peter, and suspect it may be some of that that was taken from Juan and Roger.

"But I guess you have your own problems now with the auditors being here all week. I hope things turn out for the best. If you need me sometimes for extra work, you know I'd be more than happy to help. I've plenty of time on my hands now."

"Yes, I'm afraid I could have more trouble than I want. You'll find out soon enough that a large amount of money is missing from the accounts and, at this point, I'm not sure who to suspect. Mr. Christou is on his way home from that trip we sent him on and he's probably the only one who might have some idea who to blame. Between that and worrying about you and Peter, I'm ready for a long vacation."

"I'm sorry you had to get involved with our problem. I tried to keep it between the two of us but when he was arrested for murder the picture changed and everything came out. Now I feel I owe you an awful lot. Peter is no longer a part of my life anyway, as far as I am concerned so perhaps I can make it up to you in some way.

"Sgt. Petrakos said Lt. Lanza is interested in me. Wouldn't that be something if I ended up with him?"

"Aren't you going to be in court next week for Peter's arraignment? Perhaps you should. No matter how bitter he is, he won't want to be alone with no moral support at a time like this."

"I really doubt it, considering how he has treated me the past 2 years. There must be an awful lot of evidence against him. Someone said that there was a girl involved too. Let them find her and have her give him support. He's no longer my concern. I'm sorry if I sound bitter, but I can't help it."

"No, I haven't heard anything about a girl, but if I find out, I'll let you know. I'm sorry you feel the way you do but I guess if anyone has reason to feel like that, it's you. Sgt. Petrakos is going to be here later today. He didn't say why; just that he had to talk to someone pertaining to the case. Between you and me I think he will be sorry when the case is closed because he won't have an excuse to come by to talk to Martha."

"Mr. Wilson, you are beginning to sound like some of the girls." and she laughed. "But I guess they have been seeing quite a bit of each other. That's nice. I like to see people happy. Another happy couple, from what I hear is Valerie and Jerry who recently got engaged. With all my problems lately I haven't talked much to any of the girls, but Martha came by today and told me I should see the huge diamond Valerie is sporting. I hope they will be happy."

"Well, if I'm going to be able to leave at a respectable time today, I'd better get back to work. Thanks again for your concern, sir."

"That's perfectly alright Stephanie. With a secretary like you I naturally would be interested in your welfare, as is Mrs. Wilson; and I hope you realize that."

Chapter 47

Ben and Marge went to see Steve at the substance abuse rehab center for the first time. He had been under their supervision for more than two weeks and had already shown signs of being his old self. He hadn't asked for a drink or drugs all that time and was willingly receiving counseling and therapy.

"Hi son," his dad said as they met him. "How are you doing? We miss you and just wanted you to get a chance to get settled before we came up here."

Before Steve could answer, his mother went up to him and gave him a big hug and kiss. "You're looking so much better, dear." she told him.

"Hi mom and dad. Thank you so much for coming. I've missed you too. It gets pretty lonely without any of the family. I really do understand though why you didn't come by to visit me sooner. I guess they have good reasons in cases like mine. How's Laura and the kids?" he asked. "I miss them too."

"They're all fine. The kids miss you very much and want to know when they can see you. They send their love and hope you are feeling better. What do the doctor's have to say about your progress?" his dad asked.

"They don't tell me too much. Maybe you could talk to them. I'm feeling much better though and the more I think about it the more I can't understand how I allowed myself to get in that condition. I've been a stupid jerk, drinking and being on drugs and going out with those awful women for so long. Believe me dad - you too mom - I've learned a long, hard lesson." he confessed. "Now I just want to make sure my system is free of all that junk so I can come home soon. I assure you it will never happen again. I can't believe I was blaming everyone else for my shortcomings. I miss the kids so very much, and Laura too. I wonder if she will ever forgive me," and he started to cry.

"That's OK son, let it out." his mother told him. "We believe you and we're just so happy you have come so far on the road to recovery.

Regaining his composure he told his parents. "More than anything else, I hope and pray Laura will find it in her heart to forgive me and drop the divorce proceedings. I'll spend the rest of my life making it up to her if she will allow me to. As for you dad, I know I've been an embarrassment to the company on different occasions, but I will be a model son and employee from now on if you will allow me to have my job back."

"Well, Steve, if Laura could see how far you have come in such a short time, she would be pleased." his mother assured him. "If you would really like to see her and the doctor says it is OK, we'll ask her if she would like to bring the children and come with us on the next visit. Don't you think that would be nice Ben?"

"No mom," he told her, "I want her to come to see me because she wants to, not because you have suggested it. And you, dad, I really mean it when I say I'm sorry for all the grief I've caused. Don't think I don't realize now what people must have been saying about me. That's all going to change and you will be as proud of me as you are of Michael," he told them. "There's just one other thing. When I do get released I will still be required to attend sessions in AA as well as Drugs Anonymous for a certain length of time. I'm not sure how long."

"You seem to have come over the biggest hurdle, so I'm sure you can do it Steve. In fact, I'm thinking of asking the doctor if we can take you over to the house for dinner some evening. If he gives his OK we will plan to have Laura and the kids there too; and Angie. We'll make it a real family affair," his dad said.

. "Gosh, that would be fantastic, dad. It would be great not to see doctors and nurses and therapy rooms, if only for a few hours. I'll be able to play with the kids before I have to return to the hospital. Do you think they will be afraid of me? I know I was terribly rough on them and even worse on Laura. And my sister. I love her too and haven't exactly been very nice to her and Alex. By the way, I didn't notice you saying anything about Alex coming to the house. Is he out of town? Is he and Angie back together again? Darn, why was I such an idiot? I just want to get well and get back to the office again.

"By the way, what's happening with the murder case? They won't let many of us, especially patients like me, have access to newspapers or the television, except for certain channels and a limited amount of time.. Have they caught the killer and, if so, who was it? Did you manage to find another job for you-know who?"

"Yes, she's working in a small office in Bangor. She thanked me very much for making it possible and apologized for the problem she caused. I don't think she will run after married men again. As for the rest of your questions, we will fill you in on everything else when we have you home for a visit. I don't think you should concern yourself with any possible outside problems at this point in your therapy. There must be a reason why your doctors won't allow you access to newspapers and newscasts on TV, so I don't want to break any rules. Just do as they tell you and get well fast. We love you son."

Chapter 48

It had been a couple of days since Ben and Marge had visited Steve. Now Ben was anxious to know if Alex had returned yet. As he was about to call his office, Stephanie buzzed him to let him know Lt. Lanza was on the phone.

"Good morning Lieutenant. What can I do for you?" Ben asked.

"I hate to bother you so early in the morning but I'd like to come over and ask the receptionist a few questions and I'd like you to be present. Do you think you could have Stephanie call her to your office as soon as I arrive? I'm on my way and will be there within five minutes. That is, if you aren't too tied up. But we really need to ask her a few more questions."

"No, we're anxious to get this thing settled too. I'll tell Stephanie to send her right in as soon as you get here. What's up?"

"You'll find out when I question her because I think you should be there too. We may be in for some surprises."

About five minutes later Lt. Lanza arrived and Stephanie called Donna to come to Mr. Wilson's office because the police had a couple questions to ask her. Assuming it was Sgt. Petrakos, who she thought was so cute, she came right up. Stephanie told her to go right on in, buzzing Mr. Wilson that Donna was on her way in.

A short time later, Stephanie called Mr. Wilson on his private line. "Sir," she said, "Don't mention my name, but Donna has those diamond earrings on again today. I thought you may want to bring them to Lt. Lanza's attention. Another thing, you might ask her about is Juan's gold watch, because I believe the watch Peter was wearing the day of his arrest may have belonged to Juan."

"Very interesting. Thank you ma'am. I'll be sure and tell him." Ben said, hoping no one suspected it was Stephanie he was talking to.

"Sit down miss." Lt. Lanza told Donna. "I have a few more questions to ask you."

"Well now, Lt. Lanza. What could I possibly contribute to your investigation that I haven't already told you, you know? I thought I told that nice Sgt. Petrakos everything when he questioned me. By the way, why didn't he come today? He's such a pleasant young man." and she proceeded to cross one leg over the other, her short skirt sliding up her legs displaying her entire thigh.

"Because that nice Sgt. Petrakos is busy with other matters," he told her in a rather sarcastic voice. "If you don't object I came this time. I will ask the questions if you don't mind, and sit like a lady, young woman. Your legs don't impress me one bit. (Mr. Wilson couldn't help but smile to himself) I want to make a quick review of what you told Sgt. Petrakos," and he read the first statement they had from her. "Is that all correct? Have you thought of anything else you wish to add at this time?"

"No sir, can't say that I have." she told him as she slowly uncrossed her legs and sat perfectly straight. He was the first man who objected to looking at her legs she thought.

"Then I had better try and refresh your memory because we have some additional information that involves you, and I think you'd better tell us what else you know. In fact, you may do it here or I'll take you to the station and question you there. Which will it be?"

"My goodness lieutenant, whatever are you talking about? I didn't kill Mr. Marcos if that is what you're insinuating," she said.

"Oh, I know you didn't but we know you were involved with the person who did. How well do you know Peter Kaknas? I don't suppose you have tried to visit him in prison?"

"Is that what dear Peter's last name is? Yes, I know Peter but would you believe I have never bothered to ask him his last name. We are dear friends, you know, and as soon as he gets rid of his terrible, nagging wife, we are going to be married." she told Lt. Lanza. "As for visiting him at the prison, no I haven't seen him - not yet anyway."

"You must be putting me on. I can't believe you accepted all the lies he told you, or, if you are such 'dear' friends that you don't know his last name. I also find it difficult to conclude that you don't read the papers or listen to TV news. If you are so near and dear to him then you should know where he was the night of the murder?"

"You're certainly not implying he had anything to do with it are you? Sure I read the papers but you guys will soon realize he is not guilty and let him go," she told the lieutenant, her sexy voice suddenly changing to a harsh, sarcastic one.

"You people have to be crazy to think he would harm anyone. Besides we were together all night."

"Just answer my questions, please. Now, think before you answer this one, miss. Did he leave your place, or wherever you two were, at all for even a little while?"

"Well, as a matter-of-fact he did go out to get some pizza and beer and then he had to stop by his office for a few minutes," she said.

"How long would you say he was gone - an hour or maybe even an hour and a half?"

"Yes, that's possible," she answered. "It's probably just about right.

"One more thing. Tell me miss, where did you get those earrings? They appear to be rather expensive ones for a working girl like you."

"Oh, you noticed them. Aren't they lovely? As a matter of fact Peter gave them to me; kinda like a pre-engagement present. As soon as he's divorced he will get me an engagement ring he told me."

"Do you mind if I look at one?" Lt. Lanza asked, and she took one off, proudly passing it to him so he could see how nice they were. Taking a jeweler's glass from his pocket he examined it closely.

"Just as I suspected. You are going to have to come to the station. I'm arresting you for possession of stolen property, in addition to being an accessory in the murder of Juan Marcos."

"You gotta be kidding. What the Hell could I have to gain by helping anyone murder him, that foreigner? Peter gave them to me and if he took them from Mr. Marcos, which I doubt very much, I had no way of knowing he did. Besides, even if he had taken them it doesn't mean he killed him."

"Who said Peter stole them? You did, not me. Thank you for relieving any doubt I may have had. Now, did you go with him when he trashed Juan's apartment? What kind of a watch was he wearing? You're in big trouble already so think carefully before you answer my questions."

"I think I'd better see my lawyer," she said, all of a sudden. "I'm not saying anything more to you."

"I think that's probably a good idea. There's the phone; and tell him to meet you at the station." In the meantime Lt. Lanza read her her rights and asked her, "Do you understand what I just told you?"

"Of course I do. Do you think I'm stupid? You're the one who is going to be in trouble when I sue you for false arrest. Come on lieutenant, let's get this over with." and she started to get up to use the phone.

"Mr. Wilson, are you willing to attest to what you've heard this morning?"

"Of course, Lt. Lanza." he answered. "After all, this young lady just helped ruin my secretary's life by running around with her husband."

"WHAT?" Donna screamed, as she put the phone down. "Peter is Stephanie's husband? I don't believe it. He told me terrible things about her and I know Stephanie isn't anything at all like that. Why that lying bastard!. What kind of a line was he feeding me anyway? And, why did he give me these earrings? Here Lt. Lanza, take them both. I changed my mind. I don't need a lawyer, but he sure as Hell does. I'll tell you everything I know about that night and what all he told me. As to the watch, he was wearing a beautiful gold watch the last time I saw him. When I asked him about it, since it resembled the one Mr. Marcos had been wearing, he said it was a gift from his mother for his birthday. That son of a bitch!. How could I have been so gullible? Excuse my language guys. I don't normally talk like this."

"Well, now you're being smart. I think we should go down to the station though so we can have someone there type up your statement." Then, turning to Mr. Wilson, he said, "Thank you so much for your time Mr. Wilson."

"You're entirely welcome. This conversation has been most enlightening. But if you want to have the statement typed here, I'm sure Stephanie would be more than happy to do it. She is an extremely fast typist and would have no trouble keeping up. She already knows some of the facts and would be delighted to know the rest. It would also save Donna from having to make a trip down there since she has been so cooperative. That is, if it is not interfering with police procedure." Ben said.

"No, not at all. As long as there is someone to notarize Donna's signature after she signs the statement."

"OK." Ben said, and he called Stephanie into his office and asked if she would mind typing up Donna's statement; that it might prove very interesting to her and answer a lot of questions about her own life. If she preferred she could type it directly onto the computer, using the machine in his office.

"Yes sir, I'd love to. It sounds very intriguing. I didn't realize Donna and I had anything in common."

When they got to the part about Donna dating Peter, Stephanie rose up from her chair and, raising her voice - at the same time shaking her fist at Donna - exclaimed, "Why you whore. Aren't there enough single men out there for you? Well, I've had it with him anyway, so he's all yours honey! To think I might have been even a little bit concerned about his being arrested. Let's finish this interrogation, lieutenant" she said as she sat back down at the computer. "This is getting more and more interesting.

"This won't take very long sir." she told Lt. Lanza, after Donna finished telling all she knew. "Why don't you have a cup of coffee with Mr. Wilson while I print this out and put it in a folder for you. Then I'll call one of our notaries."

"Thank you very much Stephanie." Lt. Lanza said to her, as he winked and smiled at her. "I think I will have some if you made it."

"Yes I did, sir." Stephanie responded, with a smile; wondering if anyone might suspect why they were being so friendly with each other. She didn't think anyone realized she had had a couple of dates with him. He was such an enjoyable man and such a gentleman - nothing at all like Peter.

While Stephanie was preparing the statement for the lieutenant, he was talking with Ben and telling him how hard it had been to talk Stephanie into going out on a casual date with him. He thought maybe she was only going to get more information about her husband's case. He then asked Ben to put in a good word for him. He really was very fond of her and hoped she would get to feel the same about him.

"I'll do what I can for you lieutenant. but you are certainly aware of what her life has been like recently. She could certainly use a good friend right about now. However, she probably doesn't completely trust men right now either, considering what has happened. But who knows what casual dates may lead up to. I'll wish you luck because she is a very lovely girl. I do know one thing, she is through with him and has filed for divorce, if that makes you feel any better."

"I guess you are right. I can certainly understand what you are saying. I will have to be patient and hope she continues seeing me. Thanks for the information about the divorce. That must be why she asked me if I knew any lawyers who specialized in divorces."

"Here you are Lt. Lanza," Stephanie said with a friendly smile, as she handed him the large envelope. "It's all set. I'll be seeing you soon."

After taking her copy of the statement from the officer, Donna turned to Stephanie. "Really, Stephanie, I can't tell you how terrible I feel about all this. I honestly never knew Peter was your husband. He came on to me so strong and never gave me a clue that he was even married until after we had been going together a while. He said some awful things about you, making it appear that you were the bad guy. I'm so sorry. Please don't hate me for it," and she had tears in her eyes.

"Forget it. And to think I shed so many tears over him; the rat. It looks like we both got a bum deal." she told Donna. "No, I can't hate you for what that bastard did. I hope they hang him by the balls for what he did. Oops, sorry about that, sirs," she said, as her face turned scarlet. (she blushed, forgetting Mr. Wilson and Lt. Lanza were still there) "I hope you don't think I always say things like that."

"Do you need me for anything else Lt. Lanza?" Donna asked. "I'm sorry I gave you such a bad time at first. If there is anything else you need me for, you know where you can find me. By the way," she added, "Take good care of Stephanie. I'm not blind you know."

"Thank you Donna. I'll remember that - about knowing where to find you as well as taking care of that pretty lady. And thank you Mr. Wilson for all your cooperation. I realize this has been a trying time for you." he said as he picked up the folder and, as he was about to leave, said to Stephanie, "I'll talk to you later pretty lady." and he left the office.

"Donna, how would you like to meet me for lunch and we can discuss and cuss the bum and exchange stories about him. Then we can gab about more interesting things. We'll meet at that little lunchroom down the block. Is 11:30 too early for you to break for lunch?"

"No, that's fine. I'd love that Stephanie. I'd say we do have quite a bit to discuss. See you there. And thanks again for not blaming me entirely for what happened. Maybe it's none of my business but I'm sure that lieutenant has it bad for you. He'd be a good catch for you, you know? See you later."

"I'd sure love to be able to listen in on that conversation," Ben said to himself.

Chapter 49

"Mr. Wilson," Stephanie called through the intercom. "Mr. Christou has arrived in his office. He should be here shortly as I had left a message that he was to report to you as soon as he arrived."

"It's about time he got here. It's almost two o'clock. But, thank you Stephanie. While we're waiting would you mind getting me a cup of coffee? This hasn't exactly been a normal day for me."

"No problem, sir." and in a few seconds she had placed a cup of coffee on his desk. Then she said, "Lt. Lanza is a very nice looking man, don't you think? His gruff appearance when he is working belies the soft-spoken, gentleman I have gotten to know away from work. He is also always extremely polite, and I think he likes me. When he first asked me out I figured it was because he felt sorry for me and just wanted to be friendly."

"Yes, he is a very nice person. As a matter of fact his feelings about you go far beyond the friendly state. He has told me so on more than one occasions how much he likes you. As soon as Mr. Christou leaves, we'll have a little chat."

In a few minutes Alex had arrived and was told to go right into Mr. Wilson's office. He sat down and was rather perplexed by the look on his father-in-law's face. He had also noticed that some of the people in his office had a rather strange look and many didn't even speak to him.

"You wanted to see me Ben? What's the emergency that had me returning so early?" he asked.

"Are you sure you don't already know? The auditors were here while you were gone and I want an explanation of their results. You do know what they were here for don't you? If you can prove to me that you are not implicated in this discrepancy they found, I apologize for suspecting you, and then we had better find out where the money went. When I questioned Angie she told me you had made some bad investments but that everything would be taken care of soon. Now, what exactly does that mean?"

"I don't know where to begin or how to explain what really happened to the money. You or the police, if you decide to involve them, will no doubt figure out how it happened so I may as well be honest and tell you everything from the start."

"I would appreciate it. First of all," Ben told him, "I want you to know that I will be taping your confession; and it does sound like that is what it will be."

"Stephanie," he called from the intercom. "Please get a taperecorder and bring it right in to me."

As soon as she gave him the recorder, Mr. Wilson thanked her and left instructions that he was not to be disturbed, under any circumstances, until they were through.

"Let's start at the beginning," Ben told him. "And try not to leave anything out. I don't think I'm going to like what you are about to tell me."

"Well, it all started when I first started dating that girl. Like I said before, she was exciting and sexy and Angie and I weren't hitting it off too well. I would buy her little gifts in appreciation of our rendezvous together and, whenever I'd have to be on a trip for a while, I'd bring something back to her."

"Those are things you should have been doing for your wife, not your own private whore," Ben told him in no uncertain terms.

"Yeah, I know. Well, last summer she had trouble coming up with her tuition so I gave her the money she needed. She said she would pay me back but I didn't really expect to ever see it again. During this time I was withdrawing quite a bit from our personal account until it started getting low and I was afraid Angie would realize something was wrong.

"Then, somehow, Mr. Marcos found out we were dating. I guess he saw us someplace, even though we were trying to be discrete about it. At any rate, he approached me one day in the parking lot and told me he was going to expose me to you and to Angie if I didn't pay him $7500 a month. He also had some pictures he somehow managed to take - a couple of us kissing in the park. I told him that amount was ridiculous; that I couldn't possibly come up with that kind of money. Then he said he'd settle for $5000 and not a penny less, and he was keeping the pictures in case I missed a payment. He said he needed the money to send back to his family in Nicaragua and he thought that was cheap considering why he was willing to keep quiet. I couldn't talk him out of it - told me it was a personal problem as to how I got it; just get it. I never wanted Angie or you to know what I was doing. Actually, I did invest some money in the hopes of making some to replace in the accounts."

"How could you have been so stupid; a man with your education and background? I wouldn't have believed you could ever do such a dumb thing. So when did you start taking from the company?"

"As soon as Marcos got greedy and asked for $25,000 for the negatives or he was going to send them to Angie. I had to withdraw from the company because there was no longer enough in our personal account. He even gave me instructions as to how I would get it to him. He wanted it in $100 bills, deliverable at a different location each month and not always by the same deliveryman. He figured that way no one would start suspecting something was going on. When he was murdered I was so relieved and was certain somehow I could get the money back before it was missed. I did manage to make enough to replace the $25,000. Then you sent me on this last trip, and I hadn't expected the auditors to show up when they did. I guess Harry is even more efficient than I thought. I had already ended the affair with the girl following that last encounter I had with Angie at your house, and you had fired her."

"Did you ever take her on any of your trips? I understand she took quite a bit of leave, claiming she had a very heavy load at school and had to stay home and catch up on her studies."

"As a matter of fact, I did. We always went to nice places during the evening and stayed at the better hotels. She was so much fun to be with that I just wasn't thinking ahead as to what the consequences might be. I didn't dream the money I was spending was adding up to so much.

"But I didn't kill Marcos. I knew that some day I would have to expose him, which would mean trouble for me too, but I hadn't figured out how."

"And now how do you expect to reimburse the company for the $195 thousand you embezzled." [Alex cringed when Ben used the word 'embezzled'] "All those years you have been such an asset to the company, and now this. You leave me in a terrible situation. I can't keep you on, you know. Your time here is terminated as we speak. Much as I hate doing this, it will have to be reported to the police and I foresee possible prison for you.

"You have hurt so many people close to you by what you have done. First it was cheating on Angie and now this. It's not just the company and the faith I always had in you, but you are leaving Angie and the children without a means of income - oh she won't be left with nothing. Her mother and I will see to that. But somehow you're going to have to think of some way to retrieve some of that money. You will never have a position of any authority after this, so how do you plan to pay it back?"

"I'm not sure. I do have some stocks that we have had for several years. I'm not sure just how much they are worth right now, but I will sign them over to you or the company. They must be worth a little over $100 thousand dollars; maybe a little more. They were being kept for my retirement.

"As for paying back the rest of it, I don't know. I know I don't deserve to ask you this, but if you would be willing to not report me to the police, and give me a menial-type position someplace, I would return most of my salary to you to pay you back. I realize it would take a long time to reimburse all of it, but maybe I'd be able to find a second job too - you know, have two jobs and give you all of the money from the second one; or another thing would be to see about borrowing some on my life insurance. I couldn't stand prison and it would be a worse embarrassment to the family than if I just stepped down and paid you back working two jobs. How about the company with whom I am bonded? Would they be willing to refund some of it?"

"That's something I will have to discuss before the Board of Directors. I'm not the only one who has to make the final decision, you know. I'll call an emergency meeting and then let you know.

"You should have thought about the possible consequences before you got yourself into this mess. Right now I'm so disappointed with you that I'd probably say 'no', and it would serve you right if you had to spend a few years in prison. It is possible that the bonding company under which you and other employees are bonded may take care of most of your liability but don't count on it. However, we must wait until after what has happened is reported to them and they decide on what coverage we have. In the meantime, I will accept your bonds as partial restitution, regardless of the outcome of the Board of Directors meeting."

At this point he turned off the recorder and told Alex, "Now I suggest you go back to your office and start packing your personal belongings. I will designate Harry as acting head of the office for now. Then your really hard part starts. I expect you to go home and tell Angie exactly what you have told me. Is that clear? I don't want her hearing it from any other source. See me before you leave the building so you can sign this statement."

"Yes sir," he said, and with a very troubled and dejected look on his face, he turned around and walked out of the office, with a look on his face likened to a dog with its tail between its legs..

After Alex left, Ben asked Stephanie to call the department heads and the members of the Board of Directors, and set up an emergency meeting for first thing the following morning. Make sure they realize I'll expect everyone to be in attendance, and on time.

"I hate to ask this of you so late in the day, but would you mind staying long enough to get this tape transcribed and on the computer. I will need the original for Alex to sign and some hard copies for the meeting in the morning." he instructed his secretary.

"I'll be happy to, sir. I certainly don't have anything special to go home to tonight. Besides, what kind of a secretary would I be if I refused after all that has been going on. I'll get right at it." Then she asked him, "Are you planning to stay and wait for it? It shouldn't take very long anyway considering how long the two of you were in there.

"Before I begin, I'd just like to tell you that I received a phone call while you were in your office with Mr. Christou. It was Lt. Lanza. As you know, I have been dating him occasionally; nothing big because I wasn't sure I should - dinner and then right home; that sort of thing. He seems to be very nice and mannerly and never tries any funny stuff. What are your feelings about my dating him, or anybody for that matter?"

"Of course, I already knew you were dating him and I think it is a wonderful idea. Why shouldn't you go out with him? You said you were through with Peter and had started divorce proceedings so I see nothing wrong with dating. I'm glad to hear you have decided to do it. In fact, Lt. Lanza asked me to put in a good word for him and I assure you, you have my approval. Good luck. Just be careful, if you decide to go out with anyone else, that you don't get someone who may try to take advantage of you at a time like this. Not everyone is like Lt. Lanza.

"As for my staying here. I have to make some phone calls while you're doing that, and I have to call my wife and tell her to hold up on supper. I'll talk to you before you leave. Alex will be up here to sign his statement anyway."

When Stephanie was almost through Ben came out of his office and, interrupting her, asked her what her plans were for supper. When she told him she didn't have any, he told her she was invited to his house for late supper. He also said Marge wasn't the type to take no for an answer, and that she should be at their house by 7:30. "You do know where I live, since you've been there before? Drive carefully, dear."

"What can I bring for supper; some salad or maybe a dessert?"

"Just bring your appetite. Marge will take care of the rest," he told her.

Chapter 50

Stephanie was at the Wilson house promptly at 7:25. She parked her car in the circular drive in front of the house, walked up the wide stairs and rang the front doorbell.

"Hello there Stephanie," a usual cheery Mrs. Wilson greeted her as she opened the door. "We are so pleased you could join us for supper tonight. I don't very often have a chance to cook for guests during the week. Let me take your coat and you go on into the living room and make yourself comfortable. I'll be right with you."

"Thank you very much ma'am," Stephanie said. "You have a lovely home. I always wished I had something like this but there just never was enough money to have a house in this area."

She then went into the living room and sat in a chair facing the fireplace. It was a comfortable looking room, which probably had seen many happy days while the children were growing up. That was one thing Stephanie always regretted - the fact she kept putting off having a family. Now she probably never would have children. While she was daydreaming, Mrs. Wilson returned.

"Stephanie, supper isn't quite ready but if you'd care to join me in the kitchen you're more than welcome. Ben is puttering around in his workshop next to the garage so there will just be the two of us girls. And please call me Marge instead of ma'am."

"I'll try." Stephanie said as she followed Marge to the kitchen. "But I was always taught not to call my elders by their first name. Besides, you are my boss's wife and I never call him Ben." Then, reaching into her big tote bag she was carrying, she took out a bottle of fine wine, handing it to Marge saying, "I almost forgot, here is a little something for the dinner table."

"You didn't have to do that dear." Then Marge added, "Oh posh. I call that a lot of poppycock. You have been with the company for so long you have every right to call us by our first name; at least here in our home. Besides, you're more like another daughter to me."

Stephanie laughed and said, "In that case I should be calling you mom." Mrs. Wilson laughed too.

"So what can I do to help, instead of sitting here like a bump on a log. Do you have an apron I may use? That's something my mom always insisted on - that I wear an apron in the kitchen. I don't very often wear one now, but since I have my good clothes on I should protect them."

"Certainly dear. Here you go. Now, let me see what you can do. I'll show you which dishes we will use and you may set the table. OK?"

Just as Ben came in from his workshop and was about to wash his hands so they could eat, the phone rang.

"It never fails. If we ever sat down to a meal without the darn phone ringing, I'd think something was wrong." Ben said as he picked up the receiver. "Oh, hi Angie. Is there a problem? What did he say? Well, maybe he just got delayed. I wouldn't worry. How are the kids? Have you had supper yet? Well, why don't you leave a note for Alex to come over here when he gets home. Bundle up the kids and bring them over here. We are just about to sit down for supper and you know your mother - always cooks enough for all the neighbors as well. Good, we'll see you in a few minutes."

"OK grandma, put on some more plates. Angie and the kids will be here in a couple of minutes."

Then, after greeting Stephanie, he proceeded to wash his hands before sitting down at the table.

"Are you sure I won't be in the way for family talk?" Stephanie asked. "Maybe I should go on home and come another time."

"Don't be ridiculous, dear. You stay right where you are. You know Angie and the children. It's not as though they were strangers."

"Did you tell Marge about our little conversation regarding a certain police lieutenant this afternoon, Stephanie?" Ben asked. "You know that nice Lt. Lanza, don't you Mother. Well, he has been calling on our favorite secretary. She was asking me if I thought it was alright for her to date and I told her certainly. What do you think?"

"Oh, I agree 100% Ben. She should be out having a good time. He seems to be quite a gentleman. Didn't you tell me the lieutenant told you he likes Stephanie very much?" Then, turning to Stephanie, she said, "You go out with that nice man any time he calls you. You're too young and pretty to be sitting around home. Besides it will help take your mind off all that has happened lately.

"I think I hear Angie and the children. Will you let them in Ben?"

When Angie and the children were all seated her father asked her what had happened where Alex was concerned.

"Well, Dad," she said, "He called and told me he'd like to come over for supper. You know we haven't lived together since he became Mr. Nice Guy to that young girl. I don't like not having him see the kids though, so I told him sure, we'd be happy to have him for dinner. He said he had a couple of things to do first and then he would be right over because he had something very important he had to tell me and it couldn't wait. Actually, his voice had a strange sound to it and he sounded rather mysterious; said to expect him in an hour or so."

"So, why are you worried? How long ago was that?" her mother asked.

"That was about 4:30 this afternoon and now, three hours later, I still haven't seen or heard from him. I tried getting his apartment but there has been no answer. Is something going on I should know about, Dad?" she asked. "I thought all this stuff about the girl was over and he was turning over a new leaf."

While the conversation between Angie and her parents was going on, Stephanie found things to talk about with the kids so they wouldn't be listening to what the others were discussing.

"I'm afraid it isn't as simple as that. In fact, I thought when you called that he had been home and told you what had happened. I would rather have had it come from him. Mother, do you think we should tell her or wait for Alex?"

"For Heaven sakes, Dad. Tell me what? As long as you've told me what you have, tell me what this is all about."

"Stephanie, would you mind taking the kids to the living room while I tell Angie what happened today?" and they immediately left the kitchen.

"Well, it's a good thing you're sitting down because I had to fire Alex today. It seems....."

"WHAT?" she screamed. "Now what the heck has he done? Was it worse than taking on some young girl?"

"Wait a minute Angie. Calm down. To me it was worse because it deeply affected the company," and he proceeded to give her all the details, then telling her there would be a special Board of Directors meeting the next morning to decide what to do about it.

"My God! How can a grown man, and one who has been treated like family all these years, do such an idiotic thing as that? I can't believe I'm hearing this about Alex, of all people. You gave him a top position in the company when he really wasn't ready for it. It's true he learned fast, but I always felt you started him out so high on the ladder because of me. Now he pulls this asinine stunt. If it weren't for the kids I'd wish him locked up and throw away the key. He let that little slut make a damn criminal of him. To make matters worse he's stupid enough to get caught and then that guy blackmails him. This has to be a bad dream."

"I hated to tell you this Angie, but I'm afraid Alex may be sitting in some bar, drinking, trying to get up the courage to face you. Well, call the kids in and let's eat supper and talk about more pleasant things for now. We invited Stephanie to the house for supper since she stayed late to get Alex's statement typed. And, if I know her she probably wouldn't bother cooking a decent meal for herself at home."

"Hi Steph," Angie said. "Sorry you had to be here under these circumstances and listen to all our problems; not that you haven't had more than your share lately. By the way, I thought you were dating Lt. Lanza, or did I hear wrong? From what I heard he is a very nice guy and is crazy about you. You deserve someone like that."

"As a matter of fact we have dated, but how did you find out? Everyone seems to know how much he likes me but me. He is working on a special assignment for a couple of days so I won't see him for awhile. He is nice, always calls me a pretty lady, which makes me nervous. I never know what to say in return."

"Just say 'thank you'. He means it too. He's told me more than once what a lovely lady you are and how much he cares for you." Ben remarked. "You know Marge, I wouldn't be surprised if this turned out to be something very serious. There could be a wedding in the future because he only has eyes for Stephanie.

"But let's finish supper before the phone rings again."

Chapter 51

It was lunch time the following day when several of the girls who had gathered in the lunchroom, made sure they had a place near Martha, Rose, Kim, and Valerie. They knew if anyone would know the latest gossip in the company, Martha would, and not necessarily because she was dating Sgt. Petrakos.

"So, Martha, bring us up-to-date on the murder case. I'm sure your sergeant. has been keeping you abreast of things," Valerie said.

"He's not MY sergeant - not really," she told them before saying, "Well, I'm sure you've all read the papers so you know that Stephanie's husband has been charged with the murder, as well as breaking and entering, robbery, assault and battery, and wife abuse. There was more than enough evidence against him to have him turned over for trial. If they can get a jury by then, the trial is set to start in ten days. Someone wants it over in a hurry, but I don't know who was responsible for that. Greg didn't give me details as to how and when or why the body was taken to the garage. I hear Donna was extremely cooperative in telling the police all she knew; especially after she found out he was Stephanie's husband."

"Will she be arrested too, and charged with anything?" Rose asked.

"I doubt it. In fact, she may be called upon as a witness for the prosecution." she said, "unless they decide her confession is as good as a legal deposition and she won't have to appear in court."

"What was the most incriminating evidence they found, or could Greg tell you about that?" Kim asked, rather timidly.

"He didn't say, but I would imagine finding Peter's fingerprints all around Juan's apartment would be one of the most important. After all, he and Peter didn't know each other so he had no reason to be there. There were many things that worked against him. I guess giving Donna those earrings was stupid. He sure hadn't counted on her turning state's evidence, but when she realized he was Stephanie's husband she was willing to tell everything she knew about him. I'll bet Peter will be seething when he finds that out. The earrings had been engraved with Juan's wife's birthdate."

"How did they know what the date meant, or that it even was a date? It could have been almost anything," Rose commented.

"Greg managed to get in touch with Juan's cousin, after finding an address book amongst the mess in the apartment. His cousin told him the earrings had been a gift from his wife. Somehow he managed to keep them hidden all the years he was in prison. His cousin said he would get in touch with Juan's brother or daughter and one of them would probably arrange to come to Maine first chance they got to claim any of Juan's possessions that are worth taking. Greg reminded him that they wouldn't be able to have the earrings until after the trial because they were evidence. Oh yes," she added, "To show just how stupid Peter was, he was wearing Juan's gold watch when they picked him up. It too had an I.D. engraved on it."

"Wow," Rose said. "How is Stephanie taking all this? She must be devastated. We haven't seen too much of her lately. She seems to be burying herself in her work, probably to keep her mind off the trial. From what I've heard, Mr. Wilson has been keeping her pretty busy these days."

"I don't know." Martha commented. "She was very hurt at first but now she's just plain mad and told me the other day she hopes they hang him. In fact, she has seen a lawyer about a divorce. From all the murder mysteries I have read, my personal opinion would be that I doubt if he will be charged with first-degree murder. You can be sure he will claim that he didn't mean to kill Juan; that he just intended to rob him. But don't quote me on that."

"Well girls, I guess I know something you don't know." Kim said, very proudly. "Stephanie has been seeing that handsome lieutenant who was here the day of the murder. I saw them go into a little restaurant in the Raymond area last week. They didn't see me, but I know it was them. And they looked pretty happy. How about that?"

"You're kidding. Our Stephanie dating that handsome hunk of a man? Why that sneak; and she didn't even tell us. Well, that's interesting." Martha commented. "I mean, I'm happy for her that she is dating, but I wonder why she is being so secretive about dating Lt. Lanza. Greg said he is a nice guy. I wonder how they happened to get together. We'll have some questions for her when we see her."

"Stephanie must be furious with Donna." Valerie said. "I'll bet she was ready to pull her blonde hair out from their dark roots when she found out Donna was the other woman. I sure would have, had it happened to me."

"Actually, I don't think so." Martha told her. "You know me and my inquisitive mind. Well, I talked with Donna and she told me Stephanie didn't blame her as much as she did her husband. Donna swears that at first he had her convinced he wasn't even married and, since she didn't know Stephanie's last name there was no way to connect the two of them. In fact, she and Stephanie went to lunch together to exchange notes about him. How about that?"

"Boy, still water runs deep," Valerie said.

"What do you mean by that," Kim asked. "What is this still water all about?"

They all laughed and then Valerie tried to explain by saying, "It's just a saying. Stephanie was always saying about how shy and quiet Peter was, and how he never liked to meet new people, when all the time, behind her back, he was anything but shy. Understand what I mean? All the time he has been as phony as a three-dollar bill. Stephanie deserves better. By the way, if you are right Kim, that she is dating Lt. Lanza, then that's why she has been looking so happy again and sporting all those new clothes and a new hairdo. I don't understand why she hasn't told any of us."

Realizing they had an audience in some of the other company girls, Martha turned around and said, "Lillian, are you girls getting all we're saying, or should we speak louder?" and they sheepishly got up and left.

"If it is true, Greg will know. I'll ask him next time I talk to him." Martha told the others. "But right now this murder isn't the only concern for the company. Between Steve being in the rehab hospital and Mr. Christou being accused of embezzling and being fired, I wouldn't want to be in Mr. Wilson's shoes right now. He must be a nervous wreck. Well, girls, we'd better get back to work"

On the way back to her office, Valerie happened to notice that the television set in the Executive Lounge was on. There was a special news flash just coming on so she stepped inside the door, hoping she could hear what was going on, but the volume wasn't up loud enough to hear much of it. The picture showed a car being pulled from the lake near White's Bridge It was a dark blue Cadillac de Ville, which somehow looked vaguely familiar. "Oh my God." she exclaimed to herself. "I hope no one was in it because they surely couldn't have survived."

Chapter 52

It was two days later when, as Ben was walking down the hall towards Harry's office, he saw Harry coming towards him. "You're just the person I wanted to see. If you can spare a few minutes, let's go to my office and talk. Or, since we are so close to yours we could just as well go in there."

"Sure Mr. Wilson. Anything I have to do can wait a few minutes."

As they arrived at Harry's office they stopped by the secretary's desk. "Penny, would you mind bringing some coffee into my office for Mr. Wilson and me?"

"I'd be happy to, sir. What will it be Mr. Wilson - black or with cream and sugar. I already know how Harry takes his."

"Black will be fine." he told her as they went into the office. "And, Penny, would you mind calling Stephanie and letting her know where I am?"

"Don't tell me you have still another problem, sir. Frankly, I don't think I could have maintained my sanity through something like what has happened here. And now Alex dying so tragically in that terrible accident. You are a strong man, sir. Have they determined just how it happened? It must have been a terrible shock to the entire family, especially his wife and children. Give them my sincerest condolence."

"Well, thank you Harry. I try to be strong. It hasn't been easy lately, as if the murder wasn't enough. As for Alex, Laura and the children are devastated, even though she and Alex weren't living together."

About that time Penny returned with a tray loaded down with the coffee, cream and sugar and a plate of little pastries. "I thought you may want something else," she said smiling.

"Thank you Penny." Harry said. "Now would you please hold my calls. Mr. Wilson and I do not wish to be disturbed."

"I appreciate your concern Harry. These past few months have been pretty hectic and I'll be glad when it's all behind me. By the way, how are things with you and your bride-to-be?"

"Things couldn't be better for us," he answered. "We have set the date and are getting married on Christmas Eve. Naturally you and Mrs. Wilson are invited, if you are in town during the holidays. As a matter of fact you are the first ones to be invited. With all the problems here we never got around to sending out formal announcements. But, since it will just be a small wedding, we have decided to invite people in person."

"You know very well we will be there. If there is any way Marge can assist in the plans, I know she'd love to help. She's very good that way. Well now, your plans will work out fine for what I was going to ask you.

"Do you think you could handle the title of Jr. Vice President and Head of Accounting? If you think it's possible, it will be my wedding gift to you. Naturally, it will mean a substantial increase in pay."

Harry just stared at him at first. Then, stammering he said, "I don't know what to say, sir. It is such an unexpected honor to be chosen for that job. I really can't thank you enough."

"So what is your answer? And why wouldn't you be the one to take over; or would you prefer I offer it to someone else?" Ben said with a big smile on his face. "You can handle it, can't you?"

"Oh no, don't do that. Of course I can handle it and, I'll take it. I'm just so pleased you have such confidence in my ability. You'll never regret it, I promise. Honestly sir, I feel like I am dreaming. I can hardly wait to tell Linda. She probably won't believe me at first. This promotion is going to mean so much for us now that we are getting married. We can plan on buying a house and get away from this apartment living."

"Well now Harry, don't you think that now that you will be an executive, you should start calling me Ben instead of 'sir' all the time?"

"I guess so, but it will take awhile getting used to, sir."

"There, you did it again." Ben kidded, and they both laughed. "Now how about you and I having lunch at the club where I am a member. And, by the way, I'll see that you will also have membership. Today will be a working lunch when we can talk in more detail about your job. You may be interested in knowing that the Board of Directors held a meeting a few days ago and unanimously approved of your assignment at that time. Because of Alex's death and the wake, I just never have gotten around to tell you before."

"Thank you Ben. I'd be pleased to have lunch with you. Where and what time should we meet?

"Twelve-thirty sounds good, don't you think? I'll stop by your office on the way out. By the way, I have an idea. Marge and I have reservations for dinner there tomorrow night - a chance for us to relax after all the problems. Why don't you and Linda plan on joining us and we'll tell Marge about the wedding. She will be thrilled to share in, not only the wedding news, but in finding out about your new position. You can meet us in the main lobby of the club about 8 o'clock, if that's OK with both of you."

"That sounds great. I'm sure Linda will be thrilled to go. As far as I know there were no other plans and even if there were, they can be canceled easily enough. This is by far the most important thing to have happened to us, except for getting married, of course. I'll call her as soon as we finish here. It won't be easy, but I won't tell her about the promotion until tomorrow night. She's going to be thrilled at having dinner with you and Mrs. Wilson."

"You are a sly one Harry. I can see we are going to get along fine. I like pulling surprises on my wife at times, even though she says I shouldn't do it - says I'm going to give her a heart attack one of these days. Actually, I think she really enjoys it. Will there be any problem telling Linda where we are going?

"Are you kidding. She has always wished we could afford to belong to a country club, so she will be thrilled to death when I tell her about it. She likes you and Marge, and she'll no doubt want to run out and buy a new dress, knowing her."

"OK Harry, I'll see you later for lunch and both you and Linda tomorrow night," and Ben returned to his office.

Later, at lunchtime, Harry told Ben he had something that was bothering him concerning the recent events with the company. Ben asked him what was on his mind.

Very seriously, he asked, "Ben, you have never mentioned Alex through all this talking we've done. Have they figured out what caused the accident? That must have been a terrible death for him. I feel I should visit Angie and express my feelings for her loss."

"I'm sure she would be happy to see you and Linda. It was a pretty bad accident. They think he lost control as he rounded that bad curve just before the bridge and, instead of going up over the bridge he plowed through the fence and into the lake. He was trapped in the car. They said he had been drinking heavily. There was also a half bottle of Vodka in the car. The autopsy showed the blood-alcohol level to be way above the legal limit for driving so he no doubt had been drinking quite a bit before getting into the car. He was probably so drunk he didn't know what was happening. He never was much of a drinker so that no doubt made it even worse. "Poor Angie; in spite of everything he's done lately I think she still loved him and now she is a total wreck. She is blaming herself for being so hard on him. The children are taking their dad's death very hard. He was always so good to them and took time to go places and do things with them. It's very hard on children their ages.

"As for the money he took, I really don't know how we will recoup that amount unless his actions would be covered by the bonding company. He did tell me he had about a hundred thousand dollars worth of bonds that he would sign over to the company. Whether he ever got around to do it, I don't know. We have to go to his apartment and see just what he had and to close it down. I guess after the funeral tomorrow morning Marge and I will take care of that. We aren't even going to ask Angie to go with us," he told Harry.

"I hate to say this Ben and I could be out of line, but do you think there's any chance he may have committed suicide. That's one of the first things the insurance company will ask. After all, he had messed up his family life, and embezzled from the company. Then, losing his job and being thrown out of his home he probably was depressed and figured he had nothing to live for."

"I doubt it Harry. I just don't think he was the type to do that. He loved life and especially his kids too much to do that. He was a strong man with the attitude that no matter how bad a situation was, there was a sensible way out. I'm sure he had been drinking to build up the courage to face Angie. After all, he did call and tell her he would see her for supper as soon as he took care of a couple of things. I really find it hard to believe he would have intentionally taken his own life."

"You're probably right. You knew him better, and in a different way, than I. I only knew him as a fellow worker; and even after working with him so many years I can't believe he took all that money."

The two men then discussed Harry's new job and his starting salary; which caused Harry to take a gulp. He didn't realize it would mean such an increase. It was agreed he would move into his new office the first of the week at which time his new salary would take effect. When Harry asked if it was alright to transfer Penny, his secretary, up there too, Ben told him certainly because Alex had been without a secretary since Beckie had left about three weeks ago, and they hadn't had a chance to hire anyone else. It would also mean an increase for Penny as she would be an executive secretary then. Harry said she deserved it. Then Ben told him exactly what was expected of him as head of the department as well as what his responsibilities as a Vice President entailed. Harry was told that he could also expect a reasonable travel allowance whenever travel was necessary. Everything sounded very exciting, as well as challenging, but he had no doubt that he could do it. At two-thirty the two men returned to their offices.

Chapter 53

A week after Alex's funeral, Stephanie arrived in the office one morning dressed in a new suit and a new hairdo. She looked more like a top executive than a secretary.

"Good morning Stephanie." Ben said as he arrived that morning. "You look extra nice this morning. Another new hairdo and suit? Are you trying to compete for my job?" and he chuckled. "You look more like your old self once more. I'm glad to see you are trying to put your life back together again, and doing a good job, I might add. I've also noticed the fresh flowers on your desk all the time. I wonder who could be sending them, especially since there is always one red rose in the center of the arrangement."

"Thank you sir." she answered. "I'm feeling great. I know I probably told you, but I saw my lawyer as soon as Peter was officially charged with murder and asked him to get my divorce through as fast as possible, which he is doing. At this moment I don't care if I ever see him again because I don't miss him. He's strictly on his own and I hope he stays in prison a long time. In fact, I am also taking action to get my maiden name back. Last night I went shopping and had my hair done and, as of today, I am starting a new life. You know Charles Lanza and I have been seeing much more of each other - two or three times a week, in fact. I figured you'd guess that he was sending me the flowers. Isn't that sweet of him? I've really enjoyed the evenings we've had together and he wants to see me, as he put it, as often as I will go with him. I wasn't sure at first if I should be dating too much until my divorce is final but then decided that was foolish. Oh, another thing. I spoke to the priest at my church and he's going to see what he can do about an annulment."

"My, you have been a very busy girl. I can't see anything wrong with you going out as much as you want since, as you say, your divorce is pending. Lt. Lanza is a nice young man and I know he likes you very much and will make you very happy. Well it sure is good having the old Stephanie back. Welcome back dear. Will this mean I'll soon be able to call you Miss Christeas again?"

"I hope so. I don't even want to be reminded of Kaknas any more. Thank you very much for being concerned about me. I don't know what I would have done there for awhile without you and Mrs. Wilson allowing me to cry on your shoulders. There was no one else I could talk to. It's nice to be back." she said, as she planted a kiss on Mr. Wilson's cheek, and then sat down at her computer ready to start work.

Chapter 54

"Did any of you guys see Stephanie this morning?" Kim asked the girls during their coffee break. "I happened to go by that way earlier and almost didn't recognize her. She looks like a million bucks - a beautiful new suit and sophisticated hairdo. You'd think she was applying for Mr. Wilson's job. Getting rid of her husband and dating the lieutenant sure must agree with her."

"I'll have to find an excuse to go to her office and find out what the occasion is," Martha said, which didn't surprise any of the other girls. "I guess you were right. She has been dating Lt. Lanza and he probably treats her like the lady she is; otherwise, why would she look so happy? I always felt she was a classy lady and wondered what she ever saw in Peter. Speaking of which, his trial started this week. With all the evidence against him, with any luck it could all be over in time for him to spend Christmas in prison, which is where he belongs."

"Then maybe the holidays will see the dawn of a new and better era for the company." Rose commented. "This year hasn't really been that great except for the weddings that took place, plus the anniversary party and Don's retirement party. Too bad all the tragic things had to over-shadow the good ones. Speaking of weddings, did any of you get invited to Harry and Linda's wedding? I think they are just planning a small one. I was one of the lucky ones."

The other girls in the group had also received one, coming to the conclusion that those with whom Harry was most closely associated at the company would be going; and then they talked about Harry having been promoted. They all agreed he was an excellent choice and they were also happy he had asked to have Penny promoted too.

Since neither Harry nor Linda had any family nearby and would be paying for the wedding themselves, they decided to each invite the same number of friends. The wedding and reception would be in Portland.

Chapter 55

Lt. Lanza was pleased with himself that he had finally smartened up and convinced Stephanie to date him. For the few weeks they had been dating, she still only wanted to go to local places and then go home right away. He was so much in love with her and even though he felt she was afraid to trust him yet, he was willing to wait and pray her feelings about him would change. After several weeks and quite a few of these casual dates he decided he was going to have to use a different approach to see if he could get her more interested in him. He had been sending her flowers but that didn't seem to change things very much. Things were moving along too slowly to suit him. He was crazy about her, but didn't want to come on too strong for fear of scaring her off and maybe losing her for good. He was getting frustrated though, wanting her love and not knowing how to get it. Finally, he decided he would have to be a little more aggressive.

As she opened the door on this particular evening, he presented her with a dozen long, stem, red roses. "Lovely flowers for a lovely lady," he smiled and added. "Did anyone ever tell you what a beautiful lady you are? In fact, you are breath-taking and believe me I don't go around making remarks like that to just any girl."

Stephanie told him to come in, thanked him for the flowers and then told him she didn't know what to say when he talked to her like that.

Charles took a deep breath and then, very solemnly told her, "Stephanie, I have to talk seriously to you. As you no doubt have heard from many people, I haven't married because I'm married to my job. That's not true by any means. For one thing I just never met a woman who would put up with me as a police officer. But most of all, until now, I haven't found anyone I liked well enough to propose to. I am very much in favor of women. It's hard for me to believe that your husband didn't appreciate you, but then I'm sure you don't want to talk about him. I'm afraid I'm sounding like a babbling idiot and I'd better stop before I make a complete fool of myself. I guess that's what happens when I look at you, It's so hard to describe just how I feel. You are such a remarkable girl and - darn it - I love you and don't care who knows it."

She ignored his last remark saying only, "Thank you for the nice compliments sir, and the lovely flowers. You are very kind," and she gave him a big smile. Every time he greeted her he had nice things to say and it made her tense up. Peter had never bothered saying nice things to her; just took her for granted. So it was something she was going to have to get used to if she continued dating Charles. "I have heard all that about you and no, I don't care to speak about you-know-who. Any subject but that." Then, changing the subject entirely, she said, "I went to the mall last night and finished my Christmas shopping early. I also bought this outfit for tonight, even though I don't know just what we will be doing. Do you like it?

"I love this time of year. Everything is so pretty and the people seem to be so happy and friendly. I seldom run into any grouchy people before Christmas. Too bad it doesn't last the whole year."

"Stephanie, please don't keep changing the subject and ignoring me when I tell you how I feel about you. It is the truth and by God before long I'm going to have you feeling the same about me. As for plans for tonight. I don't have to be back on duty until noon tomorrow. I thought you might like to go into Portland to a dinner theater. A friend of mine gave me tickets that are good for any one of the next three days. We'll use them tonight, if you are interested. We don't have to - you may have a better idea." He didn't want to sound pushy.

"No, that sounds good to me. I'm glad I dressed up a little so I wouldn't feel out of place," she told him as she rattled on about unimportant things. Anything to keep him from complimenting her. "I love to dress up anyway - makes me feel good. About the only time you'll see me in slacks and sweatshirts is around the house weekends and when I go for my morning walks, which I wasn't doing there for awhile. But now I'm back on my old routine."

"There you go again with your small talk. But, if it makes you happy, what is your old routine, pretty lady?"

"Well, three times a week I work out at a health club and almost every day I walk five miles each morning. At my age I can't let myself go to pot; if you know what I mean."

"I can't imagine you ever going to pot, as you say. You look pretty darn good to me the way you are. Now, shall we go so we won't be late for the show?"

They used his car, a light blue Mercury Cougar, and were on their way. The ride to Portland was a rather quiet one for awhile, both of them just coming up with small talk from time to time until they were almost there. Stephanie commented about Martha dating Sgt. Petrakos and Charles told her Greg was quite fond of Martha but he didn't think Martha considered him more than just a date. "I can sympathize with him." he told her.

Something was also said about the Wilson family. They discussed the trouble Alex caused for the company and they talked about his tragic death, wondering if it could have been suicide, considering what had happened.

"But what about you Steph?" Charles asked. "Are you truly happy now? Have you gotten used to living alone and what are your plans?"

"I don't mind it too much. Sometimes I get a little lonesome but most of the times I find enough to do to occupy my time. You have certainly helped a lot in that respect. If you're asking me if I ever think of Peter, the answer is a definite no. I'm happier right now than I have been in a long time. I have been considering putting my house up for sale and buying into a small condo, so I can really leave all the bad memories behind."

It was quiet again for awhile and all of a sudden Stephanie started laughing. "I'm sorry Charles, but I was thinking about what the girls were saying about you guys when all that interrogating was going on. Your ears really must have been burning."

"That bad huh? Well, we didn't mean anything personally, I can assure you. It was just our job, so we had to sound stern."

"Stern wasn't exactly the word they were using. But it's all over and now we can look back and laugh." Then turning very somber, she added, "I'm glad they were able to get Mr. Marcos' property back, especially those beautiful earrings that had such a sentimental value to them. Did you meet his brother when he was here? His name is Geraldo and he was such a nice, pleasant man. If you had known Juan, you would never have taken them for brothers. Not that I really care, but how long a sentence would you guess Peter will have to serve? I just hope he doesn't come after me when he gets out. He was very bitter and threatening me, you know. He will go to jail won't he? I'm always afraid the jury will find him innocent."

"I don't know Steph. It depends on what kind of verdict the jury comes up with. They can't possibly come up with a 'not guilty' verdict. There's too much evidence against him. If I were on the jury, and with the evidence they have, my guess would be second degree murder. Probably in the vicinity of 15 to 20 years. But let's not mention him again tonight. You don't have to worry your pretty head about him for a long time. And, as long as I am around, he will never get near you."

About that time they had arrived at the theater. He had the valet service park the car and they proceeded on into the theater.

"I'll be right back," Stephanie told him. "I have to make sure my makeup and my hair are OK. I'll meet you by that stairway over there."

"You look perfect to me. But go ahead. I'll wait for you."

As soon as she returned, the usher seated them in what turned out to be very good seats. The dinner was excellent, much better than the average dinner theater. The play was also very enjoyable. It was a combination comedy-mystery and, for amateur actors they did a commendable job. After the show the theater provided coffee and Danish pastries for anyone who wanted some before going home. They encouraged anyone who had been drinking to have some before going out on the highway. Stephanie and Charles only had a couple of glasses of wine all evening so they passed on the coffee and started back home since it was late and they had quite a distance to go.

During the course of their conversation on the way home, she asked him whether he was working Thanksgiving Day. He told her no and that he had intended asking her the same question. As they were nearing her house he told her he would call the next day to discuss it.

"We can talk about it for a few minutes tonight if you'd care to stop in for a cup of coffee before you go home," she told him.

Although it was late, he didn't refuse a chance to be with her a little longer, "Sure, as long as we don't make it for too long."

After she agreed to his plans for Thanksgiving she walked him to the door, again told him what a wonderful time she had, and thanked him for the beautiful flowers. "You made me feel like a young girl going on her first big date."

"Well, if that's the reaction you get we'll have to do it more often. I enjoyed the evening too, even when you talked about nothing important. How could I not enjoy being with the prettiest girl there?" he told her.

"You would make any girl feel good with the nice things you always say."

"But I don't intend to say them to any girl but you, my pretty lady.

"Good night Lt. Lanza, and thanks again. I'll be seeing you soon, I hope." and she gave him a big hug and a kiss before closing her door.

All he could think of all the way home was, "WOW, what a girl. That lady really is First Class. How am I going to convince her how nuts I am about her? If I were like some guys, I'd jump on her and make mad love to her. But that's not my style. Besides I love her too much. I'll just have to wait for her to come to me. I do believe I took a step forward tonight when she surprised me with that wonderful goodnight kiss. Somehow I have a feeling she's going to want more than that before long. I could be wrong but I think that beautiful girl is really in love with me but just doesn't want to admit it. Well, time will tell."

Chapter 56

Stephanie got to work early Friday morning. Christmas was only a little less than two weeks away and she still didn't know what she would get Harry and Linda as a wedding gift. She also didn't have a date and she hated the thought of going to a wedding alone. She couldn't just assume Charles would want to go to a wedding where he didn't know either the bride or the groom. Besides, he may even have to work that night. She had to admit that since Thanksgiving Day when they enjoyed a fabulous dinner in Kennebunkport, things had changed a great deal between them and she looked forward more and more to seeing him. He called her almost every day and still sent fresh flowers to her office. A girl would be crazy not to love a man like that. Could she possibly really be in love with him and not want to admit it? Peter's trial was expected to end by the middle of the following week and then it was just a matter of the final verdict being announced. She knew she didn't care what happened to him except that she wanted him locked up so he couldn't hurt her.

"Well, lady. Times have changed. It's OK for a girl to ask a guy out." she said out loud to herself. not realizing that during her day-dreaming, Mr. Wilson had walked in.

"Who are you talking to, Stephanie? I don't see anyone else around."

"Oh, good morning, sir. I feel rather silly, but I was talking to myself. I don't have anyone to escort me to the wedding Christmas Eve. I was thinking of being very bold and asking a friend of mine if he would like to go with me."

"You wouldn't be talking about that nice police officer friend of yours would you? - the one who is sending you those lovely flowers all the time? Don't worry, I got the word through our grapevine that you two have become a very steady item lately, even if you haven't admitted it to me. You certainly have my approval if that means anything. He must be taking very good care of you because it's been a long time since I've seen you look as happy and radiant as you have the past few weeks."

"He is so sweet and kind and has never tried any funny stuff - not even a really romantic goodnight kiss; at least not yet, if you believe that. I kissed him one night and since then that's the kind of a kiss he gives me. Anyway, I'll have to find out what shift he is on that day. He works all kinds of crazy hours so it's hard to plan ahead too much. If he is available, I'm pretty sure he will be willing to go with me. Mr. Wilson, I really have a problem. There I go again - coming to you with my problems. Anyway, I know I like him an awful lot but don't know if it is just because he is so good to me. I'm beginning to think I may be in love with him. How can I be sure it's not a rebound? I wouldn't want to tell him I do unless I was sure of it because I don't want to hurt him. At the same time I don't want to get hurt again either, even though I don't think this feeling is just a rebound."

"I really don't know what to tell you. Mrs. Wilson would be better at this, but if looks is the answer then I'd say you are very serious about this man. Like I told you, you actually haven't looked this happy in years. and I've known you for a long time. I think the best way is to follow what your heart says, or something like that. Like I've told you before, he is crazy about you and wants you for his wife. Believe me. He told me a long time ago that that was his goal."

"That's true sir. I'll have to give that some consideration." Then she asked him, "How is Mrs. Wilson these days? Has she finished her shopping? I'll bet she has the house looking beautiful for the holidays. She is such a talented lady in so many ways. You are very lucky to have her as your wife. Give her my love."

"Thank you dear; I will. Why don't you and your lieutenant plan to stop by some evening during the holidays. We'll be home because the whole family will be here. Michael and his fiancée will be here too. He always asks about you. We have an idea there will be an announcement from them about when they plan to get married. My goodness but the love bug has been busy this year, not just with my family but within the company. I hope all these newlyweds and engaged couples end up as happy as Marge and I are. Anyway, we'd be very happy to have you two drop by. Besides, I think Marge has a little gift for you - a 'favorite secretary' gift."

"I'll remember that, and thank you for the invitation. Now I have to call my favorite beau and see if he is available Christmas Eve.

"Hello. Is Lt. Lanza available please? Thank you. I'll wait if that's OK. Just tell him Mrs. Kaknas is on the line." While she was waiting, she got to thinking about how happy she would be to have her maiden name back after the divorce. She no longer wanted people to associate her with that name. In fact, she didn't even like to say it. "Hi lieutenant. How are you? Did I get you at a bad time?"

"What's up pretty lady? I have a few minutes."

"Why do you always call me that? I have a name you know. Anyway, what I called you about was to ask if you would be free Christmas Eve. I never thought I would ever call to make a date with a man, but I understand it's acceptable these days. I have been invited to a candlelight wedding ceremony Christmas Eve and I don't like the idea of going alone. What does your schedule look like for that night?"

"First off, I call you pretty lady because you are, and I do know what your name is. Now that that's settled, they just posted our hours for the holidays and, since I do have some seniority, I asked for Christmas Eve and got it. How's that for planning? As for your question, I would love to go to the wedding with you on one condition."

"And what may that be, sir?"

"That you spend some time with me on Christmas Day. I don't have to be back at work until 8 P.M. Christmas night. That should give us some time to do something. Do you ski? If you do, we could run up to Sunday Mountain or North Conway for part of the day."

"Yes I do, but haven't skied in a long time. Peter didn't know how and wasn't interested in learning. I went to Loon Mountain with some girl friends a few times. I may have to take a couple of lessons to get the hang of it again. I don't have my skis any more but I guess I can always rent them for that day. I do have my boots though, if they're still good. If necessary I'll get new stuff. I can see that this is going to be one of the nicest Christmases I've had in a long time.

"By the way, Mr. Wilson and his wife have invited us over to their home some evening during the holidays - whenever it is convenient for us. How about it? She has a gift for me, Mr. Wilson said."

"Sure - why not. They seem to be very nice people. By the way, who is getting married? I should know something about the happy couple."

"The young man works for T.G.I. You probably met him when you were there at the time of the murder. Harry Taylor is his name and he was just promoted to Chief of the Accounting Department; the job Mr. Christou had. His fiancée is Linda Gagne. She has an executive type position with some company in Portland and is a very nice girl. She's very attractive and dresses like a high fashion model. They make a lovely couple. You'll like them. By the way, are you working tonight? If you're not I thought maybe we could meet someplace and talk about holiday plans."

"Am I hearing things or are you asking me for another date, Stephanie?"

"Well, uh, I don't know, but I guess it does sound like I am." she stammered.

"I'm not on duty tonight and I'd love to spend the evening with you. Why don't I pick you up about 8 o'clock and we'll decide then what we'll do. First, I have a bone to pick with you. I too have a name, you know, and would appreciate your using it. I hear enough of 'lieutenant' or "sir" at work without my best girl calling me that too. OK?"

"OK, I got the message," Stephanie said, laughing. "I guess you told me. From now on it's Charles. By the way, do you prefer Charles, Chuck or Charlie?"

"Actually anything but Charlie, but I really prefer Charles."

"OK, Charles it is. Bye now." and she hung up. She really liked the nice things he always said but it made her feel strange to hear them so often. He really was beginning to grow on her but she still found it difficult to admit she was getting serious, and it bothered her.

At five minutes before eight her door bell rang and, as she opened the door, Charles stepped inside and, handing her two dozen long stem roses, said, "Pretty flowers for a pretty lady" and he gave her a kiss on the cheek. "Happy birthday my darling. Didn't think I knew did you? I thought two dozen roses would impress you more."

"Oh Charles," she said, "You're impossible. The flowers are gorgeous, as usual. But how did you find out about my birthday? You're the only one to wish me Happy Birthday today," with tears in her eyes. "You shouldn't have. Thank you very much," and she returned the kiss. "If you continue giving me all these flowers you'd better buy some stock in a flower shop; or do you already own one? Either that or I'll have to marry you so you will save some money."

"First, thank you for the kiss and your threat to marry me. I'll remember that. Second, I could never give you enough flowers but, if they are going to cause tears I may have to stop. And third, I have my way of finding things out. After all, in my line of work I have to know how to find out important information. By the way, I have a real birthday present I'll give you later. You women are strange; you cry both when you're happy and sad. Which are you at the moment?"

"Silly, you know I'm so happy and flattered that you care so much for me. Now, if you will excuse me I'll put these in water."

Charles followed her to the kitchen and as soon as she put the flowers down he took her by the hand and asked her, "Don't I get to give the birthday girl a kiss?" Before she could answer he put his arms around her and gave her a very passionate kiss, like he had never done before. "Now, my darling, how did you like that? There's more where that came from any time you want it. I hope you realize you mentioned the possibility of marriage to me, and I don't intend to forget it."

"I'll remember that. How could I ever forget a kiss like that." she said. "As for the remark about marriage, I'm afraid I have no comment." Then she asked him what he had in mind for the evening.

"What I'd like to do is one thing. But Greg Petrakos is having Martha over for a Greek style dinner - you know she's crazy about his cooking - and wanted to know if we would be interested in joining them; if that's OK with you."

"Sure, I'd love that. This may sound strange, but I'm anxious to see how Martha acts around a date. She so seldom dates anyone and when I ever found out she was going with Greg, it really took me by surprise. I don't know which one she likes best, him or his Greek cooking."

"Well, he sure is crazy about her but she doesn't give him any indication that the feeling is mutual. Did she ever give you girls a hint about her feelings towards him?"

"No, all she has ever told any of us girls is that she likes him a great deal; but the word love was never there."

"Let me help you with your coat and we'll be on our way, dear. This evening should be very interesting, but don't ask me why I said that."

Chapter 57

Stephanie and Charles arrived at Greg's apartment about 8 o'clock. Martha answered the door and took their coats, then showed them to the living room.

"Make yourself comfortable while we finish getting the dinner on the table. Greg, Charles and Steph are here," and she returned to the kitchen.

Greg came into the living room with an apron tied around his waist. "Can I get you guys a glass of wine before dinner. I just have to finish the salad and we can eat. We're sure glad you could make it," and he poured them a drink. Then he whispered, "I have a surprise for Martha tonight. I wanted you to be present for the occasion. By the way, I hope you both like Greek food because that's what's on the menu tonight," he said as he realized Martha was returning to the living room.

"Everything's ready Greg. Come on you two. You guys are really in for a treat. The menu is fabulous. By the way, we eat in the kitchen here because it is so much cozier; and besides there is no dining room." and they all followed her to the table where she told each of them where to sit.

Stephanie and Charles enjoyed the meal very much. Being of Greek decent, Stephanie had been raised on Greek food until her father passed away. Her stepfather refused to eat any of it. Charles had eaten some Greek food but not much. His father was Italian and preferred that his mother cook Italian.

The conversation at the table was mostly about things in the news, the work they were each doing and other small talk. Then outspoken Martha asked, "So when are you two getting married? You sure look like a perfect couple."

"Martha, honey, that's a very personal question. In fact, I wasn't going to say anything this early in the evening. Since you brought up the subject of marriage, I wanted our best friends to be present when I asked you to marry me. Will you Martha?" Taking her hand and looking in her eyes he said, "You must realize by now how much I love you, and you could make my life complete by saying yes."

At first Martha just sat with her mouth open. Then, very slowly and deliberately - not wanting to hurt him - she answered. "Greg, you know I'm really crazy about you, but I hadn't really thought about marriage. Don't get me wrong, I do love you, but you travel around so much and I'm not sure I could take that. It's not because you are a policeman; it's the constant travel. I want a husband who will be home with me instead of travelling. I'm afraid I'm going to have to give your question some serious thought. I would very much like to marry you some day, but not right now. I do love you though and hope you understand."

"Well, folks. I didn't expect this answer that's for sure. I was all set to put a ring on her finger and set a date and instead she threw me a curve." he responded with a hurt look and a shaky sound to his voice, sounding as though he might cry. "Martha, honey, I really do love you very much and, needless to say, I'm really disappointed. If you want to wait, I'll wait with you and hope and pray you will change your mind soon. I will always be here for you though."

After the surprise response, things got rather quiet and tense during dinner. When they finished Charles suggested they all go out to a club and have a drink and maybe dance a little. The others agreed that was a good idea,. "First though," he said, "I want you to know that today is Stephanie's birthday and I have a little gift for her which I'd like to give her at this time." thinking the tension might be eased some. He handed Stephanie a small package and told her to open it.

"Oh Charles, it's lovely." she said as she opened the box and found a beautiful gold chain with a pendant consisting of two gold hearts entwined and edged in diamonds. "Thank you very, very much. I love it. Will you put it on me please?" After he did that she gave him a kiss and thanked him again. "What a wonderful birthday; a man who says he is crazy about me and two very dear friends with whom to celebrate it. I am so lucky," and she wiped tears from her eyes.

"My gosh, Steph, it's just a little something for your birthday. Don't get sentimental on me. I think we'd better get going guys." Charles told the rest of them.

When Charles took Stephanie home a little after midnight, all he could say was how hurt Greg must be that Martha's answer wasn't a definite yes. "I hope you won't put me on hold when I decide to ask you to marry me."

"No comment, Charles." she told him as he walked her up to her door. "Goodnight honey. I'll talk to you tomorrow. Thanks again for the beautiful gift. I really love it."

He kissed her goodnight and, as usual said, "Goodnight my pretty lady. Take care of my best girl."

Chapter 58

The following day Stephanie kept thinking about the last thing Lt. Lanza had said to her before he left. He called her his 'best girl'. She certainly had to realize by now that he was very serious and not just being nice. She was still confused as to her feelings about him. Then she remembered what Mr. Wilson had told her about 'following what her heart told her'. About 4 o'clock she had a call from Charles.

"Hello Stephanie," and he emphasized her name. "What time do you get off work?"

"About 4:30 unless Mr. Wilson has some last minute work for me."

"So what are you doing tonight pretty lady? I don't suppose you have time for me."

"Well, let me think. After I bathe the five kids, put them to bed and then pick up their toys, I have to do the laundry and then I will be free." she kidded.

"Heck, I was hoping you could find a sitter crazy enough to take care of the little rascals so you could go out with me." He figured he could play her silly little game too.

"OK you win," she said. "I hadn't planned on anything in particular, except maybe going out with the nicest man on the police force if he wanted to take me out. I thought you had to work tonight."

"I asked someone to cover for me. Told him I had something important to take care of. Besides, he was looking for extra hours. Look your prettiest because we're going out someplace special. I'll pick you up at 7 PM sharp."

Going into Mr. Wilson's office she asked if he had anything special for her to do as she would like to leave on time. He told her he didn't. Then he noticed the gold chain and the hearts. "Well, what was the occasion for that? I assume Lt. Lanza gave it to you. That must have set him back a few dollars."

"My birthday was yesterday and he gave it to me. Isn't it nice? I'll see you in the morning, sir."

"Oh my gosh. What kind of a boss am I to forget my secretary's birthday, after all the years you have worked for me. I guess all this confusion lately has left me thoughtless. I'll make up for it, I promise. Now go home and have a good time with your date."

"You look ravishing as usual," Charles told her when Stephanie answered the door. "If you're ready, let's go. I made reservations for 8:30 at a nice place called Maria's near Portland. It's starting to snow so we don't know how the traffic will be."

They didn't talk about anything special most of the way. Traffic was slow as the snow showed signs of accumulating. He did mention that he was happy she was wearing the necklace he gave her the night before.

They arrived at Maria's in plenty of time. It was a lovely old colonial building on the outskirts of Portland. They were seated in a beautifully appointed, spacious dining room where tables were set with linen table cloths, fine china and sterling silver place settings. The service was very good, the food excellent, and they enjoyed a leisurely meal while soft dinner music played in the background. It was most romantic.

"How did you happen to find this place?" she asked. "I've never heard of it and it certainly isn't the type of place you'd go to every day. It's gorgeous in here and the food is outstanding. What a fabulous chef they must have."

"I don't remember how I happened to hear about it - it was quite awhile ago. This is the first time for me too. After all, it's not someplace you go to alone. I'd only come here with a special lady, and you're the only one who fits that description."

"There you go again, Charles, with the compliments. I don't know what to do when you talk like that. All I can say is thank you very much *and* I think you're pretty swell too."

"A penny for your thoughts Stephanie," he said to her when he saw her in a very pensive mood. "You look like you're a hundred miles away. What's that pretty head of yours thinking about? Me, I hope."

"I can't tell you," she slowly commented. "At least I don't want to. Not right now or here, anyway. I will in due time."

"Well, that sounds very mysterious. Maybe when we get home you can give me a clue or two."

The waiter, seeing they had finished their entree, approached them and asked if they would like coffee or dessert. Both of them decided they had had plenty and didn't care for anything else.

Charles picked up the check, looked at it and paid the waiter, leaving a generous tip in appreciation of the excellent service.

"Oh my goodness," she exclaimed when she got outside and saw how the snow had started to pile up. "I'm sure glad I wore my fur coat and boots. This is terrible. It's a good thing I'm not driving or we'd have to stay here for the night."

"This isn't so bad. I drive in this stuff all the time. You can get used to it and it's all in knowing how to handle your car."

By the time they reached town there were several inches on the ground and snow plows had already started doing their job.

"It's still early Stephanie. Since we will be passing by my place before we get to yours, let's stop at my house. I'll give you a tour and then we'll have a cup of coffee before I take you home. You can also interpret that mysterious look on your face for me."

"It sounds good to me," she said.

As they neared the house Stephanie mentioned that the Wilson's home was not very far from there. About that time Charles turned into the driveway and pulled the car into the garage. He helped her out of the car and then took her hand, leading her through a door that came out into what was a large family room.

"What made me think you had an apartment? This is a house and a big one, in a very nice section of town. Why do you have such a big place, and who takes care of it?" she asked.

"Aren't we full of questions tonight? It was the family home. My parents had it and when they died a few years ago it was left to me. I couldn't see selling it and going into an apartment - figured some day I might decide to get married." he told her. "Come on with me and I'll show you around." As they returned to the family room he asked her, "Do you like it? I personally think it is a terrific house. You were wondering why it's so clean. I have a lady who comes in once a week. She does an excellent job.

"By the way Stephanie. I have never heard you mention any family. Do any of them live near here? If it's none of my business just tell me."

"Oh no, it's no secret, or anything. I really don't know where or if anyone is still living. My father died when I was in grade school and my mother remarried when I was sixteen. I never liked the man she married. Then, in my senior year he molested me, but when I told my mother what he did she wouldn't believe me. As soon as school was over and I graduated, I took my savings - I had always worked summers and part-time while going to school and put my money in the bank - and left upstate New York, which was where I grew up. I went to Biddeford, Maine and found a job. I don't know why I chose Biddeford. I always had a fascination about the ocean and the thought of living in New England. I went to school nights while working days. When I finished school I moved here and went to work for Mr. Wilson.

"Even though I wrote to my mother several times to let her know where I was, and sent her birthday and Christmas cards, I never heard from her. I let her know when I moved here and tried to call her. Her husband always answered and said she wasn't home and hung up on me. I even invited her to my wedding when I married Peter but got no response. So I have no idea where she might be. I had an older brother with whom I was very close, but he was killed in an accident while he was in the service in Hawaii, of all places. He too did not approve of mother's new husband.

"At this point, I figure my mother knows where I am and has certainly read about the trial or seen it on TV. If that isn't enough to get her to contact me then nothing will."

"You poor darling. You've certainly had more than your share of unhappiness in your life. Well, I hope someday to change all that. Now let's change the subject. Tell me, what do you think of my house?

"It's a lovely home. I don't blame you for not wanting to give it up. But it is lacking something. Somehow when you see all this space you expect a bunch of kids to come running down the stairs, and toys all over the place."

"Thank you my pretty lady. That would be nice. Maybe in the near future it will happen. Oh dear, what a terrible host. Here you've been walking all over the house with your coat on. Give it to me and I'll hang it up," and he took it and put it in the hall closet.

"Now, beautiful. I want something from you," and he looked her straight in the face. "I think you know what it is. All this time I have been seeing you and wanting you, I have behaved like a perfect gentleman and didn't even give you a good kiss goodnight until recently. I was afraid I wouldn't be able to stop there."

Before she had a chance to respond, he reached out for her, took her by the hand and pulled her close to him, put his arms around her and gave her a big hug, at the same time giving her a long passionate kiss. At first she struggled but she soon succumbed to his attention, relaxing and cooperating completely.

"Don't try and say, 'this is so sudden'. I have wanted to do this since the first time I laid eyes on you when you were standing at the dessert table. Remember? You don't know how much I wanted you for my own, even back then. And, maybe this is a terrible thing to say, but I was actually happy to be able to arrest your husband, and prayed that there would finally be a chance for me to get to know you. I think someone up there likes me.

"I realize that was a selfish way of thinking and I know too much has happened in your life lately to expect you to feel as strongly about me. I am sure of my feelings but I want you to be 100% sure before you commit yourself. Do you realize what I am saying or do I sound confused? I love you so much it hurts and hope some day that you will express your love for me. There, I told you how I feel and I'm glad."

"Oh Charles, I don't know what to say. You are so sweet to me and I'm not used to such treatment. One part of me tells me I love you too, but the rest tells me not to hurry into anything and to be very sure I have truly found a man I can not only love, but trust implicitly. Can you understand that? In fact, that was what the mysterious look was all about - trying to figure out which part of me I should go with."

"Of course I understand Stephanie, and I'm betting that the half who loves me will be the winner - and soon I hope. That's the trouble. I understand but at the same time it's so frustrating. For so long, I have wanted to take you in my arms and never let you go. I don't know what I would do if I lost you now. I've waited so many years for just the right girl and I know you are the one who could make this house a home."

"Please Charles. Don't say anymore. I need more time to think. My life has been so mixed up and now, even though I'm feeling good about things, I have to be sure it will last."

"Stephanie, don't be shocked or hate me, but please let me make love to you. I'll be very gentle and you'll realize how much I really love and want you, and that I can make you happy forever. You'll never have an unhappy day with me. My love is forever.

What do you say? You'll never know how many times I've had to come home and masturbate, after an evening with you."

"Please don't, Charles. Not yet. I don't want to lose you but I don't think we should have sex yet. In fact, I don't want to," she told him, deep down wishing he would go ahead and undress her and make burning love to her. "I have never believed in sex before marriage and I'm certainly not going to start now."

"I understand my darling," and he didn't say anything more about it, respecting her wishes. About an hour later he looked out the window to discover the snow had stopped and the streets had been plowed, so he drove her home, this time putting his arm around her and giving her a tender goodnight kiss and, again telling her to take care of his pretty lady.

Chapter 59

Christmas Eve - Harry and Linda's wedding

When Charles greeted Stephanie at her door, he stared at the beautiful lady in front of him and asked her if she was trying to outshine the bride.

"Do you think this is the wrong dress to wear honey?" she asked, as he gazed once more at the form-fitting, pink sequined dress that emphasized her perfect figure. The hem line was just above the knees. It was a simple style with a slightly rounded neckline and long, fitted sleeves. She wore a diamond choker and dangling earrings. Her hair was arranged in a very smooth, sophisticated French twist with a diamond studded comb for decoration. "If you think I am overdoing it, I have another dress I could wear. We still have time for me to change."

"No, my darling. I can't explain how gorgeous you look. You are breathtaking but I'm sure all eyes will be on the bride tonight. Let's go."

When they got to their table, Stephanie introduced Charles to all the people at their table. Rose and her sister were there as were Carlos and his wife, Melanie, who was pregnant and due any day. Someone suggested they should have invited a doctor. Then Martha told them they could have Dennis's wife, Janet deliver the baby if she went into labor. Janet was a pediatric nurse and would know what to do. Martha and Greg were supposed to sit there too but at the last minute Greg was sent out of town so Martha was alone. Edward Swanson, from accounting, and his wife Anna made up what was to be the fifth couple. In all there were almost a hundred guests at the reception, which turned out to be bigger than planned.

"Don't you think Mr. Wilson has been looking tired lately?" Martha asked Stephanie. "I hope all this bad publicity hasn't been too much strain on him."

"Yes, I thought so too. But he told me it was just the late hours and so many parties leading up to Christmas. He told me I sounded like a mother hen telling him he should take it easy and get more sleep. In fact, he said I sounded like his wife."

The wedding party was ready to enter the reception room and, as the band started playing, 'Here Comes the Bride', everyone stood up and applauded while Linda and Harry were introduced as Mr. and Mrs. After everyone was seated the best man offered a toast to the new couple. About half way through the meal, the best man stood up again and told everyone he had an announcement to make.

"Ladies and gentlemen, Happy couples must be contagious in T.G.I. this year. I couldn't let the evening pass without recognizing another couple who have to be almost as happy as Harry and Linda, and I'll bet that before they are back from their honeymoon, these two will be announcing their engagement. Folks, I give you Lt. Charles Lanza and Stephanie Kaknas."

"I like that man." Charles whispered to Stephanie. "He knows when two people belong together."

"How about it Chuck? Am I right or not?"

"Well, if I had my way the answer would definitely be 'yes', but this gorgeous lady by my side is still playing hard-to-get. However, this day belongs to Linda and Harry so let's not talk about Stephanie and me for now."

Later, just as they were getting up to dance, Martha interrupted Charles and Stephanie to say, "OK you two. This seems to be the year for lovers and weddings in the company. Stephanie, you should know by now this handsome guy is nuts about you and, wearing that sexy, exquisite dress plus that fancy hairdo must be driving him crazy. So why don't you give up and say yes?"

"Martha, when you're ready to admit your true feelings about Greg and say 'yes' you'll marry him right away, then I'll answer your question," an angry Stephanie responded. "In the meantime Charles and I would like to dance while they are still playing our kind of music. Besides, I don't see your sergeant around here tonight - lovers' quarrel?" and she turned to Charles and practically dragged him to the dance floor.

"Whoa, the lovely lady has a temper. I love her even more when her eyes flash like that. Don't pay any attention to what she said, my love." and he held her tightly, giving her a tender kiss on the head as they danced.

"Don't get me wrong, Charles. I like Martha but there are times when she is just too exasperating, and thinks she has to make everything her business. I don't care to talk about it. I guess

I shouldn't have been quite so hard on her. She's used to being told off though. I knew Greg had been called out of town, so I'll apologize at the office."

After a few quiet minutes Harry cut in. "Mind if I dance with this nice lady?" and Charles let her go, saying he couldn't refuse the groom a dance with his girl. About half way through the number he said, "You look gorgeous tonight." Then he remarked, "OK Steph, when are you going to give in to Charles. Everyone can tell by the way he looks at you that he adores you. And I've certainly seen the difference in you lately - bright eyes, nice smile for everyone and happier than I've seen you in years. Don't tell me it doesn't mean love has conquered."

"Come on Harry. What's with everyone? You're all so anxious for us to get married. I just got rid of a good-for-nothing jerk. I don't intend to plunge into another marriage without giving it a lot of thought. Now, I don't want to hear anything more about Lt. Lanza and me. Case closed!" and she turned around, left the dance floor and went to the ladies room. When she finally felt she had cooled down and didn't show her anger, she returned to her table. She sat there alone trembling with anger. Thank goodness everyone else was dancing so they didn't see her. She then ordered a Vodka Gibson and drank it fast, almost choking over it. As she was just finishing a second one, Charles returned to the table.

"What are you drinking, Stephanie? I didn't realize you ever had anything but wine."

"Well, when the occasion demands it, I go for the hard stuff, sir." she commented, glassy-eyed and rather impatiently. Since she wasn't a drinker, the liquor went to her head fast. She apologized for being so sharp and said she wished people would not try to plan her life for her. "Am I being too touchy Charles? I don't mean to be - really my dear, I don't," and her voice sounded a little slurred.

"Oh, Oh, I think my pretty lady has had too much to drink. Maybe a cup of black coffee and some dessert will help you," and he proceeded to watch her slowly drink a large cup of coffee with no argument. "I don't think you are being touchy honey, but I do think everyone cares about your future after what has happened. They just want you to be happy, the same as I do. Don't be too hard on them."

"I'm sorry officer. You're probably right," she answered with tears in her eyes. It seemed that quite often when she would get in a melancholy or sad mood she referred to him as officer or sir instead of by his name, and he had learned to recognize those times.

At that point he didn't comment any further, knowing that if he said anything to her in her partially intoxicated state, she would probably start crying. Instead he made sure she had some more coffee and a small piece of wedding cake and soon she was starting to get back to her old self.

"Charles, I think I should apologize to Harry for walking off the dance floor the way I did," and she proceeded to find him. "Harry, I wish to apologize for behaving so badly. That was a terrible thing for me to do."

"Don't worry about it Steph," he told her. "I understand, but you didn't give me a chance to tell you how truly ravishing you look tonight. You must be driving Charles crazy with your glamorous look. Linda was also remarking about what a beautiful woman you are. Now, that should sure boost your ego, having another woman compliment you like that."

As soon as the next number finished it was time for the bride to throw her bouquet. Everyone urged Stephanie to join the single ladies. Much as she really didn't want to she felt she should be a good sport so she joined the others. Where did it land? Right in Stephanie's arms, of course. She said she thought it had been a conspiracy and it was meant that she should catch it, even though she felt it should have gone to Martha.

Chapter 60

Christmas Day

After exchanging gifts with each other, at which time Charles gave Stephanie a pair of beautiful diamond and emerald earrings, in addition to a bottle of her favorite perfume. She presented him with 18 karat gold cuff links with his initials engraved on them and two lovely wool, winter sweaters.

Charles and Stephanie left early for the drive to North Conway for skiing. The snow was powdery and perfect for skiing, and the weather wasn't too cold. It didn't take Stephanie long to get used to the skis and in no time it was as though she had never been away from it. They had a fantastic day together, skiing the slopes, and then rolling and laughing in the snow and throwing snowballs at each other. Stephanie couldn't remember the last time she had such a relaxed time and she completely forgot the bad memories of the past few months. Her only thoughts were of how wonderful it was to be with Charles. She always felt so relaxed and he was so easy to talk to. She went to bed that night dreaming of what a terrific time she had with him. She asked herself if she had really fallen in love with him. It just wasn't normal to enjoy someone's company so much without it being love.

After Charles took Stephanie home, he returned home feeling that Stephanie was getting to care more and more for him. He thought how wonderful it would be if he could win her over by the new year. Many times he felt embarrassed when he'd have an erection just seeing her and thinking about having sex with her.

Since he had to work most evenings, they only had a couple of short dates the week between Christmas and New Years. One evening they did manage to go to the Wilson's where they had an enjoyable visit. Marge gave Stephanie a beautiful gold lapel pin that would look good on any one of her stylish suits. Later Marge managed to get Stephanie aside in the kitchen and asked her how things were going. Stephanie told her everything was wonderful and she was very happy.

"Tell me if it's none of my business dear, but you look so beautiful and happy these days. Ben and I both care you know. It must be love the way you have been. I've noticed that beautiful necklace you wear constantly, with the hearts on it. That must mean something. Do you think Charles may pop the question sometime soon? Ben says he wishes you two would hurry up and get married, so he can relax. The suspense is getting to be too much for him. and he is looking forward to giving you away, in case you're interested."

"If you promise not to tell a soul, I really feel I do truly love him. He is such a wonderful, gentle person. I know when a day passes and he doesn't call me, I wonder why and I'm miserable. If he had his way we would have been married long ago. It has all been my fault due to my uncertainty. But I guess I will say yes when and if he asks me. Between you and me, he told me he wants me to be 100% sure of my love for him before I tell him I love him. Only then will he ask me to marry him," she admitted. "But remember, it is our secret."

Marge gave her a kiss, told her how happy she was for her, and that she wanted to be the first to know when she accepted Charles' proposal.

Since they both had to work the next day they didn't want to stay too long, so they said goodnight to the Wilson's and thanked them for a lovely evening. Mr. Wilson gave Stephanie a beautiful belated birthday card with a check for $500 and a note of apology for forgetting her birthday. "Buy yourself something nice," the note said. On the way home Charles told Stephanie he had something special planned for New Year's Eve, unless she had someplace in particular she wanted to go. She told him whatever he had in mind was fine with her.

The week was spoiled however, when Stephanie received a phone call early the following morning at work. It was Angie. "Oh, Stephanie," she sobbed. "My dad had a heart attack last night shortly after you left, and was flown to New England Medical Center in Boston. Mother went with him. They are doing by-pass surgery this morning, They tried Angioplasty but it didn't work. I'm so worried because he's had so much on his mind the past few months."

"Take it easy Angie. I'm sure he will come out of it OK. I'll have to admit he has looked very tired lately and wasn't his chipper self when we were at his house last night. He's a very healthy man though, otherwise, so I'm sure he will be fine. Is there anything Charles or I can do for you? If you want to go to Boston for a day or two I can take some leave and look after the kids. I wouldn't mind it at all. It is a quiet period at work."

"No, I wouldn't ask you to do that. Besides Michael and Jennifer are still here and would help me if I needed it. I couldn't do anything down there anyway. Mom will keep us informed, but I knew you would want to know about it. The doctors seem to think he will be OK but will probably have to cut down drastically on his work schedule. Mom has pleaded with him lately to turn the business over to the younger men, but you know my dad. Maybe this will get him to do it."

"Yes, I sure do know how he is, and much as I would miss him, he should step down. Well Angie, keep us informed. If I'm not at my own house I will be at Charles' place," and she gave Angie his number. "Take it easy. We'll all say a prayer for him. I'll call the hospital sometime later this afternoon when he's had a chance to be out of recovery and find out whatever I can. As soon as he comes home we will be over to visit him. When you talk to your mother be sure to tell her we asked about him and we will keep in touch. In the meantime, take it easy."

Chapter 61

New Year's Eve

Lt. Lanza had invited Stephanie to his house for dinner instead of their going out. It had been snowing again and the streets were slippery, so he decided to have a nice, quiet dinner - catered - and then they could sit by the fireplace afterwards and chat, and he could tell her about his promotion. They would wait and watch the New Year come in at Times Square. Then he planned to have her spend the night and he would take her home the next morning. He just hoped she would agree to what he had in mind for them.

"For gosh sakes Stephanie," Charles commented, after a delicious dinner, as they were sharing the big couch in front of the fireplace. She was sitting at one end and he was lying with his head in her lap. "With all that has happened this evening, I forgot to tell you what I was going to tell you at dinner. In fact, dinner was to be sort of a celebration. You can no longer call me lieutenant. I just made Captain which means more money and a bigger office. How about that?"

"Fantastic! Congratulations Captain Lanza. That does have a nicer ring. It couldn't have happened to a nicer man. I really mean that Charles," and she bent over and gave him a big kiss. "Hmmm, I was just thinking, the way we're sitting here one would think we were an old married couple," and she laughed. Then, realizing what he had said earlier, she added, "As for my staying here; I didn't plan on staying so I don't have anything else to wear or any toilet articles."

"That is a nice thought honey - our being an old married couple. But, about staying here - no problem. When my sister visits with her family - they come up here for a couple of weeks each summer - they always leave stuff in her old room. I'm sure you'll find something there, and the connecting bath has plenty of supplies. She is a little shorter than you but at least you won't have to wear your good dress. By the way, did I tell you you looked exquisite tonight, as usual.? OK, gorgeous, let's go up and I'll show you her room."

"What a beautiful, big room this is. If this is your sister's room, the master bedroom must be tremendous. If I'm not being too inquisitive, what business was your dad in? He must have been very successful to have such a lovely home."

"He was a very successful lawyer with a firm that had offices in New York, Boston and Portland. He did OK and always loved Maine so he did most of his work out of Portland. As a matter of fact, he was hoping I would study law and I think he was disappointed when I chose the police force, but we always got along together and he respected my choice."

"And look at this bathroom; it's bigger than some bedrooms." Stephanie hadn't noticed that the bathroom was located between two bedrooms.

They returned to the living room and during the evening they talked about Mr. Wilson. Stephanie was so happy that he had come through the operation so well and would only be hospitalized for a few days. After he came home he was to have complete rest. Marge would see to that. She hired a practical nurse to be there most of the day. No one would expect him back in the office for awhile and then definitely not full time. Stephanie wasn't sure what effect that would have as far as her job was concerned. She and Charles already decided that as soon as he was home a couple of days they would plan to stop in and see him. He would be pleased to see them together and looking so happy.

As the New Year was about to ring in, Charles stood up, held his arms out to Stephanie and said, "Stand up pretty lady." As she did he gave her a big hug and a kiss. "Happy New Year my dearest. The best of everything for both of us for the coming year. I love you with all my heart." She also wished him the best for the new year.

It was almost 1 A.M. when they finally decided they should go to bed. Except for talking about Mr. Wilson, they hadn't really discussed anything important and at times just sat quietly, holding hands and listening to soft music on the CD. As she was about to enter the bedroom she was to use, she noticed Charles entering the next room down the hall. He said he wanted to be close by in case she needed anything. He had never brought up the subject of sex again since that one night, and she was happy he respected her feelings.

Stephanie reluctantly checked the drawers and closet (she hated looking into other people's dresser drawers) until she found some shorty nightgowns and picked out a pretty pink one. His sister had good taste in clothes she thought. There was also a long, warm robe in the closet which she placed on the chair next to the bed, in case she found a need for it. She brushed her teeth with a new brush she found, still in the original wrapper, took a shower and went to bed. As she lay there she thought about how wonderful Charles was and what a perfectly marvelous Christmas season she had had with him. She told herself she was a darn fool for not letting him know how much she cared for him. Not once had she allowed herself to mention she <u>loved</u> him, even though she thought she might. He had expressed his great love for her in many ways and he was so gentle and sweet. "Listen to yourself dummy," she whispered to herself. "You know darn well it's love. Admit it." She lay there in deep thought for a few minutes. Then suddenly she sat up and announced out loud to herself. "I do. I do. Darn it, I do love Charles. Why have I been so stupid? He's one in a million. No, he's one of a kind." She then smiled to herself, pleased with her sudden awakening, and she lay down and closed her eyes, about to go to sleep. Her voice was so loud it had carried through into Charles' room and he came running through the bathroom into her room.

"Is something wrong honey? I could hear your voice all the way into my room, but I couldn't understand what you were saying. Are you sure you're OK."

"I'm fine Charles. I guess I was talking in my sleep." Then, with a quizzical look on her face, she said, "I didn't realize these two rooms were connected by the bathroom. You could have come in here anytime you wanted."

"That's right, but you know I wouldn't have unless you called me. Goodnight honey," and he kissed her on the forehead and returned to his room.

The following morning he slipped on his robe and went to her room. "Hey sleepy head. It's time to get up. If we're going to have breakfast together before I have to leave for work you'd better get up. Did you sleep well?" he asked as he sat on the side of the bed, looking at her. "Do you realize you are just as beautiful when you first awaken?"

"I had a wonderful night - slept like a log. It's a very comfortable bed. If you will allow me to get out of bed, I'll get dressed. But first, as long as you are sitting there I could use a good morning kiss." and she sat up and threw her arms around him, forgetting, at the moment, about the flimsy nightgown she was wearing.

"Well, that can certainly be arranged," he told her as they were about to indulge in a very passionate kiss, at the same time thinking there had been quite a change in her behavior over night concerning him, and it didn't seem to bother her that she was sitting close to him with very little on. He slipped out of the bathrobe he had on, and put his arms around her, getting a thrill out of feeling her skin through the thin nightgown. "I know I've said this many times, and I hope you never tire hearing me say it, but I love you very much." and he gave her a long, burning kiss.

"Oh Charles, my darling. I've been such a fool. I love you too and should have realized it long ago. Don't ever let me go," and she hugged him tightly.

"Are you sure you mean it sweetheart? You know nothing would make me happier, but I want you to be certain in your own heart when you tell me. I couldn't stand to have you change your mind now."

"I do, my darling, I do. I've never been surer of anything in my life. I just don't know why I was so stupid and was fighting it so long unless, unconsciously, I was thinking of all the abuse I went through."

"My precious, you know you will never have another day of abuse as long as you are with me. I won't let anyone hurt you. Since you are so sure of your love," he tossed the bathrobe aside and knelt down on one knee in front of her, with only his shorts on. "Stephanie Kaknas, will you marry me?"

She stared at the tall, muscular man in front of her, his handsome face sending shivers down her spine. Then, with a coy look on her face, she informed him, "No," leaving him with a terrified look on his face. "Stephanie Kaknas won't, but Stephanie Christeas certainly will." Then she looked at him and said, "Do you know you look silly there on your knee and only a pair of shorts on? Boy, when our kids ask us how you popped the question, the answer should be interesting." She then got serious, looked him straight in the face and said, "I'd love to marry you Charles Michael Lanza, any time you say."

"Oh my God girl, you nearly scared me to death. Don't ever do that to me again." As he got up and sat next to her he said, "I'm trying to be very serious and you come up with something like that. By the way, when did you get your maiden name back?

I like it much better, but I'll like it even more when you are Mrs. Charles Lanza. And how did you know what my middle name was?"

"I have my ways of finding things out too. As soon as my divorce was final, I not only requested and got my own name back, through the court, but I talked to my priest and he is going to see that the marriage is annulled. Under the circumstances he said there should be no problem getting an annulment so we can be married in the church. When all that happens I feel I will be starting a new and better life. Isn't it wonderful?"

"And you have been keeping all that a secret? Well, one other question I have to ask you Stephanie. Do you have any compunctions about marrying a police officer. Many girls do and, as a result, the marriage doesn't always last long because the wife can't take the hours and stress of worrying when her husband goes out on a call. I want ours to be an exception."

"It will be, my darling. We'll prove to the others it can be done. Sure I'll worry. If I didn't, I wouldn't love you. But then either one of us could be walking across the street and get hit by a car and killed. When your time comes there's nothing you can do about it."

"I'm glad you have that attitude. Stephanie, my life, I didn't think it was possible for me to be so happy. Your acceptance has thrilled me no end. You excite me so much sitting there with just that little nightgown on. Please allow me to make love to you this morning to show you how much I love you. I know I told you I wouldn't bring up the subject again. I will be very gentle."

"No Charles," she exclaimed, as she grabbed the robe and put it on quickly. "I'm sorry, but as much as I'm anxious for us to make love, I always promised myself I would never have sex with anyone until I was married. I didn't do it before and I certainly am not going to weaken this time. I love you too much; and I feel it cheapens both parties to do that. Please respect my feelings by waiting until our wedding night. If you love me as you say you do, you will also be willing to wait. I shouldn't have chosen this flimsy nightgown, just in case you did come in here. So I guess it's partly my fault. You don't love me any less do you?"

"OK sweetheart. I'm not crazy. Of course I still love you. I shouldn't have been so selfish as to ask. I will go back to my room now so we can both get dressed and ready for breakfast," and he reached over and kissed her. "See you in a little while darling."

When they were about half way through breakfast Charles excused himself for a minute. When he returned he told her to close her eyes and give him her left hand. He slipped a ring on her finger then told her to open her eyes.

Her eyes went wide open, as did her mouth. "Well my darling, say something. Do you like it?"

"I'm crazy about it. It's gorgeous. What did you do, rob a bank for it? You must have spent a year's pay on it. Oh honey, it is just too much." She held out her hand and admired the huge emerald-cut diamond. Then glancing over at him she said, "Hey, you must have been very sure I was going to say yes to your proposal."

"I bought that ring more than three months ago, shortly after I first saw you. It's all I ever thought about - the time I could put it on your finger. So, I guess I can assume you're pleased. I'm glad you like it. I was lucky it's the right size too. That was the hard part." He then asked her how soon they could plan on getting married and where.

She told him they could start to make plans right away, that she was sure the annulment would be final very soon. However, she would like to be married in her church, St. Demetrius Greek Orthodox Church in Biddeford.

"That's no problem," he told her. "In fact, I always felt a family should worship together so I'm willing to convert and become Greek Orthodox. My mother was Orthodox but converted for my dad."

"Thank you very much. I'll have to arrange for us to talk to the priest so we can see what we have to do, and to set the date. I'd like to be married on Valentine's Day, if possible. I hope Mr. Wilson has recovered enough by then and is able to be there. He wants to give me away. His wife told me when we were there the night before he got sick"

"I guess Mr. Wilson knew what was good for you before you realized it," he told her. Then he said, "I'm sure that as long as he doesn't run into any complications he will be able to do it by then. And that sounds like a good date. If I'm not mistaken, Valentine's Day is on Sunday this year, which would work out just fine. Honey, I can hardly wait. Time is going to go by so slowly. At last the house is once more going to see activity, with happy people in it. Do you plan to sell your house? I'm assuming we will be living here."

"Of course we will live here sweetheart. As far as my house is concerned, at one time I thought I might keep it and rent it for extra income. But I changed my mind. We don't need the aggravation of being a landlord, so I'll see an agent right away about putting it up for sale. Besides, there are too many bad memories that go with it. What do you think Charles? It is a nice house so it should sell pretty fast if I ask for a reasonable amount. I don't know what I will do with most of the furniture, but we have time to worry about that."

"I agree with you. We don't need it. Now Stephanie, I need to ask you a very personal and maybe touchy question," he told her with a very serious sound to his voice. "We haven't discussed this but are you able to have children? We aren't exactly kids you know and I've wondered why you didn't have any. Do you like children?"

"Of course; I love children. Peter never cared one way or another so I made my career come first and figured children could come later and maybe he'd want them by then. I was on the pill for many years and, considering how things turned out, I'm glad I was. I gave them up well over a year ago when he lost interest in me, except to use me as a punching bag. But I'd give up my job any day, if necessary, in order to have children. I am still considered of childbearing age but not for many more years. You did ask me because you want them too, didn't you?"

"I sure did ask for that reason and we are certainly going to enjoy trying to have them. I'm sure that, as much as we love each other, we shouldn't have any trouble producing some beautiful kids. You know, pretty lady, I've decided we were definitely meant for each other all along. We have so much in common. Why did it have to take so long for us to meet? Someone up there wanted us to eventually get together and I thank whoever it was. I just wish they had arranged for it sooner."

"Maybe they felt we'd appreciate each other more that way," Stephanie suggested.

"Gosh, look at the time. I've got to get you home so I can get to work." Then, all of a sudden he said, "I'm going to ask Greg to be my best man if that's OK with you. I'll be seeing him later today."

"That's fine with me. I thought I would ask Martha to be my Matron of Honor. Who knows, we might give them ideas? Well, not Greg. He's just waiting for her to say the right word, I think, and they would get married. We'd better get going, honey. I don't want you to be late for work."

As soon as she got home, Stephanie went to the phone and immediately called Angie to give her the good news. She told her when she talks to her mother it was OK to tell her, and then tell her dad he'd better hurry and get well so he can give away a bride on Valentine's Day. He will know what you mean and I'm sure that will raise his spirits.

Angie told her her dad was already in real good spirits and has been complaining because they won't let him go home for a couple of days yet. "He is always asking about you and Charles," she said. "I'm sure he will be very pleased with the news, but not too surprised. If I know him, his comment will probably be, 'It's about time'."

Chapter 62

It was mid January and very few customers were in the "Place to Meet" cafe across from the plaza near T.G.I., when Martha and Greg walked in about 11 o'clock in the morning. It had snowed again the night before and some streets were not too well plowed. Greg and Martha hadn't seen each other in almost three weeks, she having been away for two weeks, since the day after Christmas, and before she returned he had to fly to Washington, D.C. Most people had recovered from the holidays and it was business as usual. However, they were meeting for lunch to catch up with the events of the past three weeks. Greg had to be at work at 4 o'clock or they would have waited until evening and gone someplace special.

Martha had been in Nebraska visiting her sister and family. She had been asked many times to spend the holidays there, so this year, since Greg had to work, she decided to make the trip out west. Before her return Greg had to leave for ten days. He was quite perturbed over the fact he had missed out on most of the holiday season.

"Welcome home Martha." he said as soon as he saw her. "It's nice to see you again. I missed you," and he gave her a hug and a kiss. "How was your trip and the visit with your family? They must have been happy to see you."

"Welcome home yourself, Sarge. It's nice to be back. The family was disappointed that I wasn't able to make it for Christmas Day but when I explained that I had to attend the wedding of a co-worker, they understood and we all had a great time. My brother's wife is a fantastic cook and it seems we were eating constantly. But it was fun; a real Christmas atmosphere with a big tree and the house decorated. Their four children are such a delight - good kids and were fun to be with. But it's always nice to come back home. So," she said, "I guess there's been plenty happening around here the past few weeks."

About that time the waitress came to take their orders at which time Martha just ordered a salad with vinegar and oil dressing, and a diet coke.

She noticed a strange look on Greg's face and said, "Sorry, but I have to get rid of the holiday pounds."

"If you say so my dear, although I don't notice any difference. You look just as good to me," he kidded. "Now for the good stuff. I guess you know my boss just made Captain. But the biggest surprise was getting engaged. I didn't realize he and Stephanie were that serious. Well, actually I knew he was very serious. It just took awhile for Stephanie to realize she loved him too. I'm real happy for both of them. I haven't had a chance to talk too much with Chuck. In fact, you probably know more about their wedding plans than I do, since you've been back longer than I have."

"Yes, I had dinner at Stephanie's house one night when Charles had to work, and she filled me in on everything. It's all so romantic. I think I'm a little jealous of her. Anyway, they became engaged New Year's Day and if you haven't seen the rock he gave her as an engagement ring, you should. Just be sure you're wearing sunglasses. It is fabulous. She also has asked me to be her Matron of Honor, which thrilled me to pieces. I understand you're going to be the Best Man. They are hoping for Valentine's Day for the wedding.

"So what happened with Peter? I hope they gave him the maximum possible sentence. I haven't bothered to try and catch up with all the news since I got back and I certainly wasn't going to ask Stephanie about it. How are the Wilson's doing after all the bad publicity they were involved in?"

"Well, three days after Christmas the verdict was returned for second degree murder. Guess he convinced them he didn't intend to kill Marcos. When he hit him it just happened his head hit the base of the light standard and killed him. But he didn't have to rob him too." Then he told her, "He was given a 15-20 year sentence with a chance for parole in 12 years. As far as I'm concerned he got off pretty easy. He should have had some additional time for abusing his wife so much, but she had never brought him up on charges of abuse. She was afraid to at the time, but I'll bet had she known he was guilty of murder she would have done it. Stephanie is very concerned about when he gets out, that he may come after her. Maybe by that time he will forget about wanting to hurt her. I'm sure Charles will take good care of her and make sure no harm comes to her.

"Have you heard how things are with the Wilson's?" he asked. "I heard he had a heart attack but I haven't been able to find out how he is. They are really a nice couple. One would never think they were well-to-do; they are so down-to-earth. I suppose you heard that Harry, the groom, was appointed head of your accounting office. That surely must have guaranteed him a good raise. I understand the Wilson's gave them a very nice wedding present. Sorry I wasn't able to make the wedding."

"Yes, I know about that." Martha told him. "Stephanie always did say she can't imagine working for anyone else. His wife likes her a lot and has invited her to their home several times.

"I had called Steph a few nights ago since I never had a chance to go to her office - this was before I went to her house for dinner - but I stayed away from the subject of Peter. We didn't talk much about Harry's wedding either. I think she was mad at me, and others, at the reception because everyone was bugging her about when she and Charles were going to get married. When I talked with her the other night her main concern was how Mr. Wilson was getting along; in addition to her wedding plans. He is home now and doing very well. She also told me Steve has straightened out remarkably. That rehab hospital did wonders for him, but the fact he was anxious to get well and cooperated all the way, helped too. He is certainly a different person at work - polite, cooperative and very pleasant to everyone. Laura decided to drop the divorce action and he is living at home once more. He gave Laura a gorgeous diamond and gold necklace and is bending over backwards to make up for the way he was before. They just left for two weeks to Aruba on a second honeymoon. I think that's wonderful and I'm so happy for them. Of course Grandma Wilson is taking care of the kids; as if she doesn't have enough to do with her husband still recovering.

"Angie is the one I feel bad for. Even though Alex embezzled all that money and was cheating on her, she was actually willing to forgive him and take him back. She and the kids took his death pretty hard. It was decided his death was an accident due to drunk driving even though the insurance company tried to say it was suicide; probably because it was a big policy. The holidays were especially hard for her. She has been working part-time - mother's hours - at the plant but she wants to get something different - something in the journalism field, I understand.

"They found the bonds that Alex said he was going to sign and turn over to her dad to help pay him back. I understand his life insurance policy was a quarter of a million dollars, which he had taken out many years ago. He wanted to make sure his family would be well taken care of in the event of his death. Angie wants part of the money to go to the company, but if they were bonded I would think that would take care of some of it anyway. I don't really know just how that works.

"So now that we have brought each other up-to-date on both the good and bad stuff around here, I'm sorry you had to miss the wedding Christmas Eve. It was very nice."

"I'm not trying to knock Harry and Linda's wedding," Greg told her. "But when Steph and Chuck get married it will not only be a big one but the ceremony will be beautiful - long and very impressive. There is nothing like a Greek Orthodox wedding. Charles told me they were hoping for Valentine's Day and he wants me to be his best man. That's great, that we will be standing up for them. By the way, did Harry say where they were going on their honeymoon?"

"They went to Hawaii where they planned on cruising around the different islands. I think they planned to be gone three weeks, so they should be back at work any day.

"Another thing I forgot to tell you," she added. "As soon as Stephanie's divorce was final she went through the court to get her maiden name back and she is having her marriage annulled. I'm not sure what her maiden name is but I'm almost sure it is a Greek name, since her dad was Greek. Her mother was of Spanish and Dutch decent."

Yes, I know about that," he told her. "As a matter of fact Stephanie is already using her maiden name. You guys may now refer to her as Miss Christeas. I guess she forgot to tell you when you were talking to her. It's strange that I should be telling you so much news about people with whom you work. Charles told me some of this stuff.

"So, my friend," he said, "Now that we are up-to-date on all the T.G.I. problems, what are we going to do today? We don't want to waste it but it's too cold to do much outside, unless you ski or ice skate, and I'm not much good at either."

"No, neither am I," she told him. "I've never been much for winter sports. Were you very busy after I left on my trip?"

"At first it was rather quiet. I guess even the criminals decided to take a holiday! Even New Year's Eve wasn't as bad as it has been at times. Some guy beat up on his estranged wife and her boy friend, but they'll be OK. I guess the guy decided if he couldn't have his wife he didn't want anyone else to have her either. Some people nearby heard the commotion and broke it up before anyone got seriously hurt. But we get that kind of stuff all the time. Then they sent me to Washington, D.C. on a special assignment. I get stuck with things like that every so often, and I hate those trips. I'd much rather stay home and just get involved in normal police duty.

"But now back to us. What are we going to do to celebrate being home again?" Before Martha could answer him he had a message on his beeper to call in.

"Let me make this call and see what's going on. Then we'll decide what we're going to do. I hate these interruptions."

When Greg got through talking he didn't have a very happy look on his face. "Damn it honey. Looks like the big boss at the precinct has decided for us, what we are going to be doing - for the next two weeks, in fact. I have to report back to the station. Seems they need some officers who speak Greek to go to Athens. There's some problem at the embassy with some Americans who got in trouble. The Greek government has turned them over to the Consulate and we have to go bring them back to the States. I've been on these crazy assignments before but not for quite awhile. If it were at all possible I'd take you with me and we could see the country, but there wouldn't be a chance for that on a trip like this. I guess I won't see you for a couple of weeks. We'll make up for it, I promise."

Martha was suddenly speechless and didn't really feel like finishing her lunch. As they were leaving the cafe she asked, "How soon do you have to leave? Aren't we ever going to have any time together any more? This is why I hesitate accepting your proposal. I hate these damn trips you're always going on. You will be back for the wedding won't you?"

"Oh, I've already told the boss I have to have leave on that weekend. But I'm afraid we won't have any time now, honey. As soon as I can pack, the chief's sending a car to take me to Logan Airport to catch my flight. Everything is already arranged. I'm afraid I'll have to say so long right here.

They embraced for a few seconds and gave each other a kiss.

"Take care of yourself Sarge. I'm going to miss you a bunch. Don't take any wooden Drachmas," she told him, with a forced smile on her face.

"I won't. And you take care of my best girl; and stay away from cops. I'll miss you too. So long and give some serious thought about my proposal. I do love you. Things will change soon if I have my way." he said as he got in his car and left.

As Martha slowly returned to her office all she could think of was, "Gosh I'm going to miss him. Wonder if I'll ever see him again. With my luck he will probably find some cute little Greek girl and forget about me. Oh well, back to work."

Chapter 63

February 14th had finally arrived - the day of the big wedding. Of all the weddings among employees at T.G.I. that had taken place this past year, Stephanie and Charles' was the one everyone looked forward to the most. They all thought so highly of Stephanie and felt so bad about what had happened to her, they were thrilled when she found someone who was so much in love with her and would treat her like she deserved to be.

Mrs. Wilson had insisted on helping with the plans. With Ben recovering from his surgery, it wasn't easy, but he had insisted they do it and Marge had a practical nurse in each day to help Ben. Then she hired Olga to arrange for the reception, realizing it was rather short notice, but it didn't seem to bother Olga and her staff. Marge was aware of Stephanie's unhappy childhood, following her father's death. She liked Stephanie very much and treated her almost like another daughter. As their wedding gift to Stephanie and Charles, she and Ben arranged and paid for the reception.

Charles' younger sister and her family flew in from Colorado for the wedding. It was a surprise to them as she originally didn't think they would make it. At the last minute she had called to let him know they would be there but wouldn't be able to stay very long because the children would have to get back for school.

"What do you think of my bride-to-be, Sis?" Charles asked Kristen. "Don't you think she is wonderful? I didn't dream I would finally find anyone I could love so much."

"She is lovely, Chuck. I'm very happy for you. I was talking to her and she is a very nice person. She's not only beautiful but intelligent and I can tell she loves you very much. You are very lucky and we wish you all the happiness in the world, don't we Larry?" Before her normally quiet husband had much of a chance to respond, she said to her brother, "You are planning to have a family I hope."

"Oh definitely. We have hopes for a big family. In fact she mentioned that my house needed a houseful of kids to make it a home. Kristen, I never thought it was possible to be so happy. In fact, I'd just about given up ever getting married. I'm so glad you could come to the wedding and that you approve of her. Don't you think mom and dad would have loved her too."

"They would have adored her. Dad would be so proud that you picked the right girl. From what you told me about what has happened to her recently, in addition to her unhappy childhood, I can't imagine how any man would want to treat her so badly. He really must have been a monster. But, if you stop and think about it, if he hadn't abused her and then murdered that man, then you wouldn't have found her; if that makes any sense."

"I guess that's one way of looking at it, Sis, but it sure broke my heart when I saw her with her beautiful face bruised all over. But everything is wonderful now and always will be. Well, Kristen, it's time to get to the church. I haven't seen Stephanie today because it's supposed to be bad luck. She and Martha and the rest of the girls are at Martha's place. Steph didn't want to leave from her house, so Martha suggested her place. It's too bad we didn't know for sure you were coming so you could also be part of the wedding party."

"No problem. I'm just happy we were able to come. At least we included Tina in the wedding party as a flower girl. She was thrilled to death and told me she thought Uncle Charles was very lucky because Aunt Stephanie was the most beautiful lady she ever saw; except for me. You can't argue with a 6 year old."

"OK big brother. Let's get going. Your bride awaits you."

Chapter 64

Meanwhile, back in a small town in upstate New York, a middle-aged lady was sitting in her living room all alone, watching national news.

"Now ladies and gentlemen, we present our weekly human interest story. In a little town in Maine a modern love story has evolved. A young police officer has won his Cinderella. It seems a few months ago he had seen the girl of his dreams, a lovely lady, who, unfortunately was already married. However, her husband was soon involved in a murder, found guilty of murdering a man who worked in the same company as the lovely lady, in addition to being guilty of wife abuse. One thing lead to another and, after many rough hurdles the lovely lady and the handsome investigating officer will be married today in Biddeford, Maine."

The cameras then scanned the crowd waiting to go into the church. A reporter asked a young girl (just happened to be Kim) why she was so thrilled about this wedding, and why she thought it was a prince and princess type story.

"Stephanie is so beautiful and had a husband who constantly beat her up. When the officer was assigned to investigate the beatings and the murder, he instantly fell in love with her but she was afraid to get involved with another man. All her friends and her boss finally convinced her the young man was honest and really loved her."

"Is there anything else you can tell us about the young lady?"

"I know that deep down she wished her mother could have been here. She has tried for many years to contact her but she never answers her letters or cards, she figures she is either happy with her step-father and can't be bothered with her or she has passed away and her daughter has never been notified. I am so happy for Stephanie and Charles today," and then she stopped and said, "Look, here comes the limo." As Stephanie stepped out, Kim said to the reporter, "Isn't she beautiful? I have to go now."

"Yes, she certainly is a lovely bride. A wonderful love story come true. And now back to the studio."

"Yes indeed. It is a truly lovely story. It pleases us to be able to air happy stories rather than riots and murders. Many happy years, Stephanie and Charles. And that is our news for tonight."

"Oh Stephanie, my baby. Had I only known. All these years I have wondered where you were and if you were happy. I was so wrong about you and what you told me about Wayne. If only I could get out of this marriage, but he has threatened to kill me if I try to leave him," the lady sobbed. "If only I could find a way to contact you, I will."

Chapter 65

The Wedding

Stephanie looked ravishing as she nervously followed her four attendants and flower girl down the aisle to the music of Lohengrin's Wedding March. Her beautiful size 6, Yolanda wedding gown fit her 5 foot 8 inch frame perfectly. She carried a bouquet of white roses and stephanotis, with one single red rose bud in the middle and ice blue streamers. Martha, her matron of honor and Angie, Laura and Vickie, the bridesmaids, all wore ice blue satin cocktail length dresses that matched the streamers on the bridal bouquet. They carried sprays of red rose buds. Tina looked adorable in a long yellow dress with short puffy, lace-trimmed sleeves and a picture hat. She had a big smile for everyone as she slowly walked down the aisle scattering red rose petals along the way.

There wasn't a dry eye in the place as the beautiful bride slowly approached the altar on the arm of a very proud looking Ben Wilson. Charles was wiping tears from his eyes as he watched his pretty lady who would soon be his wife. He looked very handsome in a powder blue tuxedo, standing straight and proud; appearing even taller than his 6 foot 3 inches. His wish had finally come true and in a few minutes his pretty lady would be Mrs. Charles Lanza.

When they arrived at the altar Mr. Wilson lifted Stephanie's veil, smiled at her and gave her a tender kiss on the cheek, (she had tears of joy on them) wishing her and Charles a long, happy life. He then took a seat next to his wife who had been watching him every step of the way, showing concern that he might be overdoing it.

As usual the wedding ceremony was very long but impressive, and anyone who had never attended a Greek wedding thought it was magnificent. The crowns the bride and groom had chosen were gorgeous and, the music they had selected for the soloist was most inspiring. Everyone raved about what a lovely ceremony it was. Both video and still cameras recorded every precious moment.

As soon as the limousines carrying the wedding party arrived at the reception, the photographers were waiting for the happy couple and their attendants. One hundred eighty guests attended the especially bedecked reception hall, where Rose's sister Olga did her usual excellent job in catering and decorating - which included the usual Greek pastries (Kourenbiethes, et al). The band did an outstanding job as they played both Greek and American music equally well, getting raves from many guests.

Greg made a very impressive best man and was honored that Charles asked him to take on the role. At the same time he couldn't take his eyes off Martha. He always felt she was an attractive woman and he thought very highly of her, but today she was extremely lovely he thought. Her usual manner of dress was very conservative, to the point of looking matronly. However, the gown she was wearing at the wedding made him realize she had quite a figure. In addition, the very sophisticated hairstyle she had chosen for the day, made her appear much younger and very desirable. Every time he looked at her he felt a chill, thinking about how much it would mean to him if she would change her mind about marrying him. "One of these days I'm going to have a very serious talk with her," he thought. "Somehow I've got to get her to change her mind." In the meantime he couldn't keep his eyes off her.

As soon as everyone was seated at the table Mr. Wilson gave an extremely emotional toast to the bride and groom, and reminded Stephanie that he had predicted this wedding long ago. He told everyone how he couldn't love her any more if she were his very own, and was elated knowing she was going to be so happy. Then, kiddingly, he told Charles he would have him to reckon with if he didn't keep her happy. Finally he told everyone he had better be quiet and, much as he hated to, he would have to leave. "My big boss insists I go home and get some rest. I don't know who bosses me more, Marge or the doctors and nurses. So long everyone. Have a good time." Then, turning to the happy couple he said, "Enjoy your honeymoon kids. We'll see you when you get back - love you." Before he left the podium he kissed Stephanie and gave Charles a hug, again telling him to take good care of his bride.

A few minutes later Greg stood up to give the traditional best man toast, wishing them a long, happy life together. He told everyone how much Charles wanted Stephanie from the very first time he saw her. "No two people were ever meant for each other as these two dear friends of mine are. And to think they chose this particular day - Valentine's Day, the day for lovers - for their wedding, in my estimation, says a lot."

About halfway through the meal, Charles stood up and asked to make a toast. "Friends, I don't have to tell you how much this day means to us. However, I want you to know that my dear friend, Greg, is hoping that this lovely lady next to my bride will soon honor him with a 'yes' answer to his proposal of marriage. Don't you think they would make a wonderful looking couple?" Everyone applauded and cheered for Greg and Martha.

All Martha would say was, "In due time. Today is Stephanie's and Charles' day, not mine."

Chapter 66

The Honeymoon

Following the reception they changed into going-away outfits. Stephanie wore a pale blue form-fitting silk dress with lace ruffles at the neck and wrists. It was gorgeous. The happy couple was then driven by limo to Boston and checked into the bridal suite of the Four Seasons Hotel. They would be staying there for two nights before going to Logan International where they would leave for Europe. After landing in Frankfort their itinerary would take them to Heidelburg and Munich, Germany, followed by a short flight to Spain for three days. Their next stop would be to Rome and Florence Italy for four days. The last stop before returning to the states was to be Greece where they would spend two weeks, which included a 10-day cruise around the islands. Stephanie had always wanted to visit the country of her father's ancestors and the region about which he talked so much. They planned to be gone a month altogether.

After checking into the hotel, (and getting an ovation from people in the lobby, seeing such attractive newlyweds) the bellhop then took their luggage and escorted them to their room, opened the door to the beautiful honeymoon suite and placed their bags inside. (A huge arrangement of red roses was on the cocktail table in the living room.) Charles gave the bellhop a generous tip and told him to have a good evening. He then lifted his bride up, carrying her slender body, with ease, over the threshold. "Welcome to the bridal suite Mrs. Lanza." He gave her a big kiss and reminded her once more how much he had looked forward to this moment. "I love you so very much pretty lady" and he gently put her down.

"Well, I see they left chilled champagne for us. We wouldn't want it to get warm, would we? Let's drink a toast to each other, darling."

He popped the cork and poured a glass for each of them. As they sipped it they stared at each other with love in their eyes, neither saying a word. There were never two happier people.

After finishing the second glass, Charles took the glasses and put them on the table. He then wisked her off her feet and carried her to the huge heart-shaped king-size waterbed in the beautifully appointed bedroom of the bridal suite.

"This is where I have wanted you since I first saw you. I thought this moment would never come. Come into my arms my darling." As they embraced he pulled the zipper of her dress down and slowly slipped it off of her shoulders. She kicked her shoes off. Her dress slid slowly to the floor and as she stood facing him in her sexy, white lace lingerie, he held her close and smothered her neck and upper breasts with kisses, while she closed her eyes thinking of how wonderful her life was now and how much she loved Charles.

As he slowly undressed himself she proceeded to finish disrobing, displaying her curvaceous, body to him. She was so beautiful - long slender legs, so well endowed with firm breasts, a small waist and hips just the right size. He could hardly wait to have her in his arms on the bed so they could make love for the first time. As he looked at her standing near him, her long, dark hair recklessly covering her shoulders and partially hiding one of her breasts, he shuddered with excitement as his desire to make love to her increased.

"Stephanie, my darling wife, Come to me." and they both lay down on the bed, tightly embraced. She too was so excited she shivered at the thought of finally having sex with him. After spending several minutes of kissing and fondling each other in very special areas he told her, "My love, I am so crazy about you, I was afraid this moment would never come."

They then proceeded to culminate their marriage vows by having intercourse for the first time ever.

"Oh my darling," she cried out. "I love you so very much and am so happy we waited for our wedding night. It has meant so much more."

"Thank you my darling for caring so much. You'll never know how much it means to me to hear you say that. I too am happy we waited, even though I was afraid at times I wouldn't be able to hold off until the wedding. I've wanted to feel the thrill of intercourse with you for such a long time. I hope you won't ever get tired of us making love together. It is so beautiful when two people love like we do, and they indulged in one more very passionate kiss.

They finally separated and Charles suggested, "Let's shower, get dressed and have something to eat sent to our room. Then we'll decide what will come next."

As they sat on the couch. Stephanie seemed very quiet and when Charles asked her, "Why so quiet my sweetheart?" she told him she was so happy she was afraid she was dreaming and that someone might pinch her and she would find herself back in her own house. "Don't worry my sweet. This is real and you will never have to return to your house and the bad memories you left behind," he assured her; and he kissed her neck and lips and gave her a gentle hug. Then, to relax her even more he mentioned the beautiful roses the hotel had put in the room. "They must have realized that is what I always give you," he said.

In a little while there was a knock on the door and room service was there with a delicious gourmet dinner for them. They ate it slowly and then finished the champagne, constantly gazing at each other but not saying much of anything.

Then, as they were sitting next to each on the couch, talking about the wedding and reception. Stephanie asked Charles if he thought his sister liked her.

"She sure does. She told me you were a beautiful lady and I couldn't have chosen a nicer person for my wife. I told you I had a smart sister and that she would like you. You scored very highly with Tina too. Kristen said Tina is normally very shy and doesn't go to very many people but she told her mother she thought 'Aunt' Stephanie was beautiful and she loves you very much."

"Didn't Martha look beautiful, Charles? And from the look on Greg's face, I think he was wishing they were getting married then too."

"Yes. I didn't realize what a lovely woman she is when she isn't wearing such plain clothes and her hair isn't fixed up. I can understand Greg's feelings about being put off. Well, maybe things will change for them soon."

Since it was getting quite late they decided to go to bed. Again, they helped each other undress, stopping often to kiss each other. After getting into bed they were so excited neither of them could sleep so Charles suggested they just cuddle up very close to each other to help them relax so they could go to sleep. In a very short time they were sound asleep in a tight embrace..

The following morning, as she lay awake on her back, Charles leaned over and kissed and gently fondled her shapely breasts. Then he proceeded to kiss and suck them. She enjoyed every second. "You are so beautiful I just can't get enough of you.. I knew I wouldn't be disappointed in our lovemaking. We had to be made for each other. How can I express just how deep my love is for you?"

"Oh my darling husband, you don't know how wonderful it sounds for you to call me your wife. I love you so much and can't understand why it took me so long to realize it. We lost so much wonderful time together because I was so stupid."

They finally got up, showered and dressed and then went out for breakfast. The weather was seasonally mild for February so they walked around the area near the hotel and later had dinner at the Legal Sea Food restaurant nearby.

That evening was spent making love to each other, trying various ways to express their love. They never seemed to get enough. It's as though they felt they had to make up for lost time. The following morning they had a late breakfast and then had to pack to leave for the airport. As soon as they finished they decided there was time to make love one more time before they left for the airport, since they wouldn't be able to again before they arrived in Europe, both thinking that would be a very long time. They would be flying most of the night, making it impossible to get romantic.

After making love one more time, as usual coming to a climax together, he asked her, "How do you feel now my darling, my pretty lady? These two days have been the happiest of my life. Don't ever let me go," and he smothered her with kisses. Then, realizing time was getting short, they hurriedly dressed. Charles then called the front desk to let them know they were checking out and to get the limousine for the airport.

By noon they were on their way to the airport and to what proved to be a very romantic honeymoon. Not only did they visit many interesting places everywhere they went but they found the little village from which her father's ancestors came, which proved to be a very pretty, quaint place. The cruise proved to be particularly relaxing and very romantic. The captain dedicated one evening to the newlyweds, surprising them by introducing them to the other passengers. The entire trip included many moments of torrid lovemaking, all of which seemed to be more wonderful each time they indulged in it.

When they returned home they found that friends had moved all of Stephanie's personal things out of her house. The real estate agent with whom she left it had sold it during their absence. She had decided to leave her furniture there, telling him the furniture was included in the price of the house. He was delighted to hear that because the new owners were also newly married, had no furniture and thought hers was beautiful. She wanted nothing around to remind her of her former marriage and none of her things would have gone well with the furniture in her new home anyway.

Charles's house was so much nicer than hers and could only hold happy memories. The master bedroom in the house was very large and beautifully furnished. Actually, Charles had Stephanie pick out new furniture before they were married and while they were on their honeymoon some of his friends came in and got everything ready for the newlyweds return. His housekeeper also helped, wanting to know if she would still have her job because she enjoyed working for him in such a lovely house. He assured her - Mildred was her name - that he would expect her to stay on. To relieve her mind he introduced her to Stephanie who also assured her she had a job for as long as she wanted it.

"How beautiful the bedroom turned out, Charles. Everything is so well coordinated and it is so bright and cheery. I just love it."

"Yes, it did turn out very nice, didn't it? Now what would you like to do our first day back home? We aren't due back to work for a couple of days. You may want to call the Wilson's and see how Ben is getting along. Then we could stop someplace for some lunch if you'd like. There's also a big bunch of mail to look through - most of them cards of congratulations I imagine."

"They can wait until later. Maybe this evening. Yes, I will call the Wilsons in a little while. As for something to eat, I don't really feel like it. My stomach feels a little strange, and my period is late."

"Yes, I noticed you didn't have your period during the entire month we were away.

"Wow! Could we possibly be lucky enough to have made us a baby already?" he asked. "I sure hope so my darling. And to think we were worried about it. Well, you just take it easy and we'll do whatever you want; that is, after you give me a big 'welcome home' hug and a kiss."

"I thought you'd never ask." and they embraced tightly, kissing each other in their usual passionate way. "Thank you honey, for being so concerned. I do feel good enough to try out our new bed by making love for the first time in our very own home. Gosh that sounds good to be able to say 'our' home. No one knows we are home yet, so we won't be interrupted by phone calls or anything."

It didn't take long before they were undressed and were in their own bed in their very own home, taking very little time before coming to a tremendous climax. All the while they constantly expressed their love for each other and how happy their life would be as Mr. and Mrs. Charles Lanza.

He then leaned over her so he could kiss her breasts. After sucking and licking on her nipples, he asked her, "When we have our baby do you plan to breast feed? For now they are all mine but I'm going to be very jealous of them whenever the baby is hungry," and he reached over and kissed them again.

"OK little mother-to-be, let's get dressed and go someplace for lunch. Then we'd better get to a grocery store and start acting like a married couple."

"Good idea Captain Lanza. But we shouldn't get our hopes up about a baby, until we can be sure. After all, just doing all that traveling in foreign countries could cause me to be late. I'll have to admit though, the queasy stomach does look very suspicious. Will you still love me when I'm fat and clumsy?"

"I'm betting you are pregnant and will kill that poor little rabbit when they test you. Of course I will love you my darling and I'll be willing to bet you will make the most beautiful pregnant lady around. Now, let's go eat and then go shopping."

"Before we go, we should check the cupboards and fridge, to see what we need," she suggested, as she headed for the kitchen.

"As for calling the Wilsons, I think our first day back we belong to each other so I'll wait until tomorrow to call them." Then, checking out the kitchen, she remarked, "Charles, come in here. Look. We can't possibly need a thing. Someone has already taken care of filling the cupboards and refrigerator for us."

"I'll be darned. Well, that gives us the rest of the day free. Let's just go for a little drive and stop someplace out of town for lunch - someplace where we won't run into anyone we know," he suggested, and they put on their coats and left.

EPILOGUE

Six Months Later - Early August

Things are finally back to normal with T.G.I., after many months of rough times as well as some good ones.

Everyone knows Stephanie's ex-husband went to prison. Alex Christou was caught embezzling company funds and was fired. Before he had a chance to settle the accounts, he died in a tragic automobile accident. Steve Wilson was released from the rehab hospital and returned to his old job. He was a changed man; kind, loving and hard working. His wife withdrew the divorce action and he took her on a second honeymoon.

Due to the stress of all the tragic events, Ben Wilson suffered a heart attack after Christmas requiring open-heart surgery. Fortunately his recovery was a speedy one. He had hoped to return to work but his doctors insisted he wait at least six months. He left the company in the capable hands of Steve and Harry. After attending Stephanie and Charles' wedding on Valentine's Day; which turned out to be the talk of the town, Ben and Marge Wilson took an extended vacation, flying to Seattle for a few days to visit friends and then boarding a cruiseship for two weeks in Alaska. Upon the return trip they flew to San Francisco to visit Michael and Jennifer. He looked like a new man; rested and relieved of all the strain of the past year. However, he decided to just work part-time and made Steve President and Harry Vice President. The two men always worked well together, and turned out to be best friends. Ben remained Chairman of the Board of Directors. Since his retirement meant Stephanie wouldn't have a job (the other two men had their own secretary), Ben established a new position for her as an office manager in charge of all the clerical help. The company was prospering so much they hired fourteen more people before the end of June, with several fair sized contracts having been signed.

As expected, Stephanie made a beautiful bride and they had a very impressive wedding ceremony. She and Charles honeymooned in Europe and Greece and cruised the Greek Islands. Less than a month after returning they announced they would be parents by Christmas. Charles claims his wife is even more beautiful when she is pregnant. In June they had Ultrasound done as Stephanie wasn't feeling well. Everything was fine but they discovered she was having twin boys, which thrilled them both. Her doctor told her since her body wasn't accustomed to so much extra weight, he would suggest she should plan on leaving her job by the time she was seven months and take it easy. Ben was sorry to hear he would have to replace her so soon but assured her the job would still be there if she still wanted it.

Shortly after they returned from their honeymoon Stephanie received a beautiful congratulatory card from her mother. She told her why she hadn't contacted her sooner and apologized for not having listened to her about her stepfather. She promised that as soon as she could figure out a way to get away long enough to visit her she would. However, her husband watches her constantly and she is afraid of him. Stephanie was in tears, she was so happy to know her mother cared. But, she was very upset over her predicament and Charles and she are going to see a lawyer to see what can be done.

After Harry and Linda returned from their honeymoon, Harry took over Alex's old position. He did an outstanding job and Ben didn't regret having given him the promotion.

They moved into a new house in March and became members of the local country club. The end of April, Linda suffered a miscarriage. They were devastated over their loss as they were so happy she was expecting and wanted the baby so badly. Her doctor told her she should wait at least a year before attempting to get pregnant again.

In April Steve and Laura made a surprise announcement that they were expecting another baby. Their children were thrilled to death about having a little sister or brother to spoil. Laura was told, at her age, she couldn't do any lifting or bending to pick things up or she might lose the baby. The children and Steve pampered her to the point where she said they were treating her like a cripple. So far things are going fine. Steve's parents were excited over the idea of being grandparents again; but mostly he was delighted that Steve had changed so much.

Angie and the children are putting their lives back in order and managing very well. They still miss Alex very much. Angie took up writing and was hired as a reporter with the local newspaper, hoping it would eventually lead her to something better. She had always had an interest in journalism. Her kids keep telling her she should start dating because she is too young and pretty to stay home every night.

Michael and Jennifer were married in May. The wedding was in Maine, and they found a home in the suburbs of New York. After his father's heart attack Michael had applied for a position in the east, and was hired as the manager of a very exclusive gourmet restaurant in a New York City hotel. His parents were happy that he would be living closer to them, as were Jennifer's parents who were from Baltimore. Ben told them he is expecting them to do their share in adding to his list of grandchildren. They said they are working at it every chance they have!

Martha still dates Greg off and on, when he is in town. They are both looking forward to being godparents to Stephanie and Charles's babies. He has been sent on more and more assignments as a trouble-shooter in various categories of police work and has talked about the possibility of looking for some other kind of work. She says she misses Greg very much.

Mr. Wilson received a letter from a young lady identifying herself as Juan's daughter, Marguerita, whom he thought had been killed during the uprising. Juan's brother had made contact with her and told her what had happened to her father, turning over what belongings he had managed to get when he visited Lakeridge.. She was just a little girl when her father was taken prisoner. In her letter she said she wanted to thank Mr. Wilson for being so thoughtful as to see that his things were sent home; especially the earrings. She told him as soon as she could arrange it she would be coming to Maine to claim her father's remains, and hoped to meet the Wilsons at that time. She felt he should be resting next to her mother and that is the way he would have wanted it. Ben and Marge were able to make telephone contact with her and told her they would be happy to meet her, insisting that she be a guest in their home while arranging for the transfer of her father's remains. Juan would finally be going back home to his beloved Nicaragua after all.

THE END